'Haunting, gripping, and lyrical – a book you won't want to put down. Susan Crawford is a bright new star.' Deborah Crombie, *New York Times* bestselling author

'Excellent domestic thriller, extremely well written. Highly recommend!' Emma Kavanagh, author of *Falling*

'An exceptional literary thriller debut that sensitively portrays a woman struggling with bipolar disorder, and the horrific possibility that she's a murderer. Engrossing, thrilling, and page turning all the way through, this is one you won't want to miss!' Chevy Stevens, *New York Times* bestselling author

'This clever whodunit in the vein of *The Girl on the Train*, involving mental illness, marital infidelity, and murder, keeps you guessing.' Deirdre O'Brien, *Sunday Mirror*

'Great premise, and characters, and a wonderfully evocative setting, heavy with heat and suburban boredom, and the uneasy threat of not quite knowing what is going on. Really great.' Sabine Durrant

'I did not see the end coming. It was perfect. If you want a really good mystery then definitely read this.' Edel Waugh, for lovereading.co.uk

'Not a word is wasted in Susan Crawford's fast-paced, thrilling debut. As Crawford explores the boundaries of memory and sanity, the suspense steadily gathers, and in her skilled hands, readers will be left guessing until the very end.' Lori Roy, Edgar Award-winning author of *Bent Road* and *Let Me Die in His Footsteps*

'*The Pocket Wife* is a gripping domestic psychological thriller ideal for fans that like reading ASA Harrison and Sabine Durrant.' Suzanne Marsh, for lovereading.co.uk

'A gripping, character-driven mystery that would pair well with Sophie Hannah's *The Truth-Teller's Lie*.' *Booklist*

' [A] quirkily endearing debut.' *Publishers Weekly*

'This intriguing thriller will leave readers guessing until the last minute. Dana Catrell is a dynamic, well-written character whose bipolar disorder makes her both maddening and endearing. Tightly moving, fast-paced and suspenseful, Crawford's debut novel puts her on the map of writers to watch.' *RT* Book Reviews, 4.5 stars

'Descriptive, lyrical prose creates an intimate and visceral read that is both a solid mystery and a fast-paced psychological thriller.' *Library Journal*

Susan Crawford is a four-time winner of the Atlanta Writers Club award for her short fiction and poetry. Her work has been published in the literary magazines *Loves Lost and Found*, *Long Story Short*, and a short piece in *The Sun*. Susan works for the Department of Technical and Adult Education in Atlanta. This is her first novel.

# The Pocket Wife

## SUSAN CRAWFORD

FABER & FABER

First published in 2015
by Faber & Faber Ltd
Bloomsbury House
74–77 Great Russell Street
London WC1B 3DA
This paperback edition first published in 2015

First published in the United States in 2015
by William Morrow
an imprint of HarperCollins Publishers
195 Broadway, New York, NY 10007

Printed and bound by CPI Group (UK) Ltd, Croydon CR0 4YY

"If You Forget Me" by Pablo Neruda, translated by Donald D. Walsh, from The Captain's Verses, copyright © 1972 by Pablo Neruda and Donald D. Walsh. Reprinted by permission of New Directions Publishing Corp.

The right of Susan Crawford to be identified as author of this work has been asserted in accordance with Section 77 of the Copyright Designs and Patents Act 1988

A CIP record for this book
is available from the British Library

ISBN 978-0-571-32189-6

FSC
www.fsc.org
MIX
Paper from
responsible sources
FSC® C101712

2 4 6 8 10 9 7 5 3 1

*For Ben, Jessica, Cara, and Katie*

# Acknowledgments

From the bottom of my heart, I thank my amazing agent Jenny Bent, who saw the potential for this book in the beginning and has been there every step of the way. Thanks to my editor, Carrie Feron, for believing in me and for her illuminating gentle touch, to Maureen Sugden for her scrupulous copy edits, and to Nicole Fischer and Victoria Lowes for fielding my numerous new-author questions. I would also like to thank Nicola Barr, Kate McQuaid and my UK editor Katherine Armstrong at Faber & Faber.

Thanks to the Atlanta Writers Club, especially George Weinstein and Ginger Collins. Thanks to The Village Writers, particularly the guys at the Galaxy Diner as well as the owners and servers for putting up with our noisy exuberance and late stays. Thanks to Anne's critique group at the Marlay House; you are incredible! Thanks to Julie Hassell for saying *Why not?*; Linda Brazeau for her unwavering support since the Miami days; Peggy Skolnick for the nudge in the right direction; Deborah Mantella for her invaluable advice; Nancy Blum for being, as always, my first reader; Elisha Fields; Sheila Hula; Debbie Belzer and other friends and family members for putting up with my writing-related reclusiveness; thanks to Stephe Koontz for fishing lost chapters out of the bowels of my computer.

Thanks to Chief John King and Capt. Josh Sellers for their professional input and crime-scene information.

Thank you, Ben, for rescuing burned pots and runaway cats and trash can lids so I could write, for sharing me with Dana and Jack as they swelled and morphed and whispered plotlines in my ear in the wee hours.

Thank you, Lin, for showing me the magic of words and the magic bond of sisters—and for always being there for me, in spirit if not flesh.

If you think it long and mad,
the wind of banners
that passes through my life,
and you decide
to leave me at the shore
of the heart where I have roots,
remember
that on that day,
at that hour,
I shall lift my arms
and my roots will set off
to seek another land.

—*Pablo Neruda, from "If You Forget Me"*

# I

The ambulance is still miles away when Dana awakens to the near dark of evening. It wails ribbon-thin in the smog over the highway as she opens her eyes where she lies sprawled across her couch in a suburb of Paterson, a stone's throw from Manhattan but a different world entirely. She wakes to a headache throbbing at the backs of her lids, a library book lying beside her. She sits up and reaches for the book, marking her place with a tiny corner fold, giving it a little pat as she sets it on the coffee table.

Lately she can read a novel in two hours. She has always been an avid reader, but these days she can read much faster. The colors, the conversations, everything is much more vibrant and inclusive, as if opening a book releases genies trapped inside. The scenes and people between their covers sometimes seem more vivid than real life, with their sunny, pearl-toothed characters, the witty conversation, the handsome stranger squeezed into a subway car or knocking about on the street. Sometimes, when she finishes a book at record speed, Dana feels a slight letdown, as if a good friend has hung up the phone in the middle of a conversation.

Sometimes her house seems quiet as a tomb with Jamie gone. She'd hoped her son would choose a school in New York, but instead he's chosen Boston College. He's packed his things and gone away, and although Boston isn't all that far, it seems to Dana that he's journeyed to the edges of the earth. "He could have gone to Idaho," her husband says when she complains to him, so she no longer does. Instead she bites her tongue, paints walls, and rearranges furniture; she reads books and lies awake at night and understands she wasn't ready to be alone with Peter in a house without their son. When she allowed herself to think of it at all in the months before Jamie left, she told herself they'd be like couples on TV, empty-nesters walking hand in hand across exotic beaches, cooking gourmet meals, and falling into bed. She sighs. Peter comes home late most nights and often doesn't even eat, let alone cook gourmet meals.

She struggles off the couch, crossing the room in tentative steps as the ambulance careens toward her neighborhood, its siren now a whisper in the heavy summer air of Ashby Lane. The afternoon comes back to her in tiny waves—her argument with Celia down the street, the way they both had far too much to drink, a faint memory of stumbling home to fall across her sofa in a deep, sangria-induced sleep. If Celia's not an alcoholic now, she soon will be. Lately she always has a glass in her hand, sloshing liquid here and there as she teeters on her high-heeled wedges. Dana rubs her temples and thinks she might point out the benefits of AA the next time she and Celia get together. The two of them could go to a meeting in Manhattan, nearby but more anonymous than the ones in Paterson. She'll offer. She won't push, though. They aren't close enough for that.

Her head throbs, and she remembers her aspirin is in the purse she left in her car when she ran down to Celia's house at breakneck speed. The front door is still ajar, and she pushes through the screen, grabs her purse from the front seat, and rummages through it for the bottle. Outside, the ambulance is audible; its siren pierces the hum of traffic on the highway, and Dana glances up the street again, squinting in the thin light of a foggy evening. Something isn't right. She feels it, this offness of things, and seconds later the siren's wail is deafening. Standing by her car, she swallows the aspirin dry, watching as an ambulance rounds the corner and grinds to a halt in front of Celia's house. Three paramedics run toward the front door, where Celia's husband leans against the screen. Ronald. She can just make out the glare of light bouncing off his glasses as he throws the screen door wide. She doesn't stop to think; she hurries down the street, past the three houses between hers and Celia's, walking quickly on the hot concrete. By the time she gets to their yard, she's running, and her sandals slip in a wet spot, a puddle, as she turns in to the driveway. She falls against Ronald's car, throws her hands out hard against the hood to catch herself.

3

She rushes up the steps to the Steinhausers' and nearly collides with Ronald in the doorway. He looks at her, but he doesn't speak. He folds his arms over his chest as Dana slips across the threshold, where paramedics kneel on the new wood of Celia's recently renovated living room. Their heads are bowed as if they're praying, as if they're studying the grain of the bamboo floor, and Dana is aware of a pungent odor in the air, a smell she recognizes. "God," she says. "What—" And then she sees Celia.

"She wasn't breathing," Ronald says. He's whispering, as if his wife is only resting here across the foyer, her dark hair splayed out in a puddle of her own blood, as if he doesn't want to wake her. "I called 911," he says, uncrossing one arm long enough to point out the medics, crouched on either side of Celia, who lies pale and still, an oddly colored aura forming from the blood around her head, "but it was the strangest thing. I couldn't think of our address. It was only the old Wilmont one I remembered— 3189 Wilmont. From where I grew up," he continues, "in Cedar Rapids." His voice buzzes like a fly. Dana pushes in close beside Celia and feels a sorrow so intense that for a moment she can't breathe. Her neighbor looks so small and helpless lying on the floor. She must be cold—she must feel lonely with only these strange men around her, and Dana reaches out her hand to smooth back Celia's hair.

"Hey!" The paramedic closest to her grabs her arm. "Get her outta here," he says to Ronald, but Dana is already backing away as Ronald says, "There was an accident on the highway. A texter. A stupid fucking texter! Two hours we waited, sitting in traffic while my wife was lying here bleeding to—"

"Got a pulse," one of the paramedics says, "but it's weak."

Ronald squats on the rug with his arms dangling loose at his sides. He squints at something under the sofa, and then he half crawls toward it. A phone. Celia's phone, Dana notices, and she is unpleasantly reminded of their argument earlier that day.

"We better get her to the hospital," one of the EMTs says. "We're losing her."

"No!" Ronald collapses sideways, nearly knocking Dana down. He crumples up like a flower on a broken stem, and she guides him to a chair, where he sits, his watery eyes riveted on the paramedics as they rush the stretcher through the door. Dana's crying, too, but in a distant, disconnected way. It isn't real at all, this pool of blood that used to be Celia, this assault on a room she helped redecorate, these booted men stomping through, barking orders, bruising the shiny bamboo with their muddy feet. *Get out!* she wants to tell them, but they're already running the gurney to the ambulance. Ronald streaks across the room and out the door.

"I'm riding with my wife!" he yells, but no one answers.

The ambulance wheels struggle and whir in the stones of the driveway; the siren shrieks. Celia's rescuers speed

5

down Ashby Lane and disappear around the corner, heading for the hospital, but Dana knows from the way they looked at one another, from the way they were all business, that they think it's futile.

The paramedics are no sooner out the door than one set of shoes replaces another, all of them coming and going across the blemished, blood-smeared porch; policemen from an investigation unit scrape and scratch along the throw rugs in the living room, filling tiny plastic bags with items Dana can't quite see. They usher her outside, taking down her name, her address, who she is, what she's doing there, as if she's the one who is extraneous instead of all of them with their black gestapo boots, their cigarette breath. "We'll be in touch," they say.

Dana stands fidgeting on the Steinhausers' porch and takes a last look through the picture window at the living room, bright in the lights. She studies the drapes and squints at the cushions, as if the evidence is stuck inside the hard, rough cushion of the estate-sale chair or slumped along the corners of the couch—Celia would surely leave clues—and suddenly Dana feels certain she's the likely one to find them. In the house a cell phone jingles. A young policeman with red hair holds a phone up to his ear.

She and Celia were friends, neighbors, sharing piecrust recipes and gossip and yard-sale outings, an occasional languid conversation over coffee or an afternoon trek through the mall with bags in hand. But not secrets. Not until today. She closes her eyes, and images from that afternoon crowd her mind—sangria, bloodred in a glass; Celia's high, sand-colored shoes, the dog flopped beside the kitchen sink, a tiny rip in Celia's screen door; her own hand pushing on the thin wood bridge across its middle; her own feet on the sidewalk, on the street, on her driveway; Celia lying in a pool of blood, the broken vase beside her head, the kitchen knife just so above her hand. But there are gaps—the memories are quick, sharp images of sights and sounds, like puzzle pieces scattered on a slippery, shifting floor.

"She didn't make it," she hears the red-haired cop announce to the room at large. "The detective on the case'll be here in five." He lowers the phone and extends his boot, nudging the front door shut. Dana hurries home, her heart pounding in her ears, her breath a ragged, frantic sound in the stifling summer night. The reality of her neighbor's death settles into her bones and splinters through her skin. Collapsing on her front porch, she hugs her knees, rocking back and forth on the harsh, hot cement, and images of Celia's sons flit across her mind—Tommy and John Jr., spending the summer with Celia's ex on Martha's Vineyard. They'll stay there now, of course; they won't come back—they'll probably never set foot on Ashby Lane again. Her tears spot the gray flat of the porch. They make her heart beat far too fast, all these losses, these holes inside her soul. Lately every aspect of her life is blowing off like petals in a breeze. She feels as if she's in a constant state of watching them fly away, of holding in her spread arms nothing more than empty stems of missing things.

She'll call Peter, she decides, and for a second she feels a tiny bit better. Despite what she learned about him from Celia today, her husband is still a quintessential lawyer—down to earth, even though lately he's become another empty stem, another missing thing. Dana sighs. He's late again.

"Hello." His voice is dull in the clamor of what sounds like an airport bar.

"Where are you?" she says, and there's a scratching sound as Peter shifts the phone.

"I'm in a meeting."

"Celia's dead," Dana says, and she thinks of hanging up, of leaving him with this earful of drama.

"What?"

"Celia's—"

"No," he says, "I heard you. I just . . . Jesus. *Dead?*"

"Dead. God. There was blood all over the—" Dana's voice catches. She stops.

"Listen. Let me . . . I'm just going to stick you in my pocket for a second till I can—you know—till I can get out into the hall and—"

"Wait!" she says, but all she hears are the scratching, shuffling sounds of cloth against the phone, and finally she hangs up.

It isn't the big things Peter does that make her want

8

to leave him; it's more the smaller things, like sticking her inside his pocket in the middle of a thought—these demeaning, shrinking things he does that make her feel as trivial as a sneeze.

She sets the phone down and tries to piece together moments from the afternoon, to put things in some kind of order. She was there. She was involved in Celia's day, although she isn't sure exactly how. She had far too much to drink. And then the incredible death—the shocking, horrible, inconceivable death, sticking like a dagger in her heart. She closes her eyes and tries to remember the last thing she said to Celia. She thinks it was "I don't ever want to see you again."

## 2

Love is such a muddle, Dana thinks, especially for people like her and Peter in lengthy, problematic marriages—difficult enough without neighbors butting in and, now, dying. Celia had served quite a nasty little tidbit to her that afternoon, amid a lot of drunken rambling, and Dana shoves it to the back of her mind to be dealt with later. The night is oppressive; tall buildings downtown trap the heat, leaking warm air into the suburbs even at nearly nine o'clock, and streaks of pink zig and zag through the gray sky. She leans back on her hands and squints, remembers that summer in New York, staring over the Hudson River at a pink sky. "Look!" she'd shouted, pointing.

"What?" Her companion was an earnest poet from the East Village.

"The sky! It looks like Oz if Oz were pink instead of green!"

The Poet had tucked his hair behind an ear, long hair, poetic hair, and puffed on the dying ash, the sweet heat of his pipe from Chinatown, exhaled his answer with a stream of smoke. "It's only the pollution," he said. "Good old New York filth." She hadn't married the Poet. She'd married Peter instead, his fresh good looks, his blue-eyed blondness seeping underneath her skin, erasing nights spent with the dark, sad Poet in his room with the broken wall. Where is he now? she wonders sometimes, nights when the sky is streaked with pink and she is nothing but a pocket wife. She glances at the trace of color still clinging to the sky and thinks she might reread her son's collection of the Oz books—*Ozma* and *Glinda* and *The Patchwork Girl*—but it's too sad; it makes her think of the Poet and of Jamie growing up and moving off to Boston.

A set of headlights bounces over the small hill at the end of their street. Seconds later Peter's Lexus purrs in the driveway and Dana watches as he moves around inside it. The light of his Bluetooth fades away from his ear, dims in the dark car.

"I made a couple of calls from the office after we spoke," Peter says, talking as he tromps up the driveway. "Apparently Donald almost tripped over his wife in the entrance to their living room. It's a good thing Jamie's back at school. Until they find out what the trouble is, no one's really safe." His voice is strained; it splatters out around his breathing, his huffing and puffing. He stops beside where she sits, leaning back on her hands. "The police. Until they uncover what it is."

"What *what* is? And it's Ronald, by the way."

"What killed Celia." Peter fishes in his pockets for a cigarette, and Dana breathes in the sulfur smell of the spent match, the smoke she craves tonight, although she hasn't in years. It's only when her body speeds up and her mind click-clacks like a runaway train that she even thinks of cigarettes and now, suddenly, of Peter beside her in bed, the two of them smoking after sex a million zillion years ago.

"It isn't what," Dana points out. "It's who. It wasn't a meteor or a tractor that struck her down in the prime of her life. It was definitely a who." Her words sound silly, bouncing back at her from the thick night, and she crosses her arms over her chest. She shakes her head to clear it, fighting the confusion, the helplessness of not remembering exactly what happened earlier that day. Surely Peter will notice; he is a lawyer after all. "I saw her right before she died."

He turns to look at her. She feels his eyes on the side of her face. "Oh, yeah? How come?"

"I was borrowing some sugar for dessert, but we didn't get that far. We started talking, and we just . . ." She inhales deeply, holding her breath. A sudden unexpected rage tickles the back of her throat.

"What about?"

"This and that." She almost says, *You!* She almost says, *We talked about the picture Celia took of you at a table in Gatsby's, leering down the blouse of your little tart of a secretary,* but she doesn't. Do people still say "tart," she wonders? She has always liked the word. It sounds like what it is.

"What were you going to make for dessert?" Peter

puffs out a row of smoke circles and pushes himself up off the porch.

"Tarts," she says.

Peter snubs out his cigarette with the toe of a shiny, pricey shoe and stretches. "Let me put the car in the garage."

\*

At first she'd thought Celia was crazy—that she'd doctored the photo somehow out of jealousy. Ronald seemed like such an unfun, squirrelly little guy, running to the sink to wash up after their introduction, his handshake like an eel sliding over her palm. Still, the hungry look in Peter's eyes was obvious, even in the totally inferior pixels of Celia's cell, so there was no denying what she saw, no matter how or why it came to sit amid the badly taken photos that rolled ad nauseam throughout the Pic File section of Celia's phone. "Look!" Celia had screeched that afternoon, stumbling across the room in her wedge shoes. Celia was only five-one and had recently taken to pumping herself up on these silly shoes that, Dana thought, she hadn't mastered yet and so should save for emergencies.

"I'm looking," Dana told her. "They probably work together," and she vaguely remembers Celia making an unflattering, horsey sound and tottering back to the kitchen.

"They're working you together," she'd said.

13

Dana watches her husband from the front porch; she wishes she could talk to him the way she used to. If she could, she'd tell him that not remembering everything she did that afternoon terrifies her—these blank spots. She would say she's lately felt the familiar and unnerving energy of her madness nudging at the edges of her brain, pulsing against the backs of her eyes; she'd share with him the doubts and questions jammed inside her, but she doesn't. She can't. Celia's voice rattles in her brain, how she stood in the doorway to the kitchen, how she said, "Peter looked at me like he'd slit my throat if he had the chance." For a moment Dana sees a coldness in his eyes that makes her turn away.

# 3

Dana waits for the sound of her husband falling into bed. She won't bother with dinner; it's far too hot to cook and lately eating has become a hassle. There are so many more important things to do, so many more interesting things to do; she has such energy now that there's little time and, really, little need for food. And anyway, Celia is everywhere, slipping through the walls and air—Celia laughing at a yard sale, Celia handing her sangria, Celia lying silent in a bloody pool across the foyer. Dana reaches for her book on the coffee table, and a shudder moves like a current through her body. She sobs on the sagging couch cushion, dappling it with small wet dots as Peter's snores slice through the silence of the house.

She turns the air conditioner lower and makes herself a cup of tea, sits down at the dining-room table with his cell phone. It takes her a minute to figure the thing out. It's locked, but she fiddles with it until she finds the right combination of numbers—their anniversary date—and green arrow; the tiny icon of a padlock disappears, and she thumbs over to his contact list, looking for the Tart's number—or photo, maybe. She isn't really sure what she's looking for. Affairs are clandestine by nature, and Celia wasn't exactly lucid by the time Dana got to her house. "Daanaaa!" she'd called from her front porch. "Come on over! It's life or death!" She'd yelled so loudly that their neighbor Lon Nguyen had stopped washing his car, his sponge midway between a sudsy bucket and the left front fender of an aging Miata, his rubber flip-flops sinking in the mud. Celia reeked of alcohol and something fruity, standing there in her doorway. She'd rushed Dana over to a chair and shoved the picture so close to her that at first she couldn't make it out. "They're fucking!" Celia yelled.

"Where were you when you took this?" was all Dana could think to say. And, "Could I have one of whatever's on your breath?" She squinted over the photo of her husband and gulped down one sangria and then another, polishing off the bottle of vodka for good measure and feeling unusually calm until the drinks hit her all at once, making her fuzzy and far away, and she gagged on the burn of the two colliding liquors. "So where were you?" Dana said again.

"Across the room. I snapped the picture before they noticed me."

"And after you snapped the picture?"

Celia laughed a humorless little laugh. "They noticed me. Peter did. Later, in the parking lot, he tried to get me to delete the photo. He never actually saw it. I wouldn't show it to him. If he'd seen how bad it was—how unclear—he wouldn't have been so worried. 'This was about work,' he told me. 'You could have come over there. You could have met her.' He was kind of shouting,

16

and people were beginning to stare."

"When was this?"

"Monday," Celia said. "I was going to just delete it. I wasn't even going to mention it to you, but then I . . ."

"Got drunk?"

"Yeah," she says. "I guess."

"But why— I mean, it's nice you care and all, but why exactly do you care?" By this time the room was swimming, and she'd wondered how she was going to get out of the chair, let alone back home. Celia's face was nothing but a smudge, and all Dana can really remember after that is a lot of ranting about yard sales and women sticking together, struggling out of the estate-sale chair, weaving, trying to keep her balance in the spinning room, and at some point falling through the front door into the muggy summer afternoon. The next thing she remembers is waking up on her couch to a blinding headache and the realization that she'd left her purse in the car.

She scrolls through her husband's phone. She isn't at all sure what she's looking for. Pictures, maybe, that he's taken on his own. She shivers in the damp room. A chill falls like a shadow over her, and she remembers why she all but stopped drinking years before. She remembers the headaches, the migraines, the madness, and the fear that at heart she was an alcoholic like her father.

She scrolls over to his files, and Peter's pictures pop up. There are several shots of Jamie and even a couple of her—a few from his last work picnic—ordinary photos, images of pedestrian moments in a pedestrian life. She yawns. She moves to his contact list and scrolls down, trying to remember the Tart's name. Anna, was it? Hannah? And then there's a mysterious initial. "C." Celeste? Cynthia? On impulse she hits the number beside it, and there's a faint click as her call goes straight to voice mail.

"Hello," an oddly familiar voice says. "This is Celia. You know what to do."

Dana hits redial and listens to the recording, and then she hits redial again. Peter's hidden Celia's number in his phone. She'd never think to look for it here, under "C." She wouldn't think to look for it at all. She feels sick. She feels as if she's been punched in the stomach; she feels duped. She closes her eyes and sees Celia, bloody and dying at the edge of her living room while her dedicated, docile husband sat, oblivious and mired in traffic, while Dana dreamed sangria dreams four houses down. It makes sense now, the way Celia acted, her fury over Peter ogling his secretary in the restaurant. Dana shakes her head to clear it, but the images remain, the sounds and sights, the blood, the babbling husband, Celia's stupid voice so easily retrieved from Peter's phone. Kaleidoscopic, they separate and move and form again, each image less appealing than the one before.

*

She didn't marry the Poet because she couldn't slow

18

herself down. Lying beside him on the dingy mattress in that place with the broken wall, she couldn't relax. Night after night she lay awake, watching the rise and falling of his hairy chest, the shadows underneath his eyes, the neon light from a liquor store across the alley blinking at the sky. Like a signal, she'd told him, like a warning, and the Poet laughed. "Have a toke," he said. "It'll relax you. It will help you sleep," and the Poet stuffed his Chinese pipe with small, soft lumps of hash. It didn't make her sleep, though. Nothing did. Every week she slept less, walking through the downtown streets with the Poet, arm in arm, until late into the night, until his eyes were closing and he fell asleep exhausted on the mattress, leaving her to pace and write. Her classes flew by in a confusion of voices and raised hands—of papers written in the middle of the night, so brilliant, so eso-teric. I think I'm channeling God, she told the Poet, her body nothing more than flesh on bones. He tells me what to say. But they didn't understand—her professors, the other students. Only her dark Poet understood, and final-ly not even he could catch the words that tumbled from her brain onto the page in tiny, oddly slanted script that even she could barely read. The night he came home and found her on the roof, squatting at the edge in nothing but a slip—the night she said Jesus told her she could fly, the night she floated hundreds of handwritten pages into the winter sky over Avenue D, he'd driven her to Bellevue in a borrowed car.

The tea burns her throat. She hits redial once more and listens to Celia's voice, torturing herself with the nasal, slightly southern sound of her dead neighbor. "You know what to do."

She sinks onto the floor of the dining room and stares at the cell phone in her hand, scrolling through the contact list until she finds her son's dorm number. "Celia's dead," she whispers into his voice mail, although she doesn't think Jamie has ever actually met her. She stops; she counts to ten inside her head. "Never mind," she says. "I love you," and she holds her thumb down on the red arrow until the tiny screen goes mercifully black.

She blows on the cup, on the cooling tea, and thinks again of what Celia said—that Peter looked like he could slit her throat. Or does Dana only think she said that? She takes another sip of tea and feels a familiar rush of energy. She needs it now, this energy, this magic that has her staring at the ceiling many nights, that wakes her from her sleep and stuffs itself inside her days. It began when Jamie left for Boston, she thinks now, sitting cross-legged on the floor—after that endless, agonizing journey home from parents' weekend, peppered with Peter's mysterious phone calls at rest stops between Boston and New Jersey, her successful husband sitting on a picnic bench or standing in a clump of trees, his fleshy hand curved like a shield around his phone—"A client," he said, or "this case

I'm working on," but Dana knew he was lying.

*

After Bellevue she had not returned to school. Her time at NYU is nothing but a haze of voices and trains and pigeon crap and neon lights, of barred windows and her mother taking her back home with her lips pursed in a little pout and a prescription for lithium in the zipped compartment of her bag. The only thing Dana remembers clearly from that time is the Poet, is feeling loved, is their naked bodies in the summer, soft and pink, like peaches on the lumpy mattress, and the bright orange blanket from the Andes wrapped around them when the snow fell down outside the window.

Manic depression, the doctors said—the great magical force that turned on her and tricked her into thinking she could fly. Episodic, they said. Her mother blamed the Poet and his pipe, Camus and Nietzsche and Sylvia Plath, but Dana knew better; she knew that the madness was a part of her; she knew that it crouched along her veins. Waiting. For a while she took the medicine that made the world around her such a faded, unbright place to be, let it hold her in its sagging, dimpled arms until with a sigh she shuffled into the rest of her life, eventually trading the drug for a tall, blue-eyed husband and a world more numbing than lithium could ever be.

There were times over the years when her demons

won out, when she wore her lipstick too dark, her mascara too heavy, her dresses too short. When they did slip through—when they whispered in her ear, waking her from sleep, she drove her car into the city and looked for the Poet, who was no longer there. In corners of dark bars or perched on crumbling stoops near where he used to live, she sometimes thought she'd found him, and if she closed her eyes, it almost seemed she had—a certain look, a certain touch, a sweetness—but in morning, in the brighter light of day, she always realized her mistake.

\*

She sticks her cup in the sink; she walks to the front door and slips out onto the porch, where moths circle the yard lights. They dance and dip and buzz inside the glass, their fragile bodies knocking up against the metal sides, the tips of their wings sticking on the scorching bulbs, and Dana feels like one of them, adrenaline pumping through her veins, her nose pressed up against the glass.

She won't sleep. She knows the signs. She feels the starting of a long night of shadows just at the corner of her eye, disappearing when she turns her head, like the game she played with her cousins growing up. Freeze, she thinks it was. She was very good at it; she often won.

It's not entirely unpleasant, this restlessness, this energy, the sharpness of her thoughts, her swift responses, intuitive, clever. The clarity will in time give way to chaos. Her quick, bright thoughts will start to come too fast, will crash into one another, but she'll get help, she tells herself; she'll get help before things reach that point. Right now she needs the clarity her illness brings her. Right now the world is crystal clear, a honed and beauteous thing, allowing her to solve the mystery of her neighbor's death, to bring back the soggy, foggy afternoon, to recover the missing moments and fill in all the blanks until she knows she had nothing to do with Celia's violent departure.

It all began with that photo in the cell. If only she could see it one more time, she thinks, and shuffles the thought to the back of her mind as she steps into her sandals and locks the door behind her, sliding into the front seat of the Toyota. She'll go to Manhattan. Maybe she'll stop off somewhere for a drink to calm her nerves, and then she'll go to a bookstore downtown to browse, to clear her head, to figure things out. She thinks of the Poet. It's exactly the kind of night he would have gone out to a pub or leafed through some esoteric titles at the bookstore near Sheridan Square. Hot, sultry nights like this, he'd burn up in that apartment with only the fan whirring, loud and ineffectual, by the window.

She adjusts her rearview mirror. St. Christopher remains motionless on the visor until she turns to fasten her seat belt. It's dark inside the car, so all she really sees is a brief flicker of light, which she thinks might be his tiny metal head catching the quick glance of a passing car. She smiles. He's traveled with her many times across the bridge. He's waited patiently inside her car while she drank or ate or shopped, while she walked down lamplit streets in search of the Poet. St. Christopher has never failed her; St. Christopher has never run away. As she turns the key, he seems to shift his gaze to the left, toward Celia's house, and Dana nods. "You're right." She inches out the car door and around to the backyard, nearly tiptoeing all the way to the Steinhausers', where yellow tape crinkles in the balmy night and clues lie thick as fog inside the tainted walls of Celia's house.

She finds the Steinhausers' key on her ring and unlocks the dead bolt on the back door. She meant to return it after watching the dog while they were away—a week-end in New York, a Broadway play—but she never did. The house is damp and still—a cache of angry words and ghosts and spilled wine. She flips on the flashlight from the glove box of the Toyota and lets it play across the room; she squats down where hours earlier Ronald hunched, staring at the phone under the sofa. She thinks he grabbed it, assumed he'd grab it, but she isn't sure— there was so much noise and confusion, so much blood. She shines the flashlight under the couch, under the estate-sale chair she helped pick out; she shines it under every stick of furniture in the living room.

A car trolls down the street and stops. Its lights bounce through the living-room window, and she ducks through the house, locking the back door carefully behind her. She doesn't stop until she's in her car; she turns the key, inches down the driveway to the street.

*

The Poet came every day to Bellevue. He sat beside her
in the jumble of loud and angry voices. He held her hand
and kissed her fingers one by one as the patients lined
up for medication in small paper cups, their faces round,
blank beads on a long, thin string of fear. She took her
paper cup and smiled a thank-you, showed the nurse her
tongue and spit the pills into her hand when no one was
around. After a few days, her mother shuttled Dana off
to a private hospital on Long Island, and the Poet was
barred from any further contact. "Leave my daughter
alone," her mother told him when he phoned the house.
"If you ever cared about her at all, don't call here again.
For her sake. And, by the way," she added in a particularly venomous and untrue appendage, "the doctors say
there was so much pot in Dana's system it was no wonder
she had a breakdown," or so Dana imagines. She never
knew exactly what her mother said; it was years before
Dana knew she'd told him anything at all. She thought
he'd simply had enough, that a girlfriend who went mad
was more than he could handle, and really, who could
blame him for walking away?

*

She turns on the radio, moves her head to the music, fishes around inside her purse for the toll. Peter was right; she should have bought an E-ZPass into Manhattan months ago. She'll buy one this week, she tells herself; she can't use his car—she doesn't even want to now.

She speeds across the bridge, slick with intermittent rain. Behind her a car honks, a light, quick tap of the horn, a reminder to keep moving—a suggestion, nothing more. She glances into her rearview mirror at the tailgating car, far too close on the slick bridge. Light rushes down from a streetlamp, illuminating a small, round white face behind the windshield. In the dank and wobbly light, it's barely discernible, but for Dana, her feet planted on the threshold between brilliance and madness, the face is clear and luminescent, unmistakably the face in Celia's phone.

It's over in a moment; the car behind her disappears in traffic, but she finds she no longer wants to go into the city. She turns around, but she can't bring herself to go home. Not just yet. She'll drive around until she gets her bearings, until she slows herself down. The snoring husband she no longer trusts, the house that fills her with foreboding, another night to pace and ramble as the sun claws its way up from the ground, lighting the sky with a bright, unwelcome day—these things are bad enough without Celia strapped across the backs of Dana's eyelids, dying on a bamboo floor, her blood like flames licking out from the splayed, crimped ends of her hair.

# 4

It isn't the murder on Ashby Lane that has Jack Moss staring at the blank wall across from his desk in Paterson. The drama from the night before, the violence in a middle-class New Jersey suburb, is not particularly jarring to a veteran detective who cut his teeth in Manhattan.

It is the departure of his wife that makes him slump, listless, in his swivel chair, his eyes riveted to the ugly mint green of the station wall, to the black marks around the window. He's had no sleep. His thoughts slog through his brain, sifting through suspects in the Steinhauser killing. The husband? A rejected lover? An angry boss? No signs of forced entry, so she might have known her killer. There was an unlocked window on the side of the house, no footprints on account of gravel under the window. He picks up a pen and scribbles down his thoughts, but they are perfunctory and lackluster on the white page.

It was after eleven when he got home. Ann was still there, but only because it would have taken all the joy out of her departure if she'd left him while he crouched in the Steinhausers' living room with his evidence bag. If she'd pulled her little red Honda onto the highway as he sped toward home, her leaving would have lost its bite. Instead she'd struggled out to her car with several fairly random items, he'd thought at the time—an overnight bag and a few books, a small reading light that fastened to a headboard, her UNICEF coffee mug with ethnically diverse children holding hands around the rim.

"Where're you going?" he'd called to her, but she'd only stepped up her trek to the car, hadn't even turned around—a small blond lemming with her sights on the cliff.

Celia Steinhauser's being clubbed with a vase in her foyer wasn't something he had planned to ruin his anniversary, although he had put himself on the case. He knew the name. Steinhauser. Same as Kyle's GED teacher. He'd phoned his wife as he sped toward the victim's house and then called her again from the Steinhausers' front porch. Finally he'd called her from the lobby outside the emergency room at the hospital, where the dead woman's husband informed him, sobbing, that the vase was something they'd bought together at an art show, that Celia thought its unusually heavy weight was a good thing at the time—their dog wouldn't bang into a table and send it crashing to the floor—and that, on top of everything else, the dog went missing after Celia was attacked. Jack had patted the man on the back and slipped through the automatic doors into the swampy heat of the parking lot. "Sorry, sweetheart!" he'd nearly shouted into Ann's voice mail, as sirens clotted the air and screamed toward the ER. "I'm on my way."

At the time he hadn't realized why she didn't answer either her cell or the house phone in the kitchen, but after she'd left, when he walked inside and saw the cake from the French bakery, the scripted "Happy Anniversary" in purple buttercream, when it was, in essence, hours too late, he knew. He also knew that her anger had been building for a long time. He's never really understood the milkiness of women; he doesn't want to. He thinks it might be worse, the way they take a sharp, hard thing and stretch it into smoke and wisps of summer nights— ghosts that curl around the bedpost and lie in wait outside the kitchen door. Men, Jack thinks, deal with things head-on, and then they dust themselves off and blunder through their lives.

*

He gets up from his desk and stretches. All night he tossed and turned, and now he's dying for a cigarette even though he hasn't smoked in years. He walks into the break room and tries not to look at the half-empty box of doughnuts on the table in the middle of the room. "Hey, Rob," he says, and his partner nods, gesturing toward his mouth and then the open doughnut box.

"How's the case coming along?" he says. "The woman on Ashby Lane?"

Jack pours himself a cup of coffee from the machine, muddy and tasteless. "Night shift left a report on my

29

desk. Said somebody might've been at the crime scene last night after we left."

"Who?"

"No idea. The patrolman said there was a light inside the house, but the place was locked up tight as a drum. No forced entry. Said it was possible it was headlights coming through a window from the street behind."

"Huh. Murderer returning to the scene of the crime?"

"Could be. Anything on the missing girl?"

"They found her car not far from where she worked, stripped, with some blood on the front seat. I got two calls from Lenora at the prosecutor's office," Rob tells him. "Lenora the Luscious." He rolls his eyes. "She wants an update on both cases."

"Already? Crap!" The first assistant prosecutor has been even more of a pain than usual lately, her spike heels inches from whatever case they're on. Jack gulps down the coffee and nearly gags. His stomach is a huge knot, between Ann leaving and his eating only crusts of burned things he found in the oven in the middle of the night—the charred remains of potatoes and roasted brussels sprouts.

Probably the missing teenage girl is with her boyfriend in the city, which is usually how these things turn out, but he's hardly an authority when it comes to kids. His one remaining son is living with a girl named Maryanne in a place even felons avoid if they have a choice. Rosie's Rooms, not far from Jack's office. Jack hasn't met the girlfriend and quite possibly he never will. He hears just scraps of things from Margie, who is totally unreliable as a witness—or anything else, for that matter. If he interviewed his ex-wife on a case, he'd toss out most of what she said. Still, Margie's all he's got now, the only connection to their son. And if it's true what she told him when she dropped the ball with her AA program a few months back, he might soon have a grandchild. Sometimes he believes this, but usually he doesn't, since it wouldn't be the first time Margie's lied about a pregnancy. She told him she was pregnant a few weeks after she threw Jack out. She wasn't. It was just one of the cards she played.

He holds his pencil between the first and second fingers of his right hand, exactly the way he held a cigarette for twenty-seven years. Margie told him in a more lucid call, in which she was much vaguer about Maryanne's pregnancy, that Kyle's almost finished with his free prep courses. He's ready for the GED, which she gratefully attributed to his teacher's ability to get through to him. Ms. Steinhauser. Not exactly a common name, which is why Jack jumped on the case. His own inability to reach his son is a constant torment, a constant reminder that he wasn't there for either of his boys through all the years that led up to Joey's dying in Afghanistan, to the day he ran over a roadside bomb on some random, unremembered mission. And Jack wasn't there for Margie when their son's death knocked her off the wagon so suddenly and with such force that she, too, might have died if Kyle hadn't come home from school in time to find her unconscious and barely breathing. He dropped out right after that, in his junior year, two months to the day after his brother's death. Jack doesn't blame him. He blames himself.

He sits with his office door ajar, listening to conversation in the break room. Lenora, he decides as a slightly lilting voice drifts up the hall. He frowns. The star assistant prosecutor is an iron fist in a silk glove, as Rob has pointed out more than once, his eyes sparking at the mere mention of her name. She knows her way around the precinct—burrowed in like a little tick from the time she first hired on, earning a reputation for moving through her cases and sometimes theirs with the savvy and precision of a twenty-year veteran. She's pretty, but she's not exactly warm and fuzzy. He yawns. She looks young enough to be his daughter, but probably she isn't. Jack knows from Ann's arsenal of creams and lotions, and from the hefty charges she's run up on credit cards, that money really can buy youth. At least women think so. Lenora is cool. Impenetrable. She makes him think of the desserts in the tearoom where his mother dragged him once on a nightmare visit to see his aunt and her two giggly daughters, reminds him of the small porcelain princess tops stuck in skirt-shaped scoops of vanilla ice cream.

He looks up as Lenora and Rob approach the doorway. Their voices drift in from the hall and hang in air stale and humid from the ancient, crappy air conditioner. Lenora's voice is surprisingly slow, contrasting the quick tap-taps of her designer heels. It has a slight trace of long-abandoned southern roots. Alabama, he thinks he remembers Rob telling him. Or Arkansas.

"I'll get back to you when I hear from the parents," Rob tells her, and her answer is eclipsed by the sudden gasping sound of the A/C in its death throes.

"Morning, Jack." She pokes her head in, points her air-brushed face, her perfect nose, toward a stack of papers on his desk. "Rob has his hands full with the missing-teen case. He tells me you're working the homicide, the Stein-hauser murder, on your own for now."

Jack nods. "I'm good."

"You sure? The media's going nuts on this one. Attractive woman. Hero to the downtrodden, teacher of the underprivileged. A regular Mother Teresa. I'm already starting to get pressure down at the office. They want it cleared up quick—like yesterday." She snaps her fingers. The faint smell of flowers sticks in the damp air. "I really need your help."

"I'm on it." Jack nods again, hopes he doesn't look as lousy as he feels. He clears his throat. "Got some inter-views lined up this morning," he tells her, and she smiles. Her teeth are crazy white. He thinks again of the ice-cream princesses.

"Rob," she says. "Don't let this missing-teen case turn into another headliner," and she waves a little wave and takes off down the hall. Jack can't help himself; he fol-lows her with his eyes.

When she's left—when the clicking of her heels grows

faint and disappears, Rob abandons his post in the doorway and sits down finally at his desk. "She is really . . ."

"Yeah," Jack says. "She is really. You look like a fawn."

"I think she might like me." Rob's eyes are still a little glazed, his mouth half open. He is seriously starstruck.

"Just might." Jack drags himself to his feet. "Close your mouth, will ya," he says, and then he walks out to the break room, grabs another cup of muddy coffee, pins his hopes on the caffeine.

He swivels his chair over to the reports on the Steinhauser case. The husband is due in soon. Ronald. They met briefly at the hospital, and then there were the phone calls back and forth about the family dog that had gone missing after the murder. He senses that Ronald's hiding something, but the question is never whether people are hiding something, it's whether what they're hiding is what he needs to solve the case, especially a murder case, which this clearly is. He knows he has to be on his toes, but he feels as if he's moving through a fog; the day is thick like honey. He walks over to the men's room and splashes cold water on his face. When he gets back to his desk, Ronald is already there.

"Mr. Steinhauser," he says, and Ronald clears his throat, sticks out a shaky little hand. "Good to see you again," Jack says. "Thanks for coming in."

"Sure," Ronald says, and Jack is surprised by the strength of his grip.

"Follow me," Jack says, and together they tromp down

34

the hall to the interrogation room. "Have a seat." He reaches out, pulls a chair over closer, sits down as Ronald sags onto the chair on the other side of the table.

Jack picks up his pen. "So." He thumbs through the police report, looks at the places where he's penciled in an R. "You ever find the dog?"

"No," Ronald says. "But I'll go back tonight and search the neighborhood." He leans forward over the table.

"You got home at eight-thirty last night. That right, Ronald?"

"Yes." Ronald nearly whispers. He's leaning in so close that Jack can smell his breath, still pungent with last night's scotch; it wafts out in small, rancid puffs.

"Was that normal for you, getting home so late?"

"No. There was an accident. A rear-end collision. It was like dominoes, all the cars. This young woman, this texter, was . . . um, texting. "

"What time do you generally get home?"

"It varies," Ronald says. "Usually between six and six-thirty."

"Did you phone your wife to tell her you'd be late?"

"No."

"Why not?" Jack leans back in his seat, waving the pen like a small baton in the air over his ear.

Ronald shrugs. "I don't know why. She— Celia. My wife taught class sometimes in the evenings. I lose track of when. Lost track."

"So you thought she might be at work?"

"I guess so. I didn't actually stop to figure out if it was her work night or not."

"Why's that?" Something's definitely off. If Jack were two hours late getting home, he wouldn't even think about whether Ann was at the house or not; he'd just speed-dial her and leave a message if she didn't answer. He feels almost smug for a second, and then he remembers Ann taking off in the Honda, half the contents of their bedroom crammed into the backseat.

"Why's what, Detective?"

"Why didn't you stop to figure out if she'd be home or not?"

"I don't know."

"Hazard a guess," Jack says, and he flips the pen around again, twirling it.

"She would have been pissed," Ronald says.

"Seems like she would've been more pissed when you didn't call her. I know my wife would hit the roof if I came strolling in two hours late without calling."

Ronald shrugs.

"You two having problems?"

"Well," Ronald says, "I guess. Nothing major."

"Another guy?"

Ronald looks down at his shoes. "Not that I know of," he says, but he is clearly lying. He fidgets with his fingers, folds them in his lap.

"Your wife have any enemies you know of?"

"No," Ronald says. "Everybody liked Celia. Her

students, the neighbors, everybody."

"How about you? You like your wife?"

"Of course. I loved my wife, Detective. Always have."

"Women are funny," Jack says, and he leans over his paperwork like he's reading it. "Mysteries."

"I'm not sure what you—"

"Were you aware that Celia—sorry. Were you aware that Mrs. Steinhauser withdrew five thousand dollars from the bank three days before she died?"

"No. She— We—"

"Had a joint account?"

"Yes."

"Well, apparently she had another one. A savings. Her name only. Same bank."

"I didn't know," Ronald says, and Jack believes him.

"Was she planning on going somewhere?"

"No. Not that I knew of. Not that she told me about."

"That kind of cash—maybe she was going on a little vacation? Putting money down on an apartment?"

Ronald clears his throat. His foot taps against the chair leg, his shiny black shoe.

"Any pressing credit-card debt? Overdue bills, that sort of thing?"

Ronald squints, screws up his face like he's pondering this. "We did. Yes. We had a large credit-card balance on one of our cards, on the . . . Anyway, we'd talked—well, mostly Celia talked—at length about paying it off, or paying it down at least."

37

"Any particular rush on that, Ronald?"

"No. Well, yes. We wanted to do some traveling in the fall."

"That right?"

"She was a—you know this already—she was a teacher. A lot of her students were from South America, Central America. She spoke a little Spanish. We thought about going to Guatemala, Costa Rica—someplace like that."

"So you wanted to start out with a clean slate."

Ronald chuckles. "Well, cleaner slate."

Jack smiles, leans back in his seat. "So you can rack up the debt all over again."

"Right. Part of the marriage vows—till debt do us part."

Jack laughs. He leans in again over the table and scratches his head with the pencil. "Thing is, Ronald. Wouldn't she—Mrs. Steinhauser—wouldn't she just write a check for that?"

Ronald stops smiling.

Jack looks at his watch. One of the neighbors is due in three minutes. A Lon Nguyen. He gets up, watching Ronald rise to his feet and stand there in his shiny shoes.

"Thanks for coming in, Mr. Steinhauser. Ronald." He holds out his hand. Ronald shakes it for the second time that morning, but this time his grip is limp and sticky.

"I'm at the St. Giles Hotel, over by— You'll let me know," Ronald says, "if anything . . . if you turn up anything."

Jack looks at him. "Depends on what it is." He hands Ronald his card, tells him to call if he thinks of something that might be helpful. "Oh," he says when Ronald's stepped into the hall. "You go back inside your house last night, Ronald?"

"No. Went straight from the hospital to the hotel. Drank myself into a stupor, to be honest."

"Got somebody to corroborate that?"

"The bartender. I told him what happened. It was on the TV, the whole sordid— It came on while we were sitting there—"

"Who else has a key to your house?" Jack sticks his hands in his pockets, peers at Ronald over the tops of his reading glasses. "Anybody?"

"Not a soul. Only me. Celia, of course, and the boys, but they're . . . Wait a minute. A neighbor. Dana Catrell still has the extra key. She took care of our house a week or two ago while we were away. I was trying to . . . reconnect with my wife, I suppose. Fat lot of good that did."

*

Lon Nguyen is smaller than Jack expected. He looks like a kid, slipping in off the elevator and padding down the hall in his shorts and flip-flops. He stands for a minute in the doorway, watching people in the cluttered office as they sit for questioning or come in with reports.

"Detective Moss?"

"Yes." Jack stands up, sticks out his hand. Nguyen takes it in a brief, obligatory shake, and Jack heads back down the hall to the interrogation room with Lon Nguyen in tow. Jack can tell he hates the looks of it. A lot of people do; they get skittish in a closed room, claustrophobic. "Relax," he says. "We can leave the door open. We're just here for privacy." He goes in first and sits down, motions for Nguyen to take a seat. "So your neighbor," Jack says. "You saw her the day she died?"

Nguyen nods. "Yes."

"When was that, Mr. Nguyen?"

"It was in afternoon. I was outside. When summer is hot and so much smog, I wash my car often."

"What time was this?"

He shrugs. "Shortly after I return from work."

"Say five?"

"Maybe."

"Five-thirty?"

"More like five-thirty."

"And Celia?"

Nguyen stares at the floor or maybe at his flip-flops, Jack can't tell.

"What was Mrs. Steinhauser doing when you saw her?"

"She was yelling."

"Where was she?"

"In her front yard, out by the street."

"Who was she yelling at?"

"My neighbor."

40

"What's your neighbor's name?"

"Dana."

Jack looks down at his notes. "Dana Catrell?"

"I don't know their last name," he says.

"Their last name?"

"Dana and her husband and their son."

"Okay. So what was she yelling?"

"She tell Dana to come to her house."

"Why?"

Lon shrugs again.

"What did Celia—Mrs. Steinhauser—say, more or less?"

"'Come here right away. It is matter of life and death.'"

"Then what happened?"

"Dana close her door and run to Celia's home."

"Then what?"

"I finish washing my car and I enter inside my house."

"That it?"

"Yes. That is it."

"Did you see anyone else at the Steinhausers'?"

"No."

"Did you happen to notice when Dana Catrell left their house?"

"No. I was already inside."

"Did you hear anything? Besides what you told me, of course."

"No. Nothing else."

"All right, then." Jack stands up, and Nguyen is on his

41

feet and halfway out the door before he can even extend his hand. "Thanks for your time, Mr. Nguyen," he says as the man bolts out, mumbling what Jack assumes are parting words. By the time he picks up his notes and steps into the hall, Nguyen is nowhere in sight.

Jack stretches his arms over his head and yawns. He'll call Dana Catrell, have her come down and see what she's got to say. He hasn't spoken to her himself. One of the officers at the scene jotted down her name and phone number—said she was a neighbor, a friend, maybe; it's in his notes. At this point in the investigation, she's the last person to see Celia Steinhauser alive, and he hopes she's more forthcoming than Nguyen. Man, he'd have told Ann a few days ago, sitting at the table after dinner. It was like pulling teeth talking to that guy.

It's you, Jack, she would have said, clearing the dishes, stacking them in the sink for him to get to later. She'd turn to him, catch him on his way to the back door, trap him with her words. You're too tough on everyone, and he'd walk out back and stare at the crap in his neighbors' yard.

He stuffs all his notes on the murder into a file and walks back toward his office, makes a turn through the outside door to clear his head. As he steps into the parking lot, the air is hot and soggy. He pushes from his mind thoughts of Ann, her car bumping off the driveway onto the road, the cake at home, melting on the kitchen counter. Instead, he replays bits of his two interviews, and something about Ronald's nags at him. He can't put his finger on it. It's a feeling, that's all, but he'll check out the guy's alibi first chance he gets. He's already got a call in for the night-shift bartender at the hotel where Steinhauser's staying. And then there's the neighbor, the last one known to see the dead woman alive and the only other person with a key.

Dana scrambles eggs in a blue bowl and stirs in a few drops of half-and-half.

"Mom?" Her son watches her from his seat at the kitchen table. He's back, but only for the day; he's in the summer session, and it's tough, he tells her—the classes are more difficult, all that information crammed into a couple months. He's come home to grab some odds and ends, he's said, for his dorm room, but Dana knows it's her phone call that's brought him here. She can feel him observing her. Jamie is the sensitive one in the family, always watching for a variation in mood, like a medium, sticking trembling hands inside a house, a room, and feeling vibrations.

She turns around.

"What's wrong?"

"Well," she says, "it's upsetting, this whole thing."

"Mrs. Steinhauser?"

"Yes. The awful way she died." She stirs the scrambled eggs with a wooden spoon, scraping them from the bottom of a large cast-iron pan.

"Will they do an autopsy?"

"I guess." She empties the pan onto a large orange

plate and puts it on the table in front of Jamie. "Help yourself," she says, glancing up as Peter stumbles through the doorway and makes a beeline for the coffeemaker.

"What do you think, Peter?" She doesn't look at him.

"About what?"

"About Celia."

"It's . . . God, it's . . ." Peter pours his coffee and sits down at the table, reaches for the eggs. She's behind his chair, leaning in with a plate of bacon, so Dana can't quite see his face. She only sees Jamie watching her, studying her, and she suddenly wishes she hadn't called him the night Celia died.

They eat in silence. Peter peruses the front page of the morning paper, thumbing through to the sports section as a car honks in the driveway and Jamie pushes back from the table. His chair scrapes across the tiles and his sneakers squeak like long ago when he was little. Dana feels a stab of nostalgia. "See you guys later." He kisses Dana on the top of her head before he stacks his dishes in the sink. "You sure you're okay?" he whispers, and she nods.

"Fine," she says. "Make sure you're back in time for dinner," and Jamie turns in the doorway, gives her a thumbs-up. She stabs at a tiny edge of bacon. Across the table Peter seems riveted to the sports section. The thin newsprint shakes in his hands.

"What do you think about Celia?" Her words are loud and flat in the silent kitchen.

"I think it's horrible." Peter sets his mug down on the

45

table, and a small spurt of coffee flies over the rim onto the place mat, "as I've told you several times since this hap—"

"You didn't really know her, though, did you?" Dana takes a bite of toast. "Could you pass the jam?"

"I— Through you I did. From the times she was over here. With you."

"Really? 'Cause I don't— The jam?" She watches Peter's hand shake as he reaches for a jar of preserves; his face is pink beneath his perfect hair. "I don't actually remember her being here when you were home."

"Strawberry or . . . ?"

"Yeah," she says. "Strawberry's fine. So when were you and Celia both here again?"

"I didn't— Jesus, Dana, what is this anyway? I didn't actually write it down. 'Met Celia at six o'clock this evening. Our kitchen. Dana hosting.'" He laughs a tight little pretend laugh.

"Did you kill her?" Dana's heart is racing. She wipes her sweaty palms across the thighs of her pajamas as Peter chokes on his coffee. She watches him cough until tears run down his cheeks, and she wants him to say yes, prays he'll say yes—that she'll see a killer, a demon there inside her husband, peeking out his squinty hazel eyes. Crazily, she wills him to nod, to shrug, to raise his hands in a gesture of surrender, because if Peter killed their neighbor, then she'll know that she did not. They'll get him off, she thinks of telling him. They'll hire the best attorney in the state.

"What the fuck is wrong with you?" Peter asks when he can speak. He sounds like a frog. "Take it easy," she says, but her heart slams against her ribs. "You are so not a morning person."

"Why would you say something like that?"

Dana shrugs. "I was kidding."

"People don't kid like that," Peter points out. "Not normal people."

*

He's so different now from who he was when they first met, when Dana was twenty-two, working at a Manhattan law firm, reinventing herself—when Peter was naïve and eager, trying unsuccessfully to fit in with the senior attorneys. Or so she'd thought. Now she thinks he was neither innocent nor particularly eager. He was only new and insecure.

"We're out of sugar." He scrapes a spoon across the bottom of a large glass canister, where a damp clump of granules remains.

She nods. She thinks about grabbing his cell phone out of his back pocket—she can see the small, thin bulge of it when he leans over the counter—and scrolling to Celia's number in his contacts list. She thinks about pressing down her thumb, connecting with the message, with the "You know what to do" on Celia's recording.

She takes another bite of toast, feeling it stick to the

47

roof of her mouth, dry as dust, and she stares past Peter's shoulder out the window. From behind the oak tree at the back of the yard, a form steps onto the lawn—a hooded form in black. The hood is overlarge and moving slightly in the breeze, obscuring whatever face is there. Only the dark form is visible, stooped over in the shadows of the trees.

Dana jumps up, knocking over a glass. "There's someone out there," she says. "Look!"

Peter sighs. He doesn't move. He doesn't even turn around.

"Look! Just— For God's sake—"

He turns around finally, slowly, running his hands through his hair, but the creature in the hoodie is no longer visible; it's lost in the oaks that edge into a patch of county land, a tiny wooded plot at the far end of their yard.

"You have to get some help," Peter tells her. "You're sliding toward the— No. You're careening toward the edge."

Dana nods.

"Really," he says. "Soon. Before it's too late," and Dana nods again. She knows he's right. No matter how she feels about him, no matter what a philanderer he is, about this at least he's right, and she wonders how much time she has before the doors start closing, before her sharp assessments turn to disconnected scraps of sight and sound, before she is mad as a hatter. She hopes there's time enough to reconstruct that dreary afternoon when Celia died. "'There will be time, there will be time . . .'" Her voice is soft in the room, a sprinkle of glitter on the kitchen counter. "'There will be time to murder and create . . .'"

"What?"

"Nothing," she says. "T.S. Eliot. I was just . . ." She clears the dishes from the table and sticks them in the dishwasher, turning the large, bright dial to start. In the bathroom she tugs on a pair of shorts she finds hanging on the doorknob, runs her toothbrush across her teeth, and fills in her lips with red liner.

"I'll get it now," she says, back in the kitchen. She steps into her sandals and grabs her keys off the counter, opens the door. "I've got a few things to pick up anyway. For tonight."

"Get what now?" Peter stands behind her, gangly and awkward, like a Ken doll with cloth arms.

"The sugar," she says.

"Dana," Peter says, and she turns around. "I mean it. You really need to go see Dr. Sing."

She nods. She knows she's racing against time, that she's fast approaching an abyss, a brick wall, and that when she reaches it, she'll no longer know or care if she needs help.

As she rolls down the driveway, she sees Ronald inching past his house with his head stuck out the car window, scrutinizing the decline of his once-perfect yard. He and Celia often had the coveted yard of the month sign stuck into the verdure of their grass, but now even the yellow crime tape has begun to come loose in the wind.

49

She watches him slink past Lon Nguyen, outside washing his Miata, leaning over the soapy hood in a white sleeveless T-shirt and shorts, his flip-flops sinking in mud. Dana backs her car out of the driveway and zigzags onto the street as Ronald slows to a near stop behind her. He ducks his head around the inside of his car as if he's trying to see hers from a range of angles. In her rearview mirror, Dana watches him reach toward his glove compartment and extract a pack of Camels—at least she assumes they're Camels. "Ronald used to smoke," she remembers Celia saying. "Camels, no less, but now he wouldn't touch the things." Dana watches as he lights a match, and then she waves her hand absently toward the back window of the Toyota and speeds down Ashby Lane. Once or twice she thinks she sees him in the traffic behind her car, and she slows down, letting her foot tap on the brake until he catches up. Maybe he'll have Celia's phone with him and she can get another look at that picture of Peter.

She turns in the Root Seller parking lot, filled with sporty minivans and trendy little hybrids, and pulls quickly into a space, jumping out onto the hot asphalt. She strides to the entrance and straight through to the produce aisle, where shoppers linger over broccoli as if it's a new novel. Shopping in the Root Seller, Dana has often thought, is a little like going to a spa, with its large, abundant skylights, the soft sprays of water falling like a gentle rain at the veggie aisle, the strains of Ravi Shankar pumping through the PA system.

She makes her way past the veggies and looks up just as Ronald walks briskly through the large glass doors and strides among the lolling customers, his nose pointed forward like a bloodhound's. He disappears down a middle aisle, and Dana loiters, avoiding him. She'd once encountered him here with Celia, staring at the Rainforest Radish display as if it were a lap dance. She'd wondered then what it would be like to have a husband like Ronald, one you could take to T.J.Maxx and the Root Seller without having him pout and head for the nearest door, cigarette cravings burning in his eyes. She'd decided it might be fun but that she'd probably need a lover, too, that sleeping with Ronald might be more like a pajama party than a blush-evoking night of passion—a conviction, she now realizes, most likely shared by Celia.

When she reaches the fish section, she stops at a table of faux crab salad, where three women in aprons spoon small tufts of the fake crab onto whole-grain crackers. Behind her, someone snorts. Ronald, she thinks. She doesn't turn around to face him. Not quite yet. She moves through the sea of arms and hats, gathering this and that in quick, jerky movements. Grab the apples, grab the bag. Open the bag, insert the apples. The ambience of the Root Seller is marred by Ronald's presence. Even here where she has always felt unreachable, at peace among the cabbages and the German cheese, even here Celia's death hangs like a guillotine above her head.

For a moment he disappears, and Dana thinks he might

have left. Maybe he wasn't even following her. She grabs a bunch of organic bananas and heads back to the cart she's left in the pasta section. And there he is, his face buried in her purse, his pudgy fingers riffling her wallet. For a second she's torn between confronting him and watching to see what he's doing.

"Ronald!"

"Oh," he says. A line of crimson peeps over the open collar of his shirt and moves to his cheeks. "I was . . . You left your purse wide open in the cart here."

Dana stares at him.

"Somebody could just come along and—"

"Go through my stuff?"

"Yeah."

"Much like you were doing?"

"Hey," he says. "Hold on here. I was zipping it for you." He moves away from Dana's cart, his hand stuck out like a traffic cop's, his glasses knocked off center in an obvious collision with the display of herbal sunblock a store manager is rushing to put right. "I thought that was you back there in the fish section. I had to laugh," he says, "at the absolute absurdity of that woman serving fake anything in a store whose whole purpose is to be genuine in this minefield we live in, this maelstrom of margarines that won't melt or attract bugs no matter how long they're left outside the fridge." His words are light, bantering, but his eyes are cold and squinty in his puffy face.

Dana stares at him, placing her hand across her purse

as if it were a small, active child who might escape. Was he after her cash? Could he possibly be that destitute? No. He was looking for something. She can see it in his eyes. He's lying his balding head off, but instead of anger, she feels fear. Is Ronald trying to cover something up, a thought she finds the teensiest bit comforting? Or does he suspect she killed his wife? Is he searching for the proof inside her bag?

"Ronald," she says, "I am so sorry. About Celia. It's so awful I can't even begin to imagine how you must—"

"Thanks. That means a lot," Ronald says, "coming from you." For a moment neither of them speaks.

"Umm," Dana says, "what do you mean?" Her voice cracks.

Ronald shrugs. "Just that . . . you were so special to Celia," he says, but Dana can't tell if he's being sarcastic.

"I wasn't that special. We were . . . we were friends," she finishes in a barely audible voice.

"Yes." Ronald nods. "So where's your husband? Peter, is it? Paul?"

"Peter. He isn't here, actually. He's at home." Her voice, which she now has somewhat under control, thunders across the aisle.

"Oh," Ronald says. "Too bad."

"Do you know Peter?"

"Well," Ronald says, "no. Not really. No. I'd like to, though. I'd really enjoy meeting him."

"Oh." Dana pushes her cart forward to check out and begins unloading it in the speed line. She wonders if

Ronald has happened upon the photo in his late wife's phone and decides by now he probably has, that he's likely in pursuit of Peter to see if his is the unclear face in Celia's cell. Dana feels a slight wave of relief, a second or two of normal breathing, until it occurs to her again that she's the one he's watching. Observing. Stalking.

"So is he around much these days?"

"Not really. Why?"

"I just . . . I was thinking we could all get together, but then I— Sometimes I forget she's gone."

Dana stares at him, at the way he fidgets with the objects in his hands, his slinky, half-crazed eyes. He's acting very weird, although, really, he always seemed to her a little off. Still, the husband is often a prime suspect in a murder like Celia's. She remembers this from many late-night Law & Order reruns, and she reminds herself that stereotypes exist for a reason. She wonders how much Ronald knows about his probable cuckolding. If he's found the photo in the phone, he's also found the almost certain cluster of calls to and from Peter. Has Ronald pushed his fat little thumb down on Peter's name—or possibly a simple "P" for the sake of clandestiny—and reached Peter's answering machine? Has Ronald started putting two and two together? Is he on some sort of mission to avenge his dead wife? Dana looks away. She avoids his eyes, hard and scanning, always scanning—the aisles, her face, scanning, scanning, scanning. He seems out of control. He seems slightly crazy. She studies the contents of her shopping cart, fiddles with her purse strap. "Will there be a service?"

Ronald shakes his head. "We can't do anything until they finish the"—he takes a deep breath—"the autopsy. Here," he says, and he hands her a business card.

"Thanks." Dana drops it into her bag. "You'll let me know, then?"

"Sure thing," he says, which Dana thinks is a totally odd thing for him to say, all things considered. Or possibly it's the cheery way he says it, the inanely pedophilic items he's sticking on the conveyer belt.

"These yours, ma'am?" The cashier holds up a box of carob-covered animal crackers and a rubber duck.

"Umm . . . no," Dana says.

"They're mine." Ronald moves closer. "My stepchildren—" he starts to say, but Dana swipes her debit card, reaches for her receipt, and picks up her bags.

"Ronald," she says, "do you by any chance have Celia's cell phone with you?"

"What," he says, "here?"

Dana nods.

"No," he says. "I left it back in my room. Why? Why do you ask?" He turns toward her, and his face is red in the natural-childbirth lighting of the Root Seller. He looks like someone else for a minute; he looks like a stranger. Confrontational, like a road-rager pulling alongside her on the highway.

"I'd like to look at her photos."

He scrunches up his face; his eyes are tiny circles, like drills boring. He opens his mouth to answer, but then he snaps it shut, leaving a small, slightly boozy bubble in the air between them. "Do you have my key?"

"Yes. God! Here." She reaches into her purse and pulls out an overloaded key ring. The colorful braided attachment Jamie made in eighth grade swings madly as she struggles to free Ronald's key. "I forgot I had this," she says, thrusting it toward him.

He frowns. "You sure about that? I—" But before he can go on, Dana grabs her bags.

"Bye," she calls out, and disappears through the automatic doors, nearly running across the parking lot. It will push her over the edge if she has to spend another minute with Ronald, who is clearly now an angry, scary man, probably a millisecond from accusing her of breaking into his house the night Celia died. The bigger issue is how he knows this. Was he inside, squatting by a couch or flattened under a bed as she streaked, clueless, through the house? The thought makes her shiver. From her car she watches him walking through the parking lot, clutching his small cloth bag with the root seller lettered in red across the outside, with the duck's bill caught on the top and the rubber face of his purchase peeking out like a tiny spy. As she watches, secure behind sunglasses that cover half her face, Ronald pauses to stare at her car across the sea of asphalt, shaking his head and appearing to point toward her before he aims his key repeatedly in the direction of the already winking taillights of his car.

Dana sits in the Toyota, trying to see the insides of her purse from Ronald's perspective. His purchases—the animal crackers and the rubber duck—weren't the sorts of things a desperate man would buy in lieu of bread. So it definitely wasn't money he was after, fumbling through her wallet in the pasta aisle. Pictures, she thinks. Of course. Ronald was looking for a picture of Peter. But why did he stare at her so strangely, push-buttoning his car locks so many times the taillights flashed like Times Square? She jams the Toyota into drive and crawls out of the parking lot. For the first time in several days, she moves slowly, the car's wheels barely turning on the burning black of the asphalt. She wants to put as much distance as possible between her car and Ronald's.

Up ahead, traffic is nearly stopped, and Dana feels herself lifting off from her front seat to float above the other cars. She feels her arms move out from her sides, allowing her to hover in midair for a moment, looking for the source of trouble on the road ahead. "Stop it," she mumbles. "Get it together, Dana." She inhales deeply and switches on the radio. On NPR an author is discussing his new book. "The absolute worst is when everyone else knows but you," the author says, and Dana feels a chill go up her spine. She stabs at the radio, pushing the same button over and over in her panic, in her need to stop the voice. "Everybody knows," the author mumbles as she finds the right button. "It's always best to face what you've done."

## 6

Be careful on the way back," Dana says after dinner when the barbecue pit is lined with doused embers and Jamie's Nissan putters in the driveway. Above them dark clouds streak toward Boston. "Take your time."

Jamie nods. "I will."

"It looks stormy going north." She glances at the bag of cookies she's stuck on top of his backpack and a few books Jamie grabbed from his bedroom. She'll tell him later when he calls. "Take a look on top of your bag," she'll tell him. "I left something there for you. Your favorite—oatmeal chocolate chip!" She's done this ever since the summer he was nine and traveled to Nebraska with Peter's sister; it's become a tradition. "I'm planning to have a brunch this coming Sunday," she says, "for the neighbors. For Ashby Lane," an idea that has only now popped into her head. "I'd love it if you came."

"I don't think so. Thanks, though," Jamie says, and he adjusts the rearview mirror but doesn't leave. He motions her closer, and when she leans over the car window, bending her ear to his lips, he whispers, "Are you sure you're all right, Mom? You seem a little—"

"Tense," she says, backing away a step or two. "It's just

the . . . killing happening so close to us, to someone I—"

"Maybe you should go see that doctor in Manhattan."

"I know," she says. "Maybe I'll go this week," and Jamie nods.

They stay that way for a minute, motionless, the car idling on the hot pavement until finally Peter thumps the roof of the Nissan with the flat of his hand. "Drive safely, son," he says. "Call us when you get into Boston." The car slides back toward the street, and Dana looks up at the dark gray of the clouds, sweeping like hair across the sky. "I love you!" she yells as the car bumps off the driveway onto Ashby Lane, and Jamie waves. "I love you," she says quietly as he takes off down the road and Peter slinks inside like the enigma he's become, already reaching into his pocket for his cell phone. Dana stares at Jamie's car until it disappears, wondering how to glue back all the splintered pieces of her marriage, wondering if she even deserves a husband at this point—if she even wants one.

Has he heard her, this man who was her little boy such a short time ago? Blink and they're gone, people used to tell her. They grow up so fast. But she never believed it. She thought Jamie would always be little, jumping out from behind a chair to surprise her or creeping into their bed at night when he had a bad dream. "I love you," she says to the air.

Peter's in the bathroom with the door closed. He's nearly whispering, but lately Dana can hear anything. She can hear everything. She can hear pins dropping.

Sometimes the chirping of a bird in the next-door neighbor's yard or the barking of a dog blocks away keeps her awake, drives her to the bathroom for bits of cotton to stuff inside her ears. It isn't only sounds; she sees things far more clearly than before. Sometimes she sees the outlines of things, the ghosts of things, not only the bones.

". . . need to see you," Peter's saying, and Dana stops in the hallway to listen. The bathroom is such a silly place to go for privacy, she thinks. There's such an echo in the tiled, hard room, so many walls and corners for a voice to ricochet. "It's important," he says. "I really need to see— . . . I know. Crazy, huh? Right down the street from— . . . My wife is—Dana is—even putting on a goddamn brunch to try to figure out who. She thought she saw somebody in the trees in our back— . . . Right. Probably. Ghosts. . . . Listen," he says after a pause. "Call me on my cell. Or no." He stops, and Dana hears a swishing sound, as if he's turning toward the bathroom door, as if he senses her there, her new bionic self, picking up every single sound. "I'm turning off my phone, so leave me a message. Let me know when we can get toge— . . . Like I said, I really need to see—" There's another pause, and then he says, as Dana moves so close her ear is nearly on the door, "Make it soon." He stops again. "You, too," he says, and his voice is lower suddenly, soft. Loving. Dana feels as if he's slapped her across the face.

She hears the sound of his cell being tossed onto the back of the john. She hears him rearrange his clothes.

She hears his hand on the doorknob, but by the time he steps into the hall, she's already in the kitchen, swiping a dish towel over the counter and staring at the pile of plates and glasses. She watches Peter cross the hall and lower himself onto the sofa in front of the wide-screen TV he purchased last Christmas. "For us," he'd said, but she rarely watches it. It seems so upsetting, all the noise and colors and laughter. Dana has already decided that when she divorces him, she will gladly give Peter the TV.

"Who was that on the phone?" she calls out from the kitchen. "Who were you talking to?"

"Oh," he says, "Ted Johnston from our office. I was trying to get some inside information on Celia," he says. "Being a lawyer comes in handy sometimes."

"So why were you hiding in the bathroom?"

"I wasn't hiding."

"Yes," she says. "You were. Call him back, then. Call him now."

"Who?"

"Ted Johnston!"

He shrugs. "You really need to get yourself in to see that shrink."

She bends over the sink, plunging her arms up to the elbows in hot water, and wonders why she even cares what Peter does. Tears burn her eyes, and she tells herself she's crying because Jamie's left, and partly it's true, but mostly it isn't. Mostly it's Peter, even though she knows what he's done—what he's doing—is hardly an anomaly. Husbands leave their wives all the time for younger, bouncier, rosier-cheeked women with perkier breasts. It happened to Josie from book club. She'd sobbed out all the sordid details in the middle of a Map of Tulsa discussion, and there's poor Wanda across the street who lost her nitwit of a husband to a twenty-something who served him coffee every morning at a local diner. Still, Dana hadn't seen this coming.

In part she blames herself; she blames her mood swings, her indiscretions, her general fucked-up-ness that changed who Peter was, who they both were all those years ago, locking fingers on the subway as the train lurched down the track, running up four flights of stairs to their apartment, undressing as they fell across the bed. She knows that no one has ever loved her quite as much as Peter, and she wonders if it simply ran out at some point, like water spilling from a large, bright cup, leaving them little more than strangers, their marriage only picked-clean bones.

Thunder rumbles somewhere far away, a low hum in the distance. The wind picks up, whistling through the leaves, and something scrapes ominously against the back of the house. Maybe the althea plant, climbing like a beanstalk toward the bedroom window. She takes a deep breath; she wipes her eyes on the back of her arm and squints outside a kitchen window thick with thermal glass. She stares into the dying gray of dusk, scrutinizing every foot of the yard, taking in the plant beside the bedroom window as it creaks and bends inside the wind. On the surface everything looks the same—no hoodied creatures peering out from the brush behind the house—but Dana feels exposed as she gazes out at the backyard; she feels a pair of eyes observing her, hidden beneath the surface.

"I think Ronald was stalking me at the Root Seller," she announces, standing in the kitchen doorway with her arms folded across her chest. Her hands drip soapy water on the tiled floor.

"Why would Ronald be . . . ?" Peter sighs and pushes the mute button on the remote. The Giants game shrinks back inside the wide-screen TV.

"I don't know, Peter. What do you think?"

"I don't. I don't think of Ronald at all. I didn't even know his name until a few days ago, and I have absolutely no opinion on why the widower of our dead neighbor would be stalking you at the Root Seller. Perhaps the bigger question is why that would even cross your mind. And, again, you really need to get some help."

"He was buying a rubber duck."

"So?"

"So no one shops at the Root Seller for a rubber duck, never mind the fact his stepsons are teenagers."

"So what's your point?"

"He wasn't there to buy anything. He was there to confront me."

"And did he?"

"Actually," she says. "He asked a bunch of questions about you. Why would that be, Peter?"

It's dark, suddenly, in the living room. Storm clouds cover what's left of the light outside. Peter shakes his head and glances back at the TV screen, where players race at each other across bright green Astroturf.

She looks away. Sometimes she thinks he can see inside her brain, and she's suddenly afraid of what he might see now, in the gloom, where the muted football game sparks like a strobe in the darkened room and lightning brightens the sky over the highway. She's afraid he might see guilt welling up behind her eyes, might sense it the way a dog smells fear. And there is that, too. Fear of her own husband.

She won't confront him now about his involvement with the Tart and, clearly, Celia. She has enough on her plate, having to deal with that detective in a couple of days, the appointment she's discussed with no one. When he called to ask her to come in, she hadn't allowed herself to think about it. "Sure," she'd said, almost casually, as if she and Wanda were planning a last-minute lunch in town. "See you at ten." She hopes she can pull it off, that her guilt won't leak through and spill across his desk, painting her as the ideal murderess. She plays with the rip in the blue chair; she pokes at the ugly, dirty yellow of the cotton batting. Her hand looks strange there on the chair arm. It looks old.

*

She didn't know Peter when she was a sophomore at NYU. She'd not yet met him when she squatted at the edge of a roof near Tompkins Square and tried to fly. She's told him only bits and pieces of her stays at Bellevue, her lost scholarship, the pages of her manuscript scattered over Avenue D, her stitched and bandaged wrist. The girl who tried to fly had been expunged when she took a job in Peter's office, typing briefs for Mr. Glynniss or Mr. Hudgens or the other senior law partner whose name she no longer remembers. Peter thought she was beautiful then; he told her he was enchanted by her, by her long light hair, her eyes, her thin fingers on the keyboard. He loved her fragility, he said. And she loved him. Not the same way she loved the Poet—not that desperate, passionate, aching love that nearly killed her. It was different with Peter; she was different with Peter—capable and steady, her heels clicking across the glossy, ancient floors.

When they started going out, their conversations were mostly about work, both of them floundering in the day-to-day routine of a law firm older than they were. They helped each other. In time Peter settled into his niche, sipping bourbons in expensive bars after hours with one or the other of the senior attorneys, sharing celebratory cigars with the now long-dead third partner in the heavy mahogany of his office. Their relationship shifted from empathy to lust and finally love, climaxing in a traditional wedding in an old Episcopalian church not far from the office. Dana wore a long white gown from Saks and booked an uptown hotel for the reception; their wedding cake was three-tiered, delicate with yellow roses; her mother wept behind her hand, and bridesmaids tossed birdseed as the newlyweds ran from the churchyard to the car.

But she eventually came back, the girl Dana thought she'd buried long before, the student with her scattered words—the broken girl from NYU came back when Jamie was a few months old. She lost her baby weight and several more pounds, shrinking down to skin and bones. She didn't sleep; she didn't eat; she roamed through the apartment, checking endlessly on Jamie as he lay dreaming in his crib; she drank coffee and chain-smoked outside on the street.

One night Peter found her curled up in fetal position on the floor in the baby's room in the dark, her eyes riveted on the monitor beside the crib, her hair uncombed, her body smelling of sweat and fear. He called a neighbor from downstairs to baby-sit, trundled his young wife, frail and vacant-eyed, to the hospital a short cab ride away, where an intern told them that hormone fluctuations had most likely triggered a manic episode. The intern peered at Dana's thin form in the tiny cubicle. He gave her shots and pills and sent her home with names of counselors and doctors for therapy and follow-ups and tests, with prescriptions scribbled across small white papers.

She stayed on lithium for several months, and eventually the sadness went away. The skinny, frantic girl from Bellevue tucked herself back into the past, and Dana soldiered on. But something integral was changed between them; something irretrievable was lost. She sensed that Peter would never love her with quite the abandon he had before her breakdown—that he would never trust her with his child, his house, their lives, exactly as he had before. And if, in the long, black nights that followed, he rolled up on one elbow to kiss her softly on the cheek, it wasn't passion that propelled him but curiosity or fear, the need to take stock of his unstable wife, to gauge her ability to stand upright inside their wobbly house of cards.

Peter could have left her many times throughout their marriage, when her energy became a raw and frightening thing, when she drove to the city in the middle of the night and stayed away, leaving him to explain the inexplicable to Jamie—to placate this child who cried for a mother who sparkled and shined and burned out like a shooting star—who came home shrunken, crying in a darkened bedroom. She came back a broken thing, so broken even Jamie couldn't fix her with his poignant, frantic offerings over the years—the clay handprint from preschool, the crayon drawing of the three of them together, Dana a small stick figure between the two of them, a cheerful sun shining down from the corner of the page.

It was Peter, always Peter, who took her to the doctor

and drove her home again with a set of new prescriptions tucked inside her bag. It was Peter waiting, watching, times when the days came and went, screeching like an accordion folding shut and opening, in-out, in-out, scraping by, until she was herself again. She has always been thankful to him for this, for these sacrifices he's made. She will always feel a tiny bit of love for him because of them. Even now, with his duplicity hanging like a drape between them.

She sighs, standing up without using her hands or arms to get out of the chair. In the kitchen the phone rings, and she moves toward the sound, stiff, like Jamie's toy soldiers lying somewhere at the back of his closet. "Hello?" She presses the phone tight against her ear, turning her back to the living room with its raucous football game. "Did you run into rain," she says, "going back? Did you find the cookies?"

By the time Dana hangs up, Peter's fallen asleep on the sofa and the eleven-o'clock news has replaced the ball game. The lead story is an interview with a ballplayer who's limping toward the camera with a pulled hamstring. Dana reaches for the remote in Peter's hand, sticks it on the coffee table, carries his glass back to the kitchen as on TV the first assistant prosecutor is introduced in a follow-up story from Friday. The Steinhauser murder case is top priority, she assures her interviewer; they will leave no stone unturned. She's working hand in hand with Detective Jack Moss, she says; they're very close to making an arrest. Dana sets the empty glass in the sink, listening. She grabs the counter; her head buzzes and spins. Her insides lurch painfully, and it crosses her mind that maybe the fish Peter grilled for dinner was bad—maybe Ronald tampered with it somehow when he was bending over her cart. She closes her eyes and counts slowly to ten, trying to regain her balance as on TV the interview ends.

# 7

First Assistant Prosecutor Lenora White is standing in the office when Jack gets to work, and he's a good twenty minutes early. She is such an A-type personality. He watches her from the hallway. She really is attractive, especially this morning, silhouetted in the light drifting through the grimy window, and for a minute he forgets how angry he was, watching her on TV. She stands across the room from Jack's desk, staring out at the gray of the buildings, the ominous clouds, the reluctant sun as it struggles up behind the hustle-bustle of traffic.

"What can I do for you, Lenora?"

"Sorry. Didn't mean to be intrusive, but I told Rob I'd meet him here before work. I've got something on the Mancini case."

"The missing girl?"

She nods. "Some family issues have turned up. Just wanted to fill him in."

"Coffee?" Jack can hear the machine coming to life across the hall. "It's bad, but it's caffeine."

"Sure," she says. "Mind if I sit?"

"Hey." Jack gestures to a cruddy swivel chair beside his desk. "Make yourself at home."

*

"How's the homicide coming along?" She takes the coffee cup gingerly from Jack when he comes back, blows on it as he sets down his own cup, dropping several creams and sugars on his desk.

He shrugs. "It's coming."

"Such a push for us to— They run that damn picture 24/7, the photograph of Ms. Steinhauser—Cynthia, is it?"

"Celia."

"Right. Celia. Anything turn up yet?"

"Not really. Strange goings-on the night she died. Looks like someone was inside the house. We've got some tests being run by forensics, but nothing's back yet. I'll keep you in the loop."

"Put a rush on it?"

"Done," Jack says.

"Great. This coffee is a little strong," she says, and she adds another three creamers, stirs it with her index finger. "You guys need a woman's touch around here."

"That an offer?"

She looks up. "It all depends," she says. "You'd have to make it worth my while."

Jack smiles. Down the hall the outer door thunders back into place. "Must be Rob," he says.

"Right on time." Lenora glances at her watch— simple, Jack notes. Cheap, even, not the glitzy type he'd imagine her wearing. No bling.

71

"He's a good cop," Jack says, and Lenora takes a sip of muddy coffee.

"I know he is." She looks up through a thick batch of lashes. "Rob's a great guy. Still . . . he doesn't have the whole James Dean thing going for him."

"Who does?" Jack grabs his briefcase, starts to head out. He'll let Rob have the office for his meeting with Lenora.

"You do," she says, and she takes another sip of coffee.

*

She's pushing hard for both these cases to be wrapped up, the homicide and the missing teen, but Jack knows better than to rush things. He's got to get this right even if it means reining in the assistant prosecutor. It's a big case, complicated. He flips through his notes. He sent a patrolman back to the Steinhausers' the morning after the cop thought he saw a light on inside, just in case they missed something in the dark the night before, and he found a few footprints around the back door, maybe new, maybe not so new. The cop photographed them and delivered them to Jack's office sometime last night. They're not the best photos. About the only thing he can tell is that they're small—either a woman's or a small man's. Again, the neighbor with the key seems the likely one. Even if what Ronald's told him about drinking all night at the hotel turns out to be a lie, he's a fair-size guy and Lon

Nguyen is very small, but he didn't have a key. Almost certainly the footprints belong to Dana Catrell, the neighbor four doors down.

Rob ran the priors on the suspects, but not much came up. Nothing at all on Dana. There was an old drug arrest on her husband—cocaine possession in college—but the charges were dropped. Lon Nguyen was clean as a whistle. Ronald's first wife died in a car crash shortly after they were married, but nothing looked suspicious there. The real shocker was Celia herself. She had one arrest when she was a kid in West Virginia for aiding and abetting, the apparent getaway driver for her boyfriend, who served three years for holding up a gas station with a fake gun. Celia was released after she cooperated with the police. Mother Teresa takes a tumble.

Jack gets up and pours himself another cup of coffee. The footprints, the lying husband, the Bonnie-and-Clyde teacher bleeding out in her foyer, Ann putt-putting out of his life, and pressure from the prosecutor's office to wrap things up quick. He can already tell this case will be like herding cats and that Rob will have his hands full tracking down the missing teen. What Lenora said in the TV interview rankles him, but he didn't mention it when she was in his office. He tells himself he was just about to, but then Rob came in. Jeesh, he thinks. Man fucking up.

# 8

Dana rolls over, staring at the wall, listening as Peter showers and dresses, sitting up as he turns on the coffee-maker in the kitchen. His voice on the phone is muted. "Noon," she hears him say, and then the coffeemaker snaps and percolates, and she lies back down until she hears the front door close behind him. His Lexus purrs toward the street.

She glances outside the living-room window, where clouds are fluffy and white, and then she closes the blinds. The daylight makes her anxious. Nights are bad enough, with her sleeplessness, with her constant prowling and reading, but the brightness of morning is worse. Noon, he'd said on the phone, presumably to the Tart. She'll drive to Manhattan. She'll go to Peter's office at noon—a little earlier, so she can watch him, see who it is he meets, get a look at the Tart in broad daylight.

At a little after ten, she heads for the city, driving slowly toward the offices of Glynniss, Hudgens and Catrell in the staid brick building only blocks from Central Park. She creeps along the streets, pulling in to a pricey garage and grabbing the receipt.

It's nearly noon when she reaches the street and takes

a few steps in the direction of Peter's office. She remembers a tiny park in the midst of a collection of buildings catty-corner to the law firm—two wooden benches in a makeshift garden, a nod to greenery in the smog and clutter of the city. She steps off the curb; there's something just at the edge of her vision. A car turns onto the street and slows down for a second as if it's watching her, as if the car itself is alive and trolling for prey—as if it is surprised to see her standing there, unexpected and enticing. It speeds toward her, and for a second she's paralyzed with fear. She screams. She turns and runs back to the curb, and then she flies backward, her feet barely touching the asphalt. The car speeds past, and Dana disappears behind a clot of parked cars, ducks down beside a large truck. "Five-two, five-two," she says aloud, struggling to concentrate, to keep at bay the terror threatening to engulf her. A five and a two, all she managed to remember of the numbers on the license plate.

She unfastens her hair clip, lets her hair fall down across her face. She sticks on her large sunglasses and takes off the shirt she's thrown on over a tank top. Her arms are sickly pale in the sunny summer day. She crumples her shirt inside her purse and picks her way across the street, on the lookout for a nondescript sedan, a dark car hurtling down the street or squealing around a corner.

She reaches the small bench at three minutes to twelve and sits, staring across the street toward the door of Glynniss, Hudgens and Catrell. It opens only seconds later, and Peter steps out onto the sidewalk. He walks quickly to the curb, his hand a visor over his eyes as he stares first to the right and then the left, up and down the street as if he's looking for a taxi, but he makes no move to approach the two or three cabs that lumber by him through the noon traffic. Dana watches from behind her hand, pulling her hair across her face. She watches as a dark sedan pulls to a stop alongside her husband. She watches as Peter rushes to duck inside. The traffic shifts and snarls in the wake of this unwelcome interruption, the stopping of this car in the middle of a midday rush. Dana stands up, walking to the curb at the edge of the small green space, her hair blowing away from her face, leaving her exposed and unprotected as she squints across the street at the back of the sedan, at the five and the two on the license plate.

She stumbles toward the garage, gulping polluted summer air. She trips over a crack in the sidewalk, glances at the trees strewn in among the buildings, blossoming and green, brighter, newer than the lost Dutch elms. The traffic snarls. Horns honk. The city is a sneer. A smirk. Peter's city now, no longer hers. Once she's safely back inside her car, she doesn't want to move; she feels reluctant to leave the dark garage, afraid she'll be spotted pulling out to the street, but after what seems an eternity, she starts the car. "Here goes," she whispers to St. Christopher, lurches up to pay, and speeds toward Paterson, her eyes riveted on the road ahead.

Once home, she drinks a glass of wine, and for several minutes she sits on her sofa, the blinds closed tight against the day. Finally she picks up the phone to call Peter, even though she isn't sure how much to tell him of the morning's strange events. For all she knows, he wants her dead. Or mad. Or are his lame attempts at hiding his affairs making him look guiltier than he actually is?

"Hello," she says when he answers. "Are you back?"

"I'm here at the office," Peter says. He sounds puzzled. "Why?"

"I tried to call you around noon," she lies. "They said you were out."

"Who said I was—"

"So where were you?"

"At lunch, I guess. With Josh. Josh Reinhardt? He's one of my clients, wanted to talk about his trial coming up."

"Murder?"

"Tax evasion," Peter says, and he laughs.

Dana hangs up. A light blinks in the hallway, on the desk in the foyer—a tiny flicker, a lightning-bug wink, but when she turns her head to look, the defunct lamp is dull and dark beneath its opaque shade, and Dana knows that time is running out. She feels the madness knocking at her brain.

# 9

The idea of a brunch was at first merely a last-minute attempt to get Jamie home for the second time in a few days, but after giving it some thought, Dana decides it's a good plan in spite of its iffy origins. She doesn't think any of the neighbors were particularly close to Celia, but even so it has to be distressing to know that someone on their block was bludgeoned to death in her own living room, a shock to the entire street to lose one of its residents in such a brutal, baffling way. The funeral is on hold for the time being, due to the investigation and presumably the autopsy, and since there's no memorial service planned as yet, for the neighbors who actually knew Celia, the brunch will serve a dual purpose.

Dana will have an open house so they can talk about what's happened, so they can drift from room to room, nibbling on croissants and marmalade, and not feel cornered the way they would at a dining-room table. They'll speak more openly about their dealings with Celia. They'll let things slip, so Dana can reconstruct the day her neighbor died, understand the wheres and whos of things, and ultimately put the pieces together.

She still has Ronald's number. She has many numbers,

written down on scraps of paper lying flat against the bottom of her purse. They belong to people she found comical or brilliant, people she thought she'd like to see again, to meet for coffee in town. In the sparkly period at the onset of her madness, she is magnetic, sensual, alluring. People are drawn to her. Before she drowns inside it, she rides the wave of effervescence; she is gregarious, fun, the clever friend, the unfettered lover, the ideal companion. For a brief, bright clot of time, she shines, making deep but fleeting connections with people she meets in line at the post office or waiting for a tune-up in town. When days later she finds these papers, these cell-phone numbers and e-mail addresses, she often doesn't even remember the faces connected to them.

She assumes that not all the invitees will come. Twelve, she figures. Fourteen tops. She isn't even sure she wants the neighbors chatting with one another, possibly mentioning that Peter's never home or that they'd seen him sneaking through the back door of the victim's house. Still, she invites them all; she'll cast the deck and let the cards fall as they may.

She polishes the dustless wooden bottoms of her chairs and thumbs through Brunches for Bunches, a cookbook she discovered on a yard-sale jaunt with Celia several months before. On the way to the grocery store, she stops at a bakery and picks up some croissants and cinnamon rolls and then, on impulse, a few raspberry crullers. She'll make scrambled eggs, she decides, and maybe fry some bacon. Do her neighbors eat bacon? She opts for veggie sausage and turkey-bacon strips, orange juice and the pastries she's brought from the bakery. It's not, after all, about the food. It's about transparency. Clarity.

*

Ronald is the first to arrive. Peter shakes his hand and settles him on the living-room sofa while Dana putters in the kitchen, scrambling eggs and popping croissants into the toaster oven. Orange juice sits ready in a cut-glass pitcher on the dining table beside a large bouquet of daisies.

"Hi, Ronald!" She stands in the kitchen doorway. Sweat sticks tiny curls of hair to her forehead; the air conditioner drones gamely.

"Dana," he says, but he seems reluctant to take his eyes off Peter.

"So you two meet at last," she says.

"What's that?" Peter cups his hand around his ear as if he hasn't heard a thing, and the gesture is an unpleasant reminder of their trip from Boston, of his white hand locked around his phone. Around the Tart. Around the lilting voice that titillates and lures.

"Ronald asked about you the other day at the Root Seller. I thought I told you. Anyway, he's been very anxious to meet you."

"And now it seems you have," Peter says in a jovial, neighborly voice, but even from the kitchen Dana notices

80

the slight tremor in his hand as he bends to line up the pillows on the sofa.

"Yes." Ronald draws himself up straighter. He stares at Peter's face, his eyes small and dark, like raisins stuck in dough. "I've seen you before," he says. His voice is low and tight, a bit menacing.

"Oh," Peter says. "Probably in the hood." Again he uses this strangely jolly voice that Dana doesn't recognize.

"I don't think so." Ronald squints at Peter. "No. It was somewhere else," he says as Peter walks over to the door where Wanda and her two boys are visible through the screen.

"Hey," he says, a little of the jolliness gone from his voice. "Good to see you, Wendy."

"Wanda," she says. She slides past him and waves at Dana in the kitchen doorway.

Lon Nguyen is the next to arrive, with his wife, who speaks no English, and the two of them debate at length in Vietnamese before Lon takes one of the cinnamon buns and sticks it on a plate. He's wearing flip-flops as usual. Dana hasn't seen these before, and she wonders if he has a pair for whatever occasion may arise—if so, these would be the brunching flip-flops, a tad festive with a sky blue thong. She scrambles another batch of eggs and pours them into the frying pan as the front door opens again.

"Hello," she calls. People bubble through the front door, and Peter stands back. He bows, makes a sweep-ing, welcoming gesture with his arm as the Steinhausers' across-the-street neighbors swarm over the threshold. Clearly Dana has underestimated. There are at least twenty-five people milling through her house, oozing into the kitchen, where she stands dishing up plates of scrambled eggs and dying for a Bloody Mary. She hasn't given a brunch in years, and after today, she promises herself, she never will again.

She glances up from the skillet to see Peter standing in the doorway, his hair sticking up on top. She thinks fleetingly of a rooster. "What?"

"Oh," he says, "nothing, really. The office sent a clerk over with a discovery for a trial we're working on."

"Where is he? Or she?"

Peter backs up, takes a quick look at the living room. "She. And she's on the couch," he says, "talking to Wanda. Can you manage for a few minutes while I look it over—make sure it's all there?"

"What trial?" Dana snaps, but the eggs are sputtering and crinkling at their edges, so she turns back to the stove. By the time she takes them out to the table, Peter has disappeared and Wanda is alone on the couch. Lon Nguyen makes his way through the crowds, and Dana remembers the signs he posted on telephone poles and stuck on the outsides of mailboxes several months before. lon nguyen, block captain, they said, and there was a phone number, presumably his, that she'd not bothered to jot down before she tossed the thing into the recycling bin. He isn't exactly a walking advertisement for Neighborhood

82

Watch groups today—not at this makeshift wake for the bludgeoned, dead component of his block.

She picks up a fake sausage. "Sorta sausage," Jamie calls it, and she chews on the rubbery morsel, swallows it down with a thimbleful of orange juice, all that's left after the sudden gush of guests. She spots Ronald by the bookcase in the hall and makes her way over to where he thumbs through a book. He's inches from the bedroom, and his eyes aren't really on the book. They're scanning again, as if he's looking for something.

"Did you have enough to eat?" She stares down at where he's squatting on the floor.

"Yes." He nods. "Good sausage."

"Did you try the eggs?"

"I'm vegan," he says. "You have some interesting books."

"I do." Dana glances at the title in his hand. "But Bugs in Your Backyard isn't really one of them. Would you like a Bloody Mary?"

"Yes," he says, turning back to the book, "I'd love one."

Dana finds some slightly aging tomato juice in the refrigerator and adds quite a bit of vodka, along with horseradish and various herbs and spices she finds in a cabinet. It's getting noisy in the dining room. She swishes everything around inside the two glasses with her index finger, making her way slowly through the crowds in the three rooms between her and Ronald, who now seems focused on the bookshelf for something more illuminating.

"Thanks." He sips at his drink. "Do you know all these people?"

"No. In fact . . ." Dana surveys the living room from where she leans against the wall. "I know Wanda and her boys and Lon Nguyen, and that's about it."

"I've seen the guy in the Dockers," Ronald says. "He lives across the street from us. From me. And Nguyen, of course. He's the one who started our Neighborhood Watch."

Dana nods. "Which really needs to be more . . . um, watchful."

"Yes."

"By the way," Dana says. She leans over so she's nearly whispering in Ronald's ear. "Do you have Celia's phone with you?"

"No," he says, back at the book. "Why? What is it with you and Celia's fucking phone?" Dana sees he's suddenly stopped reading. His eyes are frozen on the page. His jaw twitches. His ears are red, and a little rash begins to zigzag upward from his throat. Still he doesn't look at her.

"Nothing." Dana takes several steps backward. "Really," she mumbles. She trips on the edge of the rug. "God. I was just— Actually . . ." She clears her throat and speaks in what she hopes is a commanding tone, despite Ronald's sudden and alarming mood shift. "I was wondering if she still had the photos of the two of us. There were several," she lies, "of us hamming it up

84

for the camera. We were friends, you know. It would be nice to flip through and reminisce."

Ronald shrugs. On the other side of the living room, Peter is escorting someone out onto the porch—the clerk, she supposes. Is he screwing her, too? Dana moves forward for a better look, brushing past a snag of neighbors as the door opens. She inches through the crowd as Peter steps outside with his visitor, and Dana studies the back of the departing head as best she can through all the people between her and the doorway—tallish brunette.

Lon Nguyen touches her sleeve with the tips of his fingers. "We are leave now," he announces. His wife stands waving and smiling at the front door. Wanda, too, is waving. She's mouthing Thank you and making an I'll call you gesture with her thumb and pinkie as her boys spill loudly into the yard.

"Thank you all for coming," Dana says. She taps a crystal glass with the edge of a teaspoon, and a twinkly sound fills the suddenly quiet house. A couple of minutes later Ronald walks briskly toward his car, neighbors crowd the street in their brightly colored summer clothes, and Dana closes the door, heads for the sinkful of soapy water.

"I'm taking a nap!" Peter yells from the living room. "What a freak show that was," he calls out after a few minutes. How about that Donald character!"

"Ronald?"

"Right. Celia's husband. Did you see the way he was looking at me? Like I ran over his dog!" Peter's voice lags on the last few words, and when she peers around the counter, she sees he's already asleep, his shoes lined up toe to toe beside the couch. Dana gives the glasses a cursory rinse and sticks them in the dishwasher. Clearly Peter noticed Ronald's weird behavior, too, even taking the cell-phone picture out of the equation, which Ronald certainly has. If she intends to see the thing again, she's obviously on her own, and by the time she starts the dishwasher, she's decided to take a trip into Manhattan to find the phone herself.

## 10

It's nearly two when Dana tosses her apron into the washer along with several place mats and a dish towel. She wanders into the living room, where Peter's snores ripple loudly through the house, eclipsing the music from the CD player near the foyer. Did anyone even hear it, she wonders—the eclectic mix of seventies and eighties music she'd so carefully chosen, the dribs and drabs of ancient blues and modern jazz? Peter hadn't picked out anything. In fact, except for his announcement in the kitchen doorway and his presence during the first few minutes, she has no idea where he even was during most of the brunch. For all Dana knows, he was in the backyard, squatted near the picnic table with his phone.

She yawns. Someone's left the front door slightly open, and she tugs on the doorknob. She grabs her latest novel from the desk just inside the door in the entryway, and when she opens the book, a piece of paper falls out—a shopping list, she thinks at first, or an old deposit slip, something she's used as a bookmark. But there's writing on it, tiny writing she can barely make out. "Fair eats, but your little brunch doesn't begin to pay the piper. Better watch your back."

Fear rips through her, surrounds her—a strangling, suffocating fear. She clutches the tiny piece of paper and closes her book, setting it on the coffee table as if a sound, a movement made too quickly, anything at all might set off an explosive, fatal retribution. She eases herself off the chair and over to Peter, snoring on the couch. She reaches out and touches him, a light, silent touch. The snoring stops for several seconds before it resumes.

"Peter?" She calls his name softly. She glances around the room in case whoever wrote the note is still inside, sunk into a corner. "Peter!" she says, louder. This time the snoring stops. His eyes pop open.

"What?"

"Someone was here!"

"Many were here."

"No—" Her voice breaks. "No," she says again. "Someone else was here, someone angry with me."

"We basically tossed them out," Peter says, sitting up with an exaggerated groan. "They'll get over it." His eyes are droopy; his perfect hair is one big cowlick.

"No," she says. She shakes his arm and holds the scrap of paper up in front of his face. "Read it!"

"Read it? I can't even see it! Where are my—"

"Here," she says, and she hands him her reading glasses.

"'Fat ears—'"

"No," she says. "God." She sticks on her glasses. "'Fair eats, but your little brunch doesn't begin to pay the piper. Better watch your back.'"

88

Peter yawns. "What the hell does that mean?"

"It means—" Dana stops. She doesn't know, actually, but clearly she was right: Someone's watching her, threatening her, hating her. She chews on her cuticle. "It means, Peter, that someone's stalking me, planning to kill me for all I know. It means I'm scared shitless!"

"I meant, did you offend someone? Hit a garbage can? Play your car radio too loud?"

"Well, yes. I mean, obviously I have. Offended someone. In fact, maybe whoever I offended is crouched somewhere inside the house."

"Why would they be?" He yawns again.

"Why would someone kill Celia?"

After a minute or two, Peter gets up and shuffles from room to room.

"You have to really look," Dana says, kicking at the drapes. She checks all the coats in the hall closet and behind the shower curtains in both bathrooms. She can hear Peter thumping around their bedroom, and when she hears him trip over an amp cord, she knows he's checking Jamie's room.

"Nothing," Peter says, back on the couch. "Do you mind if I finish my nap?"

"No," she says. "Well, yes. Actually, I do. We have to figure out who left that note," she says, but the only answer is a rumble of far-off thunder and an indecipherable murmur from her husband. She rereads the message, checking the paper for other writing, a label, a number—anything that might provide a window into the world of whoever wrote it and left it for her. There are some fragments of numbers—a receipt, too ripped for her to tell where it came from. She thinks about Ronald at the Root Seller, the odd way he acted, trapping her there in the aisle. She thinks about the neighbors milling here and there, with faces she has never seen. She thinks about how guilt tugs at her, wakens her from fitful, insufficient sleep, and then she thinks about the hooded figure staring at her through her kitchen window from the backyard, the scraping sound she thought was the althea plant beneath the bedroom window—how she scrutinized the yard to no avail, but still she knew—still she felt the eyes just somewhere underneath the surface of things, watching. Waiting. Hating.

She wonders: If she could pull back the too-large hood on the figure in the yard, whose face would be there, hidden in its breeze-blown folds? A wayward teenage gangster looking for an open window or an unlocked car? Celia's killer? Worse, would she have seen Celia's ghostly, anguished face lurking there or, worse still, her own?

*

Dana tiptoes out to her car while Peter snores on the sofa. Not only does the note terrify her, there's the meeting with the detective on Celia's case the next morning. Questioning the neighbors, he'd told her on the phone.

It's standard. She wonders, though. Lately nothing in her life is standard; nothing is the way it seems. She hasn't mentioned it to Peter, even though she knows he could come with her; he could act as her lawyer. But would he? Could she find out things about her husband if she meets this cop—this Jack Moss—alone? Things she couldn't learn with Peter there beside her? Storm clouds hover overhead, turning the sunny day into a gray and early evening. She grips the steering wheel and drives toward town, pulling sloppily in to a parking space outside an all-night diner. She sits for a moment in the hot dampness of the front seat. A sign blinks and buzzes overhead, bathing both her dashboard and St. Christopher in slightly blue fluorescence. jessie's din, it says, the last two letters bashed out by some misguided soul or a wayward baseball from the vacant lot next door.

Over the years she's come to Jessie's when she couldn't sleep, when her insides buzzed and jiggled as if she'd stuck her finger into a wall socket. She's come here for years, times like this when she's run out of friends to call in the middle of the night—and really, who could be expected to listen to her endless babbling at 3:00 a.m.?—when nudging Peter awake only makes him pull the covers tight around him and turn toward the wall. She comes to Jessie's when she's feeling manic and wired. It's so much better than a bar, she tells herself—told Peter when he cared enough to ask where she was going—better than drinking herself into a stupor, even though she's done exactly that more times than she can count. It scares her, though, the drinking, the thought of becoming an alcoholic like her father, dead at forty-one, the strange way he died. Baffling, really. He traveled all the time. He often rode that 9:15 from Philly.

It's been almost three years since she's come here, sitting in this same back booth with the cracked red plastic, the table with its ugly speckled pattern, the nicks along the edge, the thankfully bad lighting. She reaches for a napkin, slips a pen out of her bag, vaguely aware of the waitress approaching. She smiles. Glenda is a beacon in a dark night, an island in a soupy sea of humanity—the drunks, the homeless, the misbegotten, the heartbroken and lonely. The crazy. Glenda the Good.

"Hey!" she says. "Dana! Haven't seen you in ages!"

"I know. I've been—" Sane, she thinks. I've been a little too sane for Jessie's.

"What can I get you?" Glenda pockets a tip from the next table and glances back at Dana. "Decaf?"

"Yeah," Dana says. "Wow. You have a memory like an ele—"

"Got to in this business."

"My neighbor," Dana says. "She was murdered."

"Oh! God! The one on Ashby Street? It's been all over the news."

"Lane," Dana says, "but yeah."

"Be right back." Glenda sighs, heading toward the cash register, where several customers are lined up in the faulty, greenish lighting of the entrance as Dana clicks her pen open and closed and open again.

"Notes," she writes across the napkin top. She draws a line down the center, dividing it in half. "What I know," she writes at the top of the first half. "What I don't," she scrawls at the top of the second, and she underlines both headings. She has always been organized. When Jamie left for college, it was Dana who helped him pack, setting aside her feelings about his opting for Boston instead of NYU. She was the one who pored through manuals, who researched every school in the Northeast, printing page after page of statistics, leaving them neatly clipped and stacked by state on Jamie's desk. She focused on the minutiae of the thing and closed her eyes to the reality. By the time they drove up with him to college, a sad little caravan, she and Peter chugging along behind their son's Nissan, she was exhausted. At the orientation dinner, a torturous affair, she drank too much and laughed too loud, embarrassing her son with her rambling. When they left, she leaned heavily on Peter's arm, nearly comatose by the time the taxi dropped them off at their hotel near Copley Square, the first good sleep she'd had in weeks.

Under the first heading, she writes "I was there, I was angry, I was drunk." She chews on the end of her pen and adds, "I don't remember chunks of the afternoon, Ronald has Celia's phone, Peter and Celia together, Peter and the Tart together," and, as an afterthought, "Peter is such a prick!"

93

Under the second heading, she writes, "If or when I'll be implicated in C's murder." She stops, glancing up at Glenda moving toward her. "I am on a train to Crazy," she adds to the first list, and then, in capital letters, "I AM THE LAST KNOWN PERSON TO SEE CELIA ALIVE!"

"Here you go." Glenda sets two cups of coffee between them. "That one's decaf."

"Don't you have to . . . ? Aren't you . . . ?"

"Taking a break. Everybody needs a break," she says.

"Even Glenda the Good."

"I like that. 'Glenda the Good.' The Wizard of Oz, right?"

"It's actually Glinda," Dana says, but Glenda doesn't answer.

"I'm so glad you're here." Dana leans forward on her elbows. "I was afraid you might be off."

"I'm never off," Glenda says. She takes a sip of coffee. "Why?"

"My neighbor," Dana says. She looks around the restaurant. "I think I might have killed her."

Glenda rips a packet open and lets sugar sift into her cup. "Never liked that fake sugar," she says. "The devil you know is better than the one you—"

"Did you hear what I—"

"You didn't," Glenda says.

"You don't understand," Dana says. "I was there. I was— I can't remember half the afternoon."

Glenda opens a creamer and stirs it into her coffee.

"Honey." She takes a slug of coffee; she leans forward so their noses nearly meet across the faded sparkles of the Formica. "A couple years ago, you thought you were Mary Magdalene."

Dana considers. "That was different. I was feeling . . . guilty or something."

"As opposed to now." Glenda takes another swig of coffee. Dana fiddles with her cup.

"You also thought you were Judas Iscariot come back in female form. There's a theme here."

"But this time—"

"Listen." Glenda stands up. She takes one last slug of coffee and straightens her hair, reties her apron. "If there's one thing I know, it's people. And you're no killer."

"Thanks," Dana says. "Really. I think I'll just sit here for a while, jot down a few more notes." She takes a small sip of decaf. Thank God for Glenda. She doesn't judge. She never judges, but she's always here—so much more real than all Dana's other friends, times like this when her brain whirls and snaps, when her girlfriends seem nearly drugged, fiddling and fussing and slugging through their lives. Glenda says only what Dana needs to hear.

She writes down on a second napkin whatever comes to her, things she didn't think she remembered. She writes in a tiny, slanted, barely legible scrawl, very different from her usual neat and careful writing with its closed o's and carefully crossed t's. She must be channeling, she thinks, accessing some buried part of her subconscious, where things like Celia's heavy makeup wait to be pulled up from the murk of the day she died—the bright gash of crimson lipstick drunkenly applied, making Celia's mouth a large, bright, crooked oblong. There was an odor, too, something vaguely familiar that Dana can't quite place; she jots that down as well. And the vase—a heavy, thick-sided piece. She'd touched it idly, picked it up to see, and even empty it was heavy. A lovely blue, a cobalt blue like the sky deepening into night, and then a memory bull-dozes through, disturbing and intense. She stops writing. She drops the pen as if it's on fire. She stares at her hands, folds them on her lap beneath the table as two policemen sit down at the counter and look at her across the diner, a lingering, appraising glance. She hums a vapid, tuneless sound to drown the memory dredged up from the muck of her subconscious.

She carefully folds the napkins and sticks them in her bag, avoiding eye contact with the cops, who have swive-led on their stools to face her. She leaves five dollars on the table and hurries past the officers, waving in the gen-eral direction of Glenda at the register. She hums again, more loudly, sliding into the front seat and turning the key. St. Christopher gleams in the light from the broken sign as Dana struggles to forget how she'd stared at the yard-sale vase just before the drinks kicked in. The mem-ories are there, though, clear and cruel, and she thinks of the moths singeing their wings in the yard lights, recalls the moment she stared at the blue vase, the moment it was crystal clear to her exactly why Celia was upset and why she'd captured Peter and the Tart inside her phone. It comes back, too, the anger that encompassed her before the alcohol kicked in, before it fogged her thoughts and made bald spots inside her mind, how she'd wanted to pick up Celia's lovely hand-thrown vase and bash her over the head.

She tries to tamp down this totally unwelcome memory. She concentrates on the traffic, on counting the bricks in the building. She thinks about the note, the strange writing—a cruel joke, maybe, a nasty neighbor. "Glenda the Good," she says, and she repeats it. "Glenda the Good, Glenda the Good," like a mantra. She says it all the way home.

## 11

By the time the doors close behind her at the station, Dana is already halfway down the hall. Reaction formation, she thinks she remembers from one of her countless psychiatric sessions, this rush toward the detective's office, when what she wants to do is turn around and run in the other direction or flatten herself under a desk. She's terrified of this meeting, but she wants to put it behind her.

She hikes up her skirt, too loose and slipping down around her hips; her lack of interest in food has taken a toll. She finds the ladies' room and ducks inside, rooting around in her purse for a safety pin, tucking the waistband together and snapping the pin in place. She glances at her face in the mirror, and then she looks away, afraid that if she looks too closely, she'll see a murderer lurking there in the glass. She pulls out a modest, humdrum shade of lipstick, leaning over the sink to apply it, careful to look only at her lips. Satisfied, she blots them on a tissue and steps back from the mirror, concentrating on breathing until she's in the hall.

The walls are gray and formidable, and she tries not to look at them. Instead she looks down at the floor, and the linoleum squares frighten her. "Detective Moss?"

She stands just inside a large room in front of a bare-bones desk that reminds her of grade school. His name is inscribed on a wooden rectangle.

"Yes." He gets up, leaning over the desk to shake her hand, and she pulls her sweaty fingers quickly over his palm, like a crab scuttling, she thinks.

"Thanks for coming in," he says, and Dana smiles. "This shouldn't take long. We can stay here if you'd feel more comfortable," he says, glancing around the empty room, and Dana nods.

Jack Moss shuffles through some papers and looks up at her over the tops of his glasses. Drugstore glasses, she guesses, and she thinks of Peter spending hundreds of dollars on his, of his prescription sunglasses sitting in an understated, overpriced leather case, of her own large, plaid Foster Grants from Walmart.

"I spoke with your neighbor. Lon Nguyen. He said you were with Mrs. Steinhauser on the day of her—"

"Of her demise. Yes, I was."

"Could you tell me about that afternoon?"

"It was—let me think—it was hot. It was really hot. Very foggy, though."

The detective leans back in his seat. He holds a pencil between his thumbs, stretching it out like a little log in the air. "I'm not so much interested in the weather as—"

"I know. I'm just trying to bring back the whole—you know—ambience of the afternoon."

He presses the pencil more tightly between his thumbs.

"So your neighbor? Mrs. Steinhauser?"

"I was just getting home from picking up some books from the library. I'd put a couple on hold, and they'd— Anyway, she called me over. Celia. She was teetering on those stupid wedges out in her yard. 'It's a matter of life and death,' she said. So I went over to see what she wanted. I guess Mr. Nguyen told you."

"Yes."

Dana stops talking. She can feel herself speeding up. She looks at Moss across the desk, at the furrow in his forehead, the black down along his arm, his brown eyes, his hair that was probably almost black before it started turning gray. There's something about him that soothes her in spite of the reason for their meeting. He reminds her in his dark, mysterious way of the Poet. He leans over his desk toward her, and she feels the heat coming off his body in the sweltering office. She wants to reach out and touch him with the tips of her fingers. She crosses her legs, and her foot bobs up and down. She can feel sweat starting under her arms. "It's so hot," she says.

He nods. "Nothing like Jersey in the summertime. So what'd she want?"

"She wanted to show me something." For the first time since Celia's death, Dana feels visible, transparent. She feels that Moss really sees her, her imperfections, her raw and jagged edges, her sharp, incessant thoughts.

"What did she want to show you?"

Dana takes a breath and holds it in. Her heart speeds

up, beating so fast it's like one long beat. Like contractions right before a baby comes. Did Ronald show him the picture? Does he know about Peter and the Tart?

"She had some pictures of her . . . of her boys," Dana tells him. "Of herself and her boys. One of them just had a graduation recently. Tommy," she says, "from junior high, and she . . . um, she took some pictures of that. And then there was one of two people sitting at a table, a man and a woman. The guy looked like Peter—like my husband. 'Look at this!' she said."

"This was in her phone?"

"Her cell phone. Yes. Did you see it?"

"Did I see what?"

"The picture. If so, you'd know—well, sort of know— what my husband looks like. He's very handsome. He's blond. He has very expensive hair. Like John Edwards," she adds, realizing the irony. It crosses her mind that Peter and the Tart could have a small blond child stashed somewhere.

"No," he says. "I didn't. So what was life-and-death?" Jack chews on the end of the pencil.

Dana shrugs. "She was—Celia was—a little tipsy. More than a little."

"Why was that?"

"Who knows?" Dana inches back a tad on her chair. "She'd had quite a bit of sangria."

"Was it some sort of occasion?"

"I don't know. Maybe. There's always an occasion if

you want one, isn't there? I mean, there's always a reason for sangria if you teach Hispanics," Dana says, and Detective Moss looks up. "Wait. That didn't sound right," she says, but she has no idea how to fix it. She focuses on the wall directly behind his desk. She wants to tell him all she knows about her neighbor's death, to spread the moments of that day like cards across a table, to hand over the guilt hanging like an albatross around her neck. She wants to tell him that together—with his knowledge of the case and her energy they could surely solve—

"Did you two argue?"

"We . . . I had some sangria, too. I actually had quite a bit, too. I can't really remember what we talked about. Mostly about the pictures. Particularly the one picture. Whether it was Peter or not."

"And did you argue?"

"People do all sorts of things when they're drunk," Dana says. "But I don't specifically remember arguing. I mean, we weren't exactly on the same page that day. . . ."

"How's that?"

"She'd had quite a head start," Dana says. "She was a good half bottle in when I arrived."

Jack Moss sits forward as if he's suddenly realized he's late for a meeting. "Was she alive when you left?" he says, and Dana nods.

"I was completely shocked," she says, and she reminds herself that this, at least, is untainted truth. If Moss insists on a lie-detector test, she'll be fine on this particular question. "I was completely shocked," she says again, "when I saw her lying on the floor. Absolutely blown away."

"Is there anything you'd like to add?" Detective Moss takes his glasses off and taps them against the palm of his hand. "Anything that might shed some light on your friend's death?" His eyes are far more sensual without the glasses—softer, even in the harsh glare beaming down from the ceiling.

"We weren't all that close, really," Dana says. "We went to yard sales together, that sort of thing."

"Noted. Did you happen to go back to the Steinhaus-ers' the night Celia was killed?"

"No." Dana leans over to pick up her purse that's fallen on its side on the dirty linoleum floor. "Why?"

"You had a key? Have a key?"

"Umm . . ." Dana looks above her right eyebrow as if this is the toughest question yet. "I did. Yes. From watching the—"

"But you weren't in their house the night of the killing?"

"No. And I gave it back to Ronald. I ran into him at the market the other day and I gave him the key."

"Did anyone else have access to the key when you had it? Your husband? Any family members? Friends?"

"Well," Dana says. "Not that I can . . . Peter—my husband—actually had access, but he didn't . . . actually go anywhere that night. He got home late and went straight to bed."

Jack Moss nods, looks back at his notes. "Anything you'd like to add?"

"No," Dana says, and again she can say this with all honesty. She looks Jack straight in the eye and says it again. "No. Nothing." He jots down something she can't see and stands up. Dana gets up, too, extending her now slightly trembling hand.

"If you remember anything," he says, "even if it doesn't seem important . . ." He reaches into his pocket and pulls out a small white card with straight-up-and-down lettering. Black. Simple. The kind of card Dana thinks she would have if she had cards. "Anything at all, you give me a call," he says, handing it to her. "And thanks for coming in."

"Thanks for having me," she says. "I mean. God." She feels her cheeks grow hot. She shakes his hand in what she hopes is a no-nonsense, earthy, androgynous sort of shake.

"Anytime," he says, and he smiles.

"Oh." She's halfway to the hall when she remembers. It's a tiny thing. A tidbit. "There was an odor," she says, "in Celia's house."

"When?"

"When I came back. When the paramedics were working on her, when she was bleeding there on the— I was pretty focused on her, so it wasn't until later I remembered, but it was very distinctive—very familiar, actually."

"What was it?"

"I don't know—almost like perfume, but really bad perfume. And another smell, like rubbing alcohol."

Moss jots something down in his notebook. "That's what I need," he says. "That kind of thing. So if you remember anything else . . ."

She nods, trails her hand behind her in a small wave. She concentrates on walking slowly until she's out of his office and down the hall, and then she nearly runs to the heavy door, jogging across the parking lot to her car. When she is safely on the highway, when she has completed her impossible mission, she doesn't feel what she thought she would. To her surprise, she doesn't feel at all like celebrating after clearing this hurdle with the seasoned detective, that they even managed a little joke at the end of the meeting, her sweaty fingers cold inside his warm ones, his brown eyes lingering on her face. Instead she feels deflated. She feels as if she's robbed a bank and managed to get away and that she's holed up in a Caribbean hotel, stacking bills in piles of thousands, but that all she can see is the teller's face behind the glass, shocked, frightened, while a blue-haired patron clutches her heart.

The Toyota plows through traffic and speeds along the highway. For a second, Dana thinks of her father, just a flash before she shuts him out—his skinny body always in motion, always rushing. Even in his car, he was always in a hurry, always speeding until that last night, his angular face thrust toward the windshield, his boot holding firm on the brake, the rumble of the train, his frenzied energy contained, stopped. Ended.

One strappy sandal eases off the gas. She drifts into the rightmost lane, allowing other cars to whiz past, allowing herself to unclench her toes, to wonder why she wanted Detective Moss to discover all her secrets, this man who talked with her and didn't see the darkness, like thick, black ink, hiding in her veins, behind her eyes, coiled and waiting to swallow her whole.

*

She sees Peter walking quickly along the driveway to the house, and he's already talking by the time he reaches the dining room, by the time he tosses his briefcase on the couch. He's still wearing his hat, and he looks comical, standing there ranting with his little beret bobbing on his perfect hair. It goes with the Lexus, he said when he bought it from a hat store near his office, but it doesn't at all. It goes with the convertible he'd planned to buy, opting, in the end, for the more sedate, conservative sedan. Dana sets down a potato and wipes her hands on the sides of her shorts. "Sorry? I didn't really hear what you—"

"I got a call today!" he bellows from a space of bare wood between the living room and the dining room, "from that detective. Jack something."

"Moss," she says, but she nearly whispers the name. "His name is Moss."

"Moss. That's it. He wants to question me about Celia's death."

Dana feels her stomach lurch. "Maybe you should get an ascot," she says from the kitchen doorway. She takes a deep breath and slices a potato.

"Why?"

"To go with the beret."

"I tell you I'm a possible person of interest in a murder investigation and you tell me to buy an ascot?"

Dana shrugs. She drops the potatoes into boiling water and stares at the bubbles in the pot. "It's not such a big deal," she says. "They're interviewing everybody. All the neighbors. I talked to Moss this afternoon."

"And you didn't think to mention it?"

"I didn't want to worry you." She grabs a bottle of vodka and pours several shots into a glass. "Drink?" she says, and Peter nods.

"What'd he want?"

She takes a tiny sip and hands her husband the glass. "Nothing, really. He wanted to know if I'd seen anything odd that afternoon—you know, anything out of the ordinary."

"What'd you tell him?"

"Well. I said no. Not really. I told him I was over at the Steinhausers' that day." Her hands tremble at her sides, and she balls them into fists as he wanders toward the bathroom. She wishes now she hadn't mentioned the picture in the phone, but how was she to know which information had been shared and which had not? Peter will be furious. She thinks he might be mad enough to

107

leave, to pack his bags and take off to a hotel in Manhattan, where he can be with the Tart every single night, where he can turn to her in the light of a TV screen filled with baseball and tell her how his wife betrayed him, giving out his name the way she did, exposing their affair the way she has. She feels a chill go up her arms, making goose bumps, even though it feels like 105 degrees and puddles sizzle on the sidewalks. It scares her, the thought of Peter leaving. She wonders vaguely if she'll fall apart without the glue of her husband, without his body there inside the house, later—in a few days or hours or weeks—when her mind begins to splinter as it has before, when her madness gets a toehold on her life.

She wants to call him back. She wants him to dispel her fears, she wants to pick his lawyer brain until she knows for certain whether she's a murderer or not. She wants to lay her head across his lap and close her eyes and sleep there with the rain tapping on the skylight. But Peter has become a mystery, a man with Tarts and neighbors' phone numbers hidden in the call log of his cell, a man who scared Celia into saying, Peter looked at me like he'd slit my throat if he had the chance, her face so close that Dana could see the tiny veins beside her nose.

There is so little, now, to hold on to. She closes her eyes and listens to the bubbling water, to the sounds of Peter closing the bathroom door. She thinks of Jack Moss, solid as a rock behind his mammoth desk, this man with gentle, sensual eyes, who may well end her marriage in the morning, poking around about the stupid photo of Peter with his Tart.

# 12

Jack ducks in for coffee at a little dive on Market Street on his way in to the office. He'll take a minute, try to center himself, as Ann would say, collect his thoughts that splinter off in different directions, not at all his MO. Moss likes to have a plan; he likes to be sure, and usually he does, usually he is, but variables keep shifting. And to top things off, there's the overzealous first assistant prosecutor on the steps of City Hall, news cameras flashing, her airbrushed-looking face on the news. I'm working hand in hand with Detective Moss. We're very close to making an arrest.

Except they're not.

"Jack?" As if his thoughts have pulled her there, Lenora stands beside him, bending over the creamers and plastic spoons. She smiles. Her eyes are large and gray. Soft.

"Hey," he says. "Got a minute?"

"Just," she says, glancing at her watch. "I have a meeting."

"Okay. This won't take long." He pulls out her chair, sets their coffees and bagels on a two-topper with vines etched into the metal of the table, the matching chairs. "Saw you talking about the Steinhauser case on TV last week. I meant to bring it up the other day in the office, but then Rob came in and—"

"I mentioned you." She looks at him sideways from behind her cardboard cup. Steam wisps around her face.

"Right. Noticed that."

"'Hand in hand with Detective Moss.'" She smiles.

"So where's Frank in all this? Shouldn't he be the one updating the media? Usually it's the prosecutor who—"

"He was detained," she says. "He was at the capital for the day, so I filled in for him like anyone else would."

"I'm not so sure about that," Jack says. He frowns. She was grandstanding in that interview, playing to the cameras. She'll climb her way to the top if she has to impale us all on her million-dollar heels to do it, Frank had told him a few months back.

She takes a dainty bite of her bagel. "I know that Frank is your friend."

"I don't know if I'd say we were friends, exactly. I think he's been a great prosecutor. I like the guy. I respect the hell out of him."

Lenora nods. "I know you do. I like him on a personal level, too. He's got a great sense of humor. Smart, but not so tough on crime. If you look at the stats, crime's been going up in Passaic County for years, largely due to Frank's—I don't know—laid-back attitude. We're losing face. We look bad. If he ever leaves—if he should step down—I'd really like to . . . have the opportunity to turn things around."

Jack takes a bite of his bagel, stares out the window at a crowd of kids on the sidewalk, pants low on their hips. He thinks of Kyle. "You said we're closing the Steinhauser case."

She shrugs. "We are at some point."

"Right." Jack folds his paper napkin into fourths, unfolds it again. "But we've got quite a ways to go before this is a wrap."

Lenora leans back slightly from the table, peers at him over her coffee cup. "You don't like me much, do you, Jack?"

"Not true," he says. He looks at a painting on the wall over her left shoulder. "Not true at all."

Lenora fiddles with her cup, picks at her bagel. Knocks a few crumbs onto the plate. "My father was a judge," she says after a couple of seconds—says it out of the blue, as if she and Jack are friends, as if they're in the habit of shooting the breeze over coffee. "Little backwater county in south Alabama. People respected him. Everyone loved him—everyone—and he earned it. He was a fair man. Kind. A—what?—man of the soil? He knew farming like the back of his hand, but he became a lawyer instead and then eventually a judge."

"Huh."

"I worshipped him. Wanted to be just like him. I'd stand at the window every night. Summer, winter, bright sun or pitch dark—I'd stand there waiting, watching for his car to pull up in the driveway. 'It's Daddy!' I'd call to my mother. 'Daddy's home!' and I'd run out the front door. He used to let me carry his briefcase, and I thought that was such a big deal, such an honor or something, carrying this beat-up old leather—" She stops. She takes a few sips of her coffee, finishes it.

"He happy you followed in his footsteps?"

Lenora crumples the cup in her hands, looks up at the door; her shoulders slump. "I'd better head back," she says. "It's getting really . . ." She stands up, pushes the metal chair under the table, and leans there for a minute. "He died," she says. "Massive heart attack when I was twenty. I'd dropped out of college to marry some loser I ended up divorcing a year later, but I always thought . . . I mean, not completely—my father had health problems for a while, for years, so it wasn't totally because of . . . Still. It didn't help, what I'd done, disappointing him like that. It didn't help."

"I'm sorry," Jack says. He starts to get up, but Lenora motions for him not to.

"No," she says. "I'm sorry. I shouldn't have . . . gotten so carried away. Dredging up all this crap from the—"

"It's fine. Really."

She grabs her bag off the table, forces a little fake smile. "Stay on the case," she says. "We'll talk soon," and she darts out the door onto the sidewalk. In the bright sunlight, her hair is streaked with gold.

Jack takes his time leaving. He slides his chair out of the way, drops a few bills on the table—the fake iron, the glass top—and for a minute he sees something in Lenora he hadn't seen before. He smiles, shakes his head. Odd, these things she's told him, these small pictures she's flung across the table, these glimpses of the Alabama girl she used to be, falling for the wrong guy, breaking her father's heart. Is that what pushes her, drives her? Guilt? Remorse? Atonement? Ambition? All of the above? Could Frank be stepping down? He'd alluded to it not two weeks before. Thinking of throwing in the towel, he'd said, but Jack had only laughed. Told him he'd believe that when he saw it. Of course Lenora'd want to take his place.

# 13

Jack is ready for the neighbor's husband when he comes down to the station. He's heard the man's name. In fact, they might even have met at some point, some state event or dealing with a legal issue. Jack thinks most lawyers are a little sleazy, a little compromised, but he knows he's prejudiced, that his late and hard-won education has made him look askance at people who had it easier. By the time he started college, he had two kids and a failed marriage, a job paying next to nothing down by the docks. He'd barely squeaked through high school, married young, had a son, got a welding job, had another son. "My life is a Bruce Springsteen song," he used to joke, but it all started falling apart by the time Kyle was two, with Margie getting weird and vague on him, drinking every night while he was at work, dabbling in drugs, he found out years later, after the damage to their sons was pretty much done. She kicked him out when Kyle was still small, and even though he went back once or twice to try to make it work for the boys' sake, in the end he'd packed the ragtag remnants of his things and walked away.

He's lived in Paterson a long time. He sees strangers sometimes on the street, and they'll walk over to shake his hand. "You helped my boy," they'll say. "You gave him a break when he needed one," and he'll smile, but in his heart he knows he failed his own sons, that he's got one dead and one he's dead to.

He spots Peter Catrell coming in the door, and even though the office is empty, Jack takes him to the interrogation room. With this guy he'll do everything by the book. "Follow me," he says when they've finished the formalities, when they've sized each other up. The lawyer sniffs, trots along behind him down the hall.

He takes his time opening the door, arranging chairs. He looks at the man across the table and tries to figure out why he's so familiar. He puts him in different settings—cocktail parties and courtrooms—but nothing fits. It was somewhere recent, somewhere in the last few weeks.

"Have a seat," he says, and Peter sits, setting his briefcase on the chair next to his and reaching over to touch it, like it's a pair of ruby slippers that can take him back to his world, where he's somebody, and out of Jack's world, where he's not. "You're probably wondering why I called you down here."

Peter shrugs. "I'm sure you'll let me know, Detective Moss."

A smart-ass. "Where were you on the afternoon your neighbor died?" he says, and Peter doesn't flinch.

"At work."

"Anybody see you there? Say, between five and eight?"

"Yes," Peter says. "Several people."

"Names?" Jack takes out his pen and plays with the button. The point clicks in and out in the silent room.

"Actually . . ." Peter leans forward slightly. "I spent part of that time with the first assistant in the prosecutor's office."

"Lenora White?" Jack clicks the pen a few more times. He hooks his fingers inside his collar, loosens it. In light of what she's just told him—the vulnerability she's just shown—the thought of this guy working with Lenora on anything really bothers him.

"Yes."

"Fine." He writes down her name. "I know her," he says. "Anyone for the rest of the time?"

"Am I a person of interest?"

"Everyone's a person of interest," Jack says, "until they're not."

"Guilty until proven innocent?"

"Not at all." Jack leans back and tilts the chair onto two legs.

"Gail Lawson," Peter says. "Phil Brewer. John Hillman. And Frank Gillan? The prosecutor? He was with the other one, the first assistant. Lenora White."

"Okay," Jack says. He's scribbled down the names. "Thanks."

Peter touches his briefcase again, runs his finger along the seam of it.

"Tell me about the picture," Jack says.

"What picture?"

"The one in the phone." He's gambling, but sometimes gambles pay off. He watches Peter, the way his eyes move back and forth in their sockets, looking around the room, unconsciously seeking out the door. Bingo.

"What phone?"

But Jack has seen in his eyes that he knows. "Celia Steinhauser's."

"What kind of picture?"

"Of you," Jack says, and he stops playing with his pen to look Peter directly in the eyes. "You and your secretary."

"Sorry?" Peter's eyebrows knot together. "Picture? Cell phone?"

"Mrs. Steinhauser had a picture of you in her cell phone," Jack says, although he knows he's over his head.

Peter shrugs. "If she did, she never showed it to me."

"How well did you know her? The deceased?"

"I didn't know her at all," Peter says. "My wife knew her." He leans back in the chair, quits touching his brief-case.

"Were they friends?"

"They were—yes. I think they were fairly close."

"Really? 'Cause your wife—Dana, right? Dana didn't seem to think they were all that close. 'We went to yard sales together,' she said." Jack looks up from his notes.

"Women," Peter says. "Who knows how their minds work?" And Jack remembers Dana's nervousness, her foot tapping in the air, the fear in her eyes, like she was

118

a wild animal, cornered, looking for an escape. Still, he'll take her word over her husband's any day. This guy has probably said five true things since he sat down, and one of those was his name.

As with Ronald, there's something off, but he can't quite pin down what it is. Moss is on a fishing expedition, and Catrell's been a lawyer long enough to sense this. He's beginning to relax a little, slouching in his seat, observing Jack, studying his shoes, pricing his bad haircut, glancing down at his own manicured hands. "You got me there," Jack says, and he smiles. "Been married long?"

"Over twenty years," he says, and Jack thinks, Okay, so six true things. He thumbs through his notes. "I've seen you somewhere," he says. "Court, maybe?"

Peter smiles. "Could be. I seem to live there lately."

"Or maybe a cocktail party, somebody's wife's gallery opening? Could be just about anywhere."

"Same circles," Peter says.

"Not so much. Overlapping circles, maybe." Jack plays with his pen. He has this weird feeling again, a memory right there at the edge of his mind. Names he's not so good with, but otherwise he has a phenomenal memory, and he never forgets a face. "Listen," he says. He stands up. "Appreciate you coming down."

"Sure thing." The other man stands up, too, and they shake hands, a tense, quick handshake.

Jack sits back down, listens to the muffled sounds of the lawyer's shoes along the worn linoleum in the hall, the shushing sound of the door opening into the outer office, the squeak of it closing. He shuts his eyes, and they are everywhere, these images of his sons, of Margie, of his first marriage, and he doesn't understand why— why now—but he knows they're leading him somewhere. He just has to let it play out, all of it—the night Margie went into labor with Joey, the childbirth-class lingo, the "Breathe! Breathe! Pant!" rolling off his tongue, the way she looked at him, like she could kill him, as in a way she did. It just took her a while to do it. He's never forgiven himself for not fighting for his kids, for not getting them away from Margie, probably never will. He opens his eyes, stares at the wall, and there they are again, standing at the funeral, the rain coming down, Margie a mess and Kyle a stranger. He's grown up now. Taller than Jack and tough. Jack could see it in the set of his jaw that day, the squint of his eyes, the way he took the folded flag when his mother couldn't.

After the funeral Jack pulled out all the stops trying to reach him, but Kyle never answered his phone, never called him back. Jack still tries; he'll try until he's dead and gone. He tried a couple months ago—tracked him down at his night class and hung around outside the GED room like a fucking psycho, lurking there in the dark of the hallway, but he didn't care. He has no pride when it comes to Kyle.

He sits up straighter in the hard-backed chair. His eyes close. He brings back that evening, that last time he saw his son, the last time he was rebuffed, and there's another figure lurking there—another father, he'd thought at the time—a few yards down the hall, leaning up against the institutional gray of the high-school wall. In his memory the figure turns, takes a phone out of his pocket, and strolls, talking, back and forth in front of the closed door of the GED room, and Jack knows it was there he first saw Peter, there in the poorly lit high-school hall the night Jack waited, slouched against the bitter walls, his legs crossed at the ankles, his arms folded over his chest, over his badge, over his heart.

So Catrell was involved with Celia. Jack will leave no stone unturned to find out how. More concerning is the wife. Jack shakes his head. He sticks his notebook into his briefcase and fastens it. He liked Dana; there was something different about her, something mysterious. "You're a sucker for lost souls," Ann always told him, and it's true. Dana was funny, too. Jack likes that in a woman, a sense of humor. Still, hell hath no fury. If her husband was involved with Celia, there's no telling what she might have done. Dana was inside the house that night, he knows it. He knew it the minute he asked her. The question now is why she went back and why she lied about it.

*

He calls Kyle's number, and he can almost see his son's phone ringing into a rented room. Rosie's. He knows the place well, with its ancient moldy air conditioners cutting on and off every few minutes, spitting out stale air. Between going there on calls and living there himself once upon a time, he knows that the rooms are tainted with the kind of dirt that can't be cleaned, that can't be swept away or dusted off the tops of things, a glaze of petty thievery and gloom, of dankness and weed and cheap wine oozing in the fabrics of things, lumpy mattresses sprawled on unwaxed floors.

"It's me," Jack says into the voice mail. "It's your dad, Kyle. Call me back as soon as you get this. It's a police matter. I need to ask you a couple things about your GED teacher. Call me on my cell," he says." He repeats his cellphone number three times, and then he hangs up.

He wonders if there really is a baby coming, if Margie was telling him the truth—if they decided to go through with the pregnancy. If, if, if. He wonders how much Kyle remembers about him, this father who left when he wasn't much older than Kyle is now—if he remembers Margie stumbling over chair legs with her paper skin, her eyes without pupils, grabbing up all Jack's shirts and jeans and underwear when he went to work, tossing it outside into the yard, the mounds of clothes strewn through the grass—his secrets, his family, his life, reduced to ripped T-shirts and graying boxers fading in the sun.

His cell rings, and the screen lights up with kyle, even though Kyle's never given him his number. Jack saved it after Margie wrote it down for him at the funeral and stuck it in his pocket as they were leaving the cemetery, Kyle several yards ahead of them, grief-struck and stooped like an old man. "He might need you," she'd said.

"Kyle?"

"Yeah."

Jack can hear the whooshing of a match being lit and the sudden intake of air as Kyle inhales.

"How are you?"

"Fine," Kyle says, and he exhales. "I'm fine. So you said something about my teacher?"

"Yeah. Right. What's her name?"

"Celia Steinhauser. Mrs. S, we called her."

"Huh. Thought I remembered that."

"She's dead."

"Right. I'm working on her case. I was wondering . . . did you notice anything different in the days before she died? Anything unusual?"

"No." On the other end of the phone, Kyle exhales.

"How about the guy in the hall the night I came down to see you? The guy on the cell? Shiny shoes? Nice suit?"

"Yeah," Kyle says. "I do remember that guy. He came to meet Mrs. S a few times. But that was a while back. He just . . . stopped coming."

"Huh."

"So is that it?"

"I guess so. Thanks. Son?"

A lighter snaps open. He hears the flame catch. "Yeah?"

"Call me," he says. Kyle grunts something he can't

123

quite make out, and Jack ends the call, leaves his son to lie down on a mattress stretched out across a floor, to stare at a dingy ceiling and share or not share with his girlfriend whatever it is he knows about this teacher found dying in her own living room. And Jack's gut tells him Kyle knows something. From the way the kid sounded on the phone, Jack would say he knows a lot.

## 14

Sometimes Dana thinks she's channeling the dead—her friend from college, defeated by uterine cancer at forty-one, her favorite aunt, her twelfth-grade English teacher. Sometimes she can hear her mother's voice as clearly as if she were standing in the room next to her. It comes through as a thought, and she is always far more pleasant than she was when she was alive. "Good job," she might say when Dana completes a crossword puzzle on a Friday when they're harder than usual. Or, "Do you still have that old recipe for lemon cakes that Aunt Julia used to make?" when Dana can't decide what to fix for a potluck. Their relationship has improved greatly since her mother's death, but her father is a different story. Her father rarely enters her mind. Neither his voice nor his memory is welcome. It isn't so much who he was, it's the madness he's already poured into her ear, transmitted to the marrow of her bones, the illness from his own despotic father, his depressed, midwestern mother. And if he steals inside her dreams, they're never good ones. They never walk together through the park, her small pink hand in his large tan one; they never feed the ducks at the pond at the end of the street where she grew up.

In her dreams her father is always angry.

The circumstances of his death disturb her, the sudden, shocking way his car was hit by a train crossing to New York from Philadelphia. There was nothing left of him, her mother wailed into the phone to anyone who would listen. "We'll have a closed casket." Dana wondered at the time why they needed a casket at all if there was nothing left of him. Would it be for the collection of old black-and-white photographs he kept in the bottom drawer of his dresser, or for his wedding band, or the poetry he wrote, sitting at the desk in the living room, a small lamp illuminating the words he scrawled in a frenzy and then ripped up the next day, tossing the tiny pieces high into the air to rain down on the rug? She wondered if the casket would be buried with the bottles of gin he kept hidden under the front seat of his car and in the kitchen cabinet behind the brown sugar or with his anger that exploded sometimes on Sundays if she took too long getting ready for Mass. She wondered if the casket would be filled with love he saved up all those years and didn't have the chance to give.

Dana thinks these things work backward from the way they should, these things of death. Had they been close, had they enjoyed the father-daughter chats, the hiking trips and Little League, she would have missed him more when he was gone. But she would at least have these things to pluck out and remember, these sweet moments to sprinkle like a trail of bread crumbs through her life.

Instead she has always felt regret about her father, a great, vast emptiness in place of love. If she could go back in time, she'd do things differently. She'd understand his urgency, his speed; she'd see that he was trying to outrun the great gray cloud that made him sit vacant as a broken doll, his restless hands still and folded, at the kitchen table. His absence didn't have a starting place. Her father is a gust of wind.

Lately he slips inside her brain, her father on the railroad tracks in his old Pontiac. He's trying to tell her something. She can see it in his face, in the way he bends forward toward the still-unshattered glass of the windshield. In the seconds before his death, he's trying to warn her. It isn't the first time. Before her illness really gets a grip, Dana always sees her father's face. She sees the Pontiac, and sometimes, in the distance, she can hear the train whistle, but only faintly. She never sees him die.

And if it was not an accident, her father's blue car panting on the railroad tracks at the edge of town hours after he was expected home, if, as a witness said, it was as though he were waiting for the train to come, if the anger and the alcohol inside him finally dragged him there to die, Dana doesn't want to know.

*

She pours a drink for Peter and tamps down her desire to take a few swallows. It's his favorite, a martini straight up with two olives from a jar at the back of the fridge, a little old but still the green ones he prefers. She sits at the dining-room table, afraid of what he'll say, afraid Detective Moss has told him what she said about the cell-phone picture. She glances at the kitchen clock and sees he's nearly two hours late. She hears the garage door open, and she stands up, taking several deep breaths and stirring the vodka with her pinkie. She sticks some fish under the broiler and pops a bag of half-frozen broccoli into a pan of water as Peter stumbles through the screen door; sweat drips from his forehead and down along his jaw.

"Martini?"

"Thanks." He takes the drink and gulps it down as if it's water, as if he doesn't realize it won't quench his thirst.

"Another?" she says, and he nods. Dana walks back to the kitchen and roots around inside the slimy plastic carton of olives for a green one. "So how was your meeting with Detective Moss?"

"Okay."

"What did he want?" She keeps her voice light as she walks into the dining room with the martini and sets it down. She concentrates on the wood grain in the table-top, avoiding Peter's eyes.

"To find Celia's killer." He takes a gulp of his martini. His face is red, his perfect hair damp and limp.

"Are you all right?"

He looks at her, and she looks away. She looks at the

peeling paint on the ceiling where water once leaked in around the skylight. Her heart lurches in her chest.

"Why'd you do it?" he says, and Dana looks over his shoulder at the window in the living room.

"Do what?"

"Tell Jack Moss I was connected to that woman down the street?"

Dana doesn't answer. She picks up Peter's empty glass and fills it for the third time, making it a little stronger than before. The olive falls through the liquid like a stone, and she thinks of Virginia Woolf stuffing rocks inside her pockets and wandering into the river. She has always thought Virginia Woolf was a hero, simply walking off the way she did, in such a gracious, graceful way.

"Why'd you tell him Celia had a photo of me in her phone?"

"That isn't what I said."

"But close enough, right? Close enough for him to have me on the fucking hot seat this afternoon!"

"I just told him that was why I was over there that day. I told him she wanted to show me a picture she'd taken. I said I couldn't tell if it was you or not, it was so bad."

"Why would you say something like that?"

"Because," Dana says, "it was the truth." She says this with a thread of self-righteousness, ignoring the doubt she now feels, the slight regret, an inkling that she said it out of anger—out of the pain of having been deceived.

"Celia had a picture? Of me?"

"She had a picture." Dana isn't sure where she wants to go with this. "I don't know if it was you or not."

"So why would you tell him something like that?" Peter polishes off his martini and looks up. His eyebrows are furrowed. He looks hurt.

Dana turns back to the kitchen where water boils and broccoli bobs along the waves. She closes her eyes. Celia's voice roars in her left ear. *Peter looked at me like he'd slit my throat. . . .* Dana sees now what her neighbor meant. He's used to having his way, Dana thinks. He's used to winning, so when something goes awry, he's at a total loss.

"What's wrong with you anyhow?" Peter snarls from the dining room. He probes around the bottom of the glass for the olive. He pops it into his mouth and sits staring toward the kitchen. "You need to go see Dr. Sing. In fact, I'll—" He stops. He shifts on his chair and stares down at his shoes as if he's never seen them before. "You're not sleeping," he says. "When I wake up, you're never in bed."

Dana chews on her cuticle, tearing it slightly, surprised that her husband even notices she isn't there beside him on the bed, that he's observed her absence while he wheezes and snorts and thrashes in the sweaty sheets.

"And now telling the chief detective on a murder case that I'm involved in a mur—"

"That's not what I said." She stares at him, at his bleary, rheumy eyes, and wonders if that wasn't exactly what she said, by implication if not precisely in those words.

130

Peter looks at her. He chews on an olive.

"I had to . . . you know, have an actual reason for being there."

"So you invented this stuff about a picture?"

Dana doesn't answer. Now that Peter knows she's seen the photo that Celia took, he also knows she knows about the Tart. She wonders if he'll offer an explanation, and then she realizes he can't, not without admitting there was a photo. She wills the martinis to knock him off his game, to muddle his thoughts, to make him talk. Do your job, she thinks, staring at the now-empty glass, at an olive stretched out flat against its bottom.

Peter snorts. His head weaves slightly.

"I'll check on the fish." She gets up, moving quickly back to the broiler, where the halibut is black and curling at the edges. "So what'd you tell the detective about the photo? That I was lying?" As an afterthought she mixes yet another martini and deposits it along with the food on the dining-room table.

Peter grunts. His shoulders are sloped, his head bowed, his eyes barely open. She's clearly overshot. His fork dips here and there on the plate, stabbing bits of food, the uncooked broccoli, the burned fish. After a few minutes, she stands up and sweeps away their nearly untouched food. She scrapes the remains into the compost bag that she will later empty in the backyard on the heap of lush and fecund rot. She will scrape and dig and cover up the fish bones, the bright green of the broccoli heads with her

131

hands, tucking them under a collection of plant debris, and she will think of Celia being buried deep inside the earth or of her ashes flying from the hands of people standing on a mound of sand on Martha's Vineyard.

"Coffee?"

"Naw," Peter says, and his voice is thick, dripping onto the table. He pushes up from his chair and shuffles to the couch.

"Wait." She doesn't want him there with his slitty eyes staring up at the ceiling. She doesn't want him draped across the middle of her night. "Why don't I help you?" she says, and she moves toward where he lies face up on the sofa, like a playing card. "Let's get you to bed, and you can take a little nap. You'll get a second wind," she says, and hopes she's lying. She helps him to his feet, tugging him down the hallway to the bedroom. He sags onto the edge of the bed, and she undresses him, plumps the pillow, and gently sets his head down, feathers melting beneath the weight, and then she reaches into his pocket for his cell. He glances up at her, and there's something in his eyes—an accusation, she thinks, but he turns to face the wall, and in a matter of seconds he's snoring; small breathy puffs of vodka sing out through his nostrils into the clammy, stale air of the bedroom.

*

She sits on the sofa. She looks outside the window, where

the sweltering afternoon has edged into another rainy night, and thinks about what Peter said, that she's been acting crazy, that she hasn't been sleeping, and she can't argue with that. Time is running out for her. If she didn't know before this afternoon, the vision of her father on the railroad tracks has sealed the deal.

The rain picks up, a colossal summer storm, beating on the windows and the skylight, tapping on the door, and she shivers, thinking of Jack Moss, his eyes so like the Poet's. Her foot taps against the wooden floor; her heart races and runs, stopping from time to time, missing a beat and rushing to catch it up, a ragged thing, her heart. Now. Lightning flashes on the street, illuminating a figure in a slick, dark jacket before it's swallowed by the night. She slumps down on the couch cushion below the bay window, out of sight. Is he back, this monster, stealing what little sanity she has left? For a few seconds, she wavers between running to wake up Peter and calling the police, but in the end she does neither. In the end she walks across to the kitchen and pours herself a glass of vodka, nearly the last of the bottle, and she stares at it, knowing that it will calm her down, steady her nerves.

She sets the glass on the coffee table as the wind whistles through the trees, catches in something loose, a shingle or a gutter, making creaks and tremors, and she knows that these sounds, these squeaks and groans and murmurs, are only the storm, but suddenly she isn't sure. Everything scares her now, everything is a threat. She reaches again for the glass, but she doesn't pick it up. She won't drink the vodka. She will never touch the stuff again, she tells herself, until she knows for certain what she did or didn't do the last time she drank it.

She grabs Peter's phone and scrolls to his call log, thumbing down the list of names and numbers, searching for the ones from Celia—the steady stream of missed calls from "C," but there is nothing there. She feels dread, like a band tightening across her forehead. Confused, she flips back through, but the calls from Celia are no longer there, snuffed out as surely as Celia herself. Or were they ever there? Did she only imagine them? She feels panic, an icy hand at the back of her neck. She glances at the vodka on the counter, only slightly out of reach, but she looks away, scrolls through Peter's list of contacts. She finds the "C" and breathes a sigh of relief, pushing her thumb down on the letter and listening to the reassuring ring of Celia's phone. She wonders if Ronald's changed the message. She wonders why he hasn't disconnected it, whether he's using it himself or if one of Celia's boys on Martha's Vineyard will someday take it over, all the records wiped clean, all the photos intact, except the one of Peter and the Tart.

"Catlin and McCaffey Law," a male voice says. "Please leave a message at the beep, and we'll return your call as soon as possible."

She tells herself it's only a mistake. She thumbs back to the contact list; she pushes "C," but once again a man's voice tells her she's reached Catlin and McCaffey Law. He must know, she thinks. Peter has to know she's checked his phone. Or at least it's crossed his mind she might at some point check it. Or that the police will. Now that the detective knows about the photo, he could easily request Peter's phone, his call log, all of it. Of course he'd cover up this obvious link to the dead woman—the dead married woman. Or did she only imagine Celia's number in her husband's phone, Celia's ghostly voice reaching through the fog of death to haunt her?

She turns off the cell. The rain is winding down. It's still falling, but the wind has nearly stopped. She concentrates on slowing her breathing. The backs of her hands rest on her knees. "It's raining cats and dogs," her mother used to say, and she repeats the phrase inside her head. It's raining cats and dogs. When she was a child, it gave her nightmares, that expression, the ensuing images of her beloved cat, their dead dog, her neighbor's litter of puppies, all of them falling from the sky and landing—smashing—on the ground. She has never fathomed what sort of madman, what sort of sadist, would think up such a twisted, haunting image. She reaches behind her, opens the window wide, lets the rain fall nearer to her, trying to lose herself in the sound of it, the gentle, soothing patter.

Lightning darts across the sky, and again a figure lurks there in the street. It stares up at her front porch, at the living-room window, and this time it doesn't scare her. This time Dana feels anger surging through her—anger for the lost, baffled way she's lived her life; for the father who deserted her; for her enigmatic, cheating husband; for the cruel, disabling illness wrestling with her mind. This time Dana's on her feet and out the front door. The screen bangs back in place and flies out again on a drift of wind, but she is off the porch and halfway down the lawn before it slips back into place, before the sky has even shifted back to black.

# 15

She reaches the street in a few quick strides. The figure is moving in the direction of the Steinhausers', crossing the thin side yards, the coiffed lawns, moving toward Ronald's untrimmed bushes, his front yard strewn with unpicked roses. It moves through the wet night like a vapor. "Wait!" she yells, but thunder roars and rumbles, slices off her voice. The form continues, walking more quickly now, his jacket flapping out at the edges.

"Stop!" Anger propels her forward, and she runs along the street, intent on exposing the hooded figure intent on proving it's real.

The mystery figure turns around, and they stare toward each other in the blackness of a cloudy, moonless night.

"Dana?"

"Yes." She slows down, but she doesn't stop. She continues moving toward the figure dripping in the rain.

"What you are doing?"

"Lon?"

"Yes!" he yells over the sound of the rain. "What you are doing out here?"

"What are you doing out here?"

"I am block captain," he says, still in the high-pitched,

reedy voice. Lightning flashes on the roof across the street. "If I do my job better, maybe Celia—"

"No." Dana stops. In the light from the streetlamp, she can see his face, his eyebrows raised, his mouth a thin, grim line beneath his hood. "It wasn't anybody's fault," she says. "Certainly not yours."

"It was her killer's fault," he says, and Dana nods.

"So why are you out in this horrible—"

"I am watching out my window," Lon Nguyen says, "and I see someone in your yard."

"My yard? Our yard?"

He nods.

"When? Just now?"

He shrugs. "I could not find my raincoat right away, but when I did, I come right out."

"And did you . . . ?"

"No." He shakes his head. "My wife say my nerves are bad. Since Celia is killed. She say I should stay away from windows—that I am seeing ghosts."

"You're not alone," Dana mumbles. "I see them, too."

Lon Nguyen looks puzzled. He takes a step forward, and they are nearly nose to nose. Dana thinks that if this were a movie, they would kiss. "Who?" he says.

She shrugs. She looks back toward her house, where she's left the front door open wide. Behind it the living room is lit up like a stage. "I don't know," she says. "A figure in a hoodie. In our backyard. At least I thought so."

"A hoodie?"

"A jacket. Like yours."

A porch light goes on at Lon Nguyen's house. Dana can see his wife's head poking out the front door, her words streaming through the rain in Vietnamese.

"I will walk you back," Lon Nguyen says, but Dana waves him away, hurrying to her yard through the lightning bolts that drift like tiny bombs across the sky.

\*

When the rain has nearly stopped, leaving a light fog in the air, a thin layer of mist to hover over the hedges, the neglected, unmowed grass of the backyard, Dana falls into a restless sleep. She dreams bright, colorful dreams of falling animals and cars, of wandering in a lush, green world where tree trunks are translucent, where the bark is crystal clear. She can see roots, like veins, inside the trees, sucking water up into their branches, into their bright lollipop leaves, round and sharp and see-through. She can hear the murmur of the flowers, the whisper of the wind, the sudden inching-up of the grass. In her dream she looks behind the row of lollipop trees, across the empty fields, and sees the blue vase that killed Celia growing up beneath the flowers. In the few seconds between sleep and waking, she can feel the heavy smoothness of the vase in her hands—a memory that forces her awake to lie still as a stone and try to bring back when it was exactly that she held the purchase that her neighbor showed her with such pride. "It was a steal,"

Celia had said of the art-sale piece that killed her, picking it up carefully from a shelf near the foyer. Was it at that point Dana held it? Was it then she felt its cool, flat surface? Or was it on the afternoon Celia died?

She moves in tiny increments to the edge of the bed. Beside her, Peter snores. His watch says 3:17. She roams back to the living room and grabs the New York Times, finds the crossword puzzle in the back of the third section. She wanders to the kitchen for a sharpened pencil and curls her legs beneath her on the couch. The answers come to her easily, as if her brain is finely tuned, as if the dreams have made her smarter, and she fills the squares in quickly, moving on to the KenKen, which she also does with ease. Keeping busy helps her focus. The crosswords and sudokus, the KenKens—all these tiny, trivial things— they help her, they keep her sane, keep at bay the dread that hovers thick as smoke just above her right eyebrow. She places the completed puzzle page on the coffee table as outside a dog barks, running down the street toward their house and stopping out in front. The barking becomes louder. Threatening. The dog growls and yelps, and Dana thinks she hears the sloshing, swishing sound of someone dashing through the wet and slippery grass. She presses her hands over her ears. She hopes it's Lon Nguyen out there in his flip-flops, making his rounds, or that the paperboy has stopped to grab a quick, illicit smoke, leaning his elbows on the handlebars of his bicycle.

## 16

Peter doesn't say good-bye before he leaves for work. When she's certain he's gone, Dana rolls out of bed and showers, glancing afterward at her thin frame, her small breasts, her long, stick-thin legs. She sits on the toilet lid and stares at the mirror, concentrating on one small area at a time—lashes, lips, cheeks—as she applies her makeup, preparing to carry out the plan she made the day of the brunch.

When she's satisfied, she walks back to the bedroom. She checks the closet, a quick, appraising search, stopping at the short black dress she bought at Macy's on a whim. For a night out with her husband, she thought at the time. She sighs now, thinking of how different things were then, or seemed to be at least. She pulls the dress over her head and lets it fall just at her knees, feels it sway against the backs of her legs as she glances toward the mirror on its wooden stand in the middle of the room.

She walks down the hall to the third bedroom, where Jamie's electric guitar and amps still stand, where sheet music lies in lonely piles across the tops of things. She hates it now, with him away at school, hates the silence of the room, this empty tribute to her son. She moves over to

Jamie's computer, still sitting on an old desk in the corner, and she Googles Manhattan hotels. She waits while myriad options pop up on the screen. Ronald wouldn't stay just anywhere. It would have to be very clean, with an excellent bedbug rating. "He speaks in haikus," is what she remarked to Peter the day she met Ronald. It was the way he arranged his words, chirping them out in small, sharp, colorful chips of sound.

Midway through her list, she finds him at the St. Giles Hotel, where a rushed desk clerk offers to put her through to the room.

"Thanks," Dana says, "Room 2—"

"Five-twenty-two," the voice informs her, and Dana jots the numbers on a small pad, ripping off the square of white and folding it into fourths.

She hangs up while the phone rings into Ronald's empty room—she's sure he's back at work by now—and shoves the folded paper into her purse. In the kitchen she pours herself a cup of Peter's leftover coffee and nibbles a half-toasted frozen waffle, washing it down with several swallows of the coffee, bitter and too strong, the way Peter likes it.

She locks the front door and sits for a moment in the driveway, the sun beating down on her car, shining in its aging maroon glory, dappled with bumper stickers in the brightness of a day wiped clean from storms the night before. She backs out of her driveway, glancing down the street where yellow crime tape clings to the ragged, browning hedges of the Steinhausers' once-perfect yard. There is no one there. No cars. No cops. She wonders if their dog came back on his own. If so, she wonders if he knew what to do. If Celia should be murdered, she imagines Ronald telling him ahead of time, neighbor's. Door. Howl. Whimper. Food bowl. It's all good.

*

She and Peter stayed at a pricey hotel in midtown as a treat for her birthday several years before—the Marriott, she thinks, although she's no longer certain. She'd reveled in the luxury of ordering in, of breakfast in bed, of the outstanding view. Like old times, Peter said, although they both knew it wasn't. Even so, it was festive, romantic, getting away, staring out the seventh-floor window at the tourist sights. "This is wonderful," she'd gushed, but then it turned, with Peter beside her, pointing out MOMA and Saks and various other points of interest as if she hadn't recognized them, as if she were an idiot, a small child. He seemed so pompous—sneering, she'd thought, in his inimitably demeaning way. There was another time, a cocktail party in a large downstairs room—his office party. Christmas, she thinks, but she's forgotten the hotel. She turns on the radio, and the car plunges through a puddle, sending water sloshing off the road, and her heart pummels against her rib cage.

She can't drink coffee. Not now, especially Peter's

coffee, thick as sludge. The radio seems too loud, the music too confusing, the song too vibrant, and she stabs at the off button as Michael Jackson continues to sing through the car. This is it! She glances at St. Christopher, a pleading, desperate look, and he seems to nod as Michael Jackson fades back through the radio, a trail of blue light sucked inside the dash.

She chews on her cuticle. Her foot trembles on the gas pedal, and she shakes off her shoe. She shakes off both her shoes—black sandals with heels—and she imagines Celia coveting them, trying them on, wavering across the room in them, dangling her cell phone with the photo of Peter and the Tart, screaming, They're fucking! She imagines herself saying, You can have the sandals, Celia. You can keep the sandals. She sees the hotel up ahead and touches her foot to the brake pedal, slowing the car to a crawl. "But not my husband," she says now, completing her musings. "You can't have Peter."

She knows what she has to do as she pulls in to a garage a few blocks up the street from the hotel. Still, she hasn't yet decided how to do it. She'll wing it. Dana has always thought well on her feet. On the fly, as they used to say, by the seat of her pants. Lately when she thinks things through, she sees them from every angle, too many angles, too many possible outcomes, and she loses confidence. She fumbles. She drops the ball. She fails.

She slides her bag over her bare arm and steps onto the sidewalk. She has to get inside Ronald's room, even though security is tight these days, especially here in the city. She straightens her skirt and thinks of Gwyneth Paltrow slipping in and out of cabs and lobbies, gliding past doormen and nosy streams of concierges. She stands straighter, tossing her hair over her shoulders. Her sunglasses cover a large portion of her face. She could be anyone, walking up the sidewalk toward the heavy doors. For all they know, she is a star. She could even be Gwyneth.

As she nears the building, a doorman steps outside. "Good morning," he says, opening the large front door and stepping back for her to pass. He smiles. "Welcome!" She walks past him toward the concierge, the clots of men and women. They look odd to her, cartoonish, and Dana knows that this is a dream. This is her dream from the night before, the lollipop trees, but somehow she is here inside it. She's walking through it; she has to find the phone. If the picture is there the way she remembers it, then she will know she was sane that afternoon—that things occurred the way she thinks, at least the parts she can remember. If, on the other hand, she imagined the entire afternoon that began with Celia showing her the photo in the phone, then she was totally unhinged that day. She could have done anything, including kill Celia. First she'll find the photo, and once she knows that part of the afternoon was real, she'll go from there. She'll have a starting place. It will spark her memory, prod her through the blank spots. She'll also be in Ronald's room. She'll see what else turns up.

She stops.

"Yes?" A young man stares at her through thick black-framed glasses. She wonders if they'll pop out at her, if the eyeballs will leap out on springs.

"Terribly sorry to bother you." She fidgets with her dress, takes off her dark glasses. "This is a little embarrassing."

The young man leans over the curved smoothness of the counter. His eyes are large behind his lenses. Yellowish. Dana looks away.

"I spent the night here," she says, "last night. It was lovely."

The yellow eyes squint slightly. The young man leans farther across the counter.

"I'm afraid I've left my cell phone in our room," Dana says, "and I've already turned in my key. I have to catch a flight out," she says, "so I have to get my phone, and I think Ronald's probably left for work by now. My husband. He probably isn't there."

The desk clerk's cartoon lips curve upward at their corners. Dana stares at her shoes. "It was room 522," she says. "Could I have the—"

"I'm sorry," the desk clerk says, stepping back a pace or two, "but I can ring the room if you like. Your name?" He holds the receiver to his ear.

"Sarah Steinhauser," Dana says. She has always liked the name Sarah. Had she and Peter had a daughter, Dana would have named her Sarah. It's a strong name, she has always thought. Dana is an odd, pale, wispy name.

"ID?" His eyes spring here and there around the room. Dana rummages through her bag. The lobby is filling up with people. The young man looks alarmed. Three women clamor at the counter. He disappears briefly, reappearing with a slim gray key card. "ID?" he says again as a small group of people nears the counter.

"Thank you so much," Dana says. "You've saved my life," and she grabs the card, turns toward the elevators, lined up in a straight, neat row on the other side of the lobby. She thinks she hears him, thinks he calls out, "Sarah! Wait!" but she doesn't turn around.

## 17

When the elevator doors close behind her, Dana breathes a sigh of relief. She reaches over to press the button for the fifth floor, and the elevator zips seamlessly upward, not stopping until, with a dull dong, it arrives at Ronald's floor.

"Excuse me," Dana says, and she pushes past a gaggle of cartoon passengers. She moves to the front of the elevator, stepping out before the doors have fully opened. She moves quickly down the carpeted hall, avoiding the busy, teeming patterns on the rug. When she arrives at 522, she inserts the key card in the lock, and the reassuring click is loud in the silent hallway.

There's no one in sight. She pushes the door open and slides inside, closing it behind her. The room is not impeccably neat, as she'd imagined it would be. Instead Ronald's things are scattered everywhere—his boxers, his wrinkled shirts and khaki pants. Newspapers lie across a second queen-size bed, open to articles about Celia—a small piece on her life as an adult-education teacher, an earlier article that Dana has already read about the death itself, and a sheet of hotel stationery with a short, handwritten section of an obituary she assumes Ronald has written. "Loving mother and mentor. Funeral arrangements pending completion of police investigation." Dana shudders. Several pairs of socks are scattered willy-nilly on the floor, and the bathroom is a nightmare tangle of shaving paraphernalia and robes, of dental floss and toothpastes and brushes. Ronald even thought to pack a whitener booster, which Dana finds impressive, if surprising.

The room smells of alcohol and peppermint, of old stale wine stuck to plastic motel glasses, of unwashed socks and sneaker insides. Hotel, she thinks. Wine. Smells. Death. Life. Socks, as she sorts through a pile of clothing on a desk. The rubber duck lies on its side on a long, low bureau next to the TV, and Dana reaches out a finger, touches it lightly on the head. She tears through the piles of papers, of clothes, of shaving equipment. Everything, it seems, is here but Celia's phone.

She glances at her watch. Eleven-fifteen. She wonders if Ronald comes back to the hotel for lunch, if he brings a salad upstairs every day, if he sits at the small, cluttered table eating and penciling in a crossword puzzle from the Times—if he'll come back to this cramped, rank-smelling room to catch Dana thrashing through his personal belongings in her high-heeled sandals and her sexy black dress. She hopes not. She wishes she'd memorized Celia's cell-phone number, wonders if she ever even had it. She opens the dresser drawers, working her way through pajama bottoms and socks.

She sits down on the bed where Ronald sleeps, and it gives slightly under her weight. For a crazy minute, Dana thinks she might be able to sleep here in this anonymous place, where everything is topsy-turvy and foul-smelling, where nothing is expected of her. She even closes her eyes, stretching out across the bed. Her feet in the black sandals cross over each other precisely at the ankles, and she spreads out her arms, feeling like Jesus being cruci-fied. She thinks of St. Christopher nodding on the visor. "Please," she says. "Please." She whispers it. She opens her eyes. Something peeks out from the gap between the mirror and the bureau, something black. Dana crosses herself and mumbles, "Please, please, please," as she picks her way across discarded clothes, trips on a loafer, and grabs the black, half-hidden phone.

"Thank you, God. Thank you, St. Christopher," she says, "or . . . well, Christopher." She closes her eyes. She sees Celia punching the code into her phone, the way her fingers crossed the number pad in a diagonal line from upper right to lower left. Twice. Three seven, three seven. The screen springs to life. She brushes her finger across the backdrop—Celia's boys in Martha's Vineyard—and it takes her only a moment to locate the pictures, the different groupings. graduation day, the yard, ladies in morning class. Dana thinks that the one of Peter and the Tart was at the end of the graduation pictures. She scrolls through them, but she doesn't see it. She scrolls back through again, to make sure, but there are only several shots of the two boys, looking gawky and prepubescent; of Celia, pretty and thin in a pastel, sleeveless dress; of

Ronald, standing with the boys. She scrolls ahead, thumbing through a collection of plants—close-ups of Ronald's roses, the sprouts of a spring garden in their backyard. Nothing. She thumbs through again, going backward, going more slowly. She moves to the group of women in Celia's English class—the Bolivians and Peruvians, the Somalis and Bangladeshis, the Afghanis, the Romanians, the Chinese—women sitting at a table filled with food from all the countries represented in the class. They look happy. Celia looks happy. A Christmas party, Dana guesses from the way they're dressed, or maybe an end-of-term party. She zooms in on Celia's smiling face. Was she sleeping with Peter then? Was she meeting him in dark bars or motel rooms after her night class? Were they sliding into each other's front seats in the parking lot, Celia scrambling across the cold, dark leather of Peter's car, her skirt hiked up, his hairy-knuckled fingers tugging at her bra? Dana scrutinizes each of the party pictures, and then she thumbs back through the photos, from beginning to end, until she's sure that Peter and the Tart are not there.

She turns off the phone and falls back across Ronald's unmade bed, cluttered with wadded, rumpled bedding. She stares at the ceiling, and it seems to be dropping lower and lower. The walls creep inward, until she's lying in a tiny space, a claustrophobic cell. There's nothing to anchor her here or anywhere—there's nothing to keep her going. If the picture wasn't real—if the photo of Peter and the Tart did not exist—then likely nothing she remembers from that day is real. Not only are her memories of Celia's actions on that afternoon a sham, but memories of her own as well. She gets up quickly, before the ceiling covers her, before the walls enfold her, crush her. She wipes her prints off the phone and sticks it back on the bureau. It's of no use to her now. Or was it ever? She runs her hands through her hair, but she avoids the mirrors that seem to be everywhere in this encroaching room. She glances here and there, on the table near the window, on the cluttered bathroom counter, making sure she hasn't left traces of her visit, bits of herself she feels are sloughing off at every turn.

It isn't even twelve when she presses the button at the elevator, mirrored and smooth in its casing. The pulley squeals, the door opens with a sharp swish, and she steps inside. In the lobby she sets the key card on the counter and looks down at her feet, avoiding the desk clerk coming toward her.

The doorman is now wearing a hat. He is a clown, Dana decides. He's wearing makeup and an orange wig. His nose is a balloon. His eyebrows are painted on, his lashes long and loopy. Bozo, she thinks. It must be a special day at the hotel. A special afternoon. For the children, but he seems serious, standing back, holding open the door. He smiles at her. His suit is silly, ruffled, hot, the buttons shiny and bright, catching the sun, throwing it back at her, blinding her with tiny spots of light.

"Thank you," she says, and she stares down at her feet.

She does not look up. She avoids his loopy eyes, his bulbous lips, his balloon nose. She stares down at the black high-heeled sandals that Celia would have coveted and thinks they're worth four husbands. Twelve Peters.

"Have a nice day," the clown says, Bill W. says, his nameplate blazing up at her as she nods and turns right, fairly running down the sidewalk to the overpriced garage.

She flips on the air conditioner in the car, aiming the vent up toward her face. The air is warm, but at least it's moving, blowing wisps of bangs off her forehead. She knows better than to turn on the radio, but the voices come out anyway. Reproaching voices, warning voices. Songs and pieces of songs bounce off the dash and circle the inside of the car, settling in the gaps and lines, the broken places in the roof, settling like paintings, like filmstrips, and she leans back, stares at the colors, floating and merging, and it's as if she's sitting in the Sistine Chapel, not an old maroon Toyota littered with bumper stickers. She closes her eyes.

She'd pinned her hopes on finding the photo in Celia's phone, this picture Peter told her wasn't there. "Why are you saying this?" he'd asked her, and now she doesn't know. She has no answers. All she has is remnants and raveling threads. All she has is pictures on the ceiling of her car, photos she imagined in a phone, contact numbers that don't go where she'd thought, threatening notes and fancy cars poised to run her down. All she has now, Dana realizes, sitting in the crudely lit space, her eyes focused on the movie playing against the cracks above the visor, all she has is madness. She turns the key in the ignition. Her hands shake on the steering wheel, and she avoids her face in the rearview mirror, the face of a woman who is not what she appears to be. Loneliness engulfs her, smothers her.

She pulls out of the garage and drives slowly toward the highway. There are too many cars as she approaches the bridge, too many reds and blues and headlight eyes—too many bumpers smiling, too many grids, like white, straight teeth. She clutches the steering wheel and keeps her eyes on the road. When she has crossed the bridge, she turns toward the diner, letting the Toyota coast to a stop.

*

"I did it," she says when Glenda comes to take her order. "I killed her."

Glenda sighs. "Hang on. Let me get Hank to cover for me. Herbal tea okay?" she calls out, halfway to the counter, and Dana nods.

"Fine," she says, but her voice is barely audible.

"So?" Glenda is back, sliding over the plastic seat across the table with two cups. She pulls an electric cigarette out of some mysterious place in her apron and takes a smokeless little puff.

"I did what you said," Dana tells her. "I was proactive."

"Good." Glenda takes another little puff, squints her eyes like there's smoke.

154

"I stalked my own husband. I even went into Manhattan and ransacked Ronald's room."

"Who's Ronald?" Glenda bends forward slightly.

"Celia's husband. The dead woman's husband. I was looking for a picture in her phone I thought was there. Everything is disappearing."

"These things . . ." Glenda says, taking a puff off her electronic cigarette and glancing toward the front of the diner, where a line is forming at the register. "Maybe they're real and maybe they aren't. In either case, consider they're trying to tell you something. What was the picture?"

"My husband with another woman."

"And is he with another woman?"

"Yes."

"Well, there you are," Glenda says, sliding across the seat.

"Yes. God! Thank you, Glenda. I always feel so much better after I've talked to you."

"Just remember." Glenda leans over the table before she bolts toward the register. "You're okay, Dana. You'll be okay. You're not a murderer. Remember that."

Dana leaves a wad of bills beside her untouched cup and slips outside, where rain comes down in a lazy drizzle. If Celia's message was merely that—a message—if it never really was in Peter's phone, if it was instead her dead neighbor reaching out from the other side . . . You know what to do.

She'll call Detective Moss, Dana decides, backing out onto the road. That's what she knows she should do. She'll tell him everything—that she might have killed her neighbor in a drunken, manic rage. She'll confess to trips across the George Washington Bridge at midnight, to dalliances with strange men. She'll tell him everything and let him decide what should be done. "Let go and let God," she says, dredging up the line from an Emotions Anonymous meeting she attended a few times years before. "Let go and let Moss."

Rain begins in earnest, falling in small, plump drops that splatter on the windshield, comforting and gray, making soothing, soporific sounds. A sign, she thinks, glancing up at St. Christopher. "Thanks," she says. "Thanks for this at least," and he nods; he even seems to smile. The rain picks up. The car hits a large puddle, sending water over the windshield, blinding her for a second, and she resolves to tell him everything, this man who looks so like the Poet. But first she'll get some help, she'll go see Dr. Sing. She'll take a pill or two or eight. She'll slow herself down just a tad so she can stand it when they lock her up, when the small cell closes in on her, suffocating her. She will be the bigger person—bigger than Peter, with his unfindable, unprovable Tart, bigger than Ronald with his rubber ducks and haikus, bigger than all of them. Like Jesus, Dana knows she has to suffer, that she is here to do the unthinkable, to surmount the insurmountable, to save the clowns and the people in spike wedges, the topplers, the sinners. It is she who will rise to the occasion, she who, like the defunct saint who clings steadfastly to her visor, will surrender herself, unnamed and unremembered, for redemption.

She's nearly home, passing over the railroad tracks and accelerating through a small industrial section, when she sees a blur in the rain, a tiny white blotch that hops across the road several feet in front of her car. A rabbit, she thinks, but as she gets closer, she sees it's a kitten, that it's stopped in a small patch of grass, soaked and frightened—that it stares, not at the Toyota but directly through the driver's-side window, directly at Dana. It opens its mouth; it's saying something. She can see the words trail out into the rain like ribbons, blue and pink and gold, and she wonders if it's really there—if it's her mother or Celia trying to tell her something—to impart some wisdom from beyond. She shakes her head, trying to bring herself back, to ground herself inside the car, to collect what paltry remnants she has left of clarity, of sanity, of her mind. Jesus. She brakes too quickly. The car skids to the edge of the road, sliding in mud, and she feels for a fraction of a second as if the car is flying, as if she is flying, suddenly unfettered, unencumbered. Free. Is this what Celia meant in her voice-mail message, that Dana should join her somehow, extricate herself from the sordid mess that her life has recently become? You know what to do.

# 18

Jack Moss stares at the manila envelope on his desk. He picks it up and runs his thumb and index finger along its edges, tracing the perimeter, stalling. The crime-scene investigators lifted some prints from the front seat of Celia Steinhauser's SUV that don't belong to her or her husband. Forensics got a match, and Jack has the name in his hands. The prints were in the front seat—the door handle, the dash, the radio—but more important they were on the glove compartment—inside it, even. Whoever sat in the dead woman's car was all over it. Recently.

He's happy for the phone call that comes in just as he's begun loosening the glue at the top of the envelope. Something nags at the back of his brain. He sets the envelope down on his desk and picks up the phone. "Moss," he says, but his voice sounds scratchy. He clears his throat. "Jack Moss."

At first there is only silence, and then there's Ann. "Can you talk?" she says. "Is this a good time?"

"Not really." He swivels around in his chair so he can see down the hall. "But it could be worse."

"I went back to the house for a few things, but I'll have to get the rest the next time I—"

"Whatever you want," he says. "Whenever you want." Now that she's made up her mind, now that she's actually gone, he doesn't want to talk about it. Sometimes he doesn't want to talk to her at all.

"Jack?"

He swivels back, drops his head into his hands.

"Say something."

"There's nothing left to say," he tells her, and it sounds silly and cliché and not what he wanted to say or meant to say or what he imagined himself saying if Ann ever left him. And he had imagined it. He always half expected her to be gone when he came home at an impossible hour or missed a celebration or countless other marital transgressions he'd committed over the years.

"I guess that's why I'm here and you're there," Ann says. "Because there never was anything left to say."

"That isn't true. We had something."

She sighs. Her voice shakes. He wonders if she's crying. "I tried to make things work for years."

"Not long enough," Jack says, but even as he says it, he isn't sure it's true.

"How long, Jack? How long is long enough?"

He drums his fingers on the top of his desk. "I don't know, Ann. Maybe this is long enough."

"I miss you," she says, and it is unexpected, this raw truth, this ragged voice, his wife baring her soul somewhere on the Upper West Side, where she's hemorrhaging money into a hotel. He stares out the window across the room. Dark clouds gather off to the east. "Jack? Are you still there?"

He sighs. "I'm still here."

"Right," she says, and she hangs up.

Ann was the one pursuing him in the beginning, opening him up to the possibility of starting over only months after he walked away from his first marriage. She found him in a bar one night after his criminal-justice class at Hunter, sloppy drunk and self-pitying. She was sitting next to him, and they'd started talking—she'd started talking. Chitchat. Bar talk, but when she got up to leave, he'd found he didn't want her to. He followed her outside and convinced her to go with him to a diner up the street.

They talked a lot in the beginning, about things that seemed so important, so urgent at the time and that now he couldn't remember if his life depended on it. For weeks they did nothing but talk. They didn't kiss, they didn't even touch until the snowy, stormy night they slept together, the two of them swaying, arm in arm up three flights of stairs to Jack's hole-in-the-wall room above a bakery off Bleecker Street. They made love as the odor of cinnamon drifted up through the floor, the worn and knotholed boards, as the Russian baker made babka for the morning rush. They fell asleep to snow drifting down, soft and thick and pure, to the tinkling of the small bell on the bakery door, to the sun peeking up between the buildings.

Their marriage was a good one, but it was always

fragile. It was a safe harbor for Jack when he finished school and became a cop and, later, a detective, but he knows it was never quite enough for Ann—that she wanted it to go on forever, that intensity, the leaning over scarred wooden tabletops in late-night diners. The sharing. "You threw me over for your job," she used to tell him, and she'd laugh, but the last few times she said it, she was serious. "Intimacy issues," she'd said through the window of her little red Honda the night she left him, backing out of the driveway with the clip-on reading light from the bedroom peeping out at him like E.T. "You should really get some help."

He picks up the envelope again and turns it over several times. His hands are large; they cover the writing, the "Attention: Detective Jack Moss." He never meant to leave her on her own the way he did. He loved her. He loves her still, but it's like an addiction, his connection to his job, to his work. It consumes him.

"Work is the one thing you can control," she used to say, and he thinks now maybe she was right. Not that he can control his cases, not that he can stop the murders and carjackings and suicides or in any way affect the decline of humanity, but even Jack has to admit that work is the one constant in his life. No matter how bad things get, there'll still be a deskful of files and papers and unsolved cases waiting for him when he gets to the precinct. No matter what shape he's in, no matter what the hour, like a faithful mistress they will always be here.

There was a match on the prints, someone already in the system. A prior. He pulls out the sheet. Kyle Murphy. Jack stares down at his son's name, and he's almost as disappointed that he's not surprised as he is to see it printed there on the page. He never thought he'd be glad his ex-wife changed the boys' last names back to Murphy along with hers after their divorce, but, staring at the paper in his hands, he is. Kyle's shaky past is back to haunt him. It was this possibility that made Jack put himself on the teacher's homicide from the get-go.

When Kyle was seventeen, he was picked up on a burglary charge. Jack got a call at the house in the middle of the night. "It's Margie," Ann said, handing him the phone, turning over and inching her body away from his. Margie was another problem between them—another stabbing needle in the balloon of their marriage.

Kyle had been arrested for a robbery several miles from home, even though he never actually went inside. He tripped the lock with a card of some kind and stood watch while his buddies went in and ransacked the house. The next-door neighbor saw the whole thing through her bedroom window and called 911 with her light off and her nose pressed up against the glass. When the cops arrived, they pulled up to the neighbor's yard without headlights or sirens and walked next door; caught the kids red-handed. Kyle didn't have a prayer, standing on the porch with the card still in his hand. They nabbed him before he could even holler out a heads-up to his buddies. Jack left the boy in lockup for the night, and in the morning he called in a favor and got Kyle into a program, a youth camp in the country, away from his low-life friends, and it seemed to work. Until now anyway.

Jack glances at his partner. He watches Rob lean back in his chair, his desk phone against his ear. Jack turns the papers over, shoves them inside the envelope, resealing it as best he can, and then he slides it to the very back of his desk drawer. He retrieves his cell from his pocket and scrolls through the call log for his son's number as he walks down the hall away from Rob.

Again his call goes straight to voice mail. It's morning, still early enough to catch Kyle before he leaves to look for work or to go to GED class if he's still in it, if he hasn't already taken the test that he could pass even if he's only glanced at the pages of algebraic equations, the geometric theorems. His son has a photographic mind; he sees whole chunks of books inside his head. "Kyle," Jack says into the blankness of his cell phone, pressing it tight against his ear. "It's me again. It's . . . um, Dad. I need you to call me right away. This will all be out of my hands soon, so get back to me. Now!" He ends the call and walks to his office, drops into his swivel chair, letting it roll away from the desk. He waits. He walks across the room and stares outside, where pigeons spill along the street toward the courthouse like a trail of moldy bread crumbs, where cars are jammed up at a red light. His cell phone rings. "Hello?" he says. "Kyle?"

"Yeah," Kyle says. "What do you want?"

"You need to get down to the station. We're on Broadway. Brick building around the— On second thought. Not here. I'll meet you. You got a car?"

"Nope. I ride the bus like all the other underemployed, under-parented—"

"Fine." Jack cuts him off. "How about the diner down on Getty? Twenty minutes. I'll see you there." Again he ends the call quickly, without saying good-bye. He feels a sense of urgency; he feels trapped. He walks back to the chair across the room and stares at the black lines along the wall beside the window; they look like marks made by a bird, made by the pigeons fluttering outside the courthouse, by the claws and wings of captured things flapping against the dull, ugly green of the wall.

*

He gets to the restaurant before his son and finds a small table near the kitchen. In the noon light, even with the little bit of sunshine coming through the shuttered window, the table seems too bright, the restaurant too public, and Jack regrets suggesting this place. Even Rosie's Rooms would be a better choice. He stares at the menu. His shoes gleam in the sunlight from outside.

Kyle slips in like a thief, like a thug; he slouches in. He

glances around the room, and there's something in his eyes. Guilt, Jack thinks. The kid looks guilty as hell. He nods toward Kyle, makes a small gesture, a slight rising movement without actually standing.

"What?" Kyle slumps into the chair across the table. Sunlight brightens the brown of his eyes, picks up the blond highlights in his hair, too long, Jack thinks. No wonder he can't find a job.

"Order what you want," he says. "It's on me."

"Coffee," Kyle says. "Black."

"Get something else," Jack says, jovial, almost. Phony. "We'll have two burgers," he says to the waitress when Kyle shakes his head. "Two orders of fries." She scribbles on her pad and hurries back behind the counter.

Before his brother died, Kyle used to say he wanted to be a cop. He wanted to help kids, he said, wanted to stop them from getting shot down in the streets or in some other country, climbing over rocks or driving jeeps across land mines. He'd make parents accountable to something or to someone, so they'd have to be parents, not drunks and certainly not deserters. This is what he once told Margie and what she then told Jack. He wonders what his son aspires to now, what twists and turns his life has taken since his brother's death, his mother's relapse, the discovery of Margie's clammy body on the floor beside the couch. "How've you been?" he says, but Kyle doesn't answer. He follows the waitress with his eyes. "You take the GED test yet?"

Kyle nods.

"How was it?"

He shrugs. "I think I did all right. They'll let me know when they—"

Jack can see Kyle's hands shaking on the water glass. As if he's read his father's thoughts, he folds them under the table. He looks caught. Jack thinks again of the black marks around the window in his office, of Dana squirming when he questioned her, the funny nervous way she played with her hair.

"So why'd you call me?"

"I know you were in your teacher's car."

"So?" Kyle's legs are shaking. Even though he tries to keep them hidden under the table, Jack can see. He taps his foot.

"So." Jack leans in closer, looks him in the eye. "So she's dead. And your prints are all over her car."

"She gave me a ride," he says. "She did that a lot. Gave students rides when the class let out late. She dropped me off in town."

"So how'd your prints get on her glove compartment? Inside it, for chrissake?"

Kyle shrugs. He sits up straighter, leaning against the back of his chair, staring into space, as if the answer to Jack's question is in the air somewhere over his head. "I was looking for a Kleenex," he says, "so I could blow my nose, Detective."

The waitress arrives, putting their plates down among the tangle of silverware and coffee cups, their discarded saucers. She is awkward, setting a thick, white plate on top of a fork, throwing it off center, wobbly. "Anything else?" she says, but she's looking at Kyle.

"We're good," Jack says, and the waitress keeps her gaze on Kyle for a few seconds before she trots off toward the kitchen.

"So you're saying you went through this woman's glove compartment looking for a Kleenex?"

"She told me to. I asked her did she have a Kleenex, and she said to look in her effing glove box."

"And now she's dead."

Kyle shrugs again, a careless gesture, but his shoulders stay hunched, his foot tap-taps under the table. Jittery. "I know. It's all over the news—shots of her house, her dog. . . ."

"Unfortunate timing." Jack takes a bite of his burger and chews, gazing past his son toward the door.

"Yeah. I should plan my colds better."

"Listen," Jack says. "This was a murder, Kyle. You've got a record, and your prints are all over the victim's car."

Kyle picks up his burger and wolfs it down like a starving man. Jack notes his eyes—just like his mother's. "Next time I'll make sure my teacher's not planning to get murdered when I ask for a Kleenex. How's that sound, Jack?"

"Could you not call me that?"

"That's who you are." Kyle reaches for the mustard.

"Why don't you try 'Dad,' without the sarcasm?"

"That's actually not who you are." Kyle squirts the

167

mustard on his burger and drops the bun back on top.

"So how're you feeling now?"

"Fine," Kyle says. "Why?"

"Your cold. Summer colds are a real bitch. Hard to shake, usually."

"What's your point?"

"Sorry, son, but I don't buy your story. About the Kleenex in the glove compartment. I'm having a little trouble with a teacher telling her student she hardly knows to paw through her glove box looking for a Kleenex she'd probably have in her purse anyway."

"That's what happened," Kyle says, but he doesn't meet Jack's eyes. "How's Ann doing these days?"

Jack takes another bite of his burger.

" 'Cause Margie's not so good. Remember Margie? Your practice wife?"

Jack looks up.

"She was pretty much passed out the last time I went by the house. But no worries, Jack. She's got the TV set. She's got the pictures of the good son draped around. The whole house is a shrine to Joe."

"I could drop over there," Jack says.

Kyle laughs. It's an ugly, sound, like a wrong note. "That is just what she needs," he says. "Jesus."

"You don't know anything about your mother and me, Kyle."

"You planning to clear things up for me?"

Jack looks at his son across the table, at the longish

hair, the big hands, the skinny arms, eyes that can't hide anything—those wide-set brown eyes, the lashes like Margie's. "Naw," he says. "Let's just say I really didn't want to leave."

"So why did you?" For a second, Kyle is the boy on a battered front porch, watching him take off down the road.

"She said that was the only way she could be a good mother—if I left. 'I can't do it with you here,' she told me."

Kyle nods, smirks.

"I never stopped loving you, though," Jack says. "I never stopped thinking about you. You or Joey."

"I'm having a little trouble with that, though, seeing as you've never done anything at all for me. For any of us."

"You'd be surprised," Jack says, and he lifts his hand, catches the waitress's eye for the check. "And stay close. I'll need to question you again about your teacher."

Outside, on the sidewalk, they look off into the sky, the two of them. Like father, like son, Ann would say, and Jack knows it's true. Clouds billow up to the west. The air is still and heavy with the threat of rain, and they flounder, voiceless, their shoes crunching on gravel.

"Need a ride?"

Kyle shakes his head. "I'm right near here," he says. "Me and Maryanne."

"Your girlfriend?"

Kyle nods.

"What's she like?"

"She's beautiful."

"I'd like to meet her sometime," Jack says, "if you—"

Kyle looks down at the sidewalk, kicks at a small stone with the worn-through toe of his shoe. "Thanks for lunch."

"Anytime." Jack fumbles in his pocket for a business card. "Here," he says. "I know you've got me in your cell, but just in case," and he presses the card into his boy's big hand, drops three twenties into Kyle's pocket as he pulls away. "Hey!" he calls out when the two of them are several yards apart on the sidewalk. "Check your pockets." And when Kyle looks up, puzzled, he says, "Take care, son." He stands watching Kyle walk away, this man he last knew as a small child who gripped his hand to cross the street, who sang with him as he played the guitar at Christmas—all the carols he no longer knows—the boy who watched him pack his truck and drive away. There are secrets locked inside his son that he will never know, but the ones about Celia are right there at the surface. They'll all spill out at some point. Jack only has to wait.

He calls the crime scene unit, tells them to go back to the Steinhausers', to take prints from everywhere around Celia's bed—the headboard, the nightstand, everything. "Put a rush on it," he tells them. "And send the results directly to me." If Kyle's prints show up in the bedroom, Jack promises himself, he'll turn the case over to Rob and walk away. That's the line he won't cross, but then he shakes his head because he isn't really sure there is a line. It's killing him, though, hiding the prints from Celia's car, not saying what he knows about his son. The prosecutor's office wants an update every couple of days, a high-profile case like this one—and he's giving them crumbs. He's your son, he tells himself. You owe him. But Jack has never compromised himself like this before—not on the job. Everything else in his life is shit, but this one part of it he's been careful to keep pure as the driven snow. Until now.

## 19

As soon as she gets into the car, Dana notices something on the seat. A scrap of white paper, obvious in a car that for once is as neat as a pin, thanks to the cleaning project she devised to keep herself focused. She'd gathered up all the overdue library books and fished out the notebooks filled with scrawls and lists and stacked them neatly on the floor of the backseat. Pads and pencils are now fitted into a plastic box she purchased at Target for odds and ends. She even ran a cleaning rag across the dash and of course St. Christopher.

She reaches down to brush the paper off the seat but thinks better of it. This is how it begins, the mishmash of trash and books and overcoats. It begins with a single piece of paper that stands out, like this one, in a clean front seat. She picks it up and sticks it in her purse.

Something catches her eye just as she's turning the key in the ignition, her attention already moving to the gas-gauge needle, barely budging from its lying-down position on the E. She sees something—a dab of color— and she looks back at the paper, stuck now to the damp outside of a partly empty bottled water in her bag. She peels it off the plastic and stares at the same tiny writing she saw the day of the brunch.

She takes her reading glasses out of her purse, moving in small, robotic increments, as if a decisive shift might rouse the author of the note from a nearby hedge or send him springing from the trunk of her car. She stares at the scrap of paper in the bright sunlight. "You will pay for what you did, you crazy, deadly bitch." Even with the teensy writing, she can read the message easily. This time the note is clearly a threat. The first one . . . well, bad enough—but this one is much more ominous. She feels her brain sparking, emitting bright flashes that fizzle and die, misfiring like a bad engine. She cringes, slumping down in the seat. The steering wheel stares at her, the Toyota logo a lopsided smile as she struggles to focus.

When she was eight, there was a note inside her desk at school. Nasty. Cruel. "We hate you"—a note left by the class bully or a boy with a crush, someone who didn't like the way she looked, who thought she talked too loudly or not loudly enough, who didn't like her mother's car or that her father had died a sudden, violent death—a bevy of girls, she imagined, with perfect hair and blouses tucked neatly into the Catholic plaid of their skirts. She'd folded the note carefully again and again until it was a tiny thing, a square the size of a pea, nearly invisible, and then she'd slipped it back inside her desk. She never told a soul. It terrified her, though, knowing that someone was there, at the back of the room or passing her in the corridor—someone who hated her. Her present fear is heightened by the resurrection of this hastily buried memory, and for a second, in her panic, she wonders if the author has been with her all along, stalking her far into her adult life.

The air conditioner spits out puffs of cool air. The radio news is barely audible. The voices scare her. She turns it off, but she can still hear it, a soft, indecipherable hum.

You will pay.

She takes off her glasses and sticks the note back in her purse— beneath a flap inside her wallet—and edges her car onto Ashby Lane. There is nowhere she really wants to be, but her own house is the place she least wants to be, now that this person has access to her car and, even more frightening, her house. She drives in circles around the neighborhood, gripping the steering wheel until her knuckles are white. Did someone see her with Celia the day she died? Did someone see her leaving the Stein-hausers' or watch from the clot of trees in her backyard as she stood at the kitchen sink scrubbing her hands before she fell across her couch in a drunken stupor? Or is it something else she's done, some minor, unin-tended offense– Christmas lights left up too long or an overlooked potluck invitation? Dana feels a shiver up her spine. You will pay. You will pay. Her fingers tremble on the steering wheel. Her heart flutters and skips. She feels light-headed and faint. Paralyzed with fear.

She thinks maybe she'll drive to the police department and hand both notes over to Detective Moss. She even

174

turns around and drives several blocks in his direction before she pulls in to a BP station and stumbles out to pump gas into her now completely empty tank.

Back in the car, she concentrates on a broken neon sign in the parking lot next door, on the thunderclouds that cover everything in gray, and then she pulls out her cell and calls Peter.

"Dana?" He sounds annoyed. "Listen, I'm really . . . we're really slammed in here today. I—"

"Wait," she says. "This is important. I found another note."

"Another what?" She pictures his puffy hand around his phone. "I can't really hear you."

"Well, step outside, then. Go to the john." Pretend I'm the Tart or a client for five fucking . . . "I really need to talk to you."

"Okay," he says after a few seconds have gone by. "I'm outside. Now I can hear you."

"I got another note. Like the one in my book. Like the one the day of the brunch."

"In the house?"

"No. It was on the front seat of my car."

He pauses. "It goes without saying, if you locked your car door—"

"Right. So let's let it go without saying. Anyway, it was on the front seat of my car when I got in it this morning. That same writing, that weird, teensy—"

"What time?"

"What time? What difference does it make what time? I don't know what time. Ten, maybe."

"What'd it say?"

"'You will pay for what you did, you crazy, deadly bitch.'"

"What the hell does that mean? What'd you do?"

"I don't know," Dana says. "I don't know what I did. Maybe I did something horrible."

"Like what?"

"Like . . . I don't know . . . like something really . . ."

"Look." Peter's hand makes little ruffly noises on the phone. "Maybe this is just you, Dana—your Catholic stuff. Your overactive guilt."

"Is making me . . . what? Hire someone to write me scary notes?"

She hears him breathe in deeply. She hears traffic and the sound of smoke drifting in and out of his lungs.

"I'm trying to come up with a way to put this delicately."

"Because you're always so delicate when it comes to my feelings," she says.

"Okay, then," he says, and he takes another toke. At least it sounds like a toke. Dana wonders if they get high at Glynniss, Hudgens and Catrell on their lunch breaks, if Peter and the Tart sneak off to the boardroom together to light up, if maybe she's the daughter of one of the senior lawyers.

"Is she a Glynniss?" Dana says, but Peter's talking,

too, so he doesn't hear her. "What?" she says.

"I said maybe you wrote the fucking notes."

"Thanks." Dana pulls the phone away from her ear. "Thanks for the delicacy."

"On the note I saw—the one from the brunch—the writing was so tiny," he says as she fumbles for the off button, "it could have been anybody's, really. It—"

Dana sticks her phone inside her bag and stares at the sign with the missing letters, but this time she doesn't cry. This time she shivers in the soggy summer heat, remembering her own strange, tiny writing on five hundred sheets of paper drifting over Avenue D decades before.

# 20

The kitten she rescued from the highway bounces down the hall, barely touching the floor. Dana pats the cushion, and the kitten flies across the room, landing on the couch beside her. He hisses when she tries to pet him. He hurtles through the air and out of sight. He is feral. It will take some time, the vet told her, for him to come around, and he might never make a good house pet. It's ingrained in feral cats, he said, this craziness, this fear. But she's lucky he's so young, this one. She was lucky to have spotted him in the rain, tiny as he is. She calls him Spot, partly for this reason and partly for his markings, like black dots across his fur. At the back of his head, a long, thick splash of black looks like a haircut on an actor from the twenties. She reaches out again to pet him. She understands his ambivalence—approach, avoid, approach, avoid—he cleans her hand with a pink sandpaper tongue.

She leans back, shifting her body so her long legs fall over the arm of the sofa. Maybe she'll close her eyes for a minute, and maybe, just maybe, she'll fall asleep. Her lids feel heavy. The kitten dashes across the living room. She smiles as he skitters underneath the sofa and reemerges with something hanging from his mouth. With great effort Dana rouses herself, stumbling toward him as he shoots into the dining room. "C'mere, you," she says, laughing, falling after him, her body nearly horizontal as he leaps and darts. Something tumbles from his mouth, lands on the carpet.

Dana picks it up. An unopened pack of antiseptic wipes. "Silly," she says, "you are such a silly—" She rips them open. She's had her hands all over the cat—who knows what he's been into?

She stops. The odor wafts up from the plastic wrap and nearly gags her. Oh, my God! She reaches out behind her, finding the blue chair with her hands and backing slowly into it. The odor from Celia's house fills up her brain— her neighbor's fancy living room, her bloody body on the floor, that odor, that poignant, crappy-perfume odor, like these wipes stuck underneath the sofa, these stupid things she carries in her purse. She often buys the scented ones to mask the smell of rubbing alcohol. She remembers buying lemon wipes and, at some point, rose—probably lavender, too. She always carries them with her. Or did until . . . She tries to think back, tries to remember if she had them after the day Celia died, tries to remember if she stuck them there under the sofa in a drunken fog. She drops her head into her hands, covers her eyes with trembling fingers. All along, the odor lingered at the edge of her perception, played with her head, that faint, vague scent. All along, it was familiar. Eventually it would have surfaced—as she walked through Target behind a germ-

179

conscious shopper, watched Wanda wipe the sticky face of one of her sons, or pushed through the turnstile of the train—anywhere at all she could and would eventually identify the scent. But here, under her own sofa in her own living room, the recognition makes her sink into the cushions of the blue chair, terrified because everything she's found so far, everything she has unearthed or stumbled across, points to her being Celia's killer. She closes the pack of wipes, traps the odors back inside, tosses them on the desk in the entryway. Everything is gray around her, all the color sucked out of the room. She only wants to sleep, only wants the world to fade, to recede, until she figures out what she should do.

\*

It's a quarter after nine, and Peter hasn't come home. In the kitchen the dishes are stacked in a small pile near the sink and a ruined stew is caked to the inside of a large orange Martha Stewart pot. Dana scrolls to Peter's number in her cell.

"Hello," he says, and traffic rumbles in her ear.

"Where are you?"

"I told you." Peter sounds annoyed. "I told you this morning I was meeting a client after work."

"No." She sighs. "No you didn't."

"And then when we talked later—when you called about the . . . when you called, I told you we were slammed at the office and I mentioned I'd be late again."

"Not true."

"Did you make the appointment yet with Dr. Sing?" he says, lowering his voice. "The appointment you were going to make a week ago!"

"Yes," she says. "I made it for next Friday," which is nearly true. After her discovery of the wipes, she did call the office, but she got distracted by something, by Spot climbing up the drapes or by something in the yard, by the disapproving sound of the voice on Dr. Sing's machine. She will, though. She has to.

"I'm on my way home," he says after a pause. "I'll see you in a few minutes."

She hits a button, and her phone fades to black. Did he tell her he'd be late? She tries to summon up the tiny bits of talk they exchanged that morning, but she doesn't remember Peter saying anything at all, except would she please move her car—it was blocking the garage. And certainly nothing was mentioned during her call about the note.

She considers going back to the St. Giles. She remembers how easily sleep came to her there when she was sleuthing—or it would have anyway, if she had let herself relax—even in all the tangle of dirty clothes and rumpled covers. She thinks about running into Ronald in the coffee shop next door or a diner up the street—he has to eat somewhere—and engaging him in idle conversation. "We're fumigating our house," she might tell him, or "Peter's doing some renovating in our kitchen, so I decided to come here. Small world, eh?" She imagines getting chummy enough to ask again about the picture in Celia's phone—if he saw it at some point, if he deleted it. And Dr. Sing is only two train stops up from the hotel.

She keeps her eyes shut, listening to Peter's car purr in the driveway as he opens the garage door and pulls inside. In the end she doesn't leave; she lies horizontally across the bed, hoping he'll sleep in Jamie's room or on the living-room couch. In the end she's afraid that questioning Ronald will only add to her distress, her craziness, her uncertainty—that the photo in Celia's cell was no more real than Bozo greeting her at the hotel or Michael Jackson's voice after she turned off the radio.

She hears the front door squeak open and then the hush of her husband walking in his stocking feet across the living room and into the kitchen. She hears the click of the stove as Peter relights the burner under the pot of stew, the sound of water streaming from the faucet into the caked vegetables. At some point she drifts off, awakening to the odor of cigarette smoke drifting through the half-closed window. She inches off the bed and wanders to the kitchen, where Peter's stacked the dirty pots in the sink, a small and unexpected favor, and then she hears his voice. He's in the backyard. He's moved from under the bedroom window to stand on the brick patio on the other side of the porch door, and she moves closer, lulled by the hum of his words. She hears him say, "I can't guarantee anything at this point." Dana takes a step away, back toward the darkness of the kitchen. "I understand," Peter says, and then he sighs, an exaggerated sigh. "I understand completely. You could. Exactly. Jeopardizing your— . . . Of course. It's— . . . Just keep me on speed dial," he says, "and I'll— . . . No," he says. "No. I won't call. I'll wait to hear from you. Just let me know if anything . . . if there's anything— . . . Okay, hon," he says, and Dana takes another step back, another step away. "Good-bye, then. It's been—" The talking stops. Peter sighs again, but this time it's a relieved-sounding little sigh. She hears the striking of a match, and a small flash of light pops briefly into the blackness over the patio. "Good riddance," she thinks he says, but she wouldn't swear to it.

She tiptoes back to the bedroom and falls across the bed, wanting to escape, wanting not to be here in this house with notes she's possibly written to herself, with hand wipes reeking of lavender and guilt, with a husband who's chosen the worst moment of her life to have an affair. She closes her eyes against the topsy-turvy world hers has become, and when she opens them again, the clock screams one-fifteen.

She tosses and turns for a few minutes, and then she gets up and walks out to the living room. Peter lies on the couch, his shoes and socks at odd angles to his body, as if he's kicked them off. He's hung his pants over the back of a dining-room chair, and judging from the empty lager bottles on the table, he's had quite a bit to drink. There's something else. An odor that eclipses the beer. She sniffs.

Lately her sense of smell is amazing. She walks over to the couch where Peter snores explosively, spectacularly, and she bends over, inhaling flowery, sweet perfume. Lilac. She sniffs again. Yes. Definitely lilac. She knows what Peter would say. She knows he'd look at her, down his own ungifted nose at her, and say it was a client's perfume, or that a co-worker hugged him out of gratitude, or that one of the paralegals in the building is young and untrained in the art of perfume application, so the odor wafts daily up the hall and sticks to all the lawyers. He would remind her to go see Dr. Sing, but his overheard phone call lets her know that "hon's" perfume now clings to Peter's clothes, reminders of what might have been their final tryst, residuals of a parting hug or a quick greeting in the lobby of a hotel—heavy and cloying. I hate you. I hate both of you, she whispers, leaning over him so closely that a small sprout of ear hair tickles her lips.

She glances at the table, at the green bottles lined up along its marble top like short, stout trees. She finishes off the last few swallows of beer in one of them and gets up to take them to the kitchen, knocking Peter's pants off the back of the chair in her haste.

Her fingers feel thick and clumsy as she bends to pick them up, to hang them neatly over the chair. She sticks her hand inside the pockets, one by one. She thinks of packing some clothes in a suitcase and running away from the husband she hates at this moment with a passion and might, for all she knows, kill before the night is out. She can no longer trust her judgment.

Her hands tremble violently. The house is suddenly dreamlike, black and white and gray, as if she's staring at an old photograph, as if she is no longer here. Peter's pants shake between her fingers, and a receipt of some kind falls from one of his back pockets. It flutters to the fake Persian rug that runs the length of the dining room and lands faceup at the plushy edge, in the middle of a rose with a greenish vine looping out from the bottom petals. Dana gathers the squat bottles in her shaking hands and sticks them in the recycling bag beside the garbage in the kitchen. On her way back through the dining room, she picks up the paper from Peter's pants and fiddles with it, folds it into fourths, glaring at him as she walks to the bedroom.

She pulls on a pair of jeans and stuffs the paper into her pocket. She pulls a purple tank top over her head and packs without giving it a great deal of thought. She grabs random items. These days she doesn't have to think about the ordinary things. They just occur. They are managed by some separate part of her brain that seems to always be operating—a default thinker—as she centers on the more important, pressing aspects of her life. She tucks a dress inside the bag along with a pair of slippers from Bloomingdale's, jeans, and three tops she finds lying on a large, untidy pile on the bedroom floor. She plucks a nightgown off the bedside table and hurries to the bathroom, filling a makeup case with shampoos and mascaras and several jars of face creams.

When she's finished, she slides into her shoes and zips the overnight bag. She scribbles a note for Peter, more lines from Prufrock, a nod to the lilac, clinging like tar to his clothes. "Is it perfume from a dress that makes me so digress?" She turns to the door, closing it quietly behind her.

She slings her bag onto the seat and glances at St. Christopher, staring down at her from the visor. He winks. He nods toward her lap.

"What?" she says, and he nods again. Winks again. "There's nothing there," she says, and turns the key. She can feel him nodding as she backs out to the street. She can feel his eyes in the dark car, and she pushes in an old CD, pats her pocket with her left hand. It makes a crinkling sound, and she reaches inside for the scrap of paper that drifted out of Peter's pants. "This?" she says, and even in the darkness of the front seat she can see St. Christopher nod.

When she gets to the end of the street, she pulls over, letting her tires crunch along the grassy border of the Brinkmeyers' lawn. She opens the car door for light and smooths the paper out on her thigh. "It's only a bill," she starts to say, but she reads it anyway. "Days Inn, room 156," it says. "August 23. One king. Nonsmoking. $189.99."

Dana reads it again. She sits for a minute in the glow from the small, glass-plated ceiling light, and then she folds the receipt into fourths again and tucks it back inside her pocket, hooking the open door with her foot, letting it swing shut, letting the overhead glow sink back inside the ceiling. She sits, still as a statue in the balmy, breezy night until a light goes on in the Brinkmeyers' bedroom, and she edges off their lawn to the sidewalk.

She leans her head in her hands and cries—for the husband that Peter was, for their child who is now a man, for the family they once were. She turns off the ignition and sobs in the dim light from a streetlamp. And when she can focus on the road, on driving to the city, on digging up her innocence if it is there for the digging, she brushes her hair back with her hands and runs her fingers under her eyes, collecting remnants of mascara.

"Well," she says, glancing up at St. Christopher, even though she can't quite see him in the once-again-dark front seat of the Toyota, "at least he wasn't at the Marriott." She pulls back onto the road and heads for the highway, reaching over to restart the music—vintage Journey, fiddling through to the song about the boulevards and streetlights, the smoky rooms, and she sings along, almost a whisper at first, but her voice rises in the darkness of the car. She speeds up, rambling down the highway to New York, and then she opens the car window, lets the wind ruin her hair, the cool air, the smallest breath of autumn, and she turns the music up higher, sings louder. The wind flies up from the water, and she feels it all around her, feels it blow through her skin, consuming her. She is the wind.

## 21

Jack Moss checks his messages for the fifth time that morning, but there's nothing. Nothing anyway that interests him, nothing from Ann. He thinks about his lunch with Kyle. The kid is tough—he's had to be—and it was easy to see he holds his own. He reminds Jack of himself at that age. Still, Kyle is hiding something—something pretty big unless Jack's way off. His story didn't cut it, but it wasn't that. There's something more important that Kyle has no intention of telling him, and it scares the shit out of him when he thinks about what that might be.

It will take a lot of time, he thinks, a lot of thought and energy, but somehow he'll win over his son, somehow he'll make it up to him, all those years he felt abandoned, all those years alone with a reeling, alcoholic mother, him and Joey. Even if Kyle's guilty, he is still Jack's son and Jack will do what he can. He already has. He's already compromised himself more than he ever dreamed he would. His work is sacred. But, in a totally different way, so is his son, and the guilt on both fronts is eating him alive.

He sighs. He and Ann weren't able to start a family of their own, although they tried for years. There were countless trips to countless specialists, thermometers dictating when they could make love, until love was no longer really in the equation—the full moon this, the new moon that, this position, that position, boxers not briefs. Oysters, not burgers. Dark chicken and so much salmon he still gags when he smells it. Cutting back on after-work beers. He did it all. They did it all, but nothing worked. In the end they gave it up. They put in for adoption, but the list was as long as the Lincoln Tunnel, the conditions rigorous. He was too old, she was too needy, their house too cluttered. . . .

After Ann's second miscarriage, after nearly five months of serious depression, the throwing-away of the thermometer, and with Jack's fiftieth birthday looming, Ann drove down to the pound and adopted a puppy—nearly as complicated a process, she said later, as adopting a child—printed "HAPPY BIRTHDAY, DADDY" in large capital letters on a card she tied with a pink bow around its neck, and presented Molly to him at the breakfast table. He loved the dog. They both did. They both do. They'll have to work out her custody at some point, and the irony is not lost on Jack that he will beg for weekends with the dog when he let his boys go without a fight.

"Anything new?" Rob says from his desk.

"On what?"

"The Steinhauser case? Hey," he says. "You okay?"

"Yeah," Jack says. "Sure. I'm okay." He gets up, grabs his keys. "I'm going out for a minute. Got something to check on Ashby Lane."

"Want me to come?"

"I'm good on this trip," he says. "You've got your hands full with the missing kid."

When he's nearly to the Steinhausers', it starts to rain, a flooding, blinding rain, and he inches along the road, looking for street signs through the curtains of water. He doesn't remember exactly where the street is in all the twists and turns, nearly hidden now inside the fog, barely visible in this pounding rain. It's an older subdivision with abundant, massive trees that occasionally obscure mailboxes and house numbers and the few sporadic road signs.

He finds the street and makes a slow turn, nearly hitting a black Lexus swerving up the wrong side of the road. "Watch it, you asshole," he snarls at the closed window, at the pouring rain. He glares toward the driver of the other car, and even with all the water he recognizes Peter. "Figures," he says, and he thinks about turning around, pulling him over, giving him a ticket, but he'll concentrate on the murder. There's something really shady about Peter—he stinks—but Jack isn't sure it has anything to do with the case.

It's the wife who looks guilty.

He pulls up to the Steinhausers' and stops the car, peering through the rain at the front porch, at a small white blob by the door. When the rain slows down a little, the white blob hops off—a rabbit, he thinks—and he remembers what Kyle said about the Steinhausers' dog, that it was in the pictures of the house they showed on TV, but it wasn't. Jack was there when they shot the crime-scene footage that was later on the news, and the dog was missing, much to Ronald's distress. It didn't show up again until the next evening, when Ronald went back to look for him and discovered him sitting at the front door, disheveled and dirty—skittish, Ronald said, which was unlike him. Seeing the rabbit on the porch has jogged Jack's memory, bringing back this small detail that Kyle dropped into their tangled knot of conversation. So Kyle lied about where he'd seen his teacher's dog. If he didn't see it on TV, then where?

The lies are stacking up in other areas, too. The cell-phone picture wasn't in the phone. He'd checked Celia's cell at the station himself after interviewing Dana; he'd called Ronald and had him bring it down. All the other pictures were there—the ones of Celia hamming it up for the camera and several shots of her boys, a few confusing blobs that the husband said were plants and parts of plants, and, Jack suspected, several of Ronald's thumb.

But no sign of the couple described to him in such detail.

Was the photo in the cell phone deleted? He watches the rain streak down the windshield and thinks it would be pointless for Dana to make up such an elaborate story. Why not just say she went to the Steinhausers' to help her friend with a recipe or lend her eye shadow or one of a million other things women help each other with? Why bother making up something that could so easily be checked, so easily disproved? So long-winded and difficult to keep straight? If she'd wanted her husband to look guilty, why not just say that the afternoon she died, Celia called her over—which the neighbor corroborated—to tell her they were having an affair and Peter'd dumped her? Why go to all the trouble about a photo in a fucking phone? Far more probable that Ronald's lying. The guy is obviously covering up something, so it makes sense he's deleted a photo in his late wife's phone. Maybe the techies can pull it up—he'll have Ronald bring it in again. Or was Dana simply wrong, confused?

He tugs his jacket over his head and runs to the neighbor's house across the street. At first there's no answer, and then a woman comes to the door. She's small and pretty and clearly wary of his presence there on her front porch.

"Christine Reich?"

"Yes?" She doesn't open the screen, and who could blame her after what's happened practically in her front yard? He shows her his ID, his badge, tells her he knows that the men questioned her the night of Celia's death, that he'd just like to ask a couple follow-up questions.

"All right," she says, but she doesn't sound too sure. Neither does she invite him in. Water drizzles through the cracks of her overhang and streams down Jack's collar. "Like I told the officer before," she says, "I was out of town that week. I wasn't home when my neighbor was . . . was so brutally— I wasn't home."

"Right. Got it." Jack glances down at his notes. "This isn't about that night in particular. Did you ever see anyone coming and going from the Steinhausers'?"

She gives him a funny look. "Of course."

"During the day, I meant."

"Sure."

"Who?"

She shifts her weight onto one leg and juts out her hip, crosses her arms over her chest. "The boys' friends, the neighbor down the street—Dana, I think, is her name— two or three other women—friends of Celia's, I guess. They'd pull up in their cars."

"How about lately? Any unusual visitors?"

She starts to open her mouth, and then she snaps it back shut like a turtle, standing there in her green slacks, her little green print tank top. Jack waits. He taps his pen on the memo pad, doesn't say a word.

"There was someone else."

"Yeah? Who was that?" He keeps his eyes on the pad like he's only half listening, the little dance he does with skittish witnesses—makes them think it's their idea to spill the beans, not his.

"I guess it's been a few weeks now, but there was this guy. He used to come over in the afternoon—lunchtime, maybe—and take off after a couple hours."

"His car?"

"He never drove. He was on foot. I always knew when he was walking up to her front door, because her dog would bark."

Jack feels sick. On foot. Kyle would be on foot.

193

"Could you describe him?"

Christine shrugs. "No. Not really. I wasn't all that interested."

"Was it a kid? One of her students?"

"No," she says, and Jack is so relieved he could rip through the screen and hug her. "I don't think so. From the back anyway, he looked like a grown man. Medium height, medium everything, pretty much. Usually wore a hat—more of a cap, a beret." Somewhere behind her a baby wails. "If you'll excuse me," she says, and Jack nods.

"Thanks," he says, with a little more enthusiasm than he's meant to, and she snaps the heavy front door shut and clicks the locks in place before he's even turned around.

He walks up the block, passing Lon Nguyen's house to knock on Wanda Needles's door. Both Lon and Dana mentioned her being outside the afternoon Celia died, but he strikes out there. Wanda just that morning started a new job, a teenage baby-sitter tells him through the screen door, and he leaves his card, asks her to have Wanda call him.

By the time he makes it back across the street, the rain has nearly stopped. The air smells clean and wet and heavy with the scent of flowers, like too much perfume. Water slides down from the leaves and from the Steinhausers' roof, running into puddles next to the front steps, soaking into their flooded lawn. Steam floats up from the street, enfolding Ashby Lane.

He flips his key ring toward the car just as the rabbit flies past and stops several feet away at the edge of the sidewalk, only it isn't a rabbit. It's a cat, he can see, now that it's finally still and the rain no longer blurs its features. It's a kitten. He squats on one knee, and the tiny creature runs to him, climbs into his lap, clings there with its needle claws. He reaches down to pet the spotted head, and the kitten moves back, quickly, biting his hand. "What a little scrapper," Jack says. "Where'd you come from anyway?" He figures it's a stray that Celia was feeding, maybe she and some of the other neighbors. There was no mention of a kitten in the reports, only the dog. On impulse Jack picks up the biting cat and sticks it in his car. He turns the key, and his back tires catch in the gravel at the side of Ashby Lane. The kitten presses its nose against the glass of the backseat window, its front paws on the padded insides of the door, its large ears aimed at the front seat, where a blues song oozes from the radio.

His cell phone buzzes on the seat, and Jack reaches over to grab it. Rob.

"Hey," Rob says, "Jack. What do you know? That guy—that Peter guy—he phoned in this morning about his wife." His voice is patchy with static.

"Oh, yeah? What'd he say?"

"That she took off. He just wanted to let you know— us know—on account of the case, I guess."

"When?"

"Last night."

"Good for her," Jack says. "Unless he's got her buried in the backyard."

"The husband's a lawyer, right?"

"Right. She leave a note?"

"Yeah. But it was strange, according to him. Part of a poem. It didn't sound like her at all, he said," and for a second Jack feels a shiver, like an unwelcome premonition, up his spine.

"He bring it in? The husband? Did he bring it down to the station?"

"Uh-uh. I had him read it to me, though. I wrote it down, if I can find . . . Yeah. Here it is. 'Is it perfume from a dress that makes me so digress?' "

"Weird," Jack says. "Listen. Thanks for the update. I'm headed in now," but he stops for a moment, sits in the Crown Vic, even though the rain has stopped and the sun is popping out from the clouds. It didn't sound like her at all, the husband said, and Jack can't help remembering how oddly Dana acted in his office—funny, but jumpy as hell. Familiar, although he can't put his finger on just why.

He's heard neighbors describing suspects in murder investigations the same way Peter just described his wife—There was something off; he wasn't himself, or She was so sweet, and then all of a sudden, she was like a different person. He's heard statements like these far too often to take lightly what Dana's husband said, even if he is a total jerk. Is he trying to frame her, or has Dana gone off the rails, and if so, where the hell is she?

# 22

On her second morning at the hotel, Dana encounters Ronald on the busy street outside. He's dressed in a business-casual outfit, a tie but no jacket, and he's heading down the street.

"Ronald!" Dana darts after him. Her heel catches in a grate in the sidewalk.

"Dana?"

"Yes. We keep running into each other."

"Well." Ronald stops. "I don't know if I'd say that."

"No," she says, "I guess not."

"What are you doing here?" Ronald looks confused. He runs his hand through his hair in what might have been a suave, rock-band gesture but instead leaves him with a deer-in-the-headlights look. His overgelled hair stands stiff and upright, like a small wall.

"I'm staying here. I'm at the St. Giles. Room 316. They're fumigating our house."

"No kidding! I'm staying there, too." Ronald falls into step beside her. "I can't use my house until they've done everything they need to do with it. But it's fine. I told Detective Ross to take all the time he needs. I have no desire to go back there. Ever. 'Take all the time in the

world,' I told him. 'I never want to see the place again'—
my wife's blood splattered all over the floor, that stupid
overpriced vase smashed into smither—"

"Right. So what is 'everything,' exactly?"

Ronald shrugs. "Beats me," he says. "But they've still
got that damn tape up."

Dana looks at him.

"The crime tape? The yellow plastic stuff all over our
hedges? Don't tell me you haven't noticed. All the time
we . . . well, I really. Celia wasn't all that good a gardener,
truth be told—the work, the time, the energy . . ." He
sighs. "All for naught."

"Naught, really. You did have that 'Best Yard' sign up
for quite a—"

"A month. Yes. Last May."

"Do you want to join me?" Dana stops in front of a
little tea shop. "Cup of coffee?"

Ronald glances at his watch. "Maybe a quick one."

"Were you on your way to work?"

"Yes," he says. "Thank God for work. It takes my
mind off Celia."

He tugs at the door, and small bells jingle. Dana minces
inside. Her foot hurts from the lopsided heel; it puts her
at an odd angle. Inside, the lights are far too bright; their
auras vibrate and move in spirals around them. "So many
halos," she says, "so little time."

"Hmm." Ronald appears not to have heard her. He
scans a blackboard tacked up over the counter.

"I can see the writing on the wall," Dana quips, but again Ronald seems not to hear.

"Coffee, please," he says to no one in particular. He turns to Dana. "Two coffees?"

"Sure." She nods. "Thanks. But decaf for me."

"D'ja get that?" Ronald says to the air, and Dana wanders off toward a small table near the door. The light glares from the ceiling, making the place mats dance, making the menus glimmer. When she sits, she sees there is a man behind the counter, bent over, picking out pastries, bagging doughnuts and sweet rolls, which he hands over the counter to a woman in a pencil skirt, and Dana feels a little better, knowing that Ronald gave their order to an actual entity. The chair rocks beneath her, and the doorman from the hotel comes in. Or is that him? Everyone looks familiar, and she wonders if she remembers them from the hotel, if they've all come here for breakfast.

Moving into the hotel has proved not to be the panacea for sleep she'd hoped it would be. Clearly, it was only Ronald's room that soothed her—his messy bed, the newspapers strewn on tabletops, the shaving paraphernalia scattered across the bathroom counters—the ambience of Ronald, or so she'd thought. Now she isn't sure. She roots around in her purse for her dark glasses and puts them on. The lights retreat a little, still teeming but less brightly. The sparkles on the place mats dim.

"Here we are." Ronald slides into a chair and deposits their coffees on the table between them. "This one's the decaf," he says. "There's a D on your—"

"Thanks. Here," she says, reaching for her bag. Let me pay for mine."

"Don't be silly. I'm happy for the company."

Dana nods. "How are you doing?"

"Okay, I guess," he says. "How 'bout you?"

Dana shrugs. "You're the one who just lost a spouse." Spouse, she thinks, what an odd word. She wonders why she chose it and if she herself has also lost a spouse. If the two of them together were spice. Or possibly, all things considered, spicy.

Ronald squints back at the blackboard as if he's missed something. "I'd lost her anyway. She was leaving me. Not exciting enough for her, I guess."

Dana's mind sparks off in different directions. She wonders if Peter and the Tart tie each other up. She thinks of borrowing a set of handcuffs from Detective Moss and fastening Peter to the bedpost. Or maybe the toilet. The toilet and his cell phone. With great effort she pulls herself back to the conversation. Beneath her elbows the place mat glitters like Oz.

"How did you know Celia was leaving you?" she says, a bit more bluntly than she'd intended. Unfiltered words spill out all on their own these days.

"She said so."

"Why?"

"There was someone else," Ronald says. "There was another man."

"So she was planning to . . . what? Take off with this guy?" It must have been Peter, Dana thinks. It had to be Peter. Her heart pounds. "People say they're leaving all the time. It doesn't mean they will."

"Apparently she'd been to the bank," Ronald says. "That detective—Ross, is it?—told me she'd made a withdrawal from an account I didn't even know she had. It wasn't enough to move to California or anything, but it was enough for a couple months' rent somewhere."

"Moss?"

"Yeah. That's right. Detective Moss."

"So what happened to the money?"

Ronald shrugs. "Who knows?"

"So when did she tell you she was leaving you for this other guy?"

Ronald looks down into his coffee cup as if he were reading tea leaves. "A few days before she died. Where's Peter?"

"Peter isn't here. He's at home. In the yard or something. Supervising the . . . um, the fumigation."

She finishes off her decaf. The room is spinning, a haze of color and light—voices hum around them. The sounds in the coffee shop are deafening, and Ronald, when she glances up, looks exactly like the doorman back at the hotel. His nose is red and inflated like a balloon, like Ronald McDonald's. "To be honest," she says, "I left him home on purpose. Actually, we aren't fumigating the house. In fact, he's probably at work right now. I had to leave. I wanted to kill him, so I left."

Ronald snickers, reaches for the English muffin.

"I'm serious."

"What? About killing your husband?" Ronald lets out a light little guffaw. "That's why we have gun laws," he says. "We'd all be dead if we had guns handy during hormonal upsurges or—"

"No," Dana says. "I mean I really wanted Peter dead. I felt as if I could murder him. Have you ever felt that way, Ronald? Like you could kill someone?"

Ronald stops laughing. He looks at her across the table, and Dana feels the madness clawing its way out, spilling through her eyes. Please, she thinks, please please please, although even she isn't sure quite what she wants.

Ronald clears his throat, surprises her. "Yes," he says.

"Well, have you?"

"What? Killed anyone?"

"Yes."

Ronald laughs. "Damn," he says. "You had me going for a minute there."

"Because sometimes I think I might have."

Ronald stares at her.

"I mean, sometimes things happen so quickly—all these lights and noises." She hears her voice all around her but at the same time far away, like a TV or a radio playing somewhere in the distance, caught up in the air. An echo. "It's as if," she says, "everything is so incredibly real that it isn't real at all." She stops. Ronald looks scared. He fumbles with his wallet, taking out a couple of bills for the tip. Dana wonders if she's misjudged him, if Ronald is an innocent in all this. A victim. She'll reach out to him, tell him what she knows, put his mind at ease. "Listen." Her head buzzes, and the ceiling lights flash bright and hot. "I think this 'other guy' of Celia's might have been Peter. Celia had a picture she'd taken of him with a woman, with his secretary, actually. They were leaning over toward each other in a restaurant. It was in her cell. Celia's cell."

"Yeah?" Ronald looks down at the two bills on the table, studies them as if he's never seen actual currency before.

"Did you see it?"

"Not that I— No. Not that I recall."

"You said you thought you'd seen him somewhere before. Remember? At the brunch? You said you thought you'd—"

"Right. I did say that. It was probably on the street, though. I mean, we are neighbors."

"And then that day at the Root Seller, you kept . . . you know, you kept looking around for Peter, trying to get a look at him. Because of the picture, right? In the fucking—"

"He wasn't there that day, though. He wasn't with you, you said. How could I be looking around for someone who wasn't even there?"

"You were going through my purse!" Her voice is

203

suddenly loud in the rumble of conversations around them. Everyone stops talking or drinking coffee or eating muffins to stare at this woman shrieking in the middle of a humdrum weekday morning. "Why? What were you looking for, Ronald?"

"Nothing," he says in a very calm voice, as if he's talking to a toddler about to run into the street. "I told you. I was zipping up your purse."

"I know what you told me, Ronald. But what were you really doing? What were you looking for? A picture of Peter?" Dana can feel her heart pounding. She can feel her whole face go hot and red. She feels a sudden rage lurch through her—for Ronald, for Peter, for Celia, dead as she may be. She feels totally crazy. Out of control. "A picture of your dead wife's lover? Help me out here!"

"I can't, Dana. Jeez. Find a shrink, will you?"

"Just tell me the truth! You're telling me everything's in there that was in there?"

"In the phone?"

Dana nods.

"Sure. I guess. Unless we have a grainy-photo thief." Ronald manages a tiny, strangled-sounding laugh. "Look," he says, "I'll check again. Promise. I'll check when I get back in tonight, and if I see it—if I see anything at all, I'll ring your room. Three-sixteen, right?"

"Right." The lights blink bright and blaze down on them, melting the butter, melting her brain. The paisley curtain at the window vibrates and swarms with flowers.

People are beginning to go back to their food, to their conversations, but Dana's voice still hangs in the air. Her anger buzzes around the room like a swarm of bees. She jumps up from the table and bolts through the front door.

# 23

She wanders around for hours, losing herself in the crowds, browsing through Macy's, concentrating on her breathing until at last she's calm. In the morning she'll go back to the house that doesn't feel especially homey now, with the pall of Celia bludgeoned and bloody and extremely dead, with the unshakable feeling that someone's watching her, even as she does mundane and boring things—washing dishes or walking through the living room—with Peter at the center of her sanity or insanity, with the question of her own actions crowding her mind. At least Jamie, safely off at school, remains untainted. Pure. Light. Precious. And there's Spot, a breath of fresh air, with his needle claws and his huge ears, his boundless energy.

When the hotel receipt dropped like a crinkly little gift at her feet, Dana had thought it was a sign. Tiny apertures were going to widen; hidden things would come to light. She'd get some sleep in this soporific hotel in the city where she has always felt at home, where she has always felt alive. She would gather her thoughts, piece together the puzzle of Celia's death and find she wasn't in it.

But it's all gone wrong. According to Ronald, she

imagined the picture and so, most likely, the sangria in the glass, her neighbor in the kitchen, awareness of what was going on around her. There is only this confusion now, and anger, boiling up from nowhere, making her say things she doesn't want to say, making her wonder what sorts of things she's capable of doing. Worse, what she's already done.

She thinks about going to Ronald's room. She thinks about showing him the scar along her wrist, about smoothing things over; making him see she didn't mean to yell at him at breakfast, didn't mean to cause a scene. She thinks of shaming him, of coaxing, pleading, explaining the importance of his telling her the truth about the photo, but in the end she doesn't go to Ronald's room. In the end she understands that there are too many people implicated in this cover-up—too many unrelated people—for it to be real.

She walks back to the St. Giles and slips onto the elevator, careful not to meet the doorman's eyes, avoiding the desk clerk, the people clustered in small groups around the lobby, afraid they'll see her madness or that she herself will see bizarre, outlandish creatures lurking there behind their eyes. In her room she flicks on the TV and walks into the adjoining bathroom to wash her face, ignoring the long, bright mirror above the sink. The phone blinks, and she picks up Ronald's message. "Sorry," he says. "Haven't found the photo yet." She plays the message several times; he sounds a little off. Her gut tells her he's lying. Yet?

Either it's there or it isn't. Still, her instincts have been running right at 100 percent wrong lately. She deletes the message and falls across the slippery quilted bedspread.

*

The scar is old, a puckered white line running along the blue veins of her wrist. She doesn't remember putting it there, only the ambulance with its bright lights, its wide mouth, its loud, offensive sound like a scream. She remembers an incredible sadness, remembers missing the Poet so desperately that she couldn't bear to live without him. Is he even still alive? Sometimes she wonders; often she wonders. He would be as old as she is. He would have gray in his black hair. She sighs. The news drones on. Celia's face in an old photograph flashes on the screen and disappears, eclipsed by stories of a missing teenage girl and a carjacking turned murder outside a nearby train station.

She climbs between the sheets and watches the news. She mutes the sound, but she can hear the voices anyway. All night she stares at the screen, watching figures come and go, the sounds of voices going in and out, in and out, like whispers traveling down a hall or pictures scattered in a closing drawer—out of reach.

As soon as the sun comes up, Dana gets out of bed and showers. The hotel has lost its allure. There's no point hemorrhaging money into this place she'd thought would be soporific and has turned out not to be. She's forgotten now why she's even come here. There was the phone. And she was angry. Furious with Peter, but now she can't quite think why. She turns in her key card at the front desk and settles her bill, avoiding the frowsy orange and growing hair on the clerk, staring at her shoes as the doorman reaches out to help her with her things, avoiding Ronald, who is standing several yards away. A breeze floats through the brick and concrete, sifts through her hair, and she bends over her bag, fiddling with the buckle, making herself invisible in the throngs of people walking down the sidewalk.

When she straightens up, Ronald is beside her.

"Hi," he says. "Are you leaving?"

"Yes."

"Sorry to see you go. I left you a message on your room—"

"I got it."

Ronald glances at his watch.

"Please," she says, "don't let me hold you up."

Ronald raises his arms. "Feel free," he says, "but it won't do you much good. I've already been robbed by the St. Giles."

Dana forces a smile. "Look," she says, "I'm sorry about yesterday, losing my temper the way I did."

"It's okay," he says. "But what's wrong?" His arms are still up in the air as if he's forgotten them; she thinks of the Hanged Man in a tarot deck.

She shrugs. "I'm—how shall I put this?—having a breakdown," Dana says, and she turns and walks away, tipping the valet, who ushers her into her car; the Toyota sits idling on the asphalt. When she's settled her bag in the backseat, she glances at Ronald, who still stands staring at her, his mouth half open as if he were about to say something that didn't quite come out, his arms back in place at his sides. She fastens her seat belt, and sunlight bounces needle-thin off St. Christopher as the car rolls backward. Ronald taps on her window. She jams her foot on the brake. "What? Jesus!" She opens the window; hot air flows in; the air conditioner whines.

"Why'd you say you're having a breakdown? Were you and Celia . . . ? I didn't realize you were that close." Ronald sticks his head inside her window.

"We weren't. I'm just losing my mind," Dana says. "For starters, I imagined this whole scenario that centered on a picture in a phone that never existed."

Ronald looks like he wants to say something. In fact, he says, "Listen—" but then he stops.

"What?"

"Nothing." He steps back from the car, now at the beginning of a lengthy line of irate drivers. Dana readjusts the rearview mirror, knocked off center in the excitement of Ronald's appearing in it at such close proximity. Behind her, someone honks. Ronald takes a step away, toward the sidewalk. "It's just . . . things are often not what they seem to be," he says.

You're telling me, Dana thinks about saying. On the visor, St. Christopher smiles and shakes his head. "Thanks," she says instead. "I was exaggerating. I tend to do that when I'm stressed. See you in the hood," and she grits her teeth, crosses herself quickly, and pulls out onto a street filled with traffic and blaring horns. Behind her, Ronald becomes smaller and smaller in the mirror—a tiny, spluttering, puzzling form—until at last he disappears.

She crosses the bridge, navigates the highways with clenched teeth, and when she has nearly reached her street, she drives around the block several times before pulling, finally, onto Ashby Lane and sliding into her driveway.

The sounds around her deafen her—the claps of thunder in the distance, the howling of a neighbor's dog, the screeching of a door across the street. Inside the car stagnant air shifts and twitches in the stillness; it vibrates, moving in large, flashing circles around her. She appeals to St. Christopher, but he only winks and nods toward a notebook on the passenger seat, which Dana picks up, uncapping a pen stuck in its spirally wire binding. She chronicles recent occurrences. She revisits the list of things she knows and doesn't know, thoughts she's transferred from napkins and receipts, adding her most recent fears and sleepless nights. At the corner of the page, she sketches a bird with large, dark wings, with claws that curve around a building's edge, a roof. It tilts forward, toward the air, toward the sky, its feet digging in, binding it.

She drums the pen across the second page of writing, a strange, small scrawl, so different from her normal, careful script. She runs her hands through her hair, tucks it into a tight knot at the back of her head as thunder rumbles in a deafening cacophony of sound. She thinks of Jamie at three, pulling her pots and pans out of the kitchen cupboards, how he turned them over, beating on them with the handles of her wooden spoons, how he used the smallest, tinniest of the pots for cymbals, how it gave her a headache, all that racket, how it made her smile. And then there was Peter coming in the front door, home from work, the way he yelled, Would you two stop that noise! It's giving me a migraine! as if she, too, were sitting on the floor—as if her hands were wielding wooden spoons, as if she were a child.

"Run," she writes, "run run run," but where does a murderer go? She has savings—some money from her mother's estate, enough to live on for a few months. But then what? And what if they pin Celia's death on some poor innocent—the paperboy or Mr. Nguyen—while she nibbles croissants on the Left Bank? She marvels at the ironies. If she killed Celia over a picture in her phone and over Celia's jealousy of the Tart—and thus her unspoken admission that she was a discarded lover—then wouldn't the photo have to actually exist? Wouldn't there be a trail of phone calls between Celia and Peter? Why would she invent the picture, the words with Celia over drinks, the proof she found in Peter's cell as he lay snoring in the bedroom? Why, unless she had a far more sinister motive? "But what? Hating Celia's uncomfortable chair?" she squeaks up at St. Christopher. "Her fucking shoes?" St. Christopher shakes his head so fervently that the visor shimmies. No, he mouths, and she can nearly hear the word his tiny metal lips are forming. "No!"

When the rain begins, a series of small, light clicks against the windshield, she tugs her overnight bag from the backseat. She slings her purse over her shoulder, grabs her keys, and makes a run for the door.

Once inside, she drops the pad and pen on the desk in the foyer, and the room is airless and dark. It suffocates her. She turns on the small desk lamp, glancing at the bird she's inked in at the edge of the page, and then she notices the words she's scribbled on the thin lined paper. "Run run run." The writing is tiny and barely legible. She thinks about retrieving the notes she's hidden in a sealed, stamped envelope in her purse lining—she'll compare the writing—but then she stops. Something isn't right. Dana stands near the doorway, and she feels it like an icy hand along her spine. She feels the absence of something, and then she feels the loosening of the few thin ties that bind her to her life, the chaos and confusion she knows too well, that she has up to this point managed to keep at bay. "Spot!" She walks through the house. The litter box is empty in the bathroom, and she gets down on her hands and knees, peering under things, under couches and beds. In terror she checks the refrigerator, the dryer in the basement. "Spot!" She opens the back door, and her eyes scan the yard, and then she darts outside. "Spot!" she calls, running through to the front and then to all the neighbors' yards. The rain comes down in sheets, but Dana keeps running, keeps peering, keeps calling, the threads of sanity fraying as her voice climbs higher and louder, a small, sad siren in the thunder and rain. "Spot!"

## 24

Jack Moss fidgets at his desk. If he were Ann, he'd say the spirits were telling him to go back to the Steinhausers'. He'd say there's something off, and that the universe is guiding him back to the house again to straighten it all out. But he isn't Ann, and although he's always envied her the ability to be open to possibilities, he doesn't share it. Even so he feels compelled to return to Celia's house. It's Dana's disappearance, the timing of it. And then there's Kyle; there's always always Kyle, nagging at the back of his brain, waking him at all hours of the night, making him sit upright against the sparsely cushioned headboard, sweat beading on his forehead, with the certainty that Kyle lied to him in the diner. And he will go back there. As soon as he's finished his second round with Ronald Steinhauser.

Jack hears him come through the door, the high-pitched nervousness of Ronald's voice as he greets the officer at the front desk and then the thumping of his shoes in the hall. Jack swings his chair around, gets to his feet, and meets Ronald as he comes through the doorway, walks him down to the interrogation room.

Sometimes Jack thinks it's time for him to hang it up here while he's still got some good years left. He could travel. He could look up those cousins he hasn't seen since childhood, somewhere in Kansas now, he thinks, or Nebraska, one of those tornado states. He could spend some time with his son, with Margie, even, try to help her out, get her on her feet. His childhood family doesn't exist anymore—his mother dead of ovarian cancer several years before and his father close on her heels. He has no siblings. He won't leave, though. It's in his blood, this job; it's part of him, like his skin or his elbows.

"So," he says as Ronald drums his fat little fingers on the table between them, chews his lower lip. "So I checked out your alibi. The texter and all. That was on the parkway, right, Ronald?"

"Um," Ronald says. "Yes. I can't swear to the texting part. I was told that. I couldn't swear to it, though, since I didn't . . . of course I didn't actually see the—"

"Right. Funny thing, though." Jack thumbs through a small pile of papers.

Ronald's fingers stop in mid-drum. "What's that, Detective?"

"There was no accident on the parkway that day. Nothing major. Couple of fender benders earlier in the afternoon."

Ronald squirms. He looks at Jack, and then he looks away.

"So why'd you lie, Ronald?"

"I wouldn't say I lied, exactly, Detective. I may have been mistaken, but I certainly didn't mean to—"

"And yet you did."

"I can explain," Ronald says. His face is a funny orange color.

"I'm listening."

"I—" Ronald stops. "Do I need a lawyer?"

"Do you want a lawyer?"

Ronald studies his fleshy hands on the table. He hesitates, but only for a minute. "She was involved with someone," he says, and to his credit he looks Jack straight in the face when he says it. "She had a lover."

"How'd you know?"

"She told me so. 'I'm leaving you,' she says, right out of the blue. Took me completely by surprise. 'I'm in love with another man.' Oh, she tried to undo the damage. Later. 'I was wrong,' she says that next night, sober as a judge, wringing her hands, following me around the house like a puppy. 'Really,' she says. 'I had too much to drink, and I was— I really wish I could take back what I said.' You can't, though. You can't unsay something of that . . . of that magnitude. You just can't."

Jack isn't sure what he'd do if he were Ronald—if his wife said something like that. There were times he thought Margie might be fooling around, but he looked the other way. For everyone's sake, he thought at the time. If she'd thrown it up at him, though—stuck it like a dagger in his heart . . . "No," he says. "You can't."

"So that night—the night she was killed—I went to the . . . I went to the school where she worked. It was somebody there, I thought, or somebody she was meeting there. Before work, maybe, or after. She was coming home really late for a while there."

"So you thought . . . what? You thought she was involved with one of her students?" Jack's heart clomps like a racehorse inside his chest. Kyle?

Ronald shrugs. "I didn't know. I drove there from work that day. I knew she had a class that evening. I figured I'd just sit there and wait. I'd see if she arrived with someone, if she left with someone, if she got in the backseat of a car with someone. So I did. I backed into a parking space over to the side, out of the way but close enough to see what was—" Ronald starts drumming his fingers again. "But she never showed up. I waited and waited, and she never showed up."

"So you . . . ?"

"So I went home, Detective. I went home and nearly fell over her body."

"Why'd you lie, Ronald?"

Ronald shrugs. "Didn't want to sully her name? She was dead. Why mention her infideli— Why upset her boys?"

Jack taps his pen against the desktop, looks down at his notes.

"And I felt like it was my fault."

"How so?"

"If I had come right home that night instead of trying to spy on her, Celia would still be alive."

Jack raises his eyebrows. "Anything else you want to tell me?"

"No. No, sir."

"You kill your wife, Ronald?"

"No. No, I did not kill my wife, Detective."

"This stuff gives you a motive, is all."

"I did not kill Celia. I loved her."

"Right. I believe you did," Jack says. "You got someone to corroborate your story? That you were over at the school? Anybody see you?"

"No. That was the point, Detective. I didn't want anyone to—"

"Stop anywhere else?"

Ronald sits up straighter. "Yes," he says. "I stopped for gas at the Amoco station over near the school."

"Keep your receipt?"

"Yes," he says. "I always do."

"Get it to me," Jack says. "You can fax it in. Number's on my card." He stands up, and Ronald struggles to his feet, inching his way over to the door.

"Bye," he says in a hoarse voice, barely above a whisper, and he takes off down the hall.

"Oh, and Ronald," Jack calls after him. "Stay real close."

\*

Jack goes alone to Celia's house, a moth pulled to the faint light of Ashby Lane. Ronald's explanation for his blown alibi doesn't only put Ronald in question, it casts a significant shadow across Kyle as well. Bad enough all this rubbish about Kleenex in the glove box. Now it's looking more likely he was Celia's lover. But there was Peter, too, standing in the hall that night, waiting outside her classroom.

He turns on the radio and thinks about a case he worked years before, when the song now playing on the radio was popular, "Crazy," which is probably what's popped the case back into his head. He and Rob used to look at each other and nod every time that song came on, since that's what the case was. Crazy. A murder where nothing added up until a button in the molding under a back window led them straight to the killer. Jack's forte is finding needles in haystacks. If there's anything else in Celia's house to tell what happened to her, he'll find it.

He sees the first sign several blocks before the subdivision. missing kitten, it says in huge, neon-orange letters, and underneath there's a blown-up picture of the feral cat he picked up from the Steinhausers' yard and has kept at his house the past couple of days. spot, the sign says, and he notices the Catrells' address.

Once inside the Steinhausers', he closes the door behind him and stands for a moment in the foyer. Besides the crime-scene mess—the furniture moved around by the EMTs, the bloody footprints near the door—the house is fairly neat, which he'd noticed that first night. He smiles. He'd expect no less from a house where Ronald lived—

Ronald, who looked apoplectic at the thought of having to shake hands at the hospital. Celia, he guessed from the way she'd organized her phone photos, was probably a very ordered person, too.

He looks around the living room, and then he walks to the kitchen, where the dishwasher stands open, displaying neatly racked Fiestaware like the dishes they have at home—the different-colored plates, the bright bowls and cups, painstakingly acquired by Ann. He wonders if she'll want it now in her new place—in her new life—or if she'll want to start over, buy something different, something white and understated and expensive from Nordstrom's or Neiman Marcus. He doesn't care. Paper plates work fine for him, McDonald's wrapped in tinfoil, Styrofoam containers full of Chinese takeout—like she always said, he's never home anyway.

He walks through to the bathroom and the extra bedrooms he figures were the boys'. The shelves are full of books. Trophies crowd their tops, and posters of sports figures, a couple of them autographed, cover almost all the walls.

He stops at the doorway to Celia's room—Celia's and Ronald's, although the rumpled spread on the bed in one of the boys' rooms tells him the Steinhausers slept separately this summer. He glances around, but nothing catches his eye. He'll wait on the prints from the other day. He'll hold his breath on that one, hope to hell they're not Kyle's.

He walks back to the living room. He squats and looks at it from this new perspective, a Lilliputian view. He stands up and takes one more look around the room before he heads outside, walking through the yard. He moves slowly, checks the doors, the windows, even though there was no forced entry. The grass has grown knee-high in the front. It's greener, lusher in the small side yard where a lone tree offers shade.

Something glints in the sun, shiny and green. Jack stoops down and picks up a small glass elephant—a charm, a key-chain charm. He squats down again. He holds the tiny elephant between his thumb and index finger, turning it around. Something clicks in his brain, a picture, a memory of a long-ago September day—he and Margie and the boys walking across a fairground outside Paterson, the sunlight falling down, the crunch of autumn leaves, the barkers calling, "Try this! Try your luck at this one!" Their sweeping hands displaying rows of plastic toys, the bears and dolls and painted faces, balloons stuck to paper walls, darts and pins and plastic guns with plastic bullets. Kyle's hair, blond and fine, streaked with gold, as he tugged on Jack's hand, pulling him along the dirty rows between stands, the throngs of people, the toothless barker calling, "Hit the bull's-eye, sir, and win the boy a prize!" Kyle's pleading eyes, his pleading voice, "I want that, Dad!" his stubby finger pointing at the wall, at the smallest, cheapest thing—a prize so small that Jack had to ask him twice: "What?" he said. "Which one?" His mind snaps in on that day, that booth, that little finger pointing, that prize he won for Kyle with three shot arrows, the green elephant, its trunk held high for luck. He remembers how much Kyle loved elephants, especially this one, this glass, this green, this charm that now sits in his hand.

He breathes in the air of the yard that he now knows held his boy, held his prize on a day stained by blood, tainted by murder. He sticks the elephant in his pocket and walks to his car, and he doesn't look back. He starts the Crown Vic, keeps his face aimed at the windshield, the road. He doesn't glance at the yard where Dana reaches toward her mailbox. He doesn't see her long legs, her bare feet, her skinny arm with the white sad line running down her wrist. Just keep on keeping on, he tells himself, and heads back to the station for the two interviews he's scheduled back-to-back. This thing with Kyle is breaking his heart, messing with his sleep, with his entire life—has ever since he found Kyle's prints were in the woman's car—this knowledge he was involved somehow in a murder, and now this charm, this proof his son was at the woman's house. "Kyle, Kyle, Kyle," he mumbles. "What the fuck have you done?"

## 25

When Jack gets back to his office, the fingerprint report is on his desk. Timely. He looks it over, throws cold water on his face in the men's room, and heads for the lobby to meet the neighbor.

Wanda Needles is British. Jack knows this even before she opens her mouth. Something in the way she carries herself, he thinks, her neat and proper pantsuit, the stoic expression. Maybe it's her name. She follows him down the hall to the interrogation room and perches on a straight-backed chair.

"Thanks for coming, Ms. Needles. Appreciate it."

"You're welcome." She smiles a fleeting little smile. "I'm happy to help."

"Your neighbor," Jack says, "Celia Steinhauser. What can you tell me about the day she died?"

Wanda sits back a tad on the chair. "Not much, I'm afraid. I was out most of the afternoon. Most of the day, actually."

"Did you see her at all?"

"No," she says. "Sorry. No."

"How about Ronald? You see her husband that day?"

"No. But, again, I was out most of the day. I saw . . .

well, of course, the ambulance when it took her away to hospital. I saw Ronald then, running outside with the medics."

"Did you see anyone on your street that day? Anyone unusual? Anything unusual?"

"No," she says. "I've racked my brain but haven't come up with anything." She says the last word like it hasn't got a g. Anythin'. "The only neighbor I saw was Dana. Oh, and Mr. Nguyen. He was in his front yard, washing his car."

"And where was Dana?"

"Across the street. She was going to her car, and we waved, you know, and then she went on about her business, fetching her purse from the front seat."

"I see."

"Yes. And then she ran down the street. To see why the medics were there. She and Celia were—"

"Were what?"

"Well, I was going to say friends, but I'm not sure they were all that close, really, from some of the things Dana said. They bummed around together sometimes, bought things at yard sales for their houses when Dana was feeling—" She stops.

"Feeling what?" Jack looks up at her across the table. Unusual eyes—violet, almost.

"'Well.' I was going to say 'well.' Dana can be quite energetic when she's feeling well."

"And when she isn't?"

225

"Oh," Wanda says. She fiddles with her hair, wraps the ends around a finger. Pale hair, if pale were a color, like wheat or old grass. "She is a bit moody," she says. "But then who isn't, eh, Detective?"

"Moody how, exactly?"

"I don't know. Restless, I suppose."

"And this . . . restlessness, how does it manifest itself, Ms. Needles?"

Wanda inches closer to the edge of the chair. "I don't know, really. She walks a lot; she wanders 'round the street, drives off; I hear her car sometimes; wakes me up."

"At night, you mean?"

"Yes," Wanda says. "Late at night. But then with that husband of hers . . ."

"Not so fond of him, Wanda?"

"No," she says. "A sneak, that one."

"Ever see him down at the Steinhausers'?"

Wanda clears her throat. "We were all neighbors," she says.

"Right. So did you ever see Mr. Catrell at the Steinhausers'?"

"Well," she says, "I might have seen him leaving out of there a time or two, but I couldn't swear to it."

"During the day?"

"Yes," she says in a small voice.

"Did you tell his wife you'd seen him at the Steinhausers'? Did Dana know this?"

Wanda shrugs her shoulders. "I never told her. No.

I've no idea whether she knew."

"We're almost done here, Ms. Needles. Just a couple more questions."

"Yes?" She's already gathered up her things. There's a tiny rip in her pantyhose, at the ankle. He wonders if it will continue ripping or if she'll discover it in time. I'll just put some clear nail polish on it, Ann used to say, and I'll be good to go.

"Have you seen anything unusual lately in your neighborhood?"

"Yes," she says. "I did see someone in a . . . hoodie, is it? Lurking about. I noticed only because it's not the sort of weather for a hoodie."

"Where was this?"

"Near Dana's house," she says. "Once or twice."

"And when was this?"

"Recently," Wanda says. "In the past week or so. I called it in. Normally I wouldn't, but with the murder and all . . ."

Jack looks up. "They send someone out to your house?"

"No, actually," she says. "I guess it didn't seem that important, a little thug running about. Not exactly an uncommon occurrence these days, is it? Anyway, Mr. Nguyen has added himself to the mix. He's out neighborhood-watching in all types of weather and attire, so really it might have been either Nguyen or one of his minions."

"Still, right now if someone sneezes on your street,

it warrants a follow-up. Somebody dropped the ball on that. I am sorry, Ms. Nettles." Jack stands up, reaches out his hand, and Wanda gives it a limp little shake. "Thanks for coming in," he says. "You've still got my card if you think of anything else?"

"Yes," she says, sticking her briefcase and her bag under one arm. Together they walk out toward the front, where Peter Catrell paces back and forth as if he's in a cage, his shoes making clicks and taps on the cheap linoleum. He glances down at his watch and strides toward them; he looks annoyed. "Oh, my," Wanda says, giving Jack a quick good-bye nod. She ignores Peter, who has frozen in his journey across the linoleum and is staring openmouthed at Wanda as she slips out the heavy doors and clips along to the parking lot without a backward glance.

*

Even if the labs hadn't come in on the prints, Peter's reaction to seeing his neighbor indicates at least questionable activity on his part—something Wanda may or may not know, his involvement with Celia, clearly—and Jack is glad he scheduled their interviews to overlap. He watches Peter for a minute, notices the way his eyes follow Wanda out the door and out of sight into a jumble of parked cars in the lot.

"Morning," Jack says. "Sorry to keep you waiting, Catrell. Any word from your wife?"

228

"Yes." Peter shifts his weight, looks nervous. Lying, Jack guesses.

"She okay?"

"Yes. She's— Listen, Detective. I have an appointment; I'm a little strapped for time."

"Come on back, then," Jack says. "We're over here on the left," and Peter nods, heaves a hefty sigh, follows Jack down the hall and back to the interrogation room, where Wanda's perfume still swims in the air.

"Mind if I call you Peter?"

"Not at all." Peter looks at his watch.

"I'll get right to it." Jack takes out a manila folder and slides its contents onto the table between them. "How well did you know Celia Steinhauser?"

"I believe we've been over this, Detective. I told you, I didn't know the woman. My wife knew her."

"Right. That is what you said, but in the interest of time— You did say you were in a hurry?"

"Yes," Peter says, "I am."

"Then let's cut the crap, shall we?"

"I don't—"

"Your prints were on every inch of her bedroom. Particularly the bed." Here at least he's caught a break. The prints say Kyle was never in the woman's room.

Peter smiles a little half smile. "What can I say, Detective?"

"I don't know, Peter. You kill her?"

"No."

"Did Celia Steinhauser maybe get in your way? Cramp your style? Threaten to go to your wife?"

"No."

"Or maybe she was messing up your new . . . uh, relationship?"

"I have no idea what you're talking about, Detective. Just to clarify. Am I here so you can accuse me of sleeping with my neighbor?"

"Not at all, Catrell. You're here so I can ask you if you killed her."

"And I said I did not kill her."

"Right. But you also said you didn't know her."

Peter shrugs.

"As Ms. Needles might say, 'Bit of a sticky wicket.' "

"Are we finished?"

"Not quite. Did your wife know about your affair with the deceased?"

"I have no idea what my wife might think she knows."

"And yet you didn't make a secret of it, did you?"

"I didn't— Listen, Detective. I don't know exactly what that Wanda person told you—"

"Right. Now we're finished. Thanks for coming in."

"Is that it?"

"Yep. Stay close, Catrell. Within earshot."

*

At noon, Jack stops by the house for the kitten and tries

not to think about how quiet it will seem without him climbing up Jack's legs and throwing himself into a refrigerator with achingly disappointing contents. But it can't be helped. He grabs the cat, holds him up so Molly can see, so she won't drive herself nuts looking for him when he's gone. Spot, he thinks. Cute.

He pulls in to Dana's driveway and turns off the engine. He runs his hand through his hair and over the stubble on his chin, feeling almost self-conscious. Even though there is definitely something off about her, something a little wild, he finds Dana appealing. She's also very pretty in an unconventional way. Strangely open, he would say, except she isn't, really—at least not about the case.

He grabs the kitten, ignoring the struggling and clawing until they get to the front door. Jack sets him down and rings the bell as somewhere in the house something falls and breaks. He hears the splintering sound of glass on the floor. He shifts his weight from one foot to the other as, beside him, Spot's huge ears tilt forward like a dog's.

"Spot!" Dana is there, tugging the door open, a whisk broom in one hand. The door creaks and hesitates on sticky, swollen hinges. "Oh, my God!" she says. "Spot!" The kitten trots inside, and Moss stands alone on the porch as the screen door pops into place and Dana bends to pick up the tiny cat. "Where have you been?" She nuzzles her face against his neck. Spot pulls away, trots to the kitchen, where his bowl sits optimistically on its plastic place mat.

"Oh!" Dana turns back to the porch. "Oh, Detective Moss! I am so sorry! Please. Come in! Have a seat. I was just making some coffee." She opens the screen door, and Jack wipes his muddy boots on the porch mat. beware, it says, attack cat. He wipes his heels against the edges, careful to avoid the lettering, the picture of a huge, menacing cat in its center, the mat so new it still smells like plastic.

"Spot?" He gestures toward the mat, and Dana smiles.

"Of course. How do you take your coffee?"

"Black." He sits down on the sofa in front of a large picture window. The layout is identical to the Steinhausers', and for a second, fear for Kyle nearly chokes him. He glances through the glass. "More rain coming."

"Yes," she says from the kitchen. "Always. Summer of the rains . . . I wonder if the wet weather will . . . if we'll have a lot of snow this winter." She reaches toward a cupboard, pours dry cat food into a bowl. "We never let him out," she says, walking to the living room. She sets two cups on the coffee table along with two cloth napkins and a plate of scones. "Wanda," she explains, nodding toward the biscuits. "My British neighbor brought these over." She glances back to the kitchen as if the cat might disappear. "I have no idea how he got out."

"Maybe your husband," Jack says. "Maybe while you were away . . ."

"How did you know I was—"

"He filed a missing person on you." Jack isn't sure if she knows this, whether the husband's told her. If so, she

232

would know that Jack knew.

"Why would he do that?" Dana sits down at the opposite end of the sofa.

"Worried, I guess. It's not unusual," Jack says, but of course it is.

"I left him a note."

"Yeah?" He decides to let it go, to not dig himself into a deeper hole. "You ask your husband about the cat?"

"I haven't seen him yet. He hasn't been home since my . . . since I left New York, but maybe that's better, his not being here, his being away. Maybe he's—" She tugs at her top, pulls it higher up on her shoulders. "I guess he slept in town . . . at his office. Sometimes he does that. He gets so busy with work, so overwhelmed, sometimes he just . . ." Her gaze shifts back to the kitchen where Spot hunches over his blue bowl, his plastic place mat, where he turns to look at Jack and Dana in the living room. "Peter really isn't very fond of Spot. The other day he told me it's the ugliest cat he's ever seen. 'Maybe it isn't even a cat,' he said. 'Maybe it's a big rat or some kind of hybrid experiment gone wrong.'"

And suddenly Jack knows her husband let the cat out. He knows it like he knows his own name, like he knows that Kyle was at Celia Steinhauser's house. Peter let the cat out as soon as Dana left—he's sure of it. After their last interview, he wouldn't put anything past the guy. He stands up, shoots a wave toward Spot in the kitchen. "Bye, buddy."

"Anyway, I can't thank you enough." Dana looks up at him, and he sees that same familiar thing in her eyes. "I guess you saw my signs?"

Jack nods. "He was in the Steinhausers' yard the other day, and I thought he was a stray. I had him at my place while you were—"

"It wasn't there," Dana says. "I was wrong about the picture. It didn't actually exist."

Jack sits back down. "Then why'd you say it did?"

She shrugs. Her arms are like sticks. The sleeveless shirt she's wearing hangs on her, the armholes gap around the tops of her arms. "I was wrong. I found it. I looked in it again—Celia's cell—and it wasn't there."

"Maybe it was deleted."

"No." She shakes her head. "Unless Ronald was lying."

"Could Celia have deleted it?"

"No. That's the last thing she'd want to do. No. It was probably never there." Dana bites at her cuticle. "It's me," she says. "I haven't been quite . . . I haven't felt really . . ." Her voice wanders off, her eyes shift back and forth, her fingers drum against her knees. She is so familiar. There is something just at the edge of his—

"What did Ronald say?"

"Like I told you. He said there wasn't . . . that the picture wasn't in the phone."

"But what exactly did he say? Try to remember."

"I asked him if everything was still there, and he said, 'In the phone?' And I said yes, and he said, 'Unless we

234

have a grainy-photo thief.' " She turns her hands over on her knees, palms up. He sees the scar that winds along her wrist, and then he knows.

"He used those words?"

"Yeah. I know he did, because I remember thinking it was bad. It was a terrible picture. Who'd want it? Not that you can actually steal a—"

"Were the other pictures like that? Unclear like that?"

"No. That one was bad because she took it from way across the restaurant. At least I—"

Dana stares out the window. Spot leaps into her lap and bats at her hair. He steps into the top of her blouse, and it sags down, showing most of her breast, but she doesn't seem to notice. Jack glances at her wrist again and sees a young girl in the ER, her arm stitched badly by an intern, her eyes wild as she looked up from an ugly metal bed, her gown untied and open in the back. Over twenty years ago, when he was a rookie. They got the call. Suicide attempt. Bellevue, but there were so many people; so many crazy; so many spinning, stitched, and shattered; so many going to the psych ward. She looked so lost sitting there, so beautiful, her feet tapping against the air, her fingers drumming on the table, her eyes large, distracted. What's wrong with her? he'd asked his partner. What happened to her? Where'll they take her? His partner was an older guy, two years from retirement. She's nuts, he'd said. They'll take her up to psych. Who knows what happened to her? She happened to her. Jeez.

It's this fuckin' city, kid. It's New York. He wonders now if the girl in the ER all those years ago was Dana or only someone like her, someone lost and beautiful like her.

"I have these notes," she says, forcing him back to the present. "Threatening notes. I don't know who wrote them. Actually, Peter thinks I did."

"Mind if I take a look?"

"No. Not at all. That's why I— Maybe you'll see something I can't." She disappears for a minute and comes back with a folded scrap of paper. "Here's one of them," she says, handing it to him. His cell phone buzzes. Rob. "Hey," he tells him. "Can this wait? I'm—"

"Not really," Rob says. "It's the prosecutor's office. Lenora. She's on her way down here."

"Now?"

"Yeah. Says she needs to see us. You mainly. It's about the Steinhauser case."

"I'll be right there," Jack says. Damn. He sticks his phone in his pocket and turns to Dana. "Listen," he says. "I've got to head back to the office. How about if you come in tomorrow sometime?"

"Why?"

"Just to finish our talk," he says. "Bring both the notes. Ten-thirty okay? Get it over with?" He stands for a minute at the edge of the living room, in the entryway with the Oriental runner, the desk in the corner, the little antique lamp.

"Sure." She looks at him.

"You remember how to find me?" he says, but Dana only nods. At least he thinks so. She barely moves her head.

When he gets to the stop sign at the end of Ashby Lane, he sits for a minute, collecting his thoughts. So he was right about Ronald. "A grainy-photo thief," he'd said—but he wouldn't have known that the picture was bad unless he actually saw it. He deleted the damn thing. Jack takes out his pad and thumbs through the Steinhauser case contacts until he finds Ronald's number. He closes his eyes, calls up the note in his nearly flawless memory. He'd barely had a chance to glance at the thing before his cell phone rang, but even so—even that second or two looking at it—he's pretty sure it was written with a fountain pen, the tiny globs at the ends of the words. Peacock blue at that. Noticeable, to say the least. More than a little off the grid. No one uses fountain pens these days. Rare enough to see anything at all in script; everything's computerized. He shakes his head. Odds are the note was written by the Sheaffer he'd spotted beside a couple ballpoints on the desk in Dana's entryway.

*

Lenora White doesn't look happy when Jack arrives at his office. She's clearly been here longer than she'd planned to be. She walks across the room with her hand outstretched. Her legs are long. Her face is flawless, white as

237

a porcelain plate. "Hello, Jack," she says. "Sorry to drag you away from . . . whatever you were doing. But I was down here anyway, and I thought I'd touch base—have you and Rob bring me up to speed."

"No problem." He shakes her hand. "I was out in the field," he says.

"Working on the Steinhauser case?"

He nods. "You've changed your hair again."

"I'm impressed," Lenora says. "Most men wouldn't notice. Do you like it?" She tosses her head.

"Love it," he says, and she takes a seat on the other side of his desk.

"So what do you think?"

"What? Steinhauser?"

"Yes," she says. "We need to get this wrapped up. It's getting way too much publicity. Makes us look bad. Makes me look bad."

"Dancing as fast as I can," Jack tells her.

"Narrowed in on any of your suspects?"

"A few people at the moment."

"Who?"

"The husband, for one," Jack says. "Ronald."

Lenora nods. "Who else?"

"We're looking at a couple of the neighbors," he says. "Following up with forensics."

"Okay, Jack. Stay on it." She smiles, stands up to go. "Walk me down the hall?"

"Sure," he says. The phone rings on his desk. Shit.

"Go ahead," Lenora says. "Get that. Rain check on the walk." She takes a few steps down the hall in her sexy heels, and then she turns around. I'll be in touch, she mouths, forming the words with her perfectly heart-shaped lips. Her fingers flutter in the air as she clip-clips toward the lobby. Jeez. Women.

## 26

Jack hesitates before he hits the send button to complete his call to Kyle. Once they talk, he knows there'll be no turning back. It will all be out there. He swivels in his chair, listening to the creak of the aging springs. He watches Rob collect his lunch and move toward the break room before he touches the green arrow, sends his voice over to the cheap rental in downtown Paterson that Kyle shares with Maryanne, the room that grips the two of them in its flimsy, peeling walls, its scratched wood floor.

"Jack?"

"Yeah," Jack says. He rolls the chair in toward his desk, bends over the phone. He wishes he could just toss the piece of green glass in the river and walk away from the case, let Rob take over. Jack's kept him in the loop on everything except Kyle's role, whatever the hell that is. But he can't. He can't let it go. He thinks about Dana, about the scar along her veins, about Spot standing beside him on her front porch, his ears wide as parachutes. He thinks about Peter in his classy jacket, his leather briefcase next to the chair in the interrogation room, the way he kept glancing down at it, as if he had far more important things to do. More appealing things. More exciting things. Like screwing his wife's friends. "We need to talk," Jack says.

"I can't talk now, Jack. I'll have to call you back."

"It's about the case." Jack toys with the glass elephant, sticks it in his pants pocket. "Half an hour," he says. "The place on Getty."

"Wait! It's my girlfriend," Kyle says. "She's not feeling well. She's—"

"This can't wait." Jack opens the door to the hall. "This isn't a request, son," he says, and before he clicks off his phone, he's already in the parking lot, opening the door to the Crown Vic and dying for a cigarette.

When he gets to the restaurant, he walks straight to the back and finds a table where the sun slanting through the windows won't throw them into the spotlight, where the shadows will cushion them, where he hopes to find out whether or not his son is a killer.

Kyle looks distracted; he looks disheveled and crazed. His hair is wild and way too long, his eyes are bloodshot, his shirt rumpled as if he hasn't changed it in days, as if he's slept in it. But then again it's clear he hasn't slept at all. Jack watches him slump across the restaurant, studies him through his sunglasses, checks the kid's pupils.

"What's wrong with you?" He doesn't bother to stand up. He makes the smallest, slightest forward movement and settles back in his chair. "You look like hell."

"I didn't get much sleep," Kyle says. "My girlfriend— like I told you on the phone—Maryanne—" His eyes are

241

glazed, darting around the room, and Jack thinks maybe the girlfriend really is pregnant. Maybe there's a problem with the baby.

"What's wrong with her, then?" he says, but Kyle doesn't answer, and Jack pulls out the glass elephant, stands it up on the table between them. Light from the table lamp bounces off the tiny prisms, casting emerald patterns on the wall behind his chair. Kyle's face goes white.

"Where'd you find that?"

"Where do you think?" Jack pushes back from the table; he rests his forearms on the place mat as the same waitress from last time rushes over, pad in hand. mindy, her nameplate informs them, an etching on a brassy square. "Two burgers," he says before she can speak, before she can twist a lock of hair around a finger, before she can look up at Kyle from under her long lashes, sizing him up, his thin frame, his large dark eyes, his scruffy hair. Handsome in a rugged, rebel way, he looks younger than his twenty-four years—the type of guy women want to mother. "Two fries. Two coffees. Black."

She glances across the table, but Kyle only nods, and Mindy sighs a nearly imperceptible sigh, a small puff of disappointment, deposited with the silverware and napkins.

"I don't know," Kyle says when Mindy's whisked away their unused menus, when she's scribbled down their orders, when she's taking languid steps toward the kitchen. "Suppose you tell me."

"Really?" Jack leans forward over the table; he looms like a pro. It's a sudden move, a surprise. Kyle's eyes are saucers in his thin face. "Under Celia Steinhauser's living-room window."

"No kidding." Kyle slouches in his chair, but he doesn't look at his father. He gazes around the restaurant. He glances at his watch. He takes out a cheap go-phone, scans his messages. He shrugs. His lips are pale, his hands shaking. "I can't do this now. I have to get back to Maryanne."

"I can't pretend this isn't happening, Kyle. I have your charm. It was at the crime scene!"

Kyle's phone vibrates. He glances at the screen. His face, when he looks up from the phone, is ashy white. "Like I told you," he says, "I can't do this now. Arrest me tomorrow. I'll even come down to the station if you want. Here!" He sticks his hand in his pocket, pulls out a stack of bills. He tosses the money on the table, knocking over the sugar canister and the salt and pepper shakers. "Sorry," he says, and he sets them back up. His hands shake as he grabs the small pile of cash and gives it to Jack. It's clipped together with an address he's printed on a piece of paper, along with a phone number and a woman's name. Lucy Bancroft.

"What's this?"

"Listen," he says. "In all these years, I never asked you for anything."

"What is this?"

"It's first month's rent and the deposit," Kyle says. "All

243

you have to do is drop it by the office and give it to that woman, the one on the paper there. Lucy something, and pick up the apartment key."

"What's the rush?"

"I want them to have a place to go if I can't . . . if something happens to . . ." Kyle gets up, bumps into Mindy as she arrives at their table with a tray of food. "Sorry," he says. "Sorry, Mindy," and he takes the tray, sets it down on the table.

Jack starts to get up, too. "Where the hell are you . . . ?"

"Just do this one thing for me," he says, this son he doesn't know, this boy he's never really known at all. "I have to get to the hospital."

"The hospital? Is Maryanne okay? Your mother told me she's—"

"I'll call you later about picking up the key to the apartment. Oh, and Jack." He stops. He stands at the table, and his face is sickly pale. His eyes are round and dark; they dart here and there, brown with gold flecks. His pants are too big, held up by a tattered leather belt. "I didn't kill Mrs. S."

"Where'd you get this?" Jack holds up the wad of bills, the hundreds, folded neatly into a small yellow chip clip. "Whose is this?"

"Mine," he says, but he's already halfway to the door. "Well, theirs now. And by the way," he says, when he's almost out of earshot, "I passed the GED!"

"Hey!" Jack yells. "Great! You need a ride? Wait! Kyle!"

He's on his feet. Mindy looks confused. The two burgers sit untouched on the table. "Could you wrap 'em up?" Jack says, and he tosses a twenty and a five on the table. He jostles through the crowd, but Kyle is gone, vanished, somewhere on the street, streaking toward the hospital, the girlfriend, his baby, for all Jack knows. He's almost through the door before he realizes he's forgotten the elephant; he makes his way back through the restaurant, through the aisle, clogged now with dawdlers, midday shoppers, bustling with diners from nearby businesses, with friends meeting for coffee, mothers and daughters taking a break from shopping. He pushes past.

"Excuse me," he says, and his voice is gruffer than he intended, hoarse. No, the couple says, an older couple, already at the table, already sipping water without ice, their faces pink from the blustery wind outside, the sun— no, they haven't seen the charm. He gives them his card, tells them it's important. Police business, he says. Call him if they find it. Yes, they assure him, yes, of course they will. They'll keep their eyes open. He looks around, fumbles under the table, between their feet. He feels like an ass. A clod. But he keeps looking, even though he knows that Kyle outsmarted him and grabbed the charm on his way out. He leaves his card with the cashier anyway, explains his dilemma to Mindy, hands her another card. "Please! It's really important."

"Of course," she says. "It's the elephant in the room."

## 27

When Peter comes home, Dana can tell he isn't happy to see her. She can feel his anger, his unease, across the room. He pulls the door shut hard behind him.

"What?" she says, watching him from where she sits on the couch. Beside her, Spot snores on a corduroy pillow.

"You're home." He says this with a faint sneer that in the blurring of things she doesn't recognize. She only hears his words, the black and white of them.

"Yes."

"Where were you?"

"At a hotel," she says. "I was trying to get some sleep. Where were you?"

"At work." Peter just stands there. His hands are clenched into fists. "In my office. I was working late, so I slept on the couch the last couple— Did you see Dr. Sing?"

"Well," she says, "not exactly. I made an appointment. And we spoke on the phone."

"Did she call in anything? A prescription to calm you the fuck dow—"

"No," she says. "Not yet. She wants to see me first."

"So did you sleep?" He doesn't move toward the couch. He doesn't take the smallest step toward his wife. He grabs the newspaper from the coffee table where Jack Moss placed it earlier that day, when he brought it in with him. He doesn't look at her. He walks straight to the kitchen. A moment later Dana hears the burble of the coffeemaker, the closing of a cupboard door, the thwacking of the lid being lifted off a new bottle of cream.

"No," she says. "I didn't, actually."

"Why is that, do you think?" He calls this from the kitchen. She watches him as he moves between appliances.

She shrugs. "It was Manhattan. So many people."

"So?"

"So maybe that was why. There was so much noise."

"Dana." He comes back to the living room and stands for a minute with his coffee. "It's you," he says, and she thinks of the old song, the oldie goldie.

"Baby, it's youuu," she sings, and she gets up, dances toward Peter in the quiet dark of evening. Peter shifts away.

"Careful," he says. "The coffee."

"Fuck the coffee." She dances up to where he stands. She takes the cup out of his hand and sets it on an end table, rests one hand on his shoulder, the other in his palm, still hot and moist from the coffee cup. "Baby it's youuu," she sings again, taking long strides across the room, her husband rigid and weighty beside her. "You should hear

247

what they say about youuuuuuu," she croons. "They say you've never, never, ever been truuuuuuuuue."

Peter stops moving suddenly. He plants his feet—his pricey shoes, his Italian leathers—in a stance, as if he's going to box or segue into a yoga move, and Dana breaks away.

She twirls toward the dining room, her hands high above her head. She bows and swoops, her hair loose and flying down over her face. She is a tree, waving in a storm, a cloud diving across the sky, a speck of dust on the wind. She is everything and nothing, all at the same time. She is no one, and she is everyone. She stands on her toes, and she is amazed at her lightness, at her balance, at her ability. I'm channeling Anna Pavlova, she almost says, but then she sees Peter's face.

"It doesn't matter what they saaaaay," she sings, and her voice is loud and strong and true, like the Shirelles. She is the Shirelles. "'Cause, baby, it's yoooou." She ends with a pirouette. She ends in an awkward quasi split on the dining-room rug, her head thrown back, her arms reaching toward where Peter bends over the end table for his coffee.

"Is that supposed to mean something, Dana?"

"Why, whatever do you mean, darlin'?" she says, and she is awed by her own voice, by the southern lilt she's managed. It's such a wondrous thing, this new freedom, this letting-go that allows her to be all things, all people, that allows her to transcend space and even time, to escape the confines of her flesh and bones, to show her that all separation is merely illusion.

"Are you trying to accuse me of something?"

"Oh," she says. "But wait!" She stands up. She cups her hands around her mouth and closes her eyes, and her voice is haunting and sad. She is the Cure, singing on a beach with palm trees, somewhere she's never been, somewhere in a video, and the words come out and fly across the dining room to Peter in his chair, sliding his feet out of his shoes, clutching his coffee cup, as she sings these words she didn't know she knew: "I've been looking so long at these pictures of you that I almost believe that they're real. . . ."

"All right," he says. "I've had enough."

"Isn't it wonderful?"

"No," he says. "It isn't. You are crazy, Dana," but Dana smiles. He doesn't understand. He looks so small, struggling up in his stocking feet, so pitiful and lost. She wants to say, What happened to us, Peter? She wants to say, We loved each other once, but she doesn't. He looks as if he might run at her, wrestle her to the floor. He looks as if he might restrain her, and she slides sideways, dancing. She is on her toes, so light she could almost fly, so light she's iridescent—a moth, a butterfly. She moves faster and faster. She's so much faster than he is, so much lighter than he is, there in his stocking feet, there stuck to the floor. She sees him reach for her, his hands fumbling toward her as she flies forward through the dining room, past him, past the living room, but she's too quick for him.

"Stop!" He stands still again, stares at her as if she is a wild boar charging, or maybe a bird, flitting, flapping, free of its cage. "Stop! You're out of your mind, Dana, which you'd know if you had any sense left at all."

"Hmmm." Dana stops her twirling, her flying. She stops dead still in front of him, so close they are nearly touching. "Maybe just a little sense," she says, and she sticks a wad of paper, a small, crumpled gob, inside his hand and closes it, pressing his fingers in place with her own, as if she were pressing the edges of a pie, fluting the crust, trapping fruit inside, or pecans, instead of his receipt from the Days Inn. She backs away, flaps her arms. She stands on her toes, snatches her purse, and twirls toward the door as Peter makes a grab for her, two, three grabs, but she's too quick for him. He can't fly.

*

She drives out of her neighborhood without looking to either side. She concentrates on the road, oblivious to the aging houses with their alleyway yards and their fading summer gardens, to Wanda on her front porch and Lon Nguyen making his rounds. She speeds along the streets with the radio on, with St. Christopher watching from the visor. These last weeks, while the threads inside her frayed and tugged, she was afraid of Peter—afraid he'd leave her, that he'd go out one night and never come back home. But now the threads have broken clean away, ripped and floated off as if they never were. Now she doesn't care if Peter looks at her with love or hate. She doesn't need to know where he sleeps or who he sleeps with, whether he tossed the cat into the yard or if Spot found a small unnoticed gap in the basement wall, a half-closed window—a forgotten space. It doesn't matter. Everything's forgotten spaces now, and Dana, too, is sliding—Thumbelina, slipping through.

She jams her foot down harder on the gas and rounds the corner. Nothing can keep up with her thoughts; they're everywhere at once. She knows everything all at the same time, the secrets of the universe presenting themselves like gems before her. The world is alive with motion. It shimmers beneath her, above her, all around her.

She pulls the car up to the George Washington Bridge, the upper level, but she doesn't have the thirteen dollars. Never bought the pass. Shit. Traffic fans out on either side of her, stifling her, shutting her in. She eases her foot off the brake, and the car inches forward as she swats around the inside of her bag, feeling for bills she hadn't thought to bring. The traffic moves in a sudden gush, sending her to the tollbooth.

"Thirteen dollars," the cashier says. Her voice is vague, unpleasant. Her voice is cold like Peter's, her eyes already off Dana and on the next car, all of them lined up like sheep going to slaughter. Or, Dana thinks, did sheep actually go to slaughter? In such large groups? Or did they merely get sheared, only the occasional sheep going for mutton?

She looks up. "Do sheep go to slaughter?" she asks the uniformed woman in the tollbooth.

"Thirteen dollars," the cashier says again, as if there's been some sort of misunderstanding, as if Dana hadn't heard her correctly the first time. "You're holding up traffic." She reaches for something. A telephone? A gun? Dana can't see. A terror-alert button? Dana sticks her head out farther, but all she can see is the woman's side, her hand reaching forward in the tiny space.

"Please!" she yells, much louder than she'd intended. "Don't shoot! Don't call them. I'm not . . . I swear I'm not dangerous. I'm not a terrorist. I'm only disorganized. I should have thought ahead, but I'm not . . . I've not felt quite . . . well, quite right lately. But I can promise you I'm not a threat. I just—"

The woman isn't looking at Dana. She's leaning forward. Her lips are moving. Butterflies flit around her head, filling up the tiny booth. Dana jams her foot down on the gas, and the Toyota jerks forward into a sea of cars. "Oh, shit," she says. She changes lanes. She shifts from spot to spot, but it's a Friday evening, and traffic barely moves. She feels incredibly large and noticeable, her car with all the bumper stickers a dead giveaway. She imagines Peter being phoned. "She's crazy," he'll tell them. "She's a danger to herself and others. To society. To the nation as a whole. It's only the cat she likes. Adores our son, of course—she'd give her life for him. Only he and the cat are safe, and in my opinion as a celebrated lawyer—I ask you, ladies and gentlemen, I ask you to look at my shoes—the cat is suspect, too. In fact, he may not even really be a cat—a plant of some kind, a hybrid, a tracker. My friend and I, the one with the large breasts? Allow me to show you Exhibits A and B. We've discussed it, the Tart and I, and we've decided. They gotta go!" She glances at the visor. St. Christopher shakes his head.

The traffic is nothing but a snarl. Her car is stopped in the lane. A siren smears the night. She feels her body strain against the seat belt; the harness cuts into her shoulder. She unsnaps the thing and takes a jagged breath. The siren is inside her ears, inside the car. It screams and pries inside her brain. She opens the car door and steps outside. She's forgotten her shoes, but she can't feel the pavement. She's so light her feet are barely touching down. She looks out over the cars toward the Hudson, and it shimmers, it hums, it sings, eclipsing the sound of the siren with its lovely, lilting song. She climbs up the side of the bridge, and her body is an ash floating on air. She flaps her arms, lightly, delicately, gracefully, stepping out into the current so she can fly.

But something stops her, pinning her arms against her sides, tucking her wings back inside. Something lashes her to the earth; to the harsh, unyielding concrete of the bridge; to the screaming of ambulances and people; to a large woman with jet-black hair and bangle bracelets running toward her. She tries to turn around, tries to see behind her, where she's caught—a net, she thinks, she's caught in a huge net like a fish—but something stops her. This thing she can't see, it stops her. And then it whispers in her ear. "Just relax," it says. "It's over."

"No," she says, she screams, but it isn't really her screaming—it's a sad, thin wraith inside her, struggling to get free. The voice flies from her mouth and sails into the air above the Hudson, streams like the tail of a kite she made in art class as a child, filled with crumpled bows and folded magazine pictures she found stacked up on the sun porch—the blues and browns and oranges of her mother's magazines. It blew off in the wind in April. It flew away.

"No," she says again. She motions to the woman with the bangle bracelets. She motions with her eyes, and the woman nods. She moves toward Dana on the bridge, her hands outstretched. Her sari drifts around her on the wind. St. Christopher, Dana thinks, and she smiles. He's ducked inside the woman with the sari and the bangle bracelets. He's letting her know. He's found this body to inhabit for a moment, to let her know he's with her still. St. Christopher is always there. He never lets her down.

She sees her mother in the crowd. She sees the Poet and the friend who died of uterine cancer. "Sheila!" Dana screams. "Sheila! It's me! It's Dana!" But it comes out wrong. It comes out thin and wispy, another ribbon trailing off into the sky, and Sheila waves. She's wearing a tank top and shorts, and her hair has grown back lush and full. There are so many people. She looks for Peter, but he isn't there. Her car stands silent in the stack of traffic. She sees it when the crowds move, when they make a path for the EMTs, and then there is a second, but it stretches out into forever. There's a second when she flaps her arms, when she is free, when the owner of the disembodied voice has finally let her go and the EMTs have not yet strapped her to the stretcher—there's a second when she flaps her arms and they are long and graceful. They sparkle with the specks of the bay, the foam from the tops of the waves, the sparks from the tops of the world, the tiny bits of broken stars from all the universe that rest, for that one endless second, in her wings. She lifts them up, up, and they are soft, and all the world shimmers.

# 28

It's nearly midnight when Jack's cell phone rings, but he isn't sleeping. Margie left a message on his answering machine that afternoon, and he's played it so many times he knows it by heart. Maryanne's in labor—about to have the baby. It's up to Kyle to decide how much a part, if any, Jack will play in their lives, but she felt he should know; Kyle is his son, too. Jack's thought about calling her back to find out if Maryanne's okay, if the baby's okay. Kyle looked pretty rough in the restaurant, pretty ragged, and the way he bolted out is definitely cause for worry. It's late, though, and Jack doesn't want to press his luck with Margie, who usually hates him.

Sooner or later he'll hear from his son. The apartment key is on his dresser in a small ashtray he uses to collect change, now that he's stopped smoking. After losing track of the charm, he's learned his lesson. Although whether to use it or not was a choice he'd hoped he wouldn't have to make, that charm was integral to the case when or if it comes to trial. He hates to think the facts will point to Dana killing her neighbor, but Jack will go where the evidence takes him, unless . . . unless it takes him to his son, and he hopes to God it doesn't. He turns over. The bedspread lies crumpled on the floor, and the sheets are a tangled rope at the foot of the bed.

When the phone rings, he jumps. It could be Kyle or Margie; it could be the hospital. He sticks on his reading glasses and glances into his phone, but the number isn't one he knows. "Hello," he says. "Moss."

"It's Peter Catrell," a somewhat slurred voice informs him.

"Why are you calling me at—he glances at his clock—midnight, Mr. Catrell?"

"It's Dana," Peter says.

Jack sits up, props the pillow against his headboard. "What about her?"

"I was watching the news," Peter says. His voice is shaking. He clears his throat. "I think she might be dead."

"Who? Dana? Your wife?" Jesus. "You sure?"

"No," Peter says, and Jack sits up straight, swings his legs over the edge of the bed. "Apparently somebody jumped off the bridge. I don't know . . . I missed the first part of the— Anyway, the local news panned in on Dana's car. The driver's-side door was open and everything. The bumper stickers. I saw the bumper stickers, and I knew it was— Her Toyota was just there, stopped in the middle of traffic, by the tollbooths on the George Washington Bridge. She was in such a hurry, they said, she didn't even close the door."

"In a hurry?"

"To jump, I guess! To die!"

"That true? That sound like your wife?"

"No. I mean, I don't know. She was upset. We had an argument."

"About what?"

"It doesn't matter."

"Actually, it might matter." And it would matter a lot more, Jack thinks, if the argument got out of hand. Did he have more than a peripheral impact on what happened to Dana? Did Peter kill the Steinhauser woman and send his own wife over the edge—gaslight her, like in that old movie? Her face comes back to him, her stick-thin arms that afternoon, the way she looked up when he said he had to get down to the office, the fear in her eyes when he asked her to come back in the next day. He remembers stopping in her entryway, scanning the desk for details, for anything that might help with the case. Remembers his instincts telling him to stay. He wishes now he had—that he'd done something, said something, to change the course of events.

"Like I said, we had a fight," Peter says as Jack pulls a shirt off the back of a chair. She was acting really crazy, singing about a photograph. She thought I was— She found a receipt for a hotel and figured I was having an affair."

"Yeah? Imagine that." Jack tugs on his pants and tucks in his shirt. In the bathroom he runs a comb through his hair, brushes his teeth, throws cold water on his face, letting Peter babble on speaker from where he's set his cell on top of the john. "Listen," he says when he's dried his face, when he's laced his shoes and buckled his holster, when he's ready to go out the door. "Listen, Catrell. Could you hang up so I can call around, find out what's going on?"

"Oh," Peter says. "Yes. Of course. I—"

"I'll get back to you," Jack says, and he jogs out to the driveway. Inside the Crown Vic, he grabs his radio, and when a faintly midwestern-sounding voice comes on, he says, "What do we have on a suicide? On the GW Bridge? Tonight." He looks at his watch. "Last night now."

"Unidentified woman." The dispatcher's voice comes through static; the air is heavy with storms. "Five-eight, hundred twenty pounds. Light brown hair. Early forties. The car's registered to a Dana Catrell."

"Right," he says. "Suicide?"

"Attempted suicide. A commuter got out of his car and grabbed her before she went over."

Jack releases the breath he only now realizes he's been holding. "That's good," he says. "That's great. Where'd they take her?"

"Bellevue," the dispatcher says. "The ambulance was routed over to Bellevue on account of an accident on the—"

"What time?"

"Nine thirty-five."

"Thanks," Jack says. "Appreciate your help."

"Sure thing," the dispatcher says. "Have a good one."

Jack knows very little about mental illness. He knows that his mother suffered from depression the year leading up to her death and that his father was understandably depressed after she died. He suspects there was something going on with Margie when they were married—still is, probably—an anxiety issue, although he never knew exactly what it was, only that she sometimes looked like she was crawling out of her skin. She was high-strung, she used to tell him—that was why she liked to have a drink now and then. It settled her nerves, she said. It calmed her down. If anything good came out of all that nightmare mess with Margie, it was that she let the boys see what can happen when you get drawn in, give in to your addictions. She's shown Kyle how not to live his life.

Jack hits the reply button on his cell, and Peter picks up on the first ring.

"Moss?"

"Your wife's in the hospital. In the ER," he says. "Bellevue."

"She's all right?"

"I doubt that."

"But she's alive."

"Yeah," he says. "She's alive. She didn't jump. Somebody grabbed her."

"On the bridge, you mean?"

"Listen," Jack says. "I wasn't there. Suppose you talk to her about it."

"Sure," Peter says. "Sure thing, Detective. And thanks. I owe you one."

Jack ends the call and sets the phone on the seat beside him. He figures Peter's afraid Dana might say something about him or about the photograph that Jack is now certain exists or did at some point anyway. He's probably worried about his reputation, his professional image, that his wife's mad ravings might shed too much light on things he wants kept under wraps. In fact, his involvement with the murder might go far deeper than that, his distress more about his own well-being than Dana's. There was concern in Peter's voice, but though on some level Catrell clearly still has feelings for his wife, he'd throw her under the bus in a heartbeat. And, Jack thinks, turning the key and backing the Crown Vic down the driveway to the street, maybe that's exactly what he's done.

He heads for Manhattan. Dana's a suspect. He needs to question her, find out why she was on the bridge, if her suicide attempt is related to the neighbor's murder. Was she so furious about her husband's affair that she struck out? Shot the messenger? Or did Celia pick that day to tell her she and Peter had been lovers, sleeping together four doors down from where his unsuspecting wife peeled potatoes for his dinner? Was Dana drunk enough herself that afternoon—drunk or unhinged enough—to bash her yard-sale companion in the head and then go home to sleep it off, awakening hours later with no memory of what she'd done? Was that the catalyst for her break-down, the conduit for this demon that's taken over Dana's body, this frightened, hopeless entity that's slipped inside her skin and walked her to the edge of the GW Bridge—the same madness he saw all those years before, inside the girl fidgeting in a faded hospital gown with broken, fraying laces? She'd raised her arm at him, showing him a long, deep slit along her wrist, the ugly black crisscross of stitches. She'd laughed at him, an angry, mocking laugh as he stood dumbstruck at the opening of the curtained cubicle in Bellevue. "What's your name?" he'd asked the girl. "Virginia Woolf," she told him in a British accent. "Only this time they've fished me out and emptied all the stones from my pockets."

\*

He shows his badge and walks across the airy lobby with its high ceilings, its plants, its open, tiled floors closing behind him. He extends his card, says he's working on a murder case, that Dana's a person of interest; if she's lucid, it's imperative he see her.

A nurse on the ward leads him down a hall. Voices shout at him—or maybe not at him—loud, impatient voices. Demanding voices. Pleading voices. Heartbreaking. Raw—the voices of those stripped naked by disease or circumstance. Jack keeps his eyes on the perfunctory white heels of the nurse in front of him. He avoids looking to either side, avoids the anguished faces, the prone bodies strapped to gurneys, the agitated patients pacing in their temporary rooms. He glances at his watch and wonders if Ann's hotel is somewhere nearby—a subway stop or two farther uptown, a cheap cab ride from where he strides, officious and intrusive, through the yellow-walled corridors.

"She is here," the psych nurse tells him. Her voice is soft in the clamor of unsoft, undisguised emotion. She's Irish, he thinks, or Scottish. Her voice is lilting. He wants her to stay, wants her voice to fill his ears and blot out all the others.

Dana doesn't see him standing at the entrance to the cubicle; she doesn't look up. She sits, still wearing her jeans, far too baggy. She still has on the sleeveless shirt from earlier that day. Purple. The color suits her. Her light hair is a tangle, dripping from a clip that clings to the side of her head. Her face is hidden. She stares down at her hands, plays with the edges of a sheet tucked in at the end of a makeshift bed.

"Dana?"

She looks up then, but it seems an enormous effort. She sighs, pulls her eyes away from her hands and raises them to the doorway, to Jack, standing there. "It's you," she says. "I thought you'd never come." Is this how it works, this madness? Does it blur the things that came before—eclipse the days and nights and hours, the pain, the dreams, the memories she can't contain? Does it allow her to forget?

He clears his throat. "Are you all right?" He takes a step inside the room—a tiny step, a baby step, they used to say, that childhood game—Mother May I, was it? Mother, may I take two baby steps?

She stares at him; she smiles. She raises her eyebrows as if he's asked the strangest thing. "No," she says.

"I'm sorry." He stands dead still in the doorway, as if he might spook her by moving, as if she might run away, as if she might slip over the George Washington Bridge.

"Make them let me stay," she says. "Tell them I want to stay here. With you."

Jack nods. He wonders who she sees. He wonders who she's talking to, what ghost she's plucked from her past and stuck there in his body. "I'm glad you didn't jump," he says. "I'm glad you're safe."

"I've done a terrible thing." Her eyes are wide and blue. She reaches forward, grabbing at him, grabbing at the air. "An awful thing."

The doctor brushes past Jack in the doorway. "I'm sorry," he says. "Whatever it is you need from this woman will have to wait. We have to get her stabilized."

"Can I stay?"

"No," he says. "Not here. You can either wait in the lobby or come back later."

"When?" Jack steps backward, out into the hall. He doesn't want to leave, even though the place makes him crazy, claustrophobic—even though he feels trapped in this room of horrors. He wonders what it is Dana wants to tell him, but more than this he wants to stay with her. She looks so helpless and hopeless, so alone.

The doctor shrugs—the doctor or the intern from NYU—the one in charge for the moment, the one whose job it is to protect people like Dana from people like him. The person with the kind of badge that matters here. "This afternoon? This evening? Tomorrow, maybe? We'll just have to see."

"Wait!" Dana reaches out again. Her hand stretches toward him—open this time—a supplicating gesture, pleading. Her eyes are huge in her thin face. "St. Christopher! I left him on the bridge!"

## 29

Jack arrives late to the station the next morning. He's nearly always prompt, no matter how late he's out working on a case, but the night before has really thrown him off his game.

Even when he got back from Bellevue—and by then it was well after two—he couldn't sleep. He couldn't get it out of his head, Dana in the ER, reaching out her hands the way she did, the fear in her eyes blurring with that other time all those years ago, in the same hospital, the girl who couldn't have been more than nineteen. And then there was Margie's phone call on his answering machine—the likelihood that by now he has a grandchild. He's already left five messages for her, but so far she hasn't answered any of them, which doesn't really surprise him. On the way home from Bellevue, he made a few calls, threw his weight around and found out Maryanne was in St. Joseph's. He leans back in his chair and sticks his feet up on the desk. He's the only one there. Everyone's either out on the streets or not in yet. He closes his eyes, and he's almost asleep when his cell phone rings, jarring him awake.

"Moss?" a shaky male voice says. "Jack? It's Ronald. Steinhauser. It's Celia's husband. Widower."

"Ronald." Jack glances at his watch. "You on your way in?"

"No," Ronald says. "I'm . . . I'm late. I was up all night. It's terrible. If it hadn't been for her car, I'd never have known."

"Known?"

"The Toyota. Hard to miss with all those . . . with her political bumper stickers. Could be a problem, I always thought, in traffic. Dangerous, even. You never know what kind of idiot might be behind you and suddenly go into road rage. Anyway, I knew it was Dana."

"Knew what was Dana?"

"On the news. On last night's news. 'Oh, my God!' I thought. 'This is all my fault.' Unintentional, of course, but I should have been more thorough. I should have looked harder. All that doesn't matter in the end, though, does it? I'm as bad as a thug with an Uzi or a drunk driver mowing down a crowd inside a crosswalk." Ronald belches, and Jack suspects he's still a little drunk from the night before. "She and Celia . . . the way they trudged together in search of chairs and other pieces of interest if not actual . . . um, usefulness . . ."

"You've got fifteen minutes, Ronald. I'll be waiting for you in my office."

\*

When, sixteen minutes later, Ronald Steinhauser puffs

and pants up the hall and throws himself, red-faced, into a chair, Jack is toying with things on top of the table in the interrogation room. He stacks a little bunch of pencils in a pile against his steno pad. "Tell me about the photo in Celia's phone, Ronald."

"I was coming down here last night to show you," Ronald says, surprising him, "but then there was that shot of Dana's car on the news, and I . . . God, I was so . . . I closed my eyes for just a second, and the next thing I knew, it was morning."

Jack fiddles with the pencils, knocking the pile over.

"So I got up and grabbed the phone and headed for the train. I was on my way down here—at the entrance to the subway, and I took out my wallet to find your card . . . to verify your . . . with Celia dead and then with Dana— I felt like a piece of gum on a cosmic sneaker, invisible with all the hordes, all the crowds. When there are so many people, there is no one person, I was thinking, and just then someone bumped into me, and the next thing I knew, it was gone. 'Help!' I yelled. 'Somebody help!' and a jogger took off, came back with a traffic cop, but it was too late. He was gone. It was gone."

"Your wallet?"

"No. The cell phone."

"He took your cell phone and left your wallet?"

"Celia's cell phone, actually. The one with the picture."

"Of Peter Catrell and his . . . work wife or whatever?

Thought you said it wasn't in the phone. You looked, remember? I even looked."

"Right. This was another phone. One I didn't know about. But then I didn't know about the bank account either. Anyway, the picture was in it. It was . . . at least it looked like the one Dana was so anxious to find."

"Could you describe the photo, Ronald?" Jack weighs his words carefully.

"Yeah. Sure. It was a picture of a man leaning over, talking to a woman with blond hair down to her shoulders. A very busty woman, not that it matters. They were sitting at a table in a restaurant. It was difficult to tell much—the photo wasn't very good."

"As you pointed out before you saw it."

Ronald clears his throat. "Did I? I don't really remem—"

"Did you recognize them?"

"It looked like Dana's husband," Ronald says, "but to be honest, it was hard to tell."

"Well, listen, Ronald. Thanks. Too bad you can't bring in the phone."

"I know. I was devastated. 'Take my wallet!' I wanted to yell after the guy—in fact, I think I did. 'Take my wallet!' I yelled at him. 'But bring me back the phone! Bring me back this picture, whose disappearance has caused a friend to go over the edge. Literally.' "

"Well, that's a shame, Ronald. Where'd you find it anyhow?"

"In my car. Under the . . . you know, mat in the back-seat. I stopped at a light yesterday, jammed my foot down on the brake, and the thing flew out. It must've gotten mixed up with my stuff when I moved into the hotel."

"Yeah? Flew under the front seat, you mean?"

"No. Well, sort of. I heard it bounce out back there, so I fished around when I stopped, and there it was. Weird, huh?"

"Yeah," Jack says. "Weird." He tries not to smile. This guy is such a liar. And he's so bad at it. Jack was a little surprised that his alibi for the night of Celia's death checked out. The bartender remembered him vividly, though, so it was definitely Dana who went back to their house.

"Heart-wrenching about Dana. Will there be a memorial service? I know a funeral isn't possible at this point."

"Not until she dies, probably."

"Wait. I thought— Last night, on the news, they showed her—"

"She didn't jump," Jack says. "Somebody stopped her."

"Oh, my God! That's wonderful! That is so totally wonder—"

"I agree. Thanks for coming down, Ronald. Glad you found the photo."

"Can she . . . can Dana have visitors?"

"I don't know," he says. "Probably not yet."

"Well, could you see that she gets the message?"

"About the picture?"

"Yes," Ronald says. "It might help her."

"I'll see she gets it," Jack says. He knows that Ronald's story doesn't hold water, but the important thing is that he did at some point see the photo and obviously deleted it to cover his own ass. And in light of all the lies he's handed over, Ronald's making himself a prime suspect—jealous husband, first one on the scene, wife threatening to take off with another man. He doesn't seem the type, but people like Ronald have been known to go off the deep end, do a one-eighty on a lifetime of placid with one crazy, violent act. Peter's still in the running, too, with his prints all over the bedroom and his obvious lack of regard for women, including his own wife. And although Dana will be relieved to hear what Ronald's got to say about the photo, this minor revelation does nothing for her case. Too late now for it to make her feel she hasn't lost her mind. That ship has clearly sailed.

Meanwhile there are still Kyle's prints in Celia's car, the missing five grand, the glass elephant he found in the Steinhausers' overgrown yard—still the knowledge that his son knows more than he's saying about the murder on Ashby Lane. Jack stretches, locking his fingers over his head. He's listened to everyone who's streamed through the office since Celia's death. He's noted the shifting eyes, the skirted questions, the suave and not-so-suave responses, the dilated pupils, the tapping feet and babbled, rambling answers. Now it's time to figure out what matters and what doesn't. It's time to sort the truth from the lies and see what kind of picture comes to light.

# 30

Dana opens her eyes and closes them again. She doesn't move. She doesn't want to be here. She doesn't want to be anywhere. She wants to be gone, and she would be if they had left her alone, if they had let her fly. "Do you remember?" the doctors asked her when she first arrived here, in this new place outside the city, the move from Bellevue orchestrated by Peter. "Do you remember what happened to you on the bridge?" As if her interrupted flight were someone else's doing, as if it were a perpetration and not her own idea, her own last-minute plan, her own longing to escape the loose and flapping sashes of her life.

It's the colors she remembers most—the blue-black of the sky, the gray of the bridge, the spots of silver where the light hit, the white tips of the waves beneath her, the pink umbrella someone held above her head, the dark blue print of a skirt, a brown arm forcing her away from the bridge's edge, holding her firmly while the ambulance bulldozed its way through traffic. She remembers a collage of light and dark, of color and white, unlike this world of gray, where everything is muted. Her mind is a muddle, a puddle, a murk. The chaos and confusion are still there, but the bright, sharp sparks are gone, the volume turned down on her madness.

The door opens. "How are you today?" a voice says, and Dana's eyes fly open in spite of her resolve to keep them closed.

"Fine," she says, but it is such a tiny sound. "I'm fine," she says, and again it's like a scratch, a bird's wing on a window. She closes her eyes.

"Is there anything you need?" With her eyes shut, the voice could be anyone's. It could be the Poet's voice or God's. It could be St. Christopher.

She shakes her head.

"Rest. I'll check on you later," the voice says, and this time the door stays open.

Dana rolls onto her side and stares at the shiny wall. Ocher, she thinks, semigloss. The whole room is shiny; the whole ward is shiny. It's been recently painted. If she concentrates, she can even smell the paint.

This is the way the world ends / Not with a bang but a whisper. No, she thinks, it wasn't whisper; it was something else. She'll ask Jamie to Google Eliot when he comes back. "The Hollow Men." She won't ask Peter, even though the poem fits him to a tee.

She misses the clamor of Bellevue. She misses the yellow walls, the temporary cubicle that told her she was only passing through. She misses the Poet. He was there. She remembers him there, but she knows he couldn't be. "Was he there?" she says, but her voice is a sliver, falling on the rough whiteness of the sheet. Not with a bang . . .

## 31

When the door opens this time, there is no attempt to drown sound. Sneakers squeak across the linoleum and stop at the bed where Dana lies, pretending to sleep. "Hello there," a new voice says. Jamaican, Dana thinks. "Time to get up."

"No," she says.

"Can't hear you."

"No," she says again.

"Sorry. Still can't hear you."

"NO!"

"That's right," the voice says, a little pleasanter, a little softer. "That's right, honey. You have to speak up!"

"NO!" Dana yells again, "I'm not getting up!"

"It's good to be heard," the voice says, and Dana opens her eyes to a large, dark-skinned woman appraising her from the side of the bed. "But you still have to get up out of that bed."

"Why?"

"Time for group," the woman says—a doctor, Dana sees from her name tag. Dr. Ghea.

"I'm not ready for a group discussion," Dana says, but her words are garbled and wrong, circling her head

274

like mosquitoes that need swatting.

"I'm sorry?"

"What's wrong with my voice?" Dana feels as if she's somehow landed on another planet where her words are meaningless. Maybe she took off after all. Maybe she did fly away.

"It's the medication," Dr. Ghea says. "It slurs your words. Jumbles things a bit. We'll fine-tune your prescription, and soon you won't even be taking it."

"No?"

"No," she says. "You'll be on Depakote only. It just takes a while for it to kick in."

"Oh." Dana closes her eyes again. "I thought . . ."

"I know what you thought." Dr. Ghea slips a blood-pressure cup around Dana's arm, and it compresses like a boa constrictor. "But you need to stay on your meds, Dana. No more of this trying to fly off the George Washington Bridge. You've got too much going for you."

Dana chokes out a bitter laugh.

"Which you'll see if you ever get out of that bed and down the hall where you belong."

"Group?"

"Yep. I'll even bring you there myself."

"Wow," she says.

"But only this one time."

She doesn't want to go to group. She barely understands the doctor's words with all the racket in her head. And then there's the murder. Celia. Now it's coalescing.

Piece by piece, the thready, floating bits of things, of thoughts and faces, memories and words, are catching on one another's edges, coming back together, like the big bang working backward, her life an explosion in reverse. There's so much time to think, lying here on the starchy sheets, the TV in the dayroom a dull and constant droning in the background, like a fly caught in a screen.

## 32

Jack sticks his phone in his pocket and sits on a bench outside the front doors of the hospital. He tried to question Dana after checking around and finding she was transferred out of Bellevue and back to Paterson, but he was told he'd have to wait. She's getting settled in, the psych nurse told him when he tried to see her—a tall redhead wearing jeans and a T-shirt. It was only the ID hanging from a ribbon around her neck that separated her from the visitors, the mothers and sisters, the daughters and friends. marcy, her nameplate said, which Jack thought was interestingly close to "mercy," and he'd wondered, not for the first time, how people's names affect their lives—the judge named Truman, the carpenter named Buzz.

It feels like the ending of things. Even though the day is bright and the sun is blazing through the trees, it feels as if summer's edged away. The air is still. Ann, Kyle, Margie, Joey—he feels their absence like an ache in his chest.

"Jack?"

He turns around. Kyle looks different, but Jack's not sure how. He's even shabbier than the day they had lunch. His hair sticks up in tufts, and his clothes look slept in. There's something else, though. He seems different.

"Jeez. I thought you were smiling there for a second."

"Naw. Must be the sun." Kyle sits down on the bench. He glances at his watch. "Listen," he says, "my friend— my girlfriend . . ."

"Is she all right?" Jack searches his son's face. "I phoned the hospital early this morning. Did she—"

Kyle stops him. "Let's do this first," he says. "I'd rather just get this interrogation thing over with."

"Okay. Your call." Jack folds his hands. He leans back on the bench, even though he's dying to know about the baby. He takes a deep breath, forces himself into detective mode. "How'd your lucky charm wind up under Celia Steinhauser's window?"

"I don't know," Kyle says. "The dog?"

"What dog?"

"It was on the news. They showed it on the news. A mutt—small? Brown?"

"No," Jack says. "They didn't. Actually, the dog was missing for a day or two after Celia's murder."

"Oh. She must've told me, then."

"Would she describe it? I mean, why would she describe it? And why would your charm be there in the first place?"

Kyle shrugs. "I guess I left it in her car."

"Look." Jack takes out his cell. "I'm trying to help you here. If you don't want my help, you can talk to someone at the station." He thumbs through his phone.

"Okay." Kyle sighs. "You gonna arrest me, Dad?"

278

"Haven't so far."

Kyle looks back at the hospital. He glances straight up at the windows, at one of the windows, it looks like. Jack watches him from behind the black curtain of his glasses.

"Did you pay?" he says, and Jack nods.

"I did. Nice place," he says, and he thinks again of Kyle and Joey when they were little, remembers them swinging on a homemade swing, bright red, their legs pumping them higher and higher, Margie in the doorway, her hands cupped around her mouth. Thinks of the baby. He hands Kyle the key. "I like the tree in front," he says. "When you were a kid, there was this tree in our front yard. . . ."

"Yeah," Kyle says. He smiles. "Yeah. I remember. Thanks," he says, "for this." He holds up the key, sticks it inside his wallet.

"So where'd you get it?"

"What?" Kyle says. He slips the wallet into the back pocket of his jeans.

"The wad of bills?"

Kyle shrugs. He stares at the parking lot, or possibly the street, Jack can't tell which.

"I liked Celia," Kyle says. "I didn't kill her. She was nice. She was a good teacher."

"Go on."

"I needed to get out of where I was living. I needed to get Maryanne out of there. That crappy—"

"Rosie's Rooms."

"Yeah." Kyle looks at him. "How'd you know?"

279

"Your mom," Jack says. "She mentioned it."

"When? I didn't know you guys were even talking."

"We keep in touch. More so lately."

"She didn't tell me."

"Well, that's . . ." He doesn't finish. There's no point, really. It's par for the course. That's Margie, hoarding information, meting it out when it suits her. She still hasn't called him back. "So you had to get Maryanne out of where you guys were living."

"Yeah. I kept trying to find work. Every day I was out looking for something. Maryanne had a job, but she— I knew she wouldn't be there much longer. She was pregnant, so I knew we might not even be able to afford Rosie's Rooms. We might be out on the street."

Jack bites his tongue.

"I applied for every job I could find. I tried places that weren't even advertising, where they didn't even have signs in the windows, but there was nothing."

"So you . . . ?"

"So nothing. I just kept trying. Maryanne was so sure. 'You'll find something,' she was always telling me. 'Just keep looking.' Like that would change anything. I did, though. I kept looking. I was desperate. I was grabbing at straws."

Jack doesn't move. He looks out over the parking lot. He barely breathes. What Kyle says now could end him— both of them, really. How can he put his son away for murder if it comes to that? Then again, how can he not?

"So this one day," Kyle says, "it changed everything. I was walking out with Celia. Mrs. S, we called her. It was late. The class was late getting out. 'Want a ride?' she says, and I told her sure. She said she'd drop me off in town. She seemed really distracted. She kept looking in her phone. Even when we were in the car—all the time she was driving, she kept looking in her phone. I figured she was hoping to hear from the guy who used to wait for her after class sometimes—that guy you asked me about. He'd stopped coming a few weeks before. At least I hadn't seen him in the hall."

"Did you see him anywhere else?" Jack says. "Ever?"

"No." He scratches his head. "Never. Only there."

"Anyone else ever out there waiting for her?"

"Nope. Only that guy, and only him a few times. Four or five times, maybe."

"Okay," Jack says. "So you were in her car."

"She stopped at a liquor store. 'I'll just be a second,' she said. 'It's been a rough day.' And she disappeared inside. She was in there a long time. I figured she was checking her cell again before she got in line. Anyway, I was bored. I opened her glove compartment. Not for any reason, really. I was just . . . curious, I guess, to see if she had anything interesting, weed or anything. Her registration was in there, and I glanced at it. And then, just as I was closing the glove compartment, I see this withdrawal slip for five thousand dollars. No money, just the slip, but it was dated that day. That morning. Nine fifty-six." He stops. He looks up at the windows and then back at the door, at the parking lot, everywhere but at Jack.

"Go on."

"I had to get Maryanne out of that dump. Out of Rosie's. It wasn't safe. It wasn't a safe place. I kept thinking about the car registration. I kept seeing Mrs. S's address in my head. The next time I closed my eyes, it was all there, like it was printed on my eyelids."

Jack doesn't move.

"I decided to rip her off," Kyle says. "I decided to break into her house and take her money if it was still there. Not all of it—just enough to get us out of Rosie's. I'd pay her back. I would've paid her back. It was all I could think to do. I was desperate."

Then why the hell didn't you call me? Jack wants to say. Or move in with your mother? He stares at his hands as Kyle lights a cigarette.

"I walked up there from the bus. When I got close to her house, I put on a pair of gloves I bought at the drugstore. I was sure Mrs. S would be in class, but her car was still in the driveway. I figured she was running late. I decided to wait and look around her house for the money when she left. I knew she wouldn't carry it with her. She'd hide it somewhere inside, in a book, under her mattress, somewhere simple."

He stops. He doesn't look at Jack; he looks back toward the hospital. "I snuck up near the side of the house to see about the window. It was fairly low. It wasn't locked. I knew it would be easy to climb through. I didn't see Mrs. S, though. I thought it was weird she was still there. She wasn't ever late for class. Not on the nights I went anyway. I just stood there for a couple minutes, trying to decide what to do."

"What about the dog?" Jack says. He bites his lips.

"It was inside. In the house. It was barking like crazy, but not at me. There was something else going on that I couldn't see. I crouched down in the hedges between their yard and their next-door neighbors' to wait for her to leave. There was something wrong, though.

"I heard Mrs. S yell something from the back of the house—from the kitchen, I guess—and then a second later she screamed, 'What are you—' And then there's this racket, a crash, and the dog's still barking like crazy, and I move backward into the yard next door and I hide. Fuck, I'm thinking. All I want to do at that point is get out of there, and I wait for two, three minutes, maybe."

"What time was this?"

Kyle shrugs. "I don't know. I was so . . . It was way after seven, though. I know that. Her class starts—started—at seven, and I'd timed it so she'd . . . Anyway, the next thing I know, the front door opens, real slow, real quiet, and I see somebody come out of the house and take off. A second later I see the dog shoot out and run down the street."

"Was it a man or a woman you saw leave?" Jack says.

Kyle shrugs. "It was really foggy, hazy, plus it was starting to get dark. Plus, whoever it was wore a hoodie."

"Damn." Jack sits back on the bench. "Height? Build?"

"Hard to say." Kyle closes his eyes. "I'm not sure about either the height or the build. Medium, maybe. Whoever it was was bent over, huddled up, so I couldn't really tell. Dark gray hoodie, sneakers, I think."

"Where'd he—she?—go?"

"There was another little street across from Mrs. S's—a side street or something. Whoever it was went down there."

"They get in a car?"

"Yeah. I think I might've heard a car starting up. I can't remember. It was all so . . ." Kyle shakes his head. He looks away from the windows and stares at his sneakers, shabby and worn through at the toes. "I waited," he says, and Jack moves closer to hear him. "I made sure they were gone, and I went in through the window. She was lying there." Kyle stops, he chokes. "Mrs. S. She was just lying there near the door. There was blood underneath her, pooled up under her head."

"So what'd you— Did you try to save her? Yell for help? Do anything at all?"

Kyle shakes his head. Tears trickle down his cheeks. "I got on my hands and knees, to help her—to check her pulse, shake her, to do something—and then this car pulled up in the driveway. Her husband, maybe. I saw this vase lying beside her head. She was just . . . God, she was . . ."

"Then what?"

"Her purse was there, opened up on the floor, like whoever bashed her head in was looking for something. The money, I was thinking—somebody robbed her. It was there, though. In a bank envelope. Right in plain sight. I grabbed it. I didn't even think. I stuck it in my pocket, and I got the hell out."

"Out the window?"

"Yeah."

"You still had on the gloves?"

Kyle nods.

"Anything else you remember?"

Kyle shakes his head. "No."

They don't speak for a few minutes. They look off in different directions, avoid each other. Finally Jack clears his throat. "Look, Kyle." He'd bought these super-dark glasses to block the sun, to block out the world sometimes, but right now he's doubly glad they're as dark as they are. It's all there, Jack has always thought—it's all right there in the eyes, what you're thinking, and what he's thinking now is that even if his son is telling the truth, he'll have one hell of a time selling it.

"Wait!"

Jack looks up. "What?"

"Lavender," Kyle says. "It smelled like lavender."

"What did?"

"The living room. Around the body. It smelled like this lavender body oil that Maryanne wears. And alcohol. Rubbing alcohol."

285

"That makes sense," Jack says. "Alcohol erases finger-prints." Dana mentioned an odor, too, during her first interview. He also remembers seeing a pack of antiseptic wipes on her coffee table when he returned the cat. Lavender fucking wipes.

"So am I under arrest?" Kyle fiddles with his ring, the high-school ring that Jack gave Margie the money to buy the boy when he was starting his senior year, before Joey died, before their lives were turned upside down and graduating from high school was no longer a priority.

"Where's the money?" Jack wants to believe him. Even more, he wants to think he'd believe him even if Kyle weren't his son. He wants to believe his story's almost plausible. "Was that what I just handed over to . . . ?"

Kyle hesitates, and then he reaches into his pocket, pulls out his wallet. "Here's what's left," he says. "But yeah. The rest of it went for the apartment." He hands Jack a wad of bills. "I wonder what Mrs. S was gonna do with all this money."

Jack shakes his head. "So how about your lucky charm?"

"I guess it fell out while I was climbing in the window. He reaches back inside his pocket. He pulls out the ele-phant and sets it on the bench between them. "Sorry," he says, "but I needed it."

"How'd you . . . ?"

"I grabbed it off the table that day in the restaurant when I knocked all the stuff over—in all the confusion.

"You're good," Jack says, "but I wish you weren't. What'd you need it for?"

"For Maryanne," he says. "For luck."

"She all right? And the baby? Jeez, kid. Don't keep me in suspense here. Tell me about the—"

Kyle smiles. "Maryanne's fine. She's great. She and our son. They're both—" He stands up. "You're a grandpa," he says, and Jack gets to his feet. He starts to shake Kyle's hand, but he hugs him instead, feels a smile spreading across his face, feels the bones of his son's ribs. After a minute he loosens his grip, but he doesn't let go all the way. He wants to hold on, to expunge all those years he wasn't there for either of his boys. He wants to keep Kyle safe, make sure he doesn't go to jail, make sure he hasn't just produced another fatherless child, continued a tradition Jack started over twenty years before.

"Are you bringing me in?" Kyle says. He takes a couple steps toward the hospital, and Jack gives him a long look, shakes his head.

"Call me, though, if you think of anything else. Anything. And don't go far." And Kyle smiles again, says he's not likely to do that, not now that he has a baby, then takes off running toward the glass doors.

"Hey!" Jack yells across the widening distance. "Congratulations, Kyle!"

"You, too!" Kyle calls, running. His sneakers fly over the grass.

"When do I get to meet him?" Jack calls through his

cupped hands, but Kyle just keeps running. He doesn't even turn around. He shoots his arm out in a little wave behind him.

Jack might be crazy. He might be so blinded by this paternal gush that he can't think straight, but he believes his son. He'll add in what's missing of Celia's money, make Kyle pay him back over time. He'll tell Ronald it turned up, that it was hidden somewhere—behind a mirror in one of the bedrooms or stuck in the back of a picture frame.

The sun is high in the sky. Somewhere on the OB ward, his grandson lies swaddled in a blue blanket while Margie blows kisses toward the hard plastic of a nursery bassinet. Somewhere in another place, through a maze of hallways, Dana gathers all the strength she can to open her eyes and look around, taking in the slick white blandness of her temporary world, while outside on a prickly concrete bench, the new addition to a small square of stones and spindly grass, Jack sits staring into space, oblivious to the tears collecting at the corners of his eyes. He mumbles a quick thank-you to God, to the universe, to Maryanne and Kyle, promises them all he'll raise the child himself before he'll let him feel alone.

# 33

Until today Dana's had no visitors—only Jamie schlepping down from Boston the night she arrived here. She asked them not to let Peter past the desk in this new place where he's insisted she come, making arrangements for her transfer as soon as she was stabilized.

"Please," she'd begged a nurse on the crowded ward that first morning when they told her she was leaving. "I'd rather be here at Bellevue. I'd rather be in the city. I'm a student," she'd told her, "at NYU, so it's so much easier if I stay here. And my boyfriend—it's only here he can get in. It's only when I'm here I get to see him."

The nurse had smiled and patted Dana's hand, placating, patronizing. "I'm so sorry," she said. "Your husband wants you closer to home."

"I haven't got a husband. It's my mother," Dana told her. The nurse hadn't answered; she'd only bestowed a final round of hand patting and taken off down the hall.

Dana understands now it was Peter who had her transferred. She remembers her mother's death; she knows she isn't studying at NYU. She knows that the Poet is no longer in her life, at Bellevue or anywhere else. She understands that she imagined his visit.

"Dana?"

Several patients sit near her in the open area, watching a television set that blares in a corner. Three tables surrounded by straight-backed chairs are scattered here and there around the room, and three large couches skirt its edges. She sits at one of the tables, staring at the TV on the wall. She looks up at her visitor. "Detective Moss?"

"You know who I am?"

"Of course," she says.

"How are you?"

"Better," she says. Her tongue is thick. It comes out "buttr." She takes a gulp of bottled water.

"I brought you something." He reaches into his pocket and pulls out the St. Christopher medal from her visor. "I brought you a chain, too," he says. "I left it at the nurses' station."

"Thanks," she says again. "Afraid I might strangle myself with St. Christopher?"

Jack looks down at his shoes. Well, it's . . . you know . . . the rules."

She smiles. She looks at him. "Were you here before?"

"No," he says. "Not here."

"Bellevue?"

He nods.

She studies her fingers. She looks at his face. For a minute or two, she doesn't say anything. "It was you," she whispers.

"Yes. You seemed to think— I got the feeling anyway

that you thought I was someone else."

"Yes," she says. "You look like him."

"Him?"

"Someone I used to know. A poet I used to know."

Jack nods. "Do you mind if I sit down? Ask you some questions?"

"No," she says. "Not at all. I remember I was supposed to come to your office—"

"Right." Jack pulls out the straight-backed chair across from hers. It makes a scraping sound against the shiny linoleum. "Your husband," Jack says, and he sees Dana tense up. "Did you know before the day of her murder that he was involved with Celia?"

She sighs. "No. Had no idea."

"But you know now."

"Yes."

"When did you begin to think so?"

"The day she died."

"Did she tell you this?"

"Well," Dana says, "not really. But she was so . . . eager—to out him."

"With his secretary, you mean?"

"Yes. The Tart, I called her. I didn't know her name—a moot point now, of course."

"Not really." He leans toward her. "You're wrong about the picture. Ronald was in my office the day after . . . the day you came here. He said he'd found another phone—that his wife had a second phone or something

291

and he found it under the mat in his car."

Dana yawns. "So?"

"So he told me the photo you'd asked him about the other night was actually in that phone—this second phone."

"He's lying," she says. "He's just trying to—"

"I know he's lying. He's a really bad liar. But the thing is, at some point he did see the picture. He described it in detail. It sounded like the one you saw. In fact, he asked me to tell you. Thought it might help."

"It would have." Dana's eyes drift up to the TV. "For a while there, I thought if I could find that photo— I thought if I could only know it was real, I'd be all right." She smiles. "God. The things I did to find that stupid cell phone."

She is riveted to the TV set, the clapping hands of the judges. Jack clears his throat, rattles some papers. "Dana?"

She nods, but her attention is across the room on the nonsense on TV.

"If you thought Celia was involved with your husband, how did that make you feel?"

"Angry," she says. With some reluctance she turns away from the TV and looks at Jack. "Furious." And then he's the one who looks away; he has to. There's something so unexpected there behind her eyes, something so intense it could consume her, consume everything around her. For a moment it's as if the funny, fragile-seeming Dana's been replaced by a stranger, an angry, chilling entity he doesn't know and doesn't want to know.

Jack clicks his pen point in and out a couple times, looks down at his notes. "When I saw you at Bellevue," he says, "you told me you'd done something awful. At the time I figured it was just the drugs they'd given you or—"

"A delusion, Detective?" Her voice is cold. Clearer suddenly, but icy. Hard as glass.

He shrugs. "You tell me."

She turns her eyes back to the wall, to the panel, to a young man singing on a stage. She takes a breath and lets it out slowly. She fiddles with her robe. On TV a young black man croons into a microphone.

"You were angry."

"Yeah. She'd just shown me a photo of my husband with another woman. Yeah. I was pissed."

"At her or the woman?"

"At the Tart, I guess. Mostly."

"So you're saying this was a shoot-the-messenger sort of thing?"

"I guess I'm saying— Look, I don't know what I'm saying. I'm really tired. Do you mind if we do this some other time?" Dana's eyes drift back to the television. Her hands drift to her lap.

"Yes." Jack reaches over and taps her on the arm. "I do mind, Dana. This is important."

She sighs. "What? What do you want?"

"Were you angry at Celia or at the Tart?"

"The Tart. At first. But I also knew. Thought. Later . . . I knew." Her eyelids droop. She is no longer watching TV. Her body slumps forward slightly.

"Dana. What did you know later?"

Her eyebrows knot together. Her eyelids droop again. On TV the panelists hold up cardboard squares with nines and eights. The crowd applauds. A nurse heads toward them, across the shiny floor, her sneakers squeaking on the linoleum.

"Dana?"

"Everything's sort of mudd— Why would Celia care so much that Peter was with the Tart? I mean, why would she be following him around, snapping pictures of him in her phone unless they were . . . No. I knew they were lovers, or whatever. I knew they were fucking." The last word comes out louder, angry, reverberating in the sudden quiet of the dayroom. The nurse stops at their table.

"Time to go," she says. "Visiting hours are over."

"Oh," Dana says, pushing herself away from the straight-backed chair.

"What about the notes?" Jack stands up with her. "When you're out, I'd like to look at both of them."

"They're here," she says. "I have them here." Another nurse squeaks toward them in her rubber-soled shoes.

Dana shrugs. "Maybe Peter's right. Maybe I wrote them. I'm not sure. One was in my house, and one was in my car."

"Was it your handwriting?"

"No," she says, "not really. But then I wasn't doing anything the way I usually do—not for the past few weeks. And my handwriting changed once before, years ago, when I . . . in college when I . . ."

"So you have them here in the hospital?"

"Yes," she says. "They're in my purse, but they took my stuff." With some difficulty she gets to her feet, wobbling for a few seconds. "Thanks," she says, and her voice is wobbly, too, but softer than before. Dana again and not that strange, unnerving— "Thanks for St. Christopher."

## 34

Jack waits at the locked door to be let out, to head back to his car in the parking lot, to leave this place of cheery walls and frightened, medicated faces. When he turns around, the nurse is already heading toward a few stragglers still visiting, to a brother or a lover or a friend still sitting on a hopeful couch with flower-printed cushions, staring up at panelists waiting to judge another singer.

He turns to look back, but Dana doesn't reappear. He has her there in his head, that image of her, the sad, slow way she moved down the hall away from him, away from the dayroom with its large windows, its squares of thinning sunlight forming patches on the floor and glancing off the sides of things—tables and chairs and sofas. He has that image of her seared across his brain. But there's the other image, too, the rage he saw behind her eyes. He wonders where Peter is. With his other girlfriend, the one that's still alive? The Tart, as Dana called her? Does he come here at all now that he's moved his wife away from the city, away from where she begged Jack that first night to let her stay? Bastard, he thinks, and as if his thoughts have conjured Peter from thin air, the man is suddenly in front of him, so close that Jack nearly knocks him down as he plows through the outside door. "Oh," he says. "Damn. Sorry. Didn't see you there."

Peter brushes off his jacket. "What was that, Detective?"

"Nothing. I've just been to see your wife."

Peter nods. "And how is she?"

"I wouldn't really know about all that," Jack says.

"Was she able to help you in your pursuit of— What exactly is it you're pursuing now, Detective Moss? Still working on the Steinhauser death?"

"It's a murder case," he says. "Your wife and I had an appointment, but obviously she wasn't able to make it down to my office."

"I see." Peter elbows past. "Don't question Dana again without a lawyer."

"Would that be you, Catrell?"

Peter glances at the door. "No, Detective. It would not. In the first place, I'm not a criminal lawyer, I'm a tax attorney, and anyway, I'm not certain I could—"

"Could what?"

Peter shrugs. He glances at Jack and looks him in the eye for a second, maybe two. "Help her," he says. "I'm not convinced—" He stops, clears his throat. "I'm a tax attorney," he says again. "Let's just leave it at that."

\*

When Jack reaches his car, his phone beeps on the front

seat, and he picks it up. three new messages. The first is Ann. She's coming by, she says, in the morning. There are a few more odds and ends she's left at the house, plus there are several things they need to discuss—finances, her new place—practical things. It's not an especially personal message, but at least it's her voice. He listens to it several times before he saves it.

The next one is the prosecutor's office. Lenora. Professional again. Cool as a cucumber.

"If you have a minute," she says, "we need to talk about your case. I can see you anytime tomorrow as long as it's before noon or after two. Let me know." She leaves a number—her cell phone, he imagines. It's different from the office number he already has.

And then there's a message from Kyle. The baby's sick, he says. A fever. Maryanne was ill when she delivered, and they're keeping him in NICU a few more days for observation. "I'm right here," Kyle says at the end of the message, his voice barely more than a whisper. "I'm not going anywhere, but I haven't told Maryanne anything. Or Margie. Please, Jack," he says, and his voice sounds strange. Worried. "I really need to be with Maryanne. At least until we know the baby's all right. . . ." The message trails off. Kyle. Jesus.

He slides his seat back and stares out the windshield at the sky. Soon it will be dark. Soon a nurse will squeak across the dayroom floor and take her place behind a window where she'll administer the meds. Soon Dana will stand in line, stretch out her palm for pills—two, three pills. Soon her eyes will glaze over and she'll shuffle back to her room and lie across her bed, St. Christopher on the table next to her, the secrets of the night she tried to fly locked up inside her head. Something about Dana touches him, but things aren't looking good for her as far as the case goes. He calls down to the precinct to get a warrant started for the notes in her bag. No doubt Lenora wants an update.

# 35

Dana can see Peter through the glass. She sees him as she eats her dinner, some kind of poached fish she can't identify, bland and watery, a soggy sprout of broccoli, a slice of buttered toast. She sips her water, setting the plate back on the tray to be picked up later. They've let her eat in her room because of Peter's being there to visit. He stands, shifting from one foot to the other in the small space on the other side of the glass.

She sighs. She runs a brush through the tangles in her hair and walks into the bathroom, where she splashes water from the tap across her face. It's the first time she's seen her husband since her transfer here, since the night she was picked up, since he came to see her in the cubicle at Bellevue sometime before dawn. She bends over to put on the new slippers he left at the nurses' station along with several other items in her overnight bag. Small fake jewels glitter up from the yarn toes. She sighs again and walks out to the lobby to perch on the flowered couch across from the TV.

When Peter sits down beside her, Dana feels a slight shifting of things, a subtle upheaval of her insides. She wants to leave, to run away. She's learned here in this place to listen to her body, to her heart. These last days in D Ward, she's been learning to stop, to examine and absorb what makes her feel this way or that before it overwhelms her, before she reacts. She works on these things now, in group, in sessions with Dr. Ghea, these coping mechanisms.

She is one of three women in group therapy; the other four members are men. Sometimes Dr. Ghea is the facilitator, but usually it's Dr. Tim. One of the other women—Tina, she calls herself, although Dana wonders if she's made up the name, if she has another, truer, less flamboyant name she uses in the outside world—is a suicide like Dana. As they say Dana is, even though she's tried to tell them countless times how wrong they are, how different she is from them, that she had only meant to fly. "This is what I would have done if I'd wanted to die," she said one afternoon in group. She'd flung her wrist in the air, shown them her scar, let them gaze at the white, puckered line between her veins.

"Why?" one of the men said. Riley, she thinks it was. "Obviously it didn't work too well the first time."

She didn't answer. She didn't have an answer. She lowered her arm and thought about what he said and wondered if "flying" might not be another word for "death."

The walls of the group therapy room are filled with paintings that remind her in some way of Spot—wild, unfettered paintings. Swirling. Colorful. Many of them were done by patients on D Ward, some while they were locked up here, when they stood drugged and weaving at their easels, painting from memory or from photographs brought in by family members or friends or lovers. Painting what they saw around them, the cacophony of sights and sounds, the slippery blur of things, the colors far too elaborate, too daunting, too dazzling to be real, or painting what they saw through the window—the barren bleak of winter, the dead, denuded trees, the brown wisps of grass. She's begun to paint in art-therapy class. Her paintings aren't the thick, pulsating, van Gogh works she'd planned to do; they're watery and small, but she likes them.

She sees herself in Tina. She hears her thoughts in Tina's words, and in Melinda's as well—heavy, sad Melinda with her stockings pulled up past her knees, her long sleeves covering her arms but not erasing the random, unexpected glimpse of cigarette burns and pencil stabs, of toenail-scissor cuts in the soft white skin of her thigh.

And every once in a great while, Dana sees herself in one of the four men—so different from one another, so vastly different from her, and yet in some ways they are all the same, dancing on the precipice, the face in Munch's Scream, sharing the bright and naked thing that burns like a meteor inside them, that makes them want to sing, or die or, Dana finally understands, to fly.

\*

"Hello, Peter." She doesn't look away; she's no longer afraid that he can see inside her brain, and even if he could, she no longer cares. She takes a deep breath; she looks him in the eye.

"Hey," he says. "How're they treating you?"

"Fine."

"Good. That's—"

"How is Jamie? Have you talked with . . . ?"

Peter nods. "He's coming back next weekend. Do you remember him being here?"

"Of course," she says, recalling Jamie's face, the frightened look in his eyes, the earnest way he peered at her as she lay on the tiny bed in her cell-like room. She shudders. She wishes she could have stopped him from coming, from seeing her that way, that she could have spared him that at least.

Peter nods again. he sets his briefcase on the floor beside the couch.

"Why am I here?"

"You tried to jump off the George Washington Bridge," Peter says. "We've been over this."

"No. I mean, why am I here instead of Bellevue?"

Peter shrugs. "It's a better hospital."

"No," she says. "Bellevue is top-notch. This one's just closer."

"Yes." He shrugs again. "Yeah. It's closer. A lot closer to the house."

"More convenient for you."

303

"I suppose it is, Dana." He sighs.

"We talked," she says, "that first night. I begged you not to make me leave there."

"You were crazy."

"I am crazy."

"No," he says. "You were crazy. Because I had you transferred here, you are now not crazy."

"God," she says. "You are such a lawyer." Part of her is almost happy to be sitting on a flowery couch, arguing with her husband. It seems like such a normal, sane thing to do.

"So what was our illustrious detective doing here?"

"Moss?"

"Is there another one I don't know about?"

"Probably," she says, sparring, but her heart's not really in it.

"Why was he here?"

"He brought me my St. Christopher medal," she says. "It was in the car."

"Why?"

"I asked him to," she says, and Peter nods. He looks up at the TV screen.

"So how's Spot?"

"Obnoxious and feral and probably much less happy than he would be in the wilds from which you plucked him."

"The wilds of the exit ramp?"

"Well," he says. "No. He's fine. He needs a girlfriend."

"Projection," she says, and Peter studies the muffled reality show on TV. "I guess the better question would be why are you here?"

He turns to her. He looks at her, finally, in the bright lights of the visiting area. "Because, Dana, you are my wife. I'm your husband. This is what wives and husbands do."

Dana shrinks into the cushions of the sofa and stares up at the TV. "It's not enough," she says.

Peter shrugs. "This is the best I can do."

"I know. But it's not enough."

"Things change," he says. "People change."

"I know."

"I fixed the toilet," Peter says, "so when we flush it, we won't have to jiggle the—"

"Great. Thanks." There's something just there at the edge of Dana's mind, a small red stone, glinting in the mud-puddly memories of the day Celia died.

"So how're you feeling?"

"Fine," she says.

There's so little to say. With Jamie gone there is really almost nothing to say. Here, in the hospital, in the vivid, honest lights, here where they can't hide, they fumble toward each other. The TV gleams out from the corner; an audience laughs at a pouting woman in a sundress, and they stare at it because there's really nothing left to say.

She concentrates on the small red thing, letting the voices fill the space between them. She nods when Peter says good-bye, forces a smile when he kisses her on the cheek, and when he leaves, she walks him to the door, waits with him for the nurse to open it. All the while, though, she focuses on the shiny red, the sound of a toilet flushing, the way she'd bolted from Celia's living room and stumbled down the hall to pee the afternoon her neighbor died. She remembers leaning against the counter, struggling to stay upright, so drunk that it was like moving through a dream, so drunk she'd forgotten. It's only now, with Peter's talk of broken toilets, that she remembers the shiny red dot that caught her eye in the neat gray landscape of Celia's master bath. She remembers recognizing, even through the fog surrounding her that afternoon, her husband's tie clip, with its ruby stone, the one she gave him for his birthday three years before.

She slumps down on the sofa in the dayroom, wishing Peter hadn't come, wishing he hadn't chosen now of all times to be a good husband and fix the fucking toilet. If he hadn't, she might never have remembered what she saw in Celia's bathroom—Celia's lover's tie clip. Did Peter's carelessness push her over the edge that day? Did his flagrant disregard for her gift propel her back to Celia's living room in a murderous rage? Is she being stitched together here on D Ward only to remember on some bland morning or sleepless night that she staggered down the hallway to the living room and bashed her adulterous neighbor in the head?

# 36

It promises to be an interesting day. Breakfast with Lenora and dinner with Ann. Jack dressed carefully that morning. He took his time shaving, scrounging around for the aftershave Ann gave him last Christmas and splashing it liberally across his face. "You are one handsome devil," he declared, grinning at his reflection and thinking of Ann's self-help CD, the one she popped in sometimes when they went on trips together. "Empower yourself every morning," it said. "Look in the mirror and empower yourself with words."

He was surprised when the first assistant prosecutor suggested breakfast. He'd planned to stop by her office at some point that morning, but when he called her from the hospital parking lot to set up a time, she'd taken him totally off guard.

"Could you get away for a quick bite?" she'd wondered. "That way I can kill two birds with one stone. No offense, Detective."

"None taken. Where and when?"

She hadn't missed a beat. "Downtown? E.Claire's? Ten-thirty?" she'd suggested, and he'd said fine. He'd see her there. Got online and Googled the place for directions.

The warrant and the notes from Dana's purse were on his desk when he came in that morning. He's made copies of the notes, but the ones he's looking at are the originals, all tiny curlicues and peacock blue ink like they used in grammar school, snapping the cartridges in place, the fountain pens with the fine points, the girls with their peacock blue notes—the "Meet me after class," the love notes crumpled in pants pockets. The color brings him back to Catholic school, to memories of Sister Gina pacing at the blackboard, her habit flying out behind her like tail feathers on a crow. He glances at his watch.

*

He'd never even heard of E.Claire's, which turns out to be a bustling little spot, the kind of place Ann loves and that makes him feel as if he has three heads. It's overflowing with women and fussy-looking men, clustered near the door and trickling out to the sidewalk. Sweat covers his forehead. Everyone is bouncy and fresh, everyone is sleeveless and fluffy, like a collection of Persian cats. He is suddenly heavy and dark in his work clothes. He tucks his badge inside a pocket and runs his hand through his hair. The air is thick with odors, with colliding scents of pricey perfumes and aftershaves.

He looks around. Everyone is thin, like Dana, like dancers. He stares at the door, and the crowd parts slightly, letting him through, like ballerinas at rehearsal, all pointed toes and muscled calves. Probably they are dancers, Jack decides.

"One?" A woman in pink tights and a busily patterned tunic stands beside him. She moves in close to him, listening for his response in the chatter of voices. Eiffel Tower earrings dangle from her ears.

"I'm meeting someone!" he yells, and she turns away, graceful in her high heels. Her hair is long and straight; she pirouettes across the lobby, distributes menus to a gaggle of arriving teenage girls.

"Jack?" Lenora appears beside the hostess, coming toward him in the crowd. Her breasts press against a white lace blouse. Her face is flawless and young. "We're over here in back." The woman in the tunic smiles at Jack, and he picks his way through the crowd and shakes Lenora's outstretched hand.

"Good of you to come," she says.

"Glad to do it," Jack lies. They walk single file between the rows of myriad tables overflowing with bubbly laughter, with tan, thin arms and smoothies, with glitter-studded fingernails and powdered-sugar crepes.

Theirs is a small table toward the rear of the large restaurant. Lenora sits down first, her back to the kitchen. She faces the front door, the tunic-clad hostess, the arriving diners. Jack sits across from her and glances at the menu— small, he thinks, considering all this fluff and fanfare. He glances down, lets his eyes shift quickly over the names, the silliness, the Scandalous Scrambles and Devilish Duos.

A waitress appears with her pad, and Lenora orders the Turnover Trio, which appears to be two over-easy eggs and a croissant.

"Ready?"

Jack clears his throat. "I'll have the same," he says. "And a coffee. Black."

"I'll have a coffee, too," Lenora says, "with cream. No sugar, though."

"So a Jumpin' Jack Black and a Sweet Cream Dream, no shug?"

Lenora nods. The waitress scurries back to the kitchen.

"Quite a place."

"It's a little much," Lenora says, "but the service is super fast."

Jack sets his glasses on the table beside his discarded menu, sticks a linen napkin on his lap. "So what is it you wanted to know?"

"Your case," she says. "I need an update."

He avoids her eyes. He studies the list of coffees on the back of the menu.

"What turned up on the prints?"

"Interesting," Jack says, "especially the ones we got from the bedroom."

"How so?"

"Hers were there, of course, the Steinhauser woman's." He reaches for his croissant, delivered, along with their eggs and coffee, amid a clatter of silverware and festive, brightly colored plates. "Her husband's prints were all over the place, and then there were a shitload of other prints, presumably her lover's. Sorry," he says. "Pardon my French. Pun intended," he adds, gesturing around E.Claire's

Lenora smiles. She bends in close over the table, and her boobs are vastly visible. "I'd like to see the labs on those prints," she says. "Could you bring them by my office in the morning?"

"Yeah. Sure." Jack looks across the table at Lenora's nearly untouched plate. "Aren't you hungry?"

"Always." She smiles. "Trying to watch my weight." She nibbles her croissant. "What's your take on the neighbor?"

"Which one?"

"Dana Catrell. She was on the news . . . what? A week ago, maybe? I don't know if you saw—"

"I didn't." Jack reaches for his napkin and knocks it under his chair, where it sticks to the brightly colored rug. "Her husband phoned me, though," he says, nudging the napkin with his shoe. "He'd fallen asleep and— He wanted me to call around, to see what was what."

"And what exactly was what?"

"They carted her off to Bellevue."

"Terrible." Lenora shakes her head. "Is she still the last one to see the Steinhauser woman alive?"

"So far." He doesn't mention Dana returning to the scene of the crime. He's got no real proof, but almost certainly she wrote the notes he's subpoenaed from the hospital. He'll have forensics check on that later, and if he's right, he'll bring Lenora up to speed.

"According to her husband, she has a history of mental illness. Very volatile at times. And she certainly had means and opportunity to kill her neighbor if she were so inclined."

"Motive?"

Lenora shrugs. "Could be something trivial if this woman was disturbed enough to jump off the GW Bridge in the middle of a traffic jam." She pokes at her eggs, takes a small bite. "Or it could have just . . . happened. If something Steinhauser said or did really set her off, she could have picked up the nearest thing and . . ." She shrugs again. "Then again, it's possible she had no involvement whatsoever. Her suicide attempt made me look at her, that's all. Guilt can make people do weird things. So . . . really tragic. All of it."

"I agree." Jack glances at the napkin he's now managed to bump completely out of reach beneath the table. "There are a few very strong suspects," he says. "Two of the neighbors, the dead woman's husband, who wouldn't know the truth if it jumped up and bit him. Not enough hard evidence to make an arrest at this point." Jack is holding his cards close. He always does, but on this case, with his own son in the mix—with all the media hype it's generated and Lenora watching him like a hawk, grandstanding, using the case to further her career—there's no telling what she might trot over to the press. Too much too soon would blow the case sky-high. "I know you want to wrap this up, but I need to be absolutely sure. Don't want to jump the gun here."

"Of course." She places her hand on his arm. "And I respect you for that. I really do. You're a straight-arrow dude, Jack. Wouldn't have you any other way." She smiles, rummages in her bag.

"Let me get this." He reaches for his wallet.

"Don't be silly. You can get it next time." She touches his arm again, lets it linger for a few seconds. "I invited you." She laughs. She has a nice laugh. Robust, he'll tell Rob when he arrives back at work two hours late. She's got a robust laugh, when his partner comes in with remnants of a Krispy Kreme dotting his upper lip, teasing Jack about E.Claire's and savoring every word, every detail. Lenora signs the tab, and Jack slides it to the edge of the table as she grabs her compact to repair her lipstick, asks him if she's gorgeous yet.

"Definitely," he tells her. "You are definitely that."

And she is. She's every man's dream, but maybe that's the problem, Jack sometimes thinks, times like this, when she lets him know that if he came on to her she wouldn't run away. Maybe she's a little too perfect. A little too ambitious and self-serving. Still, there was that openness the other day, the things she said about her past, that vulnerability. Maybe Ann was right. He's attracted to lost souls.

They stand up, squeeze past each other in the tiny space. He'll wait a little longer before he shares what he knows. For everybody's sake. He wipes his hands on the napkin he's grabbed from the table, and it smells faintly of Lenora, of her perfume or soap or whatever it is about her that makes him think of flowers.

They part ways in the lobby. "Jack?" she says when they're several yards apart. He stops in the doorway. The light hits her, silhouettes her. "See you in my office in the morning."

"Sure thing." He turns and pushes his way out the door, afraid she'll see through him if he lingers there in the bright sunshine streaming in the windows. He hasn't even mentioned Kyle. There's no part of what his son told him he can possibly relay without exposing Kyle as a petty thief who broke into the victim's house and stole her money while she lay dying on the floor and who insists he didn't murder her. Right, he thinks. Like that'll fly.

He takes a deep breath. Tomorrow he'll get a warrant to go back to the Steinhausers' one last time. He'll examine every piece of lint and dandruff, looking for something to exonerate his son.

## 37

It's after nine by the time Jack gets home. He falls across the bed in the room Ann pretty much stripped that morning. The few "odds and ends" she mentioned picking up involved random, unexpected items—the quilt from Bloomingdale's, the table from her grandmother's farm, the antique lamp beside the bed. Even her pillow is gone. The room is little more now than a bed and a dresser. His dresser—she's taken hers. She had to hire a moving company, she said at dinner, and he wonders how much this will cost him, this spousal burglary. He closes his eyes against the barrenness of the room, of the house, of their ended marriage.

A car alarm goes off somewhere on the next block, and he rouses himself, strips off his clothes, and falls back into bed. At least she didn't take the sheets. Still, tomorrow is another day, so who knows what other "odds and ends" she'll return for, stuffing pieces of their defunct marriage into bags and satchels, tossing them onto the backseat of her car.

Molly nudges his hand with her nose, and Jack moves over on the spreadless bed, taps the mattress beside him. "Come on up, girl," he says, but Molly only sighs, sprawling loudly on the floor on the other side of the room. "Do you miss Ann?" Jack says, and Molly's tail thumps hard against the rug.

The dinner had not gone well. Ann was polite but distant, and Jack wonders if she has a boyfriend. She was distracted, checking her watch from time to time throughout the evening.

"Plans?" he'd said. "Don't let me keep you," but she'd said no. She was worried about the job she was starting in the morning, she'd told him, worried about not sleeping, yada, yada, yada. He wants to believe her, but even if there was a lover waiting for her back at the new apartment Jack has not yet seen, it's Ann's business. It's no longer his. He closes his eyes against the pallor of her face, the pallor of the dinner, the pallor of the bedroom he now barely recognizes, and falls into a fitful, dreamless sleep.

When he wakes up, it's still dark. He rolls over and glances at the clock on the floor beside the bed. Five forty-five. Summer ended quickly this year, with no warning, with no transition. One day it was hot, the next night it was fifty-three degrees. He's glad for it, for the ending of a swampy summer, but now he's freezing, lying on the bed with only thin blue sheets to stave off the cold. He pulls them tighter around him, shifts his feet under the dog's warm body, remembers Molly climbing up on the mattress sometime in the night, when the cold fell down outside and came in through the leaky walls. At dinner, Ann mentioned two or three times how much she missed

Molly, but Jack will draw the line there. She can take the clocks and bedspreads and antique lamps. He was a lousy husband—he'll eat his crow without complaint—but he won't give up the dog.

He drags himself out of bed and into the shower, emerging red-faced, with his hair standing up like grass on an unmowed lawn. He turns on the coffeemaker and plops a piece of bread into the toaster, scrambles three eggs, and cooks them in the one skillet Ann forgot to take. He smiles, remembering the morning before, the gaunt bodies clustered in the aisles of E.Claire's, the raised eyebrows and silver-polished nails, Lenora's lacy top, her breasts.

His phone has a missed call. kyle. Eight fifty-six. Where was he then? he wonders. Still with Ann? Still trying to get her to come home with him? He'd pulled out all the stops at the very last, before they left the table, before they reached their separate cars and drove off in different directions. He'd nearly begged her. "Please," he said. "Let's just try it for a week. Hell, two, three days, even," but she shook her head.

"We did," she said. "We tried it for twenty years. At least I did. You—not so much." Or was he driving home by then, the radio blaring in the cushioned front seat of the Crown Vic? "Bye, Bye, Blackbird." An appropriate choice, he'd thought at the time, turning it up louder and louder, singing along. "Pack up all my cares and woes . . ."

He punches in his code, listens to the message: "Hello, Dad." Kyle's voice is low, quiet, as if he's in a crowded room, as if it's a secret, what he's telling Jack. He clears his throat. His voice wobbles on the word "Dad," making it sound like two syllables. "I remembered something else about that night," he said. "I'd forgotten, but when I closed my eyes a minute ago, it was there. Perfectly clear. Whoever it was at Celia's house got into a late-model sedan on the side street that day. It was dark—black or gray. Blue, maybe. The light was really bad. But that's what I saw. I'm sure of that. Hope it helps." There's a pause, and then he says, "Bye."

Bye, bye, blackbird.

Jack calls Lon Nguyen from his desk at work and asks him to get back to him as soon as he can. "You can come down to the office," he says, "or just call me. The sooner the better." He leaves his numbers. "Listen . . ." Jack glances at his watch. "I'll be on your street," he says. "I'm leaving now, so you can catch me on my cell."

He stops in the break room and grabs a doughnut. Rob lounges against a chair, waiting for the coffeemaker in the corner. It whines and belches, eventually spitting out some of the worst coffee in the world. Like mud, everyone says—mostly the women in the office—tsk-tsking, smiling. Men, they say, since it's usually Rob who makes it. Rob or Jack.

"Doughnuts, Jack? You? What would Ann say?" Rob winks at a rookie officer across the room.

"Oh, I don't know," Jack says, munching. "'Eat doughnuts and die'?"

"Huh?"

318

"Or maybe, 'I'm cleaning you out. I want the dog, and by the way go screw yourself and eat doughnuts and die'?"

"Oh." Rob stops chewing. "Hey, I'm really sorry, Jack."

"Yeah. Well . . ." Jack grabs a second doughnut, wraps it in a napkin. "One for the road," he says.

"I can come along if you want," Rob says. "We caught a break on the missing-teen case. A tip. Found her in Manhattan with her abusive boyfriend. She's back home now, but who knows for how long."

"Great," Jack says. "You did good, partner. Rumor has it you've got another case coming your way. Homicide over on Broadway in the wee hours. We'll both be working it as soon as I wrap things up on Ashby Lane."

"Yeah. Saw that one when I came in this morning." Rob's phone rings, a marching ring. Lenora, Rob mouths, and Jack waves him away. "I'm okay with this," he says.

*

He pulls up in the driveway. It's a sunny day. Cool. A breeze. Leaves are starting to turn color on the trees in front, and the yard looks different. Ronald will be crazed, Jack thinks, when he sees the disarray. Jack opens the car door and steps out onto the lawn, once green and pristine, once rife with Ronald's roses and hydrangeas, but overgrown now with weeds that choke through the grass and climb across the flower beds. He likes it better this way, with the sidewalk a tangle of uneven monkey grass, the spent hydrangeas with blue flower petals strewn across the lawn, an odd, sporadic carpet, weeds oozing through cracks in the sidewalk. It looks almost Old World, he thinks. Ironically, it looks more like a home now that no one lives here. And maybe never will—not Ronald anyway. Not from what he's said.

Jack steps carefully around the yellow tape and lets himself inside the front door, standing in the middle of the living room for a minute or two. The air is cool; dust drifts and dances in sunlight streaming through the picture window near the couch. The room is still and frozen. There is no life here, no energy. He looks around, but he sees nothing he hasn't seen before.

Because of what his son said, Jack heads for the back of the house—to the kitchen, where, if Kyle told him the truth, Celia first called out to the person coming in the front door, the person who ultimately left her to die. Dishes still stand in the dishwasher. A couple of sponges are stacked near the sink. An empty bottle of sangria is on the counter, but no blood. Not a drop of blood.

He glances at the floor. With the exception of the muddy footprints, it's still clean, despite the time that's passed, despite the boots and heels and stockings that have no doubt walked through or stood, as Jack now stands, staring at a room made all the more eerie by its neat, uncluttered state, a movie set devoid of actors.

His phone rings. "Moss here." Ann used to tell him he sounded silly answering his phone like that. Like a sitcom cop, she used to say, like a caricature.

"This is Lon Nguyen."

"Oh," he says. "Hey."

Lon Nguyen breathes into the phone.

"Listen." Jack leans against the counter under the window. "When I drove up here the other day, I noticed you guys have a Neighborhood Watch sign a couple streets over."

"Yes."

"Does that go for your street, too?"

"Go for?"

"Are you part of the Neighborhood Watch group?"

"Yes," Nguyen says. "I am block captain."

"Great," Jack says. "That's great—these watch groups really cut down on crime."

"Not always," Lon Nguyen says.

"No." Jack squats down on his haunches. "Not always. So that day," he says, "the day Celia Steinhauser died."

"Yes."

"Did you happen to notice a car that evening?"

"We are in suburbs," Nguyen says. "Lotta cars."

"Right. But did you happen to notice one that isn't usually here?"

"No," Nguyen says. "But there was a car. . . ." His voice drifts off.

"Yeah? What kind of car?"

"I don't know that."

"Color?"

321

"Not sure. It was dark."

"What? The car or the . . . ?"

"Both."

"What size car was it?"

"Don't know. Medium size, maybe. It was not the car that seem strange," Nguyen says. "It was where it was park. Not in a driveway."

"Where?" Jack focuses on a small, clear speck beneath the stove. With all his heart, he hopes Nguyen verifies what Kyle said. With all his heart, he hopes his son told him the truth.

"On side street," Nguyen says.

"Which side street?"

"The one across from Celia's house."

"When?"

"Not sure, but it was drive away before the ambulance come. I did not see the driver."

"At all?"

"No. Not at all."

"Why didn't you tell me this before?"

"I forget," Nguyen says. "I forget until just now you ask me."

"Thanks." Jack stands up. "You guys keep up that Neighborhood Watch group."

"Yes," Nguyen says. "That is all you want to say?"

"Yeah. That's all. Thanks again," Jack says. "You've been a huge help."

He slides down to the floor, letting his back rest against

322

the counter. He thinks about phoning Kyle. Dad, he'd called him. Jack smiles. That was a keeper. He'd saved the message in his voice mail.

He glances back down at the one tiny piece of litter, and even that's underneath the stove. He wouldn't have seen it if he hadn't squatted down exactly where he did, if he hadn't gotten the phone call the second he did, but even so, they should have found it in the sweep. He frowns. These guys . . . It's not the first time this team has screwed up. He pulls a pair of latex gloves from his back pocket and puts them on, walks across the room, and kneels down to reach under the stove. He isn't sure what it is at first. He rests it in the center of his palm and squints at the jagged thing. A piece of fingernail.

He stands up very carefully so it doesn't roll into a vent. He holds it at arm's length, as if it might reach up and scratch him. He doesn't take his eyes off it as he grabs an evidence bag out of his pocket and seals the thing inside.

*

Jack sits in the parking lot downtown and stares at the bagged bit of fingernail. He knows it probably means nothing at all, except that at some point Celia broke a nail while she was cooking. She might have jammed it against a cupboard door or the can opener. Possibly she snagged it on a pot holder or a loose thread on her apron. Or maybe the dog passed through and when she reached to

323

grab him, she got her finger caught in his collar. The possibilities are endless, and he's okay with whatever turns up, as long as the nail's not his son's. He radios down to the station to tell Rob he'll be in after lunch. "I'm meeting with Lenora," he tells him, "at the prosecutor's office."

"Lucky you," Rob says.

"Right." Jack runs his palms across his hair, remembers the way her hand felt resting on his arm the day before—warmer than he would have thought. He straightens the collar of his shirt and steps out into the parking lot.

*

"Detective Moss?" Lenora stands in the doorway to the lobby. She looks much more professional than she did at E.Claire's the day before. She's wearing a black skirt that drifts against her legs when she turns to beckon him inside and a gray blouse with lace around the wrists.

"Thanks," he tells the secretary who's summoned her, and he immediately trips over the doorsill. Damn, he thinks. Get a grip.

"Have a seat." Lenora's all business this morning. Or mostly business. She smiles. "I enjoyed our brunch," she says, "although I don't imagine that E.Claire's is exactly your cup of tea. No pun intended."

"It was fine. Great croissants."

"I'd guess you're more of a diner kinda guy," Lenora says. She sits down at her desk.

"Yeah," he says. "Harry's Diner, actually, not too far from here. How'd you guess?"

She laughs, and her throat curves inward as she tilts her head back. Her skin is smooth and bright in the sunlight coming through the window. "I didn't get to be an assistant prosecutor without being somewhat observant. Actually, I've seen the place. It isn't far from here."

"Right." He fumbles with the file on his lap. Its contents embarrass him as he sits here in Lenora's office, her perfume heavy in the room. It all seems intimate, suddenly, these prints of Peter's on his neighbor's bed—this affair, captured now on the papers in Jack's hands. He watches Lenora's finger trail along the edges of the proof, the particulars, the moans and movements, the lust and sweat and laughter, the knotted hair and tangled legs, the passion, documented in the contents of the envelope that rests across his knees.

"Are these the prints from the lab?"

"Yep." Jack hands her the file. "The neighbor's prints are all over the dead woman's bed."

"Where?" she says.

"The headboard. The footboard, the bedposts, both of them, the— Hell, the rails . . ."

"Whose?"

"Peter Catrell's."

She doesn't say anything. Her face is blank, expressionless, but it registers in her body, the impact of his words, the shock of them, and he wonders if she, too, was duped by this asshole, if she's disappointed that he isn't who she'd thought.

"You know him, right?"

"I do." She smiles. "Through his clients. A couple of his clients. We worked on the Whitman case together a while back, and then a few weeks ago we—"

"Does this surprise you? His prints on the dead woman's bed?"

Her lips curve up on one side in a little half smile. "Not really. He— Let's just say I'm not all that surprised." She peruses the report. "What a jerk," she says. "Is he a suspect?"

"Yes."

"Motive?"

Jack shrugs. "Celia was an inconvenience? A threat to his marriage? There's an incriminating picture somewhere."

"Enlighten me."

"It's complicated."

"I've got time," Lenora says.

"I don't," Jack says. "But in a nutshell, the Steinhauser woman snapped a photo of Catrell in a compromising situation with his secretary." He stands up, walks across to her desk, where Lenora now sits, the print results spread out in front of her.

"I see." She sticks the prints back in the envelope. "Jack?"

"Yes?"

"Can you spare me a couple more minutes?"

"Sure. What can I do you for?"

"The prosecutor . . . well, Frank Gillan—you know Frank—is retiring," she says. "Did he tell you?"

"Not really." He slumps back in the chair beside Lenora's desk. "He mentioned he— Jeez. I really hate to hear that," he says, and he is. "Frank's been prosecutor forever. It sure won't be the same around here without him."

Lenora nods. "I'm in line for his position. I didn't say anything before because I wanted to be absolutely sure he was going to . . . to actually . . ." She lowers her voice as if her desk is bugged and she's divulging state secrets. "That's why I've been so— You know my thoughts on Frank, on his policy. On his attitude. What's happened to the crime rates in the county. I'd like a chance to change that, turn things around."

She clears her throat. She twirls the ends of her bangs around her index finger. "I'm having breakfast with the judge and his entourage next Wednesday. I'm hoping he'll put in a good word for me when he sees the governor."

"Take him to E.Claire's and it's in the bag," Jack says.

"That's the plan! I've even made reservations."

"You're seriously taking him there?"

She nods. "An early lunch, before the noontime rush. Great service. It's festive. Reasonable. Plus, they'll pull some tables together for a group."

"Well," he says, starting to stand, "best of luck to you."

"Wait," she says, and Jack sits down again. "I guess

327

Rob told you the missing girl turned up."

"Right."

"Have you considered making an arrest in the Stein-hauser case?"

"Yes," Jack says. He looks her in the eyes.

"The Catrell woman?"

He nods.

"Maybe you should do it sooner rather than later."

"Why is that? You know something I don't?"

"No," she says. "No I— Actually, wrapping up this murder case on Ashby Lane would make me a far more viable candidate for Frank's position. I don't mean to put pressure on you. . . ."

And yet you are. He bites his tongue, nods. "And Dana Catrell being arrested?"

"Is a good first step."

"Are you ordering me to . . . ?"

"No," she says, "of course not. But I am suggesting you make an arrest in this case soon."

"Right," he says. "Mrs. Catrell is locked up at the moment, won't be going anywhere right now. By the way, the husband? Peter Catrell? You're his alibi—one of them anyway—for the day Celia was killed."

She frowns. "That could be. We did meet," she says. "The three of us. Frank was there, too. I've forgotten the exact date. I'll have to check my calendar. The only thing is, our meeting was early in the afternoon. I don't see how he can get much mileage out of that. She stands up, extends the envelope to Jack. "Thanks," she says. "I appreciate your bringing this down. If we do a business meal again, we'll make it at Harry's. Promise."

*

At the lab he asks for the tech he knows. "George," he says. "I need to talk to him."

"He's in the back." A receptionist he's never seen before blows a small bubble with her gum, inhales it inside her mouth and chews with a series of loud snaps.

"I'll wait." Jack sits down on one of the hard plastic chairs. It's bare-bones here. There's not even a window in the tiny lobby. It's a very different world from Lenora's.

"Sure." She snaps some more as she leafs through a thick stack of papers.

"You guys backed up?" he says.

"Always." The gum smacks again, forming itself into a medium-size, mud-colored bubble. "He'll be out in a sec." Her words implode into a round of vociferous smacking as the door opens and George steps into the tiny room. She bounces out of her seat and stretches, tosses her gum into a nearby wastebasket. "Taking my lunch." Her voice is whiny and young.

"I need a favor," Jack says when the secretary's gone, when her cell-phone chat is fading down the hall. The elevator dongs its arrival, and her voice disappears behind its closing doors. "She new?"

329

"Yeah." George smiles. "She's a temp. Jeez."

"Can you get these run through quick?"

"What? For DNA?"

"Yeah."

"Steinhauser case?"

Jack nods. "I'll owe you one."

"One what?" George says. He takes the bag.

"One whatever."

"Make it one receptionist and you're in," he says. "Preferably someone over twelve and not a gum chewer."

"Sure."

"Really?"

"Of course really," Jack says. He crosses his fingers and stands up. "See if there's a match with what we've already got."

"I'll see what I can do for you, call in some favors—"

"Thanks," he says. "And, George? Keep this on the down low, will you?"

"Sure," he says, and disappears inside as Jack heads out the door to the hall. On the elevator the voice of George's temp chirps between floors, and Jack thinks of Lenora walking in her heels across her office, gorgeous and driven.

# 38

Dana sits on the small bed in the tiny room that's been her home for the past several days. She's packed her things—a few items of clothing, a toothbrush, a smattering of toiletries, three novels she hasn't touched. She's tucked them back inside the suitcase that Peter delivered on her second day here, dropping it at the nurses' station as she drifted between worlds, as she struggled to return to earth. She'd refused to see him.

She sits on the bed beside her bag and stares at the wall.

He is in the lobby. She's asked the small nurse with the kind face to keep him there. "I need a minute," Dana told her. "I need to say my good-byes." It isn't true, actually. She's said her good-byes. She said them last night, what few she had to say.

She's given out her number to exactly three patients—a man and two women from her group. She'd like to hear from them, she's said. She'd love to get a coffee, catch up when they're discharged, but she knows they won't call. She knows she'll never hear from them again, and if she does by some random stroke of luck or coincidence see them on the street or in a coffee shop or standing on the platform waiting for a train, she knows they'll look the other way, as if they've never met, as if she were a stranger on the street. It won't be anything personal. And then again, it will be as personal as tearing tiny pieces from their hearts or brains or lungs. "What happens in Vegas," she mumbles, and she runs her fingers through her hair and sighs.

She doesn't really want to see her husband. She certainly doesn't want him there inside her room, undoing all her progress with his sneers and caustic comments—with his presence. She doesn't want him picking up her suitcase or opening the car door. She wants him gone. Without her pills to calm her, she would drive to the ends of the earth to get away from him. Now, though, serene and medicated, she only wants to lie across her bed and think about the things she's recently experienced, the expanding and contracting of the world around her, the way her filters seemed to thin and finally disappear, allowing time and space to flow out of sync. She wants the quiet and the solitude to absorb the knowledge that her husband no longer loves her. A painful thought at best, but for Dana, who has leaned on Peter many times throughout their married life, turned to him in the wee hours to pour into his drowsy ear all the bizarre images her sleeplessness has conjured, it is particularly disconcerting, especially now. For Dana, time is running short. The drugs have done their tricks, they've successfully turned down the volume in her head, but they've not erased the events of the past weeks.

She knows Jack Moss will soon arrest her. She saw it in his eyes when he brought her St. Christopher medal to the hospital. When they sat together in the dayroom, she heard it in the slight hesitation, the slight catch in his voice. She knew it from the way he watched her walking to her room, unaware she could see him reflected in the glass of the nurses' window, the way he shook his head just once, folding his arms across his chest. She can't afford to loll. Lolling is for other people or for her in another time or place. Right now she'll smile and nod, the model patient, gracious and grateful. Unctuous, if need be. But once she's out of here, she'll go back off the meds that dull her, drain her energy, rein in her thoughts. She needs every ounce of drive and strength and courage she can gather. Just for a little while. She's had a chance to rest; she's had a chance to pull herself together, to regroup, as her mother used to say. She's Scotch-taped back together, and she prays the tape will hold.

The photo in the phone seemed so trivial only days before. When Moss told her what Ronald said, she'd barely blinked. It was the meds, she thinks now; they made everything seem trivial, which she supposes is the point. But now, with this great gift that Ronald handed her—risking his own neck, casting himself as the jealous husband in this eerie play—she understands. She's begun to trust her perceptions, her memory. Almost. There are still the giant gaps that afternoon, and even though she knows that her memory was accurate up to a point, it doesn't mean she didn't kill Celia. It only means she had a damn good motive.

She doesn't judge Peter. She prefers not to judge him. It isn't that he slept with her friend. It isn't that he hid it from her—that and the mysterious Tart. She now sees he played with her perceptions, marched her toward insanity, deliberately or not. But it isn't even these things, these obvious and concrete things she hates him for. It's not the thises and thats of it all—the things she can point to and say, Here is what you've done. You see? And this! And this! It's what she can't point to, what she can't exactly see, what she knows lurks there behind the shapes and textures of things. It's the gray he's made of her life that makes her hate him. It isn't what Peter has given or not given her over the years, it's what he's taken away—the colors, and music, and tastes—the sweetness of things, the bright orbs he's molded and fiddled into small, dull blobs.

She understands about the Poet, that he is a symbol. She knows now it isn't the Poet she longs for but the girl who loved him. And her sessions with Dr. Ghea have allowed her to recognize that for people like her there is a slight, thin space between happiness and madness, that it's a tightrope walk, a balance between light and dark, that she will struggle all her life to find it and, once she does, to keep it.

She feels raw; she feels vulnerable and fragile, une-quipped to deal with Celia's death, sitting like a boulder in the pit of her stomach. In her sessions she only vaguely alluded to it—Celia was her neighbor, she'd told Dr. Ghea. It haunts her sometimes, what happened. It's so blurry, that whole afternoon. She'd had too much to drink, she'd once said, laughing, folding and unfolding her hands, and that really bothers her. She'd looked up at Dr. Ghea through her lashes, giving her a chance to question, to interrogate, to probe, but Dr. Ghea had only jotted something down on a pad of paper and asked her why she'd chosen the word "haunted."

"Well, really, I could have killed her, for all I know," Dana had said, but she laughed when she said it, standing up and crossing the room to pour herself a glass of water.

Dr. Ghea hadn't brought it up again, and neither had Dana. They talked about other, less depressing things. They talked about hopeful, happy things, and she was glad the moment passed unnoticed, the hinted-at confession, but she was disappointed, too, that her demons weren't discerned, her ghosts, her guilt, that Dr. Ghea didn't pull a bottle from her coat and shake out a pill to fix her.

She stands up. She grabs her suitcase and without a backward glance walks to the lobby where Peter waits to take her home. She'll stick to her plan. She won't let anger for her husband clog her thoughts, won't let her rage derail her.

# 39

Even though she's called ahead, Jack Moss seems slightly surprised to see Dana standing there in his doorway. "Moss?"

"Come in. Come in," he says, standing up and ushering her in with his arm. He sounds too jovial for the occasion, and Dana stares down at her feet planted on the cruddy, scratched-up floor. Her father used to talk that way, sitting at his desk at the office or in the little cubbyhole room upstairs where he did his writing. "Come in the house," he used to say, swiveling his chair around to face the door. "Come in the house," even though she was either already in the house or at his office downtown, impossibly far away from the house. He always said it loudly, animatedly, as if he were throwing a party and was afraid no one would come. It was a warning, her father's overzealous welcomes. They told her he would soon be coming home later at night—that the house would smell like spilled gin, that tiny bits of poems would soon be scattered on the rug.

"Thanks for seeing me." She doesn't sit down. Without her dulling meds, she's restless once again, bright and scattered, walking a thin, slight line.

"Sure." Jack thumbs through piles of papers on his desk and pulls out a manila envelope. "Copies," it says. "Dana Catrell." "Have a seat. I can let you look at these, but I can't let you take them out of here in case they become part of—"

"It's okay. I just wanted to have a quick—"

"Right," he says. "Sit. Take a load off. These are copies. The originals are on file."

She nods. She sits down. She scrutinizes the notes, the handwriting, commits them to memory, so she can bring them back, sharp as tacks, when she closes her eyes.

"So you doing all right?"

"Fine," she says. "Never better."

"Yeah?"

"No. God."

"How's Spot?"

"Fine," she says.

"So why'd you want these back?"

She shrugs. "I feel naked without them?"

Jack looks up and smiles. Still, Dana knows he's planning to arrest her. She almost doesn't care at this point, but there's Jamie to consider. For Jamie she'll do everything she can to stay on top of things. "I kept them in an envelope," Dana says. "A self-addressed envelope. Stamped and everything."

He nods. "I saw that."

"I figured it was a federal offense to tamper with the U.S. mail, so people might be less apt to—"

"Clever," Jack says, but he's no longer smiling.

"Paranoid."

Jack shrugs. "Semantics. Mind if I ask you a couple questions while you're here?"

"Would it matter?"

"Probably not." He shoots her a little fake smile. "Did you ever figure out who the Tart is?"

"No. I was sure it was Peter's secretary, but I met her at his office yesterday when I went down to work out some things with him. Her name is Ms. Bradley. Very sweet, very demure, but not the woman in the photo. Not the Tart."

"You sure? People can change, you know. Be completely different when they aren't at work."

Dana fidgets with her purse strap. "She did seem annoyingly . . . present or something."

"Not all that hard to change the way they look either."

"And she had on this . . ."

"This what?"

"This wide, knitted turquoise thing that went around her head; I remarked on it. It was really pretty. It did totally hide her hair, though."

"So, really, she could have been Peter's . . ."

She shrugs. "For all I know, the Tart's one of his clients. But I've got other priorities at the moment. And Peter's . . ."

"Peter's what?"

"Gone," she says.

"You okay with that?" This is a surprise.

338

"As okay as I am with anything."

Jack plays with a little mound of paper clips on his desk.

"Well." She stands up, eases herself toward the hall. "Time, she fleets." Another unexpected little father saying.

"Dana?"

"I know," she says, turning around in the doorway. "I won't go far."

"Good," he says. "But I was going to say I'm really glad to see you out and about."

She wonders, hurrying down the hallway, if Jack Moss questioned her about the Tart because he's worried she might go crazy jealous and kill again. A serial husband's-girlfriends killer. He's hiding something, trying to hide something. He didn't look her in the eye—he barely even looked up—kept screwing around with his paper clips. It's probably those notes she practically forced on him. He must think she wrote them, as does Peter. As I'm beginning to, she realizes. Again she thinks of Jamie, driving in from Boston to visit her, having to see his mother shuffling through a locked-down psych ward, slurring her words, clutching a St. Christopher medal, and she's determined to keep herself together for his sake.

She sits in her front seat and looks around the parking lot. It's nearly dark, much later than she'd thought. It was an impulse, coming here to get the notes back from Moss. Now she wishes she'd never mentioned the damn things.

What was she thinking? Now they're sitting in a file somewhere waiting to be used against her, to prove she's some lunatic scrawling nasty, cryptic threats to herself in peacock blue—an off-putting color she doesn't normally use, doesn't even remember buying the expensive fountain pen. She found it in the desk drawer by the door when she was searching for clues and figured it belonged to Peter or, more likely, one of his clients. And then she kept forgetting to ask him, even though she'd left it on the desk so she'd remember.

She sits for a moment watching the sunset rage orange across the sky. She wanted to see the notes again so she could compare them to the bits of manuscript she managed to save from her manic episode in college. She has a houseful of things she's written over the years; she was, after all, an English major back at NYU. But these threatening notes were different. They were written in such tiny script, in a way she's never written anything besides the manuscript back then, the hundreds of pages she covered in smaller and smaller writing as the weeks wore on, as her madness gathered, clotting like a cancer in her brain.

Once home, when she'd first gotten off her flattening, uninspiring meds, she'd gone through every room, through every box, looking for the manuscript, phoning Peter in the end; she was that determined. And he had helped, ironically, remembered where he'd put the things she'd gathered from her mother's house after she died, during the distressing forage through her childhood things.

She starts the car. The sun slides down behind a stretch of grass. She pulls out of the parking lot and trails her hand in a small and unseen wave toward Jack's office.

Come in the house, she thinks again. Come in the house. Her father's voice, an echo down the tunnel of her ear. A warning. Rain pounds, thuds like tiny stones against the windshield, tugs down the night like a great dark curtain. Her foot is heavy on the gas. The Toyota slides a little on the slippery street, and Dana eases up, braking slightly. The car behind her shines its lights too brightly on the narrow road, and Dana speeds up again, but only a little, only enough to satisfy whoever it is riding her tail—far too close for these wet roads. In the rearview mirror, she sees only the bright lights, the high beams, blinding her. She glances in the side mirror, sees an outline, a sedan. The lights are too bright, the night too dark and rainy; she can't see a face. "Slow down!" she shouts, her voice a pin drop in the fury of the rain, the brilliance of the lights. She glares into the rearview mirror as the car speeds up again, comes within an inch of the Toyota, and she thinks about the notes: "You will pay for what you did—"

The car behind her honks, not quite a blare but more than a tap, and then it speeds up again, looming like a meteor in the rearview mirror. Dana rams her foot down on the gas, stares at the headlights as they grow larger, brighter, in the mirror. She feels a knock as the car behind her hits the Toyota—a tiny ping—or is it the storm? A branch? Dana's heart pounds; the rain falls in sheets. She looks back at the road, but it's too late. Lightning flashes, a quick, blinding zigzag that illuminates a tree branch directly in front of her, and Dana turns the wheel, a violent twist as her tires skid and slip, losing their grip, moving the Toyota in a wild sideways movement. She turns the wheel sharply back the other way, but she continues sliding, hydroplaning on the rain-slicked road. The Toyota bumps off the asphalt, grazing branches and a small clump of hedges, coming to an abrupt and jarring stop in a shallow ditch beside the road. Dana is vaguely aware of a car above her on the highway, screeching to a stop. Its headlights veer back onto the road as a second car pulls up behind it. A couple sloshes from their car toward her in the pouring rain, and Dana makes two phone calls, one to AAA and one to Jack Moss.

The couple insists on waiting. It isn't safe out here, they tell her, not for a woman alone. Not on a night like this. Not these days with all the crime. They wait inside their car, the windshield wipers swishing back and forth. Their headlights are a beacon for the tow truck, a comfort in the dark, wet night.

Jack picks up on the second ring. "Moss here," he says.

"I think someone just tried to kill me," Dana says. Her teeth chatter even though it isn't really cold.

"Who is this?"

"Dana Catrell. I didn't know who to—"

"Where are you?" A chair squeaks, and she pictures him at his desk, working late, his nice, dry office.

342

"In a ditch," Dana says. "But I'm fine. I mean, I'm not hurt or anything. The tow truck's on its way."

"What happened?" The chair squeaks again.

"I was . . . like I said. Someone forced me off the road. It was raining, and the road was slick, and this car just kept getting closer and closer, and there was this tiny whack on the bumper, just a thump, and then there was this branch right in front of me, and I . . . swerved, I guess, to miss it, and my car slid off the road."

"And the car behind you?"

"Well," she says. "They stopped, and then this other car pulled over and the first car took off."

"Did you report it?"

"I am reporting it," she says. "I'm reporting it to you."

She hears a shuffling sort of sound. She wonders if he's fidgeting with his papers or possibly the mound of paper clips. "Can you describe the car?"

"No," she says. "It was raining really hard, and the brights were shining in my rearview mirror."

"Listen," he says, and the chair is a screech in the background. "Maybe they were just obnoxious people trying to get around you. Trying to get you to speed up."

"Right."

"Is it possible? Considering what's been happening lately, you might be a little on edge."

"Yeah," she says. "Well, I should go. The tow truck is here."

"Wait," he says. "We need to talk again, Dana."

"When?" She gathers her things and pushes at the car door, and her heart leaps and dives behind her ribs. "My dance card's pretty full these days."

"Tomorrow."

"Should I go on in or ask for you at the—"

"No. I won't be in the office in the morning. I'll be out in the field. How about you meet me at E.Claire's. You know it?"

"Yes," she says. "Why there?"

"Why not there?"

"Umm. It's kind of like going down the rabbit hole for tea?"

"Oh." He clears his throat.

"Hey," she says, waving to the tow-truck driver as he backs in toward the Toyota. "It's fine. It's great. They've got killer cinnamon rolls. Or—um— What time?"

"Ten-thirty."

Dana sits for a moment longer in her car, watching as the tow truck rumbles back and forth, positioning itself for rescue. A crazy day, an insane day; it plays across her mind like a bad movie. In spite of what Moss said, she knows that what happened on the road was not just chance. Her senses are once more alert—far more so, she thinks, than his. Her intuition is sparking back on track. The driver of the car behind her was no stranger, no random driver anxious to make it to a dinner date on time. There was something in the jarring way the car came up behind her, tapped her bumper, the angry lights on high beam, blinding her, the horn puncturing the sounds of rain and night like a snarl. Something very personal. No. This time Jack Moss is wrong.

The tow-truck driver clamps a giant hook to the Toyota. The Good Samaritans wave heartily out their car window and pull onto the road as Dana yells thank-yous to them over the steady rumbling of the truck. She stands on the puddly embankment, clutching her purse, shivering. Her hands are clammy and wet. Her heart pounds. Out of the corner of her eye, she sees a car pull over to the side of the road, but when she turns to look, there's nothing there.

# 40

When Dana arrives at the restaurant downtown, Jack Moss is already waiting on the sidewalk outside E.Claire's, an odd choice, she thinks again, watching him fidget as he glances up and down the street through glasses so dark they make her think of Ray Charles. She chose her outfit carefully—a flowing skirt and a fitted top with a flowered obi belt, strappy sandals with heels. Even though she's apprehensive about why he's asked to meet with her, she's almost glad to be here. There's something solid about Jack Moss, something portlike in the endless storm of Celia's death. Dana's hair is loose and curly with the cool of autumn, the dampness of impending, ubiquitous rain. A sudden gust of wind comes up from the water, and she ducks her head, grits her teeth against the cold.

He stands outside the front door. It's less crowded this morning than it often is at E.Claire's. He stands awkwardly, checking his phone, amid thin, trim would-be nibblers, as Dana hesitates, catching her breath. She is invisible in the ocean of fluttery arms and scarves as she crosses the sidewalk.

"Moss?"

"Hi," he says. "Wow! You look— I didn't recognize you at first. Nice cummerbund."

"We women call them belts." She smiles. "But thanks, Moss."

"Ready?"

"Sure," she says, "I'm ready if you are," and together they pick their way through the trendy, flowery clientele of E.Claire's.

She orders more than she will ever eat. She orders Canadian bacon and scrambled eggs and an elaborate cinnamon roll. "Scram-Ham Shazam," she announces to the waitress, "and a cup of green tea." She notices that Jack Moss orders very quietly. He mumbles his order, and the waitress bends over slightly. "What?" she says. "Could you repeat that? It's so noisy in—" And Jack barks out the silliness, the Jumpin' Jack Black, the stack of Banan-Appeal pancakes.

"So what do you think about the notes?"

"I guess the question is whether you wrote them. I mean, do you think you wrote them?"

"I guess I could have, but I don't actually remember writing them. That's why I wanted to see them again. To compare them to something else I wrote once when I was at NYU. When I had a sort of nervous brea— I was writing a lot then, a manuscript, very tiny writing all over the pages. I found some of them—some I didn't throw out the window, actually—and I wanted to see if the writing was the same."

"Was it?"

Dana leans back in her chair and crosses her arms. "Well," she says, "it was hard to tell, but it didn't really look the same to me. Except for the size."

"I'd like a sample of your writing, too, if you wouldn't mind. I could send it to forensics to compare."

"Sure. Here." She hands him one of the scraps of paper from the bottom of her bag, one of the many names she's scrawled down.

He takes a slug of coffee the moment it arrives—the Jumpin' Jack Black—pockets the paper. "So who had access to your house?"

"Everyone," she says. "I had a brunch for the entire street."

"Wow!"

"I was a little manic." She shrugs. "I didn't know half the people who showed up. And I was stuck in the kitchen most of the time, so really anyone could have—"

"Any Scram-Ham Shazam involved?" he asks as their breakfast arrives with a loud clatter.

"Nope. Badly scrambled eggs and cold fake sausage."

"Yum," Jack says, starting in on his pancakes. "Maybe one of the neighbors was really pissed off about the food?"

"Possibly. Except there's the other note I found on the front seat of my car. I mean, the food wasn't that bad!"

"Right."

"But I don't lock it."

"Your car? How come?"

Dana shrugs. "I really love it here," she says. "The ambience."

"Really?"

"Well," she says. "No. Actually it's a bit fluffy. I have to say. It's really not my cup of tea. I was surprised you like it so much."

"Me? I hate it! Thought you'd like it."

"Really?"

"Well." Jack wipes his mouth with a floral napkin. "No. I guess not. It was the first place that popped into my head."

"Which in itself says volumes about you."

"Right."

"Do you come here often with your . . . with your wife?"

He shakes his head, chewing. "I was here once with someone from the prosecutor's office, and I felt like I was trapped inside an off-off-Broadway play I didn't quite get." He leans over the table. "I thought the customers were from some dance company in the area."

Dana laughs. "I can see that."

"Actually, my wife left me," Jack says, but just then there's a flurry of activity behind him, a crowd coming in the door. He turns around to look; everyone turns around to look. The hostess strides across the lobby with menus, obsequious and apologetic. "Right this way, Your Honor. So sorry you had to wait," even though he hadn't. Or she—Dana can't see who the hostess is talking to. She

349

seats the party quickly at three or four tables pulled together, and they make quite a stir in the already noisy restaurant. Their raised voices, the rustling of garments, the clinking of water glasses being filled and dispensed, and occasional shrieks of laughter momentarily eclipse the clatter of the other diners.

"Cotillion?" Dana takes another bite of her toast. "Prom? Or maybe they're actual dancers from one of the—"

"Naw," Moss says. "They're not skinny enough. I think that's Judge Warner and his little flock of— Oh! There's Lenora."

"Lenora?"

"Lenora White. The first assistant prosecutor I told you about. The one who—"

"Oh, yes. The one because of whom we sit here feeling dowdy and overweight."

Jack laughs. "Me, maybe. You, not so much."

"No. You're wrong there. I think all non-anorexics might feel a little— Hey. Which one's Lenora?"

He turns around in his seat. "The second one from the far end. Left side of the table."

"You sure?"

Positive," he says. "Why?"

"She's not what I expected," Dana says. Her heart flutters and pounds. "Here, I mean. This isn't what I expected. It's her! She's Peter's Ta— She's the woman in Celia's phone!"

"You sure?" he says, but he doesn't sound surprised, and Dana knows this is why she's here, why he's suggested this of all unlikely places.

"Yes," she says. "I mean, the picture was kind of not clear, and her hair was totally different. Blond. Longer. Same face, though. Yeah. I'm sure."

Dana stares across the room as Lenora bends forward, her eyes wide behind glasses she wasn't wearing in the picture. She seems to be an all-business kind of person, so unlike what Dana had imagined, so unlike the depiction in the phone, with Peter drooling down her blouse. She looks professional this morning, here in E.Claire's in her pricey faux-suede olive suit, the black blouse peeking out beneath it.

They finish their breakfast, but it's different after Lenora's bustling entrance, less amusing now that Dana knows why they are here. It's heavier between them. The lightness is gone, the banter a flash in the pan. Sizzled. Fried. She ponders what it means, this Lenora White, first assistant prosecutor being Peter's Tart. She plays with the food still on her plate. "So, Moss. Am I under arrest or what?" Her mood has changed; the morning is suddenly drab and dull.

He tosses some bills onto the table. "Just wanted to hit base with you—that whole thing last night with your car and the notes and all . . ."

"That's it?"

"For now," he says. "Oh, and it gave me an excuse to come back to E.Claire's."

Dana stands up. "Let's go over there." She wants to see the woman up close. She wants to scrutinize the face that's made a mess of her entire life, ended her marriage. She wants to meet the Tart who slept with Peter, God knew how many times, who sniveled to him on the phone while he whispered in the bathroom, his voice bouncing off the tiled walls, who made him pull over to talk at rest stops all along the New England coast, his hand cupped around her stupid words, edging Dana into madness.

"What? Now?"

"Yeah. I can't not meet her after all that's happened," Dana says, and she starts across the crowded, sunlit room with Moss beside her, his shoulders hunched as if there is no place on earth he'd less like to be than here in this flower-dappled tearoom, wending his way to the Tart's table with her lover's wife. The aisles are narrow and bustling with waitresses and gorgeous people, among whom Lenora is definitely at home. She sits with diffidence at the judge's table. Her hands are folded on the tabletop, her attention riveted on whatever Judge Warner is saying, sputtering—shouting, nearly—at the other end of the table. Dana watches Jack reach out toward her, not without some trepidation.

"Hi," he says. He touches Lenora's fake-suede-covered shoulder.

"Jack!"

"Back for more," he says.

"In the mood for Turnover Trios, eh?" She glances at

Dana. "Hello," she says, and she extends her hand. "I'm Lenora White."

"Yes. I know," Dana says. "I'm Peter's wife. I've heard so much about you."

Lenora doesn't change her expression in the least, although her face goes ghostly white and pink blotches pop up on her neck. "Good things, I hope," she says.

"Let's just say I'm delighted to finally put a face with the . . . well, with the . . . um, rest." She sniffs. "Nice perfume."

"Excuse me?"

"Your perfume," Dana points out. "It's nice. Peter wears it sometimes."

Jack clears his throat. "Enjoy your breakfast," he says, nodding toward the judge. He lifts his hand in a little wave and backs away from the table. He steers Dana toward the door, his palm flat on her shoulder, where it remains until the hostess has nodded her good-bye and the heavy door has latched itself in place behind them.

They stand together on the sidewalk in front of E.Claire's. Dana pulls a Marlboro out of her bag and lights it.

"I didn't know you smoked."

"I don't," she says. "Not usually. I'm an emergency smoker."

"And this qualifies?"

"Totally."

Jack glances at the sky. "Looks like rain," he says,

although for once it's actually clear, with white clouds puffing across a sea of blue. Dana doesn't contradict him; she doesn't even look up.

"You knew," she says.

"Knew what?"

"Please," she says. "I'm not having problems with that part of my brain. You knew she was Peter's Tart. That's why you brought me here."

"I thought she might be."

"Why? Why are you doing this?"

"I'm sorry," Jack says. He takes a step toward her, but Dana backs away.

"You're really screwing with my head. So what do you want me to say? She's beautiful? And smart, I'm sure. And she can get through a meal at E.Claire's without a Xanax? Of course Peter would prefer her to me. What more could a guy want?"

"A lot more," Jack says. "Believe me. Sorry if having you run into her seemed like an ambush. I didn't want to mention it to you beforehand because I wanted your initial reaction. Didn't want to muddy the waters."

She takes a final puff and stubs her cigarette out on the sidewalk with the heel of her sandal. "No worries." She waves her hand in the air. "It added drama," she says. "Like dinner theater. What's E.Claire's without a little black humor thrown in? Anyway, I'm glad to see she's real. That she actually exists."

He laughs, but it sounds forced; it sounds like a cough.

"Listen," he says. "Can I drop you off at your house? I have the Crown Vic."

"No." She looks somewhere past him, over his shoulder toward the sky. "Thanks, though. I think I'll just—I don't know—stroll around for a while. Buy a gun. Shoot Lenora. Catch the bus back home." He doesn't answer. He looks uncomfortable. She wonders if he might believe her. "Seriously, I've got some things to do while I'm here, but I'll take a rain check on the ride."

"Rain check it is, then. And thanks, Dana. Thanks for meeting me. I'm sorry if I made you feel— I really didn't want to upset you," he says, and she waves her hand again in a nonsensical little motion. "I had a good time," he says, "in spite of everything."

"Me, too." Dana turns and walks down the sidewalk. She can feel him watching her until she disappears inside the crowds of people in suits and tweeds and heels and pantyhose and skinny jeans and all the squares of sidewalk separating them. When she reaches the corner, she turns around, and he's still standing in the same spot on the sidewalk. He raises his hand in a wave and leaves it there until she turns and starts across the street.

Jack is at work when he gets a call from the lab. The reports are back. Extremely interesting, according to George—can Jack come down that morning? He'll be away from his office, he says, in the afternoon, but he'll be there until twelve at least.

Jack drives in with more than a little apprehension. He wonders why George said what he did, presented the thing the way he did. He thinks he knows; he's nearly positive his hunch will pay off, but there's still the nagging doubt he's wrong that makes him take his time driving down to the lab. If the bit of nail is Kyle's, he'll have no choice but to arrest his own son. The thought makes him physically ill; his reaction is visceral. The baby—Joey, they named him—is still in the neonatal ICU, but thank God he's getting better every day, Kyle says, stronger. In fact, he told Jack the doctors think they can take him home today. Kyle has been there, camped out in the hospital every minute he isn't at his new job at the lumberyard. He can't go to jail. Jack can't separate him from his son, but it's too late now. He put things in motion when he dumped his little pile of DNA at George's door, and now he'll just have to wait and see what's turned up, deal with things one step at a time.

He locks the Crown Vic and stretches, takes a deep breath before he walks inside, where he asks the gum-chewing temp to let George know he's here. His initial reaction to the early-morning phone call was to wait until after noon, when George would be out of the office. He would have preferred discovering for himself what it was that George found so interesting, digesting the lab results in a private corner somewhere on his own. No matter how it turns out the case is complicated—has been ever since he found Kyle's prints in Celia's car, ever since the morning Dana marched into his office and perched like a trapped bird at the edge of a wooden chair.

He hasn't phoned Lenora on the labs. Not yet. He wonders if George has called her. She has more clout. Certainly her orders trump Jack's lame request for secrecy. And anyway, she's gorgeous. In fact, he half expects to see her when he opens the door to the lab, but the lobby is dark and cramped and empty as usual.

"Thanks," he says when George comes out and hands him the manila envelope, sealed and neat, devoid of writing. "I appreciate this."

"It wasn't all that complicated," George says. "We already had the Steinhauser body and the labs on it. There were scratches on Celia Steinhauser's arm."

"Yeah?" Jack is already edging toward the door. He wants to pull out the labs in the privacy of the Crown Vic, with his radio off, his A/C blowing cold air in the parking lot. He wants to take his time unraveling what happened that mysterious evening on Ashby Lane, and he's certain the labs will fill in the blank spaces, answer most if not all his questions. "Well," he says. His hand is on the doorknob. The temp smacks her gum loudly from behind the desk. George steps forward. His eyes gleam with intrigue.

"Yeah," he says. "So what we—actually they—ran was the fingernail you brought in. The tissue underneath it was Steinhauser's. Celia's. The vic's. You were right about that—I'm assuming that was what you thought when you brought it in."

Jack nods.

"Plus, Steinhauser actually had some skin tissue under three of her nails that matched the DNA on the nail you brought in."

"No shit." Jack pauses. His hand is still on the knob, but George is pressing in closer.

"Yeah," he says. "But listen. Here's the kicker."

Jack is a rabbit caught in a snare. George is almost touching him. He's so close that Jack can smell his breath. His eyes are wide and bright. "You want to sit down?" He waves in the general direction of the hard plastic McDonald's-restaurant chair.

"Naw," Jack says. "Naw, I'm—"

"Okay, then." George turns and drumrolls soundlessly on his Formica countertop. "Both the skin tissue under Steinhauser's nails and the fingernail you brought in were a match with the DNA from the napkin. Soooooooooooo, unless this was a random napkin pickup, it looks like you've got your killer. It was a napkin, right?"

"Yep. And it wasn't random at all," Jack says. "Thanks again, George. Do you need these labs back after I have a chance to . . . ?"

"Copies," George says. "Keep 'em," and he turns back toward the inner half door, toward the temp who taps her own long purple fingernails against her desktop, who watches Jack through thickly lined eyes, studying him there in the doorway as he stands with one hand frozen on the knob, the other gripping the unopened envelope. A large pink bubble emerges from between her lips, nearly hiding her face for a second before bursting with a resounding pop, breaking the spell, breaking the hold this moment, this news, this office, has on Jack. He turns and heads up the hall, not stopping until he's through the outside door and trudging toward his car. Above him a cloud tears open, spilling rain down on the, pure, unblemished orange of the manila folder, dotting it with dark spots.

He stops at a drive-through and picks up two burgers— half of one he'll give to Molly. He never goes home for lunch, but this day is different. He wants to study the labs, and anyway, it's a red-letter day of sorts. This afternoon he'll wind up the case, at least his part of it. What happens next is up to the prosecutor's office and the courts.

He takes his time unwrapping the greasy burgers, acutely aware of Molly drooling beside the kitchen table. He takes his time eating, instead of bolting everything down the way he does on the rare occasions he even bothers with lunch. He pores over every detail in the paperwork from the lab. He wants to be dead sure before he makes his next move. He fixes himself a cup of coffee and takes his time with that as well, stalling.

When he's finished his lunch and has nearly memorized the labs, when he's let Molly out and back in again, when there is nothing more to keep him home, he gets into his car, where he sits for a moment in the driveway, tapping his thumbs against the steering wheel. When he's listened to three songs and a traffic update, he scrolls to Lenora's cell-phone number and pushes the little green send arrow, infinitely relieved to hear it go to voice mail. "Hey," he says. "It's Jack Moss. Meet me at Harry's Diner at"—he glances at his watch—"at two-fifteen," he says. "It's important." He sits in his driveway through three more songs, and then he backs out to the street and heads for the diner.

*

Lenora isn't wearing the sexy lace top from their breakfast at E.Claire's. She isn't wearing a suede suit with glasses and heels. She's wearing a simple black skirt, a white blouse. She looks almost demure, coming through the door of the diner with her bangs dipping over one eye.

"Hey, Jack." She sits down. He's found a little table in back, near the kitchen. It's not that big a place, only eight or nine tables and a counter. It's always full, but never really crowded. Harry's is the kind of place where people

360

come in off the street to grab a cup of coffee, and it's the best around, but Jack doesn't remember ever having to wait to get a seat.

"Hey, Lenora." He sets down his cup. He looks beyond her left shoulder at the wall; he doesn't meet her eyes.

"Sorry I'm late," she says. "I was in a meeting when you called."

"Right. Not a problem."

"I'm glad we're finally here," she says, and Jack nods.

He was acting on impulse, picking up her napkin at E.Claire's the day they met for breakfast. At first glance her signature on the bill bore no great resemblance to the tiny script in Dana's threatening notes. It was the slight exaggeration of the loops in her e's and t's that caught Jack's eye. Even that would almost certainly have gone unnoticed had he not been poring over the notes from Dana's purse only moments before he left to meet Lenora. He looks at her finally, setting the bare-bones coffee mug down on the scarred tabletop. "Why'd you kill Celia Steinhauser?"

Lenora picks up the small, square menu and sticks on a pair of glasses. "That's not my kind of humor, Jack. Why in the name of God would you say something like that? This is crazy. You're crazy. I'm leaving now, Jack. I'm going to stand up and walk right out the door and pretend I never heard you say what you just said."

"It won't work, Lenora. We've got the forensics to prove it."

She looks away from him. She sets the menu down on

361

the table and stares at it as if she isn't certain what it is. Her face crumples. She looks frightened. She looks as if she might cry. "Off the record?"

"I guess nothing's really off the record," he says. "Not now."

"Coffee," she says to the waiter. "Cream. No sugar." She watches as he walks back to the kitchen. "I suppose there isn't really any reason not to tell you," she says, and her face is composed once more, tranquil, smooth as silk. "It isn't like I had a choice, really. The woman was a lunatic. Just ask Peter Catrell. He knows all about lunatics—between Celia and his crazy wife."

"I wouldn't ask Catrell the time of day."

Lenora sets her glasses on the table beside her menu. She glances into space, into the shadows of the room, and she looks very young without her prosecutor's face, like a college student wearing grown-up clothes. "I made a mistake," she says. "I worked my butt off to be where I am—to have the job I have." Her southern accent is more noticeable suddenly; her roots peep through. "It was a terrible mistake, getting involved with Peter."

Jack nods. On this at least they can agree. The waiter sets down Lenora's coffee and disappears.

"She caught us together. Celia. She seemed really crazy to me, tailing Peter the way she did, sneaking around, following him, snapping that picture of us in Gatsby's that day. Kissing, maybe. I couldn't remember. I only wanted that stupid photo out of her phone before she put it all

362

over the Internet, the six-o'clock news, before she called my office and ruined any possibility of my—"

"Why would she?"

"Revenge? Jealousy? She was clearly literally nuts about Peter, and it would have made a tasty little news story: the first assistant prosecutor from East Jesus, Alabama, sleeping with a prominent married lawyer? Why wouldn't she? I would have lost everything I'd worked for. I'd lose my chance to—"

"Take over Frank's position."

She nods. "He was such a pushover. That's what people thought of him, of the whole department. I wanted to make us a force to be reckoned with. I wanted to—"

The waiter comes back with more coffee, and Jack covers his cup with his hand, shakes his head.

"She told me the day she . . . she told me at her house that she planned to run away with him. With Peter. Can you imagine? She thought he loved her. Even after she saw him with me. Even after she took that stupid photo, she still thought—"

"Does he know?"

"That she was a bunny boiler? A nutcase? I guess so. I mean, unless he's a total idiot, he must have known."

"About you, I mean. Does he know what you did?"

"No." She looks up. Her eyes graze Jack's and drift away, landing on the table next to theirs where three men hunch together. They talk excitedly, their words overlapping. Lenora yawns. "He thought his wife did it," she says. "He didn't think I even noticed her that day. Celia. In the restaurant snapping our picture with her phone. He's such an egomaniac, I guess he thought I was too focused on him to see anything else, that I somehow managed to miss his crazy neighbor darting around like the paparazzi in those stupid shoes."

Jack leans back from the table. "Listen," he says. "I don't think you should say any more."

"Why not? It was self-defense." She stirs her coffee even though the cream is already mixed in, even though there isn't any need. She looks up, raises her eyebrows. "She came at me with a butcher knife, weaving in those ridiculous heels. Drunk. Teetering. Totally out of her— She must have thought I was Peter at first. 'You!' she said when she saw me. She seemed really surprised. 'You?'" She takes a sip of coffee. "This is really good," she says.

"You were in her house, Lenora."

She takes another sip of coffee and sets her cup down carefully on the table. "I only wanted the phone. I told her that. All she had to do was give me the—"

"How'd you even know where she lived?"

"I followed her. She was hanging around outside the restaurant that day she took the picture. Stalking him. Stalking us. I drove around the block when Peter thought I'd gone back to my office, and I spotted her with him out in the parking lot—the two of them yelling, Celia waving her phone around. They were so busy arguing they didn't notice me. Peter was half drunk, and she was so furious

I don't think she even realized that all the people in the parking lot were watching them. I was sure someone would call the cops. She totally lost it out there. He left, finally. Peter. He just got in his car and took off. Celia sat there for a while, and when she pulled out, I followed her. I followed her all the way back to her safe, pretentious little suburban life on Ashby Lane." She smiles. "So I knew where she lived. I went back a few days later."

The sun slants in and touches them even in this back corner that Jack picked for privacy, for obscurity. He sighs. He glances at her nails, the pearly polish. "You struggled in the kitchen?"

She nods. "I tried to get the knife. She was totally—"

"And you broke a nail."

"I guess so. I was leaving; I was headed for the front door. I thought I'd talk to Peter, get him to calm Celia down and make her see how crazy she was acting—but she followed me out to the living room, teetering on these impossible shoes. She had the knife. She was coming right at me with this . . . with this knife, and I just grabbed the nearest thing and—"

"Maybe you shouldn't say any more."

"It was over that fast. In the blink of—" She snaps her fingers. "I never meant . . ."

"What time was this?"

Lenora shrugs. "I wasn't wearing a watch," she says. "I had this cheap one. You get what you pay for, I guess. The strap broke."

365

He feels his stomach plunge. He feels a giant letdown, wonders if he should have put the pieces together sooner, if Lenora threw him off his game with her . . . allure. In any case it's a waste. Brains. Beauty. She's got it all. Had it all. Even if she can pull off self-defense, her career is toast. And that was what Lenora lived for. He stands up, but he doesn't look her in the eyes; he looks slightly to the left of them. "We really need to go. Rob's waiting for us down at booking."

Lenora nods. Her hands are pressed against the coffee cup, as if she's warming them. She fiddles with her silverware, looks around the room for a minute and then she finishes her coffee and stands up to go, straightens her skirt, pulls her hands through her hair, but Jack still has an unsettled feeling. The vagueness nags at him. He's a perfectionist, meticulous. He wishes the timeline were tighter, that he knew exactly how much time elapsed between Lenora's departure and the arrival of the ambulance. Did Ronald waste precious minutes? Did he hesitate to call the EMTs out of anger or fear or, hell, revenge? Did he look at his dying wife and amble out to the kitchen to make himself a cup of coffee? Pour himself a drink? Jack sighs. He'll never know for sure. In the end, though, it was Lenora who struck the fatal blow, and if Ronald's got secrets, maybe they don't have anything to do with the case.

*

366

"So where is Celia's phone now?" she says once they're on the road, once he's Mirandized her. He doesn't bother cuffing her; she isn't even sitting in the backseat. She knows the system. She knows not to make things worse by putting up a fight. The kicker is she was damn good at her job.

"Deleted. Destroyed," he says, "both the photo and the phone, as far as I know."

"Good." Her face is pale but slightly gray, like a soiled sheet or snow in the city.

"Did you go back afterward," he says, "to Ashby Lane? Mess with Dana?"

"It was my case. Would have been my case. I went back a few times, did a little undercover work. Peter was pressuring me. 'See what you can find out,' he kept saying. 'The woman lived right down the street from us.' I was doing my job." She shrugs. "When Dana had that stupid brunch, I walked in with some of the neighbors, strolled around their living room, chatted with some British woman—stuck a few things here and there while Peter was in the kitchen brownnosing his wife, convincing her I was there to drop off some papers."

"Stuck things here and there?"

Lenora tosses her head as if she's forgotten she's cut her hair short. "My hand wipes under the sofa, a note in her book, a pen in the desk drawer, that sort of thing. I went to their street, their yard once or twice."

"Anybody see you?"

"She did. Dana did. At least I think she did. Once. In their backyard. And then another time their neighbor saw me from his window. He came out after me one night in the middle of a storm—short guy in a raincoat. And then there was the time Dana drove herself into a ditch."

"You run her off the road?"

"No! I was . . . I admit I was following her, and I did get a little . . . well, actually, a lot too close, but what happened was all her. That was all Dana. She totally freaked and lost control of the wheel, zigzagged off the road. Someone pulled over to help her, or I would have called it in. Anonymously, but I would've called it in."

"Peter ever . . . ?"

"He never saw me." She laughs a bitter little half laugh like a twig snapping. "Even when we were together, he never really saw me."

They ride in silence for a block or two. Outside gloom settles across the sky and trickles down to the street. Rain again, but today Jack will be glad for it, will welcome it; today it suits his mood. He glances across the front seat at the side of Lenora's perfect, unlined face. "So why the notes?"

"Since when is writing notes a crime?" she says. "A lost art, maybe. Not a crime. Gum?" She pulls out a pack of Dentyne Ice and extends it toward him. He shakes his head. Her eyes are blank and hard, like chunks of coal. She reaches over and turns on the radio, finds a rock station. Music surges through the car. "Is this okay?"

"Yeah," he says. "Yeah, it's fine."

She turns away. She looks out the window, where raindrops splatter on the glass and land in puddles on the road. She moves back and forth in time to the music. It's a new song, something Jack has never heard before, something Kyle would listen to. She taps her fingers against the clasp of her bag. When she moves her head again, he sees that her eyes are closed. He watches her out of the corner of his eye—watches the ice begin to crack, the fissures forming, brittle and thin as a membrane, the porcelain princess splintering across an ice-cream skirt.

He reaches for his phone, picks up the message he'd been too preoccupied to notice before, a message left while he was with George that morning, when he stood in the airless closet of a lab with no phone signal. He listens to it now, as Lenora bobs to grating techno rock, her bangs across one eye. "Hey," Kyle's voice says, and Jack manages a smile in spite of the madness of the afternoon, in spite of the racket from the radio and the unraveling of the self-contained and beautiful assistant prosecutor. "I'm working at the lumberyard this weekend," the message says, "but I've got this Sunday off. If you can come by for dinner, there's a couple people here I'd like for you to meet." And with his phone pressed tightly up against his ear, Jack can just barely hear a baby crying in the distance; somewhere a woman sings. Maryanne, he thinks, or Margie. Across the seat Lenora begins to shake her head more wildly, knocking it against the window, harder and harder. He pulls the Crown Vic over to the side of the road and radios for help, for the EMTs, gives them a location as he pins Lenora's arms against her sides and thinks of Dana bolting from her car and trying to fly.

# 42

Dana sets down the gallon can of pale gold paint she bought at Home Depot the day before. Parts of one dining-room wall are filled with swatches, and two lop-sided peach squares from a discarded Martha Stewart sample tin dapple another. She eyes the dining room, the bland paint, so faded it's difficult to say exactly what color it once was. Autumn Wheat, she thinks, but she isn't sure.

She ties her hair in a bandanna, closes Spot onto the back porch, and tugs a sweatshirt over a tank top and a pair of jeans. It's an old pair, and they nearly fit her again. They no longer fall down past her hips as they did weeks before. Newspapers sit in a thin pile on the coffee table, and she grabs the top few, spreads them out along the baseboards of the dining room, where she will soon paint. She walks back into the living room and turns on a CD. The strains of Modest Mouse float through the rooms.

Peter used to hate the way she painted. "You have to tape," he'd say, edging past the stacked furniture and paintbrushes, newspapers scattered slapdash on the floor, but she rarely did. She preferred moving the folded news-paper page along with her foot to catch the dripping paint. His way—the methodical taping, the infuriating papering of the floor—took far too long. By the time he'd finished with the preparation, she was bored with the whole project.

The room is cold with autumn settling in. A chilly fall, they're predicting on TV, but Dana likes the cold. She likes frigid mornings, frost on browning leaves, the scent of firewood up the street, the sky clear and heavy, a wall of blue. She walks across the living room, pirouetting on the Persian rug as Spot paces, looking trapped and dismal on the other side of a closed French door.

Peter hasn't been back to the house for weeks. She knows he will eventually appear to pick up what he's left there, to sort through what few things of his remain—these traces of a husband he no longer is. She knows he'll choose a random, problematic time, sliding his key into the front door and slinking inside. He's no longer welcome here. She doesn't miss him. If in the cold of late night the bed seems large and empty with only Dana there—if she wishes there were someone else beside her, it isn't Peter. The Poet sometimes or, most recently and most recurrently, Jack Moss. But if waking in the night she sighs and runs her hand along the pillows, shivering in the sudden drape of fall, it is never Peter she imagines there.

It was like a movie, Dana would say later, when she was able to talk about it all, when the turning of a doorknob, or the sound of footsteps on the porch, or seeing scraps of white paper didn't send a shiver up her spine. The story that spilled out across the front page of the paper and dominated every news spot on TV had everything from pathos to pathology. Colorful and large, the cast of characters floated nightly into Jersey living rooms— the gorgeous yet tragically unhinged young first assistant prosecutor banging her head against the window of a cop car; the tiny, fragile foreign-language teacher dead in her foyer; the married lawyer who manipulated both women at the expense of his poor, demented wife, whose suicide attempt, the papers raged, was a matter of public record, the amazing fact she'd not ended up at the bottom of the Hudson nothing more than fate. "desperate housewives" meets "law & order," one of the headlines read.

The story broke right after Dana's lunch at E.Claire's, right after her encounter with the woman shown hand-cuffed at her arraignment with a bandage peeking out beneath her bangs. Jamie was home for a long weekend when it all rolled out on the eleven-o'clock news, and he'd reached for the remote to mute the newscast, to shield his mother as the particulars of her husband's life unfolded in vivid color on Peter's wide-screen TV.

"It's okay," she told him, sighing. "I already know," and she had known some of it, thanks to Moss. She knew the highlights if not the particulars—if not the whys, at least she knew the whos and whens and wheres of things.

Jamie wasn't surprised either as he gazed at the TV and texted his new girlfriend. Peter, who had told his own wife nothing, had at least had the decency to drive to Jamie's dorm in Boston, where he'd warned his son of the unfortunate link to the highly publicized murder—Peter's slight, he said, almost tangential involvement. What Jamie would soon see on the news and what would sadly and ineptly be unrolled for the general public was mostly hype, he'd told his son. The newshounds rarely got things right.

Dana threw out every stick of furniture she'd found with Celia in their yard-sale days—a small desk, an antique phone stand, and three barstools. She promised herself she wouldn't go to Celia's funeral—a promise she broke in the end, but only when a TV camera panned in on the Episcopalian church downtown and after she'd let three of Moss's phone calls go to voice mail. Only then did Dana change her mind, slipping into a black skirt, a lackluster beige blouse, and the high, black, strappy sandals that Celia would have loved. She headed for the church with the cool of early fall blowing through the open windows and Rachmaninoff blaring from the car radio. Ducking past the cameramen outside, she slid into a pew at the very back of the church, where she listened to a barrage of eulogies and tributes to a woman Dana realized she had never really known.

Ronald was true to his word. He never moved back to Ashby Lane. The house is on the market now. The lawn is neatly mowed, if brown, and what flowers remain are trimmed and tidily deadheaded, the shutters newly painted a pale, insipid blue. She hasn't seen Ronald since the funeral, when they walked together to their cars, his wife's ashes in a lovely silver urn, his fingers trembling on the intricate design around its top. Sometimes Dana is troubled by a thought. A memory, she thinks, but she isn't sure. Considering her state of mind when Celia died, the sangria blur the day became, nothing from that afternoon is certain. Still, sometimes she can almost feel the hood of Ronald's car when, sliding into their driveway, she caught herself by throwing her hands against it. She can almost feel its warmth—tepid, really. The warmth of a hot engine cooled down over time.

She opens the paint, spills the pale gold liquid into a roller pan. With her toes she slides a slice of newspaper under the white trim along the baseboard and rolls the new paint across the dingy, mushroom-colored wall.

She steps back, examining the color. The rain pounds down outside, the windows fill with gray, and the sky is the color of dust. She rolls the paint in long zigs and zags, filling in the spaces between. Beside the window the wall is warm and bright in the lamplight. Dana paints and sings and knows, if only for that one hour, that one moment, she has found the balance that Dr. Ghea spoke of, the small, thin place between darkness and light.

Someone knocks at the door, and Dana navigates her way around the displaced chairs and corner cupboards, through the dishes from her mother's family, dusty and archaic, stacked on the dining-room table, the Spode and Haviland she's almost never used. "Coming," she calls out, and she stops to turn the music down.

It isn't Peter. It can't be Peter—he would use his key.

He'd slip in. He'd catch her there, shifting the sports page under her bare toes, her feet already speckled with gold paint. He'd stand there in the entryway, his arms crossed over his chest. "Dana!" he'd say. "You're doing it again. All wrong. All wrong. As always." Or he'd slink back to the bedroom to lie across their bed in the darkened alcove by the dresser. He would lie in wait. He'd scare her, lurking like a shadow in the murk of the rainy day. "Oh," he'd say. "Didn't mean to startle you, but it is still my house, after all. Where else would I be?"

She takes a breath and tugs on the front door, and Jack Moss stands on the slick, rain-splattered porch, his sneakers at the edges of the doormat, his trench coat open and flapping in the wind. Raindrops roll down the visor of his Mets cap and fly into the air.

"Moss?"

"Hi." He grins.

"Come in."

She steps back from the door in the tiny entry with the Japanese umbrella stand, the dark red flowered rug, and he stands dripping in the doorway. Water plops in circles and rolls along the floor.

"Here," she says. "Let me take your coat."

"Sorry." He hands it to her. He glances at the wet floor, the spots of rain across the flowered rug.

"It's fine." She gestures toward the dining room, the painted wall, the scattered bits of newsprint. "What do you think?"

"I like it," he says. "It's cheery." He steps to the edge of the living room.

"Sit," she says. "Can I get you a cup of coffee?"

"No," he says. "No. I'm just here for a minute."

"Listen." She smiles, sits beside him on the sofa. "If you've come to arrest me, Moss, this is a really bad time."

"Oh, yeah? How come?"

"The painting, obviously. I'm afraid you'll have to come back later."

"When?" He seems almost serious. He laughs then, like he's caught himself. "There's never a really good time for arrests."

"Some times are better than others. On the way to E.Claire's might not be a bad one."

"Or in the dentist's office. Seriously." He makes a move to stand, slides forward on the sofa.

"Seriously."

"There's this job at the forensics lab."

"Huh."

"Would you be interested?"

"I don't know." She cups her chin in her hand. "Should I be?"

He shrugs. "I could take you over there. Show you around."

"Yeah," she says. "Okay."

"Next week? Tuesday, say?"

"Sounds good."

"Maybe lunch afterward?"

"Hmmm." She taps her fingers against her knees. "That depends."

"Yeah? On what?"

"Where? E.Claire's?"

"Where else?"

"Anywhere in the world else. Anywhere in the universe else!"

"No kidding?"

"Nope. I'm out of Xanax."

"I'll see what I can come up with," Jack says. He gets to his feet. "Want some help?"

"What? Painting?"

"Yeah. I could tape off the trim before you—"

"Naw," she says, "but thanks anyway. I've got this system."

"Right. My ex used to . . . both of them used to . . ." He stops, takes a breath, sticks on his cap. "How are you doing these days?"

Dana looks down at her hands. She looks at Spot, darting back and forth behind the door. "I'm okay," she says. "I take it one day at a time. This is a good day."

He nods. "You deserve a whole long string of good days."

They walk together to the door, their bodies touching briefly in the narrow entryway and moving apart. "Next time you can say hey to Spot," she says.

"Nice cat."

"Not really, but he grows on you."

"Yeah." He waves toward the frantic kitten as it leaps onto the back of a rattan chair. "At least he isn't boring," Jack says, and he pushes against the screen door.

"We don't really do boring around here." Dana laughs. The rain has slowed to a steady drizzle, and she knows it's ushering in more cold. She stands in the doorway, her arms across her chest, as Jack hurries to the Crown Vic in the driveway. She waves as he backs out, as he tips his rain-soaked cap, as a little rivulet of water pours into his lap, as he yells, "Damn!" and pulls the rest of the way out to the street.

She breathes in the fresh air. The day is colder already. She leans her head back, staring at the gray-fog sky, the dazzling autumn trees. The wind blows through, making a long, sweet sound in the air, catching in the spaces between things, garages and skinny side yards and fallen, rolling garbage cans. It pulls her hair back off her forehead, slapping her bandanna from side to side. She breathes again and closes her eyes, and the wind is in every pore, on every inch of skin, but it does not consume her. When it passes, she still stands whole on her front porch, her hands reaching out behind her for the door, her feet dappled in gold.